I0646017

# HER BEST FRIEND'S SISTER

# Praise for Meghan O'Brien

### *Camp Rewind*

"Romance is on fast forward at Camp Rewind. This is a quick, satisfying read for those longing for the nostalgia of a summer camp romance." —*Publishers Weekly*

"*Camp Rewind*, Meghan O'Brien's latest offering, has the sexiness we've come to expect in her fiction, with more of a contemporary romance feel. The sex is hot and varied, as expected, with the overt, enthusiastic consent that is rarely seen elsewhere. More time is spent than usual on just making out, and wow, does that ever pay off when they hit the sheets (or the sleeping bag)."—*Curve Magazine*

### *Thirteen Hours*

"Meghan O'Brien's writing style is entertaining. She is creative and her story isn't the typical romance. It was a lovely little story with the elevator being the highlight of the story. If you want a long and very sexy foreplay then this book is for you."—*The Lesbian Review*

"Ms O'Brien has a knack for erotica and she sure isn't shy in showing it off! Goodness, this was a scorcher. I finished it about 24 hours ago and am still blushing, burning, and wanting."—*Prism Book Alliance*

"Meghan O'Brien has given her readers some very steamy scenes in this fast paced novel. *Thirteen Hours* is definitely a walk on the wild side, which may have you looking twice at those with whom you share an elevator."—*Just About Write*

"Boy, if there was ever fiction that a lesbian needs during a bed death rut or simply in need of some juicing up, Thirteen Hours by Meghan O'Brien is the book I'd recommend to my good friends...If you are looking for good ole American instant gratification, simple and not-at all-straight sexy lesbian eroticism, revel in the sexiness that is *Thirteen Hours*."—*Tilted World*

### *Battle Scars*

"As a former US Marine, I usually have a difficult time with books that try to discuss military concepts, philosophy, and events but I didn't feel that way with this book. *Battle Scars* is a quick read that drew me right in and didn't let me go. Both Ray and Carly have had emotionally devastating experiences but this book is about love and hope and dogs. Wonderful, supportive, loving dogs."—*C-Spot Reviews*

### The Muse

"Entertaining characters, laugh-out-loud moments, plenty of hot sex, all wrapped up in a really fun story. What more could you ask for?"
—*The Lesbian Review*

### Wild

"I love Meghan's take on shapeshifters...The story has great pacing and keeps you on the edge of your seat until its heart-pounding end. I can't wait for [the] sequel."—*BookDyke.com*

"I truly enjoy shifter stories but I have never had the pleasure of reading one so well written or so hot. Even for a Bold Strokes Book it was erotic and exotic!"—*Prism Book Alliance*

O'Brien "knows how to write passion really well, and I do not recommend reading her books in public (unless you want everyone to know exactly what you are reading). *Wild* is no different. It's very steamy, and the sex scenes are frequent, and quite erotic to say the least."—*Lesbian Book Review*

### The Night Off

"*The Night Off* by Meghan O'Brien is an erotic romance that is not for the faint of heart. But if you can handle BDSM that includes hard spanking, humiliation, and anal play, then you'll be rewarded with a beautiful, emotional romance. If you've been looking for an erotic romance that is super dirty but has big, big feelings, you won't find anything better than *The Night Off*. Meghan O'Brien is the queen of lesbian erotic romance, and this book is an absolute must."
—*The Lesbian Review*

### The Three

"In *The Three* by Meghan O'Brien, we are treated to first-rate storytelling that features scorching love scenes with three main characters...She hits her stride well in *The Three* with a well-paced plot that never slows. She excels at giving us an astounding tale that is tightly written and extremely sensual. I highly recommend this unique book."
—*Just About Write*

# By the Author

Infinite Loop

The Three

Thirteen Hours

Battle Scars

Wild

The Night Off

The Muse

Delayed Gratification: The Honeymoon

Camp Rewind

Her Best Friend's Sister

Visit us at www.boldstrokesbooks.com

# HER BEST FRIEND'S SISTER

*by*

## Meghan O'Brien

2017

HER BEST FRIEND'S SISTER
© 2017 BY MEGHAN O'BRIEN. ALL RIGHTS RESERVED.

ISBN 13: 978-1-62639-861-0


THIS TRADE PAPERBACK ORIGINAL IS PUBLISHED BY
BOLD STROKES BOOKS, INC.
P.O. BOX 249
VALLEY FALLS, NY 12185

FIRST EDITION: MAY 2017

THIS IS A WORK OF FICTION. NAMES, CHARACTERS, PLACES, AND
INCIDENTS ARE THE PRODUCT OF THE AUTHOR'S IMAGINATION OR
ARE USED FICTITIOUSLY. ANY RESEMBLANCE TO ACTUAL PERSONS,
LIVING OR DEAD, BUSINESS ESTABLISHMENTS, EVENTS, OR LOCALES
IS ENTIRELY COINCIDENTAL.

THIS BOOK, OR PARTS THEREOF, MAY NOT BE REPRODUCED IN ANY
FORM WITHOUT PERMISSION.

CREDITS
EDITOR: SHELLEY THRASHER
PRODUCTION DESIGN: STACIA SEAMAN
COVER DESIGN BY MELODY POND

# Acknowledgments

As always, thanks to Shelley Thrasher for her editing expertise. You make that part of the process so very enjoyable, which I appreciate.

Major shout-out to my wife Angie, who conceived of these characters and their history after I told her I would write any short story she desired as one of her birthday gifts. Yes, short story. You can see how that worked out.

To the rest of my family and friends: Thanks for putting up with me, especially when I'm in a writing frenzy. I'm sure it's not always easy.

And because this always has to happen: 1) Kathleen, apologies for not yet producing a book that you could actually assign to your students; 2) Mom and Dad, please don't read past this page!

To Angie, for her birthday

## CHAPTER ONE

Claire Barker slipped backward out of her best friend Sarah's vacant house, using her foot to prevent the round, orange tabby cat she'd come to feed from following her outside. "Stay, Willow. Your mommy and daddy will be home tomorrow afternoon, all right? You can lodge your complaints then." The baby-faced cat stared up at her and let loose an open-mouthed scream, apparently unwilling to delay her bitching about the pet-sitting service she'd received. "Sorry, kitty. I'd stay and hang out with you a little longer, but I have a hot date with my hands this evening that I simply can't miss." When Willow meowed again as the door swung closed in her face, Claire added, "That's right. I've got an even more needy pussy than you to take care of tonight."

"Wow, talk about impeccable timing. Away for nine months, and I managed to come home just in time to hear something like *that*."

Claire whirled around at the thrillingly familiar voice behind her, dissolving into a fierce blush at the sight of Sarah's older sister, Alex, standing there in the driveway, breathtaking as ever. An internationally renowned fashion photographer, Alex had spent most of the past decade hopping the globe on various assignments, only occasionally coming home to Northern California to spend time with family and unwind. The visits had become less frequent over the past three years, right around the time Claire's business venture with Sarah had really taken off. After Sarah had used a fraction of her share of their second-year, multi-million-dollar earnings to purchase this beautiful new house near their favorite stretch of vineyards, she'd offered to let Alex move into the granny unit out back so her beloved big sister would have a permanent space to occupy during her brief stopovers home.

Naturally, Claire had been thrilled when Alex accepted the offer. She'd nursed a massive crush on Sarah's sister since the tender age of twelve, when she'd first met the exotic, magical, masculine seventeen-year-old girl who always treated Claire like a real person instead of her much-younger sibling's best friend. Some of Claire's very first masturbatory fantasies had featured Alex in the starring role, usually as the dashing, experienced, older butch lesbian who was almost certainly the most perfect sexual mentor imaginable. Not much had changed in that regard, as there was at least a fifty percent chance that Alex's name would've been on Claire's lips when she made herself come tonight. Sarah's big-shot sister was Claire's ultimate sexual fantasy and the unrequited love of her life.

Which was precisely why it was so humiliating for *Alex*—of all people—to have overheard her big plans to spend Saturday night diddling herself. Even as she yearned for the earth to open up and swallow her where she stood, Claire offered a weak wave and an awkward, "Hi, Alex."

Tall, broad-shouldered, and utterly, breathtakingly handsome, Alex pulled off her sunglasses and shot Claire an easy smile. She still had the same kind blue eyes Claire remembered from childhood. Alex's jet-setting lifestyle hadn't seemed to change her all that much, even if her clothes were more expensive and her taste in women seemed to surpass any fantasy Claire could ever hope to fulfill. A hardcore engineering and computer geek since birth, Claire was a stereotypical nerd in glasses who struggled to speak eloquently when she was nervous, which was pretty much all the time when Alex was around. Meanwhile, Alex spent the majority of her time surrounded by glamorous women who'd made beauty their profession and, according to the occasional snapshots she texted to Sarah, left a trail of unrealistically pretty ex-lovers wherever she went.

Despite the disparity in their stations, at least as Claire perceived them, Alex gazed at her like she was sincerely happy about this reunion, offering a playful wink along with a gentle nod. "Hey there, Claire-Claire."

The flames in Claire's cheeks burned hotter at the sound of the childhood nickname only Alex had ever used. "Sorry, I..." Claire gestured vaguely at the door behind her, then to her car, which was parked beside a sporty blue convertible that had to belong to Alex.

"Sarah and Marcus are out of town for the week and asked me to feed Willow."

Alex's lips twitched. "Yeah. I kind of figured that out."

Unsure how to tiptoe past the elephant in the driveway, Claire sighed. "I really wish you hadn't heard the other part."

"Well, I probably should've announced myself sooner. I was just…enjoying the show." Alex flashed her customary grin that still turned Claire's knees to jelly. "Anyway, don't be embarrassed. Some of my favorite dates have been with my hand. Cheap, easy, and a happy ending is all but guaranteed. Only a fool wouldn't occasionally indulge in such luxury."

Alex had never been shy when it came to talking about sex, which was almost certainly one reason Claire found her so intriguing. Claire wasn't actually all that shy about sex either, unless she had to discuss it out loud. After scrambling for a response that would sound both casual and at least mildly alluring, she finally blurted, "It's sweet of you to assume that it's only an occasional indulgence." Cringing after she replayed the words in her head, Claire sighed and stared down at her feet. "Anyway…change of plans. This seems like an ideal time to go home, crawl under my bed, and never come out."

Alex's sweet laughter gave Claire enough courage to tear her attention away from the ratty old sneakers she'd been unfortunate enough to wear today, a beloved pair she should have replaced at least six weeks ago. Eyes twinkling, Alex held up an oversized brown bag Claire hadn't noticed before that moment, upon which was emblazoned the colorful logo of a local vegetarian-only, fast-food drive-through. "Listen, you're not the only one caught in an embarrassing situation here. I decided to stop at that new veggie joint and couldn't decide what I wanted to try off the menu first. So I ordered a garden burger and fries, and a bean burrito, *and* a personal pizza. I'd planned to sample a little of everything while trying not to eat myself sick. Which means you caught me getting ready to spend *my* Saturday night snarfing enough food for three people. Alone."

Claire managed a reluctant chuckle. "Look at us: lust and gluttony."

"Which are, coincidentally, my two favorite sins of the deadly seven." Alex wiggled the fast-food bag back and forth in an enticing manner. "Would you be willing to postpone lust for a bit to spare me from gluttony? I really could use some help eating all this food."

Still embarrassed, Claire opened her mouth intending to refuse, her go-to instinct, but instead she said, "Okay."

A grin stretched slowly across Alex's face. "Yeah?" She seemed surprised yet genuinely pleased. "Sarah said your new app is selling like crazy. And that the math-and-science-based curriculum you designed for high school girls got nominated for a big education award?" Unless she was a better actress than Claire realized, Alex appeared to be legitimately impressed by their accomplishments. "I'd love to catch up with you and hear all about it."

Relieved that the conversation had moved away from the topic of her self-pleasuring, Claire forced herself to relax so she would stop acting like a complete dork. "Yeah, this was a good year for us. Sarah has done a brilliant job with the marketing. If not for her success in getting our products noticed by the right people, who knows where we'd be?"

Alex nodded toward the granny unit, then held Claire's gaze as they walked along the path to the front door. "My sister *is* amazing, no doubt, but you're the technical whiz who actually created all that software. Not to mention designed the coursework." When they reached the entrance of the small cottage, Alex actually fumbled for a moment to find her keys. As she fitted the right one into the lock, she said the most exhilarating thing Claire had ever heard. "So *you're* amazing, too, Claire. Own it."

## CHAPTER TWO

Simultaneously glowing and flustered, Claire was glad when Alex walked inside ahead of her and tossed her keys onto a small apothecary table right inside the door. She was sure she had a silly, love-struck grin plastered on her face. "Thank you."

"Seriously. You always had that adorable, geeky-girl thing going on, but I had no idea what a freakin' super genius you actually were until I read the interview you gave to *Wired* magazine last year. I ended up passing that article around to a bunch of people at the shoot I was working on at the time, bragging that I knew you two way back when."

"When we were annoying little kids who used to bug you to drive us to the arcade?"

"Exactly." Alex swept a large cloth off the dining table, around which sat four chairs that looked like a human derriere had never touched them. "Please excuse the state of the place. I actually drove here straight from the airport. The good news is that they lost my suitcase, so at least I don't have to unpack everything tonight."

"Staying for a while this time?" Stiffly, Claire chose a chair and sat down. "Or just passing through?"

"Staying, actually." Alex tossed the bag of food onto the table in front of Claire and continued into the attached kitchen. "Take whatever you want. I'll scavenge from what's left."

Claire opened the bag and pulled out the various food items. Still nervous about being around Alex—by *herself*, even—she ate a couple of french fries but hesitated to test her uneasy stomach with more. "I'm not super hungry, to be honest."

She heard the refrigerator door swing open, and Alex called out, "Are you thirsty?"

"A drink sounds wonderful."

"Great." The distinct sounds of beverage preparation began. "So, how are things outside of work? Life treating you well?"

"Not bad." Claire stared at the open doorway, musing about how much easier it was to talk with Alex when she couldn't see her stunning face. "Pretty quiet. My brother got married in June."

"*Luke?* Really?" Alex chuckled, and Claire snickered at her obvious surprise. "Can't say I saw that one coming."

"Me either. But he fell for a nurse he met at a friend's birthday party. Apparently it was love at first sight."

"Damn. Maybe there's hope for the rest of us then." Alex strolled back into the front room carrying a bottle of red wine and two mostly full glasses. She put one glass down in front of Claire, the other next to her, then set the bottle on the table between them while raising a questioning eyebrow. "I'm afraid I don't have a lot of options until I make a trip to the store, but I can pour you a glass of water if you prefer."

Looking forward to the loosening of her stupid inhibitions, Claire picked up her glass of wine and took a long sip. "No. This is perfect."

Alex seemed pleased. "I was hoping you'd say that." She took a drink of her own, then let out a contented sigh. "I've been waiting for this moment all day."

"Fast food and wine?"

"Being home." Alex sat in the chair to Claire's left and grabbed the veggie burger, hurriedly unwrapping it without a trace of self-consciousness. "Getting some real food in my stomach." She took a large bite and moaned. The sound caused a pleasant twinge through Claire's instantly sensitive clit. Swallowing, Alex took another sip and shot her a warm smile. "The wine and the company are unexpected pleasures."

Claire took an even longer drink this time, nearly draining half the glass. She would need the liquid courage if Alex continued to say things like that. Setting the drink down, she attempted to steer the conversation back to her favorite subject: Alex. "How about you? Is life treating *you* well?"

Alex's smile wavered ever so slightly. "Life is good. Work has been steady, the locations interesting. The models...well, it varies. Still, I'm ready to slow down for a while." She paused to chew on her burger, giving Claire an opportunity to wonder what had prompted that decision. As far as she knew, Alex thrived on her life of adventure and had never considered hitting the brakes even momentarily. Picking up on her curiosity, Alex said, "I've been working on an art project for the past year. Unrelated to fashion. I've pitched the series to a gallery in San Francisco, and they want to do a show. Since I can afford to pay my bills indefinitely with all I've saved over the past decade, I figured... why not try something new?"

Claire brightened at the news. When she'd first met Alex, the older teenager's bedroom had been papered with her favorite photographs, a veritable collection of artistically staged shots and candid slices of life captured in time. Though fashion photography had launched her career in a very specific direction, Claire knew that Alex had never lost her love of using the medium for her personal expression. The idea that she was about to reclaim that passion in her professional life made Claire want to burst with pride. "That's wonderful!" she said, cheeks already warm from the wine. "I'm so happy for you. Congratulations."

"Thanks." Improbable as it was, Alex seemed almost bashful about Claire's praise. "It's been a lot of fun. We'll see what happens."

Fresh off another swallow of wine that had all but emptied her glass, Claire asked, "Will *I* get an invitation to the big opening?"

There was no mistaking Alex's blush this time. Visibly pink-cheeked, she was delicious in her sudden awkwardness. "Uh..." She chuckled and met Claire's eyes with a mischievous smirk. "I'm afraid the subject matter might scandalize you."

A surge of wetness literally trickled out to soak Claire's panties. Polishing off the last few drops of wine that clung to the bottom of her glass, she reached for the bottle, but Alex beat her to it, pouring refills for both of them after she'd thrown back the rest of her own drink in one hearty gulp. This go-round, Alex let the red liquid flow until it nearly reached the rims of their glasses. With an attempt at nonchalance, Claire took a casual sip. "Go on. You can't say something like that and then just *stop*."

Alex polished off the burger and cracked open the box containing the individually portioned pizza, which was topped with light cheese, tomatoes, and basil. "Want a piece?" Alex separated a one-quarter slice from the rest of the pie and handed it to Claire with a smirk that made it clear she was trying to stall—and that she knew Claire knew it, too.

Mellowed by her first glass, Claire snatched the pizza from Alex and took a dainty bite. Then she said, "The subject matter of your show. Spill."

"It's nothing *too* shocking," Alex said. "Erotic shots, that's all. Lots of nudes. With a major focus on the female form, particularly the vagina." She took a bite of pizza, then another, chasing the mouthfuls of food with more wine. "My love letter to pussy, for lack of a better description. I ended up shooting more than sixty women over twelve months. All ages, colors, shapes, sizes. So much variation, it was magnificent." Pizza polished off, Alex turned her attention to the practically full bag of fries. "Mind if I have some of those?"

"Please." Claire drank some more wine, hoping Alex wouldn't think she was a lush. The more she consumed, the easier this all became. "Your project sounds beautiful. I'd love to see the show when it opens, as long as *you* won't be too scandalized to have your little sister's annoying best friend there."

Alex laughed. After eating a few fries, she pushed away the food to focus exclusively on her wine. "You've never been annoying, Claire. Even when you *were* just a little kid in my eyes."

*So that means I'm not a kid to her anymore?* Claire bit her lip, almost tipsy enough to ask, but not quite. However, she *was* tipsy enough to say, "Over sixty women, huh? And how many of them did you sleep with?"

Alex's smile froze in place, the hurt reaction subtle but noticeable. "Just one, actually. I was seeing her when I came up with the concept for the shoots. She was my first model." Pausing to take a slow drink, she closed her eyes and rolled the liquid around on her tongue before swallowing. "She dumped me ten months ago. I haven't been with anyone since."

Shocked to have drawn out so much information with one teasing query, Claire wasn't certain how to respond. "I'm sorry. I can tell she meant something to you."

"I thought she did. Or rather, I thought I meant something to her." Alex shook her head and waved away the slight melancholy that had invaded her mood. "Please understand, I'm better off without her. She was a manipulative, lying narcissist who never cared about me as much as what I could do for her."

"But she had a pretty pussy?" The wine eased the way for the word to leave Claire's mouth for the first time since the driveway, but it couldn't prevent the blush that rose in her cheeks after she'd uttered it.

Alex snorted, then reached over to clink her glass against Claire's. "Indeed. She had a very pretty pussy. Yummy, too." She took another long swallow and let out a satisfied sigh that Claire suspected was partially in memory of her ex's flavor. "Too bad she was a lying, cheating jerk."

"Well, remember...there's plenty of pussy in the sea." Claire blinked, then stared at the empty wineglass in her hand. *When did I finish this one?* She looked up at Alex, who watched her with obvious amusement. *And did I really just say that?*

"On that note, how's *your* love life? Seeing anyone?" Alex followed up her question by taking another lengthy drink.

"Uh, no." Claire cleared her throat, ashamed of her excruciatingly lackluster dating life. "I tell myself I don't have time because of work, anyway, but the truth is, I never seem to meet anyone who's interested. I mean, no one that *I'm* interested in, as well."

"Well, what's your type?" Alex turned her chair to face Claire more directly, then leaned back and crossed her legs as though settling in for a long conversation. "Maybe I know someone I could hook you up with."

Claire answered with a vigorous shake of her head, horrified by the thought of allowing the woman she loved to play matchmaker. She immediately felt the effects of the alcohol, almost losing her balance and toppling off the chair to one side. Catching herself, she giggled nervously and said, "No. That's okay."

"Are you sure? Even if I haven't actually lived here for a while, I do know a lot of single women in the area. Men, too, if you wanted to spread your wings."

Claire wrinkled her nose at the suggestion. "No men."

Alex beamed. "All right, then. What do you look for in a woman?"

"I don't know." Flushed, Claire fumbled with the bottle, filling a third of her glass with more of the deep-red liquid. "I like someone who's smart, funny...and butch, I guess?"

"Oh, *really?*" Alex took the bottle from her and emptied the rest into her own glass. "Sarah told me you dated a baby butch a few years ago. Even texted me a picture of you two once." She took a sip, then added, casually, "She was cute."

Claire bought time by taking another drink, one she *definitely* didn't need. Her entire body felt warm and alive with arousal, and she feared she might say or do something she would regret. Excited to see this conversation through, yet nervous beyond belief, Claire said, "Jane. She was nice. At first."

Alex's expression darkened. "And then?"

"She said I was boring." Claire shrugged, trying to play off the comment like it hadn't stung, even though it had. "She's probably right."

"No. She's a bitch." With a roll of her eyes, Alex chugged the rest of her wine and set the glass on the table. Then she rested her forearms on her thighs and leaned forward to stare into Claire's face. "You're *not* boring."

"Oh, I don't know. I work too much, I prefer to stay in on the weekends, I hate big parties, and I'd rather sit in a bathtub with a book than go out dancing at the club *any* day." Claire drained the rest of her wine to avoid making eye contact, then placed her glass on the table next to Alex's. "Jane found that *unforgivably* dull once my new-girlfriend sheen wore off. Granted, she did come crawling back six months later when Sarah and I took the company public."

Alex snorted. "I'll bet she did." She continued to search Claire's face, seemingly unafraid to let her curiosity show. "Has there been anyone since?"

"No one serious."

"How about sex?"

Now unambiguously tipsy, bordering on drunk, Claire didn't even pause to think before tossing out the kind of smart remark she might've made to Sarah—who would've simply laughed it off. "Is that an invitation?"

The goofy smile on Alex's face became even goofier, growing lopsided and tinged with what looked like desire mixed with mild alarm. "Do you want it to be?"

Afraid to test Alex's sincerity, Claire chose to simply answer the original question. "No dating, and no sex, for two years now. Which is why I spend my Saturday nights...entertaining myself."

"What's your favorite way to make yourself come?"

Claire blinked, caught off guard by the blunt question. "Uh..."

"Shit." Still grinning, Alex lowered her eyes and shook her head. "You know what, I'm sorry. I've asked that question of the models for my project so many times now, I think I've forgotten how invasive it actually is."

Emboldened by the idea that Alex was interested in knowing something so intimate about *her*, Claire said, "I usually rub my...clit with my fingers. Sometimes I'll watch something on my computer...or read a story...but mostly I fantasize."

Alex lifted her eyes to Claire's. "Fantasize about what?"

Claire immediately shook her head. "No way. I'm definitely not *that* drunk." It would take a lot more than a couple glasses of wine for her to confess that Alex was her favorite and most frequent subject.

## CHAPTER THREE

Alex giggled, a thoroughly girlish sound that took Claire by surprise. Rising from her chair, she grabbed Claire's hand after only the briefest hesitation, helping her to stand on unsteady feet. "Well, *I'm* a little drunk. Let's move this into the front room. I'm suddenly craving a reunion with my favorite couch in the world."

Claire followed as Alex led them to a well-worn leather couch that sat beneath a large, shaded window. Abruptly, Alex dropped Claire's hand and took a running leap at the cushions, landing face-first along their length with a contented groan. "Oh, yeah. That's what I'm talking about." Pulling up her legs while simultaneously rolling onto her back, Alex scooched up to rest her lower back against the arm while waving Claire over. "Come on. Sit down with me."

Claire experienced a sudden moment of clarity in which she realized that she'd somehow managed to get stupidly inebriated with the woman she wanted to sleep with more than she wanted anything else in the entire world. Alex seemed game to let this unexpected reunion continue even as they trod closer to dangerous ground, a thrilling place where whatever they said and did might potentially alter their tentative yet longstanding friendship forever. Claire wasn't sure she trusted her own judgment, or even Alex's, so she hesitated in front of the couch, unsure what to do. When Alex's smile faded slightly and her eyebrows drew together in confusion, Claire said, dumbly, "Listen, I don't want to impose. You just got home. I'm sure you must be tired."

Alex's smile fell away completely. "Have I made you uncomfortable?"

"No!" Horrified by the thought that she'd destroyed any chance for them to be together, Claire rushed forward and sat on the couch beside Alex's feet. "Not at all."

"Good, because I would never want to do that." Alex's eyes watered slightly, the alcohol clearly bringing intense emotion to the front. "I really like you. I'm having fun tonight."

"Me, too." Claire glanced down at Alex's feet and, without thinking, pulled one onto her lap so she could unlace the boot. She fumbled slightly with the laces, her normally deft fingers clumsy. Wanting Alex to understand that even if it frightened her a little, she *enjoyed* the simmering sexual tension between them tonight, Claire murmured, "It's nice to be able to talk with you like this. Like…"

"Two adult women?"

Claire nodded, tickled that Alex actually understood. "Yeah."

"You know, I really *don't* see you as a little girl anymore." Alex exhaled with relief when Claire pulled off her boot, then her sock, and happily offered her other foot for the same treatment. "Especially after I read that interview you did. Like, seriously. You sounded so *together.* So fuckin' *smart.*" She huffed and poked Claire's thigh with her bare toes. "Smarter than *I'll* ever be."

Claire battled the urge to pull out her phone and Google her own name so she could reread the interview that had so clearly impressed her childhood crush to such an unbelievable extent. Giddily, she resisted and instead tugged Alex's second set of laces loose with renewed confidence. "Of course, you're far more *talented* than most of us could ever hope to be. Including me."

Alex yanked her foot out of the second boot and sat up to tug off her sock. "You should probably wait until after you've seen my new work before you make that call. Could be I'm just a pervert."

Claire watched Alex's T-shirt ride up to expose a thin stripe of bare skin on her lower back. "Well, I look forward to finding out."

Glancing toward the front door, Alex opened her mouth to say something, then stopped—and closed her mouth again.

Intrigued, Claire prompted her. "What?"

Alex shrugged. "I left my laptop in the car with my carry-on bag. Since I should probably bring my stuff inside the house anyway…" She bit her lower lip, then raised a tentative eyebrow. "If you wanted, I could show you some of my favorite shots right now."

Subject matter aside, how could she possibly refuse? "Sure." *Thank goodness I've had half a bottle of wine already.*

"Yeah?" Alex's obvious anxiety seemed to have sobered her up a bit. "You don't have to. Maybe it'll be too weird." When she took a deep breath, Claire could sense that she was about to change her mind. "It's probably—"

"Alex, I want to see them. *Please.*" Claire's face heated at her overly passionate entreaty the instant it burbled out of her.

Alex licked her lips. "Okay." She glanced toward the kitchen. "Would you mind pouring me another drink?" Making shy eye contact, Alex looked startlingly vulnerable in a way that Claire had never imagined seeing the woman of her dreams. "I promise not to get totally smashed. I just…need a little more courage. You'll be the first person to see most of these photos, besides the curator at the gallery."

Claire put her hand on Alex's knee and squeezed. "I'm sure they're wonderful." Standing, she walked to the kitchen as steadily as possible. *I touched her knee. Which is next to her thigh. Which is so, so close to her…* "Another glass, coming right up."

When Claire returned to the front room with two more glasses of wine—because if she was going to view an art project focused on lady parts while sitting beside Alex-freaking-Williams, she sure as hell needed another drink, too—Alex had just returned from outside. Barefoot, she carried a backpack she set down near the door and a laptop case that she brought to the couch as Claire settled back into her seat. Sitting close enough that Claire could feel the heat emanating off her body, Alex picked up her refreshed glass of wine and took two large swallows. "Okay." She put the glass back on the table and opened her laptop. Double-clicking on a folder titled, simply, *Cunt*, she enlarged the first of dozens of photos, a close-up, black-and-white photograph of an aesthetically perfect vagina. "Here we go."

They sat together in silence with the image for a few endless moments while Claire took a big gulp of wine. Grateful for the fuzzy heat that immediately spread through her muscles and loosened her tongue, she lowered the glass and said, honestly, "Beautiful."

"Unfortunately, that one's my ex." Alex clicked to the next photo, what looked to be the same pussy, but this time with long, feminine fingers exploring the delicate folds of her labia. Shot at a different angle, this one showed the plump mound of her ex-girlfriend's vulva, which was also perfect. "I still love these shots, though."

"They're amazing." Claire sipped her wine as Alex began to scroll through the photos, occasionally murmuring a quiet, "Love it" or "That's gorgeous" or "Breathtaking" about the ones she particularly admired. After a few dozen photos and half her glass of wine, Alex paused on an image of a woman's swollen labia peeking out from between her thighs, framed by her full bottom, and said, "There are a few more, but they're a little…explicit."

Now drunk enough to wish she hadn't made Alex worry so much about causing her discomfort, Claire put her glass down a little too loudly. "Go ahead. Show me. It'll be inspiration for later. You know, lust."

Alex laughed but also kind of groaned. "Okay. But when you realize that you're sitting here looking at porn with Sarah's big sister, please don't freak out and regret it in the morning. Deal?"

Would Claire regret this in the morning? *A real, live masturbatory fantasy for me to embellish and expand upon in my head forevermore?* At the moment it was difficult to imagine being sorry about anything that happened tonight. In fact, the only real disappointment would be if nothing happened at all. "Deal. Now show me your porn."

With a nervous chuckle, Alex brought up an image that Claire instantly recognized as her ex. Her shapely bottom filled the frame, each round cheek gripped by a strong hand and pulled apart to reveal her incredible wetness and the long, flesh-colored dildo the unseen wearer was using to penetrate her slick, pink vagina. Instinctively, Claire glanced down at Alex's hand on the laptop to confirm her suspicion. *Is that really a photo of Alex fucking someone?* "Oh," she murmured aloud, unthinkingly. "Uh, wow."

"I haven't actually decided whether to include these in the show." Alex clicked to the next shot while studiously avoiding eye contact. "Tell me to stop at any time."

"No, don't stop." The second photo showed a similar pose, but this time the bulbous head of the dildo only barely rested inside the ex-girlfriend's swollen cunt. Allowing herself to be carried away on a pleasant cloud of alcohol-induced euphoria, Claire placed her hand on Alex's to encourage her to continue. "Are there more?"

Alex cycled through a handful of additional shots: two fingers penetrating her ex's eager hole, a pale bottom and pussy spanked bright pink by the bare palm still hovering over the reddened flesh, and after that an entire hand disappearing between a woman's soft thighs, up to the wrist. When she landed upon a particularly striking shot of a familiar mouth pressing a wet-looking kiss against the ex-girlfriend's shiny clit, Alex waited only half a second before hurriedly clicking ahead. The next photo was no less graphic than the previous one, a close-up of the flat of what was unmistakably Alex's tongue mid-swipe across the aroused ridge of flesh. Breathing hard at the visceral rush of fantasy the sight brought forth, Claire crossed her legs to stifle the urge to rock against the cushion in an attempt to seek relief from the effect of Alex's provocative talent.

"Does that mean you like them?"

Detecting true uncertainty in Alex's lilting voice, Claire managed a small nod and a tight, "Yeah. I do."

Alex minimized the photo on-screen but, in doing so, revealed one more thumbnail Claire knew she hadn't yet seen. Without really thinking, Claire leaned forward to take control of the laptop, double-clicking on the last image. "You missed one."

"Don't—" Alex lunged for the keyboard and then froze, staring dumbly when yet another incredibly appealing image filled the screen. Shot from the neck down, the topless model had her thighs spread wide and one hand resting on her lower abdomen as she displayed herself to the camera. The woman's bare breasts were out of focus, but the lens had lovingly captured every detail of her pink, thick-lipped pussy. Quietly, Alex said, "This is another I haven't made a decision about."

Alex's tentative voice made Claire jump. "Why not? I love it." Her throat went dry as she belatedly drew the obvious conclusion. *Oh.* She picked up her glass and poured the rest of its contents down her throat. *Because it's a self-portrait.*

Alex apparently detected Claire's flash of recognition, because she snorted loudly, then buried her face in her hands as she dissolved into helpless guffaws. "Oh my God, I'm *so* drunk. I'm so drunk, and I just showed you a picture of my pussy."

Claire's breath caught at Alex's confirmation of what she was seeing. She leaned near to study the image more carefully. "To be fair, I kind of showed it to myself."

Still chortling, Alex slammed the lid of the laptop closed, then turned to hide her face in the arm of the couch. "*Please* don't tell Sarah."

"It'll be our little secret. However, you do realize that if you include that one in the show, or any of the others you took with your ex, *everyone* will see it." Claire paused for effect, knowing she was about to deliver a terrible psychic blow. "Including Sarah."

Alex lifted her head to reveal rosy cheeks, only managing to meet Claire's eyes briefly before lowering her gaze. "All right. You've talked me out of it."

"That wasn't my intention," Claire said, bleeding honesty now that she'd drenched her filter in alcohol. "You're really damn sexy, Alex. So is your pussy. I say if you've got it, flaunt it. Right?"

Alex managed to glow even redder. "You're sweet."

"I'm not trying to be." Claire squeezed her thighs together, riding the giddy high that came from suddenly feeling like the most confident one in the room—something that almost never happened to her in social situations. Clit throbbing, she realized how perilously close she was to doing something truly ill-advised. And yet she couldn't seem to stop herself from pushing ever forward, desperate to see exactly how far Alex would be willing to take their mild flirtation. "I'm just telling you, if your goal is to arouse your audience, then you should absolutely include that last shot in the show. Because it was *definitely* arousing."

Alex's confidence slowly returned in the form of a hesitant smile. "Are *you* aroused, Claire?"

"What do you think?" Claire held her breath as she awaited the answer.

"I think…" Alex paused, then exhaled loudly. With a chuckle, she said, "I think we're drunk."

"Yes." She wasn't going to deny it.

"And…maybe we should be careful."

Claire frowned, no longer all that concerned about being cautious now that she'd consumed another full glass of wine. "Of what?"

"Of doing something we'll wish we hadn't."

Despite having wrestled with the same worry less than an hour ago, Claire failed to suppress her disappointment about the sudden appearance of Alex's conscience. Unfortunately, it seemed that she *could* trust Alex's judgment after all. *Damn.* Awkwardly, Claire chose to feign ignorance. "Such as?"

"Claire." Alex's low voice dropped to a throaty murmur. "You know what I'm saying."

Made unbelievably bold by the wine, not to mention her raging libido, Claire leaned against Alex's side for a beat before moving away. "That you want to do dirty things to me?"

*I really just said that. Out loud.* Claire closed her eyes, trying to determine exactly how embarrassed she would be in the morning.

Alex shuddered noticeably in reaction to the words Claire still couldn't fathom having uttered. "Like you wouldn't believe, Claire-Claire."

Unable to look at Alex after the hoarse, stunning confession, let alone *move*, Claire struggled hard to catch her breath. To think. Swallowing hard, she finally whispered, "Is that really such a bad thing?"

"I think it might be." Despite her apparent reluctance, Alex made no effort to put any additional space between their bodies.

Light years beyond any sense of shame by this point, Claire asked, "Why?"

"You're Sarah's best friend, for one." Although Alex delivered this verdict in a somber tone, she sounded eager to be dissuaded. "You're also drunk."

"I'm not the only one. And even so, I'm not beyond the ability to give consent. Are you?"

Alex shook her head. "No, but I'm older. It wouldn't be right."

"Alex, you're thirty-two. I'm twenty-seven. You wouldn't exactly be robbing the cradle."

Blinking, Alex stared into Claire's eyes as her handsome face took on an expression of actual wonder. "Wait, you…you really want this, don't you?"

She might as well have doused Claire's face with gasoline and lit a match. "Shut up," Claire said, chagrined by how easily Alex had detected her obvious need. If she were smart, she'd put a little distance between them before she made an even bigger fool of herself. Screwing up her friendship with Alex wasn't an option. "More wine?"

## Chapter Four

A lex caught Claire's hand to prevent her from standing up to go to the kitchen. "I'm already too drunk. So are you."

She wasn't wrong. Claire wobbled a little on her feet, then sank back down onto the couch. "You're right." A thought occurred, one that made her giggle nervously. "Which means I'm stuck here for a little while, unless I call a cab."

Alex shook her head firmly. "I'm not sending you home in some stranger's car. Not like this."

Pouting, Claire said, "I didn't *mean* to get so drunk."

"My fault. I take full responsibility." Alex exhaled as she rested against the arm of the couch. "I was nervous about hanging out with you. I wanted to loosen up, but…" She raised her hands into the air and shimmied them. *Jazz hands.* Claire chortled aloud at her silent musing. Chuckling along with her, Alex concluded, "Now I'm a little *too* loose."

Claire immediately zeroed in on the bombshell Alex had so casually dropped. "You were nervous? With *me?*"

"Well, yeah." Alex scrubbed her hand over her short hair with a self-conscious lift of her shoulder. "Now that I know what a genius you are…"

"I'm still me. The geeky, bespectacled dork who used to freeze up every time you talked to her. Who *still* does."

"You *do?*"

Blown away by Alex's supposed astonishment, Claire exclaimed, "You've got to be kidding. I've always been a nervous wreck around you! You had to have noticed."

"Well, you've always been kind of quiet, but you never seemed like a frozen, nervous wreck to me." Alex sat up straighter, shifting to face Claire. "Why did I make you so uneasy? I wasn't ever mean to you, was I?"

"No." Laughing in disbelief at Alex's cluelessness, Claire didn't even press pause before allowing her loose tongue to unleash the biggest secret she'd ever harbored. "Alex, I've had the stupidest, most massive crush on you ever since I was twelve years old. It paralyzed me every time you came near. Don't tell me you never realized."

Alex's lips parted, and she drew in a shaky breath. "I really thought you were just shy. I mean, I think I knew you were a little infatuated with me as a kid, but I…I figured you'd grown out of that."

"Well, I haven't." Claire's heart thundered at the realization that now that she'd finally outed her attraction, she would receive one of two responses. *Or perhaps no response at all.* She tightened her hands into fists, queasy about the magnitude of what was happening. "And now you know."

"Now I know." Alex hesitated, then lifted her arm and let her fingers hover over Claire's. "May I hold your hand for a minute?"

Claire turned her wrist so her palm faced up, then nodded. She whimpered softly when Alex's large, callused palm pressed against hers and their fingers interlaced like the most natural thing in the world. "I'm drunk," Claire repeated, like a disclaimer. "Sorry."

"Too drunk to consent?"

Alex's husky question made it almost impossible to breathe. "Consent to what?"

"I don't know." Alex squeezed her fingers, then lifted their joined hands so she could brush her lips over Claire's knuckles. "A kiss?"

Paranoia seeped into Claire's pleasant buzz, making her worry that Alex's request could be motivated by simple pity in the aftermath of her embarrassing disclosure. "You don't have to do that, Alex. Really."

Alex's fingers flexed on hers. "You don't want me to?"

"Of course I want you to." Claire licked her lips and stared up into Alex's eyes. "But only if *you* want to, for real."

A strong, sure hand curled around the back of Claire's neck and pulled her into a tender, exploratory meeting of their lips and then, thrillingly, the very tips of their tongues. The kiss ended almost as soon as it began, eliciting a despairing whimper from deep in Claire's throat when Alex backed away. Breathing hard, Alex looked into Claire's eyes and whispered, "I want you."

Wetness literally gushed from Claire's pussy, as though her body were weeping with joy over having finally lived the exact scenario she'd fantasized about hundreds of times. Too drunk to self-censor her physical reaction, she bent slightly at the waist and twisted around, reaching between her legs with her free hand to check if she'd stained Alex's favorite couch. Never having been in such a sexually charged situation, especially while intoxicated, Claire struggled to hang on to a coherent thought, let alone respond in a way that wouldn't kill the mood. All she could manage to say was, "My panties are soaked. I hope I didn't get any on the leather."

Alex's fingers tightened on the back of her neck. Her thumb stroked the top of Claire's spine. "I'm wet, too."

Claire couldn't help but to imagine the photograph of Alex's gorgeous pussy, this time coated with slick, clear fluid and swollen dark pink with arousal. She tried to think of how to reply, but even red wine couldn't restore her vocabulary with that vision filling her mind's eye.

"You're picturing it, aren't you?" Alex smiled big. "My wet pussy."

"How could I not?" Claire breathed. "I won't be surprised if I see your self-portrait every time I close my eyes, for the rest of my life."

"Then I'm jealous." Alex brought their faces closer together but didn't allow their mouths to touch. "You'll have the memory of that photo to get you by, and I still have only my imagination to go on."

Growing more comfortable the longer they remained in the intimate embrace, Claire asked something she'd always wondered but had accepted she would never know. "Have you ever thought about me before? Sexually?"

Alex lowered her eyes, clearly a little conflicted. "Before I read that interview, only a few times. The very first was the day I took you and Sarah to the beach to go swimming after your high school graduation ceremony. There were a handful of other times after that, when I felt naughty enough to go there. Since last year, though, it's been more frequent." She trailed off, then let out an amused snort. "Especially since I've had so much opportunity to masturbate, being single and celibate."

Claire struggled to believe that wasn't simply the alcohol talking. "Seriously?"

Reestablishing eye contact, Alex pinned her with an expression so earnest that for the first time in their lives, Claire felt every inch her equal. Soberly, Alex said, "I wouldn't lie to you. I *won't*."

Claire initiated their second kiss, a sensual dance of lips and tongues that undid her every bit as much as the first had. She immediately abandoned the idea of self-restraint, not so inconspicuously rocking against the couch cushion in an effort to find friction for her achingly sensitive clit. Alex dropped her hand from Claire's neck to the middle of her back, then lower, to tease the subtle cleft of bare skin rising just above the waistband of her panties. When Claire broke away with a gasp, Alex bent and sucked on the sensitive flesh joining Claire's shoulder to her neck.

Swept up in a situation still too unreal to believe, Claire asked, "*You're* not too drunk?"

"To make out with you?" Alex nibbled on her neck, teasingly, then pushed her hand farther down the back of Claire's jeans to grab a handful of her ass. "Definitely not."

"Is that what we're doing?" Without conscious thought, Claire slipped her own hand between Alex's thighs, rubbing the crotch of her jeans before capturing her concealed mound in a possessive grip. Exactly as she'd imagined doing countless times in dozens of different fantasy scenarios. "Making out?"

Alex made a strangled noise in the back of her throat, releasing Claire so she could slump against the couch while she endured the rough handling. "What do *you* want to do, Claire-Claire? Tell me. Sounds like you've thought about this at least a little before tonight." She exhaled shakily, lifting her hips to push against Claire's palm. "After fifteen years, you must know exactly what you want to do with me right now."

Flushed from both the wine and her embarrassment over her rich inner fantasy life, Claire continued to squeeze and caress Alex through her jeans even as she groped blindly for a suggestion that wouldn't be too humiliating to say out loud. "Um…"

Alex's hand covered hers, encouraging Claire not to stop by helping guide the speed and pressure of her touch. "Or would you prefer that I take charge? Do you like the idea of surrendering control to me?"

Claire nodded a little too rapidly. *Drunk. So very fucking drunk.* "I want you to take control. I want you to..." She paused, considered the inhibitions she normally possessed, then forged ahead, relieved to discover that she didn't currently care about anything except getting off. "Be in charge. Tell me what to do. Show me how to do it."

With a moan, Alex straightened and reached for her again, dragging Claire closer to plunder her mouth with her greedy tongue. Claire felt the shift in their dynamic immediately, Alex's natural dominance taking over now that she'd been given permission to wield it. Pressing Claire back against the arm of the couch, Alex ran eager hands over her breasts, her hips, her stomach, then finally, somewhat terrifyingly, between her legs. Alex backed slowly out of the kiss, nipped Claire's chin with her sharp teeth, and rumbled, "I want you to show me your pussy."

Claire's entire body caught fire. "Just...*show* it to you?"

Alex dissolved into a lopsided grin, clearly tickled by her shock. "You saw mine."

"Yes, but..." Claire scrambled to complete a mental inventory of her personal hygiene. She'd showered that morning, thank goodness, and was wearing decent enough panties, but she hadn't trimmed her pubic hair in days. Or shaved the quarter-inch of growth under her arms. "You were prepared. I'm not."

"You don't need to prepare." Alex pushed a lock of hair behind Claire's ear, then played gently with the lobe. "I want to see you just as you are. Not a meticulously cultivated version of yourself."

"But I told you, I'm soaking wet. Like, to the point it might be a little off-putting."

Alex laughed long and hard. "I doubt it." She beamed at Claire with such authentic affection, such undeniable *desire,* that any further resistance on Claire's part felt not only futile, but unforgivably foolish. "I've seen a lot of women's pussies, sweetheart. Some of them very, *very* wet." Backing up just far enough to allow Claire to sit, Alex stayed connected with a hand cupped around Claire's breast, the pad of her thumb toying with the erect nipple. "I've never wanted to look at anyone as badly as I want to look at you right now. And that's the truth."

"But...I'm afraid I won't measure up." Claire bit her lip as soon as the breathless confession flew out of her mouth, turned off by her own lack of confidence. *If you want to be with Alex this way, you need to believe you're worth it first.* "Sorry. I know that's silly."

"No, it's not." Both of Alex's big hands clasped hers, comforting her with their sheer size and warmth. "Not silly at all." Stroking Claire's knuckles with both thumbs, Alex fixed her with a patient, empathetic expression that belied her obviously inebriated state. "I think you're stunning, Claire, but regardless of how you look on the outside, you're one of the most beautiful people I've ever known."

Slowly, Claire leaned forward to trace the tip of her tongue over Alex's upper lip. "All right, but will you take off your clothes first?"

Alex inhaled swiftly but nodded. "Sure."

"And can I have just a *little* more wine?" Claire bit down on Alex's lower lip, rolling the plump muscle between her teeth before releasing it with a sensual moan. "You're not the only one who needs liquid courage before baring her soul."

Breathing hard, Alex practically leapt off the couch, grabbing their empty glasses to teeter clumsily toward the kitchen. "Just a *sip* or two more."

## CHAPTER FIVE

As soon as Alex left the room, Claire's hands flew to her mouth and she let out a silent scream. Then a roof-raising cheer. Then, still energized, she broke into an elaborate, seated jig that ended midway through her performance of The Sprinkler dance, when Alex rushed back from the kitchen only to promptly erupt with delighted guffaws. Mortified, Claire laced her fingers on her lap, wishing for the ability to psychically retrieve her new glass of wine from across the room via some sort of Jedi-level mind magic. "That was fast."

"What can I say? I'm excited." Grinning broadly, Alex sauntered back to the couch and handed over Claire's last sips of wine. "Clearly I'm not the only one."

Claire downed the entire glass in one go. Shuddering as the heat of the alcohol flowed through her body, Claire felt wide-eyed at the realization that Alex had started to strip down in front of her. Already topless, Sarah's big sister was a veritable butch goddess, with broad shoulders, a tapered waist, and shapely breasts even more breathtaking in reality than Claire had ever dared to dream. Alex paused to grab her glass and take a few eager sips, then bravely unbuckled her belt, thumbed open the button on her jeans, and pulled the tab of the zipper down to reveal a glimpse of the black briefs she wore beneath. Once she'd tugged her pants down around her ankles, Alex glanced up at Claire with a quirked eyebrow. "Feel free to join me anytime."

Not wanting Alex to feel alone in this act of courage, Claire chugged the rest of Alex's wine and stood up to unbutton her own jeans. "Oh, what the hell."

"*Yes!*" Left only in her boxer briefs, Alex fist-pumped in celebration of Claire's commitment to the cause. After a brief pause, she lowered the boxers with a jokey, yet thoroughly seductive, wiggle of her hips. "Now don't worry, young lady. I'm a *professional* pushy... uh, *pussy* inspector."

Claire wrinkled her nose as she stepped out of her own jeans. "Don't remind me." With her bottom half clad in only a pair of black, lace-trimmed panties, Claire wobbled as a wave of dizziness left her unable to smoothly negotiate their removal. "I should sit down," she said, then collapsed onto the couch in front of Alex.

Alex knelt at Claire's feet, staring up into her eyes with the kind of tender devotion Claire had never actually expected to see directed at her outside her wildest dreams. Placing her hands atop Claire's thighs, Alex gently nudged them apart. "Show me, baby. Let me see what you've got."

Seduced by Alex's firm, commanding tone, Claire opened her legs. Instantly aware that Alex could see the large stain darkening the crotch of her panties, she tried to control the pounding of her heart while she waited for a reaction. Alex licked her lips and tightened her fingers on Claire's inner thighs, surveying her arousal with quiet reverence. Even more wetness trickled out of Claire in direct response to the heat of the hooded gaze, along with a tremulous whimper that caused Alex's full lips to twitch in obvious amusement. Claire groaned, losing patience with the drawn-out tease as the last of her uncertainty fell away. "You can take them off, if you want."

Rather than guide the panties down Claire's legs, Alex simply took hold of the sodden crotch and pulled the material aside. Fully exposed to the love of her life for the very first time, Claire stiffened and studied Alex's face to discern her honest opinion. Pure, unrestrained lust flashed in Alex's eyes, leaving her with an awestruck expression both surreal in its lack of ambiguity and powerful for the way it made Claire feel. "You're perfect."

She was far from perfect, she knew, yet Claire believed that Alex's praise was sincere. Shyly, she whispered, "Thank you."

"I want to get rid of these." Alex grabbed the waistband of her panties and tugged them down to expose the top of Claire's hairline. "And kiss you all over that pretty pussy." She fingered the elastic band, brushing her thumb across Claire's still-exposed labia with a crooked smile. "After that, my sweet, *naughty* girl, I'll use my tongue to clean up this incredible mess you've made."

Claire's chest heaved, and for a moment, she fully expected to pass out. When that didn't happen, she hurried up and, with a frantic nod, granted Alex permission to proceed. "If you really want to."

"I *really* do." Alex yanked the panties down Claire's legs with a lack of caution that only made her wetter. "Do you like having your pussy eaten, Claire-Claire?"

Claire answered with a hearty nod. "It's my favorite."

"How many tongues have touched you here?" Curling her arms around Claire's knees, Alex fit her shoulders between her thighs and dipped to kiss the swollen labia she'd unearthed by positioning Claire's body as she had. "Not just the baby butch's, I hope."

"Two others." Hissing with pleasure, Claire went absolutely still while Alex first used her fingertips to spread her open, then ran her tongue along the length of her slit. "I won't even ask how many pussies *you've* licked."

"None as delicious as yours." With a moan, Alex shoved her face into Claire's pussy—and her tongue into the tight hole.

Claire arched her spine, tilting her head back to stare up at the ceiling while she basked in the nirvana of Alex's searing mouth. She forced her attention back to her lap only seconds later, not wanting to miss the visual element of this dream come true. Rapt, she pushed her glasses higher up on her nose so she could stare into Alex's blue eyes while she watched the woman she loved feast noisily on her sodden cunt. Seemingly thrilled by the attention, Alex adjusted her position to ensure that Claire could see every last detail of the diligent tongue that swiped again and again over her painfully engorged clit. Beyond words, Claire turned her focus inward, to the silent incredulity she still couldn't seem to vanquish. *Alex is going down on me.* Alex *is going down*...on me! Crying out, she spasmed under the demanding suction of the lips now attached to her clit, then grabbed the back of Alex's head in a desperate attempt to keep that incredible mouth on her forever.

Alex pulled back slightly. "Do you like what I'm doing?" She circled her tongue around the hard ridge of Claire's clit. "Tell me what feels good."

"*Everything,*" Claire breathed. "Everything you're doing feels better than *anything* I've ever felt before."

She shivered as Alex's noisy approval vibrated through her labia, then dragged her fingernails over Alex's scalp until she raised gooseflesh on the muscular arms that held her legs open. Shuddering with undisguised satisfaction, Alex took Claire's clit between her lips and gave her a loud suck before establishing a deliberate up-and-down rhythm in an enthusiastic pantomime of oral sex, passionately performed. Struck dumb by the sheer eroticism of the sight—*I'm receiving the greatest head of my life, from Alex!*—Claire spread her legs as wide as they would go and undulated her hips to force herself deeper into Alex's mouth.

With an ardent groan, Alex pulled back to murmur, "What a nice girl you are, to get so wet for me."

Claire tried to force Alex's head back down, but she wasn't nearly as strong and lost the battle almost as soon as it began. "Please, Alex. Please don't stop *now*."

"Don't worry, sweetie. *Relax.*" Alex planted a sloppy kiss atop her clit, delivering a brief burst of ecstasy that fell just short of sending her over the edge. "I know how to take care of a needy little pussy like yours." She licked around Claire's erect flesh, then sucked the bundle of nerves between her lips with a noisy slurp. "Now pay close attention to everything I do, Claire-Claire, because afterward, I'll expect the same treatment from you."

Claire shuddered at the way Alex managed to reference the most mortifying moment of her life while simultaneously unleashing the most tantalizing dirty talk she'd ever heard spoken aloud. "I'm paying attention." She gasped when Alex went back to work, vigorously licking and nibbling and sucking until Claire's thighs began to quake uncontrollably and her entire body tensed in anticipation of a shattering climax.

Pausing only long enough to drawl, "All over my tongue, baby," Alex intensified her efforts, batting at the rigid clit she held between her lips until Claire came with a deafening roar. She grabbed Alex's head with one hand and her strong shoulder with the other, hanging on tight as the powerful orgasm ripped through her tremulous frame. Long past modesty, Claire felt little need to dampen her cries of pleasure, jerking against Alex's skillful mouth as she rode wave after wave of ecstasy to their inevitable conclusion. Staggered in the aftermath of such unexpected bliss, Claire released a weak whimper as Alex continued to lick her folds while her sated body returned to earth.

"Alex." She grabbed one of the wide shoulders that were still forcing her legs so far apart. "May I please…" Hoping to encourage the light role-play Alex had initiated, she blushed, then said, "Demonstrate what I've just learned?"

Shiny with Claire's juices, Alex lifted her face to flash a drunken grin. "You certainly may." Lowering her gaze, Alex very lightly traced her fingertips over Claire's sensitive labia. "But first…would you allow me the privilege of snapping a quick photo? Just one."

The self-consciousness Claire thought she'd shed for the night instantly resurfaced. "A photo of what?"

"Your pussy." Alex continued to fondle her while she stared steadily into Claire's eyes. "I promise I won't show it to anyone else. This one will be for me only." She slipped a fingertip inside Claire's vagina, causing them both to groan. "I just…want to remember this moment. Forever."

Touched by the wistfulness of the request, Claire surprised herself by nodding. "Okay. Yeah."

"Really?" Alex seemed at first surprised, then electrified. She crawled across the room to her backpack—granting Claire a magnificent view of her tight little ass in the process—and rustled around inside for a few moments before eventually retrieving a digital SLR camera. By the time Alex returned to her former position between Claire's legs, the impulse to cover up had grown too overwhelming to ignore. As Alex fumbled to remove the lens cover, Claire dissolved into bashful giggles and hid her pussy behind her fingers. Alex lifted the camera to peer through the viewfinder, then lowered it with a playful smirk. "Don't be shy."

"But I *am* shy," Claire said, yet moved her hand anyway.

Alex raised the camera and quickly clicked the shutter to capture the shot. Then she adjusted the angle of the lens and snapped another.

Flinching at the fresh realization that she was being photographed while bare-assed and spread open on Alex's couch, Claire protested. "Hey, you said *one*."

"Sorry." Alex lowered the camera with a grin. "Bad habit." She glanced down at the LCD display, then turned it around so Claire could see. The feminine landscape on-screen was every bit as erotic as all the others Alex had shown her, despite the intimately familiar terrain. "Look how *sexy* you are, girl."

Simultaneously emboldened and embarrassed by the genuine attraction she felt to the image of herself through Alex's eyes, Claire slowly leaned back and spread her legs farther apart. "You can take another…if you want."

Alex spent a bit more time setting up the next photo, first guiding Claire's legs into the desired position, then pushing up the hem of the T-shirt Claire had managed not to take off to reveal her bare stomach. She pointed the camera at Claire's pussy, murmuring, "This might be my favorite one of them all." *Click.*

"You should take a picture with your finger inside me," Claire heard herself say, a suggestion that sounded both shocking and delicious in her ears. She nodded to confirm her own impetuous idea, then erupted into giggles when Alex shifted her camera to one hand so she could reach between Claire's legs with the other. "I can't believe we're doing this."

Alex pushed a single finger inside her, up to the second knuckle, interrupting Claire's laughter by forcing out a loud moan. "Me neither." She clumsily aimed the camera with her free hand, forced to strain a little to click the shutter. "I'll be masturbating to *this* later."

The suggestive comment unleashed a flood of inspiration to Claire's fevered brain, and she immediately reached for Alex's camera with a pleading expression. "Lick me again, for just a minute." She batted her eyelashes when Alex handed the camera over with a smirk. "For art."

"Uh-huh." Alex pushed her hands beneath Claire's ass, grabbing her butt and lifting her swollen pussy to her mouth. "Art." She stuck out her tongue, waited for Claire to aim the camera, then dragged the tip up her labia to circle her clit.

Claire took two photos in rapid succession, eager to preserve this singular moment forever. The tableau of Alex's dreamy lips pressed to her pussy, with those desire-filled blue eyes staring up at her with unabashed adoration, was simply too much for Claire to visually process in her current state. She liked the idea of being able to revisit this experience later, when their curiosity was sated and Alex had moved on to bigger and better things. As though sensing her sudden flirtation with melancholy, Alex shoved her tongue inside Claire's opening yet again, compelling her to capture the memory with a quick succession of poorly aimed shots. She hoped at least some of them were in focus.

Alex came up for air, first to relieve Claire of the camera, then to grasp her hips and roll her onto her belly. "Turn over, baby. Let me look at that luscious bottom of yours. Stick it up in the air so I can see your pussy, too."

*Thank God I'm drunk,* Claire thought happily, setting her knees apart on the edge of the couch so she could thrust her butt in the general direction of Alex's face. "Like this?"

"Just like that." Claire heard the *click* of the camera, then felt the indescribable joy of a long tongue delving into her from behind.

"Oh," Claire moaned, backing into Alex's face as the exquisitely foreign sensation rolled through her. "Oh, no one's...no one..." She couldn't seem to articulate that this was the first time someone had buried their face in her ass.

Alex laughed, licked up to her anus, then spanked Claire's left cheek hard enough to make her squeal. "Good." She snaked her hand between Claire's legs, reaching up to give her not-yet-recovered clit a possessive tug that gradually turned into a light massage. Squirming at the still-too-intense stimulation, Claire slammed her thighs closed on Alex's arm, then burbled helpless laughter when she received a remarkably gentle bite on her rear end that instantly startled them open again. Claire rolled onto her back after Alex had extracted her hand from between her legs, smiling at the expression of mock disapproval she received.

Claire shrugged. "It's your turn, anyway."

Eyes foggy with desire, Alex nodded with enthusiasm. "Yeah, *my* turn."

# CHAPTER SIX

A lex rose to her feet and reached for the pants she wasn't wearing. Her state of undress appeared to take a moment to register, but eventually she glanced down in confusion before busting up with laughter. "They're already off."

"Yes, they are." Claire sat up and reached for Alex's narrow hips, dragging her lower body right up to her face. "Come here. I want to see your pussy again."

Alex planted her feet apart, then used her fingers to spread open her labia so Claire could take a good, long look. "Give it a little kiss for me, Claire-Claire. Just like I showed you."

Weak with hunger, Claire pressed her mouth against Alex's labia in a tender, blissfully subservient kiss. The scent she'd always wondered about now surrounded her, even better than she'd hoped, and the flavor she'd long yearned to discover finally coated her lips. Moving her face from side to side, she bathed herself in Alex's juices, savoring the arousal *she'd* helped to create. She poked out her tongue and ran it through the intricate folds concealing the source of Alex's delicious wetness, unable to suppress a moan at this realization of one of her lifelong goals. Alex let her hands fall away from her labia, allowing the slippery flesh to smother Claire's nose and mouth, so that she felt entirely enveloped by the woman she loved. After a moment, Alex nudged Claire backward to rest against the arm of the couch.

"Lie down," Alex rumbled, guiding Claire farther onto her back. "I'm going to put my pussy in your mouth so you can suck it."

Claire was shocked when she didn't simply pass out. "*Yes.*"

Alex caressed Claire's cheek with her fingers, dark eyes

glimmering with desire. "Would you like me to use your tongue to get myself off? Tell me."

"Yes, Alex, please." Chest heaving, Claire grabbed at her hips in an attempt to tug Alex into position over her face. "Fuck my mouth."

Alex dropped her head with a strangled groan, then swung her leg across Claire's chest to crouch over her waiting tongue. "We're not going to regret this in the morning, right?"

"Shut up," Claire told her for the second time that night, then strained to lick the labia that hovered only inches from her lips. "Teach me how you like to be eaten." She lifted her head to briefly suck on Alex's wrinkled folds. "Tell me what to do and I'll do it. Whatever you want."

"All right, then." Alex tilted her hips and lowered her opening to rest against Claire's chin. "Lick my labia first. Nice and soft." She pitched forward when Claire eagerly obeyed. "Good. That's *very* good." Dropping her hand, Alex twined her fingers in Claire's long hair and held her firmly in place as she rocked against her mouth. "There you go. Now slide your tongue up to my clit, all the way up—" She gasped when Claire found the distended nub and traced sensuous circles around its throbbing head. "*Perfect.*"

Falling silent, she allowed Claire time to coax her sizable clit out from beneath its hood. Once it was fully engorged, Alex used the hand that wasn't tangled in Claire's hair to part her labia and push herself even deeper into Claire's open mouth. "Take the shaft between your lips, Claire-Claire, and suck on it like it's a tiny little cock." Alex tightened the fingers in her hair as Claire did exactly as directed, with gusto. "Oh, fuck yeah. *Fuck...yeah.*" Her lower body surged against Claire's face with increasing urgency. "Oh...my...*fuck*, girl. I hope you're ready for a mouthful of cum, 'cause that's what you're about to get."

Clutching Alex's hips, Claire moaned at the searing dirty talk, at the way it intensified her ardor, made her feel literally mindless with desire. She slid her hands down and around to grab Alex's firm butt, marveling at the powerful muscles that flexed beneath her fingers as Alex pistoned ever more urgently into the tight circle of Claire's lips. The need to touch Alex absolutely everywhere overrode any sense of propriety not yet demolished by the alcohol she'd consumed, sending her fingers to explore the crevice between Alex's rounded cheeks, then the wetness that flowed from her pussy in abundance. Alex's breathing stuttered when Claire made a return trip to her anus with a newly lubricated fingertip and painted the tight pucker of muscle with the hot juices.

"I'm coming," Alex cried out, pulsing hard against her tongue. Claire sobbed happily, exuberant that she'd managed to deliver the same pleasure she'd received. Increasing the suction of her lips, she nearly came herself—again—when Alex gave her hair a rough tug and rasped, "Swallow it." She ground her pussy against Claire's mouth, hips jerking in time with the contractions of her inner muscles. "Swallow all of my cum, baby. Everything I give you."

Claire kept sucking until the hand in her hair finally loosened, and then she lapped up all the sticky wetness smeared across Alex's pussy and thighs, obediently, like a dutiful student determined to impress her teacher by going the extra mile. Alex allowed her to keep working like that for a minute or two, stroking her hair tenderly while murmuring words of affection and praise, before finally easing back.

Then Alex lifted herself off Claire's face, allowing her to sit up even as Alex collapsed backward against the opposite end of the couch. For a few, interminable moments, they stared at one another in silence, Alex completely naked and still visibly recovering from her climax, Claire with her face covered in Alex's cum. Both of them were clearly uncertain about what to do or say next.

After what felt like an eternity, Alex said, "I'll get us some water. We probably need it."

"Good idea." Claire licked her bruised lips, tasting Alex all over again. "Thanks."

When Alex got up and padded into the kitchen, Claire couldn't help but notice again that her bare ass looked every bit as delicious as she'd always envisioned. Sighing, Claire rested against the back of the couch and attempted to check in with herself and process what had just happened. *I'm so drunk.* She exhaled evenly, suddenly very eager for that glass of water. *Alex is also drunk. Obviously.* With effort, Claire sat up and searched the floor for her panties and jeans. *Maybe I should call a cab. Is that what she'll want now that we're done?*

Alex walked back into the room right as Claire picked up her panties. "Hey." She offered Claire a full glass of water and sat heavily on the couch, leaving at least twelve inches of space between them.

"Are you cold? I have some clothes I left here last time I was home. You could borrow some boxers and a T-shirt to sleep in."

Claire tossed the panties back onto the floor and took a big, wet gulp of water. *She still wants me to stay over. But will that be weird tomorrow morning? Will we do it again tonight?* Too drunk to argue, not that she even wanted to, Claire acquiesced with a nod. "Okay."

Alex smiled, seeming relieved. "Good." She stared at Claire over the rim of her glass as she took a long drink. When she lowered the water from her lips moments later, Claire was surprised to see the corners of Alex's mouth turned down in apparent disappointment.

"What's wrong?" Claire slammed back the rest of her water, desperate for hydration, and swiftly gained an uncomfortable awareness of her bladder for the first time that night. Before Alex could answer, she said, "I have to pee."

Alex chuckled. "Me, too." She nodded toward the rear of the guesthouse. "It's through my bedroom. I can show you."

"Thank you." Claire stood up, then blushed when she remembered she was still bare from the waist down. Of course, once Alex got up and took her hand, completely naked herself, Claire decided that her own nudity was a fair price to pay for the spectacular view of Alex's. When an awkward silence descended upon them as they made the short trip to the bedroom, Claire said, tentatively, "That was fun."

Glancing over her shoulder, Alex beamed toothily as she led Claire into her private domain. "Yeah. It was." She pointed to the relatively small attached bathroom, which still managed to sport a deep tub that definitely looked big enough for two, in addition to a separate shower stall. A warm hand landed on Claire's bare bottom, making her jump. Alex drew back with a sheepish smile. "You go ahead. I can wait."

Claire peed and tidied up and washed her hands as efficiently as her moderately clumsy state would allow, eager to get back to Alex before either of them had time to panic about what they'd done or second-guess what they might yet do. To Claire's immense delight, Alex was still naked when she returned to the bedroom. Lying on her back in the center of the bed with her hands folded on her stomach, Alex stared contemplatively at the ceiling but turned to greet Claire with an affectionate nod as soon as she appeared in the doorway. "Feeling better?"

Claire tipped her head. "Much."

Alex climbed off the bed, then pointed to a small pile of folded clothing at the foot of the mattress. "If you'd like to put something on."

"Thanks." It didn't escape Claire's attention that, despite having ample opportunity, Alex hadn't gotten dressed. *Does that mean she wants to go again?* "Are you tired?"

Almost guiltily, Alex said, "A little, but not really."

Claire wasn't either. "Okay. Then I don't need pajamas yet."

Alex hesitated in the bathroom doorway, biting her lip to suppress the clear joy that answer had elicited. "Before, when you asked what was wrong?"

Somehow that seemed so long ago. Claire nodded. "Yeah?"

"I was disappointed when I realized I'd never even gotten your shirt off." Alex smirked as she disappeared inside the bathroom. "I'll be back in a minute. Stay right there, okay?"

"Okay." Claire took a deep breath after Alex closed the door. "Okay," she repeated in a whisper. "She wants you to take your shirt off." She toyed with the hem and tried to calm her racing heart. "She's already eaten you out, so this should be no big deal. At all."

Except it was. Alex had spent the past decade photographing scantily clad and occasionally naked women who'd dieted and exercised and otherwise sculpted themselves into models of absolute physical perfection. No way could she ever compare favorably. It wasn't that Claire believed she was unattractive. Just...*less* attractive, surely. After having seen some of the women who'd posed for Alex, including the ex with the perfect pussy, Claire couldn't bear to disappoint her with a thoroughly average body. Not face-to-face. Not when she'd probably never be able to live the moment down inside her own head. She closed her eyes, wishing she weren't still so very intoxicated, that she could think more rationally.

"Are you all right?"

Alex's soft voice startled a gasp out of her. Bringing a hand to her still-clothed chest, Claire said, "I didn't hear you coming."

Alex leaned against the door frame, eyes sparkling. "Thanks to my ninja reflexes."

"I guess so." Blushing, Claire stared down at her lap as Alex—still without a stitch of clothing on—strode over to sit on the bed close to her side.

"Now it's my turn to ask," Alex murmured, smoothing Claire's hair away from her face. "Is something wrong?"

Claire shook her head, unable to meet her concerned gaze. Her silly fears of inadequacy were too pathetic to admit out loud. "No. I'm fine, really."

"Are you tired? I won't be upset if you've decided you need to pass out." Alex bent to brush her lips over Claire's temple. "We did expend quite a lot of energy out there."

Claire got wet all over again at the visceral surge of memory Alex's suggestive comment evoked. "No. I don't want this to be over yet." She cringed the instant the truth left her mouth. *Too needy? Too needy.*

"Good. Neither do I." Alex's fingers trailed up Claire's collarbone, along the line of her jaw. "Will you let me take your shirt off?"

Claire blew out a shaky breath. "Sure."

Alex dropped her hands to the hem of Claire's shirt, yet made no move to further undress her. "You seem nervous all of a sudden. Why?"

An embarrassingly loud bark of laughter burst out of Claire's tight throat, which only made her face grow hotter. "Well…you're used to dating models. I'm not a model."

"I've dated more than just models. In fact, I've dated—and slept with—many different types of women." Alex lifted Claire's chin to force eye contact. "But never one I've known for so long, or respected so much, or, quite frankly, wanted so badly."

This all seemed too incredible to believe. Unsure how to respond, Claire finally whispered, "This just…doesn't seem real. That you could possibly want me the same way I want you." She shook her head to clear it. *Would Alex really lie to me? For sex? Because she's drunk?* She'd never known Alex to be cruel. Especially not to her. *Or could all of my fantasies really be coming true?* She was afraid to accept that idea, in case everything changed after they sobered up.

# CHAPTER SEVEN

Alex slipped a hand beneath her thighs, used the other to support her back, then lifted Claire's body to place her onto her lap. Unable to suppress a whimper when her naked pussy pressed wetly against muscular thighs, Claire hooked her arms around Alex's impressive shoulders to maintain her balance. But when Alex reached again for the bottom of her shirt, Claire instinctively let go, raising her arms so Alex could slip the thin garment off over her head. Tossing the top aside, Alex paused to ogle her bra while she caressed Claire's back with strong, slightly callused hands. "Want me to tell you about the first time I ever fantasized about you? I felt horribly guilty afterward. You were eighteen—*just*. I was well into twenty-three."

"You said it was the day you took me and Sarah to the beach." Claire shivered, nipples tightening within the slightly padded cups of her bra. She almost wished Alex would take the damn thing off so she wouldn't have to feel the scrape of the cotton against her sensitized flesh. "I remember that afternoon. It was fun. You wore board shorts and a bikini top, and I couldn't stop looking at your stomach." She let her hand drop to touch that same stomach now. "You mostly sat under an umbrella and read a book while Sarah and I built sandcastles and played in the water."

"Actually, I sat under that umbrella *pretending* to read a book while I watched you run around in that black, one-piece bathing suit. The one with the cleavage." Alex smoothed her hand down the valley of Claire's breasts, eyes going glassy as she reminisced. "I felt like such a dirty old lady, noticing your 'budding' body for the first time. But holy shit, Claire-Claire." She brought both hands up to cup Claire's bra, rubbing her thumbs over the raised peaks. "You had the most beautiful breasts. I fantasized about sneaking off with you somewhere and pulling down the top of your bathing suit so I could see them. I tried to picture what your nipples would look like, how they would taste. I wanted to touch you so badly my pussy *ached*. That night after I dropped you off at home, I went straight into my bedroom and made myself come, wondering how it would feel to be the first one to touch Claire Barker's perfect little tits."

Forgetting her current lack of hand-eye coordination, Claire reached behind her back and struggled to unclasp her bra. "I'm sorry you won't be the first—though you would've been that day—but you're welcome to touch them now."

Alex's face lit up with an expression of outright jubilation, and she hurried to help Claire with the stubborn clasp. "Only if you really want me to."

Claire chuckled breathlessly when Alex peeled the material away and took in the sight of her bare chest with a contented sigh. Fixated on the tension in Alex's face as she first swallowed, then parted her lips and leaned closer to take a nipple into her mouth, Claire promptly slicked the smooth thighs that supported her weight with a fresh gush of wetness. Moaning, Claire cradled the back of Alex's head with one hand and used the other to trace the powerful muscles of the jaw that kissed, licked, and sucked each breast in turn. "I used to fantasize about you being my first, too. I wouldn't be surprised if we both masturbated to thoughts of each other that night."

"What else did you think about?" Alex spoke while peppering kisses all over her chest. "Like, say, when you were eighteen. You were a virgin?"

"Until I was twenty."

Alex managed a bittersweet chuckle around her left breast. "Missed opportunity."

"I can't tell you how many times I imagined losing my virginity to you—or in how many ways."

"Tell me one example." Alex kissed the side of her nipple and dropped a hand between her thighs. She nudged Claire's legs open with a careful fist, then brushed her fingertips over the slippery labia. "One secret fantasy about giving it up to your best friend's big sister."

Claire wondered if Alex could feel it every time her pussy let loose with another torrent of juices. "Okay. Remember that time I spent the night at your parents' house, couldn't sleep, and went down to the kitchen for hot tea at the same time you came home from that party on the boat? The one where you met the fashion designer who gave you your first professional photography gig?"

"Of course. That was a pretty memorable night." Alex pushed her hand deeper between Claire's legs, rubbing carefully on either side of her swollen clit. "I'm choosing not to think about the fact that you hadn't turned eighteen yet."

"True enough, but this is a fantasy I *still* have sometimes." Claire caught the back of Alex's neck in her hand and guided her mouth down to the more neglected breast. "Anyway, you and I sat in the kitchen and talked for maybe twenty minutes—completely alone, I might add, which was absolutely *thrilling* to me at the time. In one of my favorite fantasies, you take me back to your bedroom to celebrate the night you just had. Sometimes I'm completely willing and enthusiastic, sometimes I act like I'm shy and uncertain about the whole idea, even though I'm excited, and sometimes I really *am* uncertain. It depends on my mood that day, on how dirty or rough I need the story to be to get off."

Alex moaned as she guided a single digit into Claire's vagina, then a second. Her lips encircled Claire's left nipple, then her right. Murmuring, she asked, "Tell me the one where you're completely willing and enthusiastic."

"Well…I sneak up to your room with you and sit on your bed while you lock the door. I tell you I've never done this before, with anyone, and you kiss me and promise to show me what to do. You take my hand and put it between your legs, holding my fingers while you teach me how to stroke your clit. Usually I'm a little clumsy at first, but you're always so patient. So tender. Yet still firm—and demanding. You know what you need, and you're determined to train me to provide it properly." Claire groaned, arching against the strong arm that supported her back as the fingers inside her scissored before twisting to hit a spot that made her entire body sing. "My favorite part was always the oral-sex lesson. Hence my blatant attempt to live out that scenario earlier on the couch—"

Alex released the tip of Claire's breast from between sharp teeth. "That was fantasy fulfillment for us both, believe me."

Claire *was* beginning to believe her. She rode Alex's long fingers, painting the tops of her thighs with the unending river of her arousal. The digits inside her reached and stroked and caressed, and like a puppet on strings, Claire's body jerked and bucked under Alex's control. She pressed her face into Alex's neck, panting hard when the hand on her back slid lower to tease the cleft of her ass. "*Alex.*"

"This is exactly what I pictured doing that night, after the beach." Alex buried her nose in Claire's hair and inhaled deeply. "Putting you on my lap, touching you like this." She moved her lips next to Claire's ear and breathed, "Open your legs for me, sweetheart. Let me in."

Claire let her legs fall open, which—with her head spinning like it was—just about sent her tumbling off Alex's lap. Holding her steady, Alex gathered Claire closer and, chuckling, pushed the fingers as far into her pussy as she could. Claire cried out and raised her head to stare directly into Alex's eyes. "That feels so *good.*"

Alex withdrew slowly, then drove her fingers back in every bit as deliberately as she had the first time. "I know it does, baby. I like making you feel good."

"Then don't stop." Claire squirmed on Alex's lap, wishing for friction against her throbbing clit. "Keep fucking me."

Alex hummed throatily. "You love having my fingers in your pussy, don't you?"

"Yes!" In desperation, Claire dropped a hand to tug on her nipple, hoping to spur on the orgasm she knew was coming. "*Please.*"

Alex brought up a thumb to brush against her clit, a mere tease. Claire groaned and lowered her own hand between her legs, using her fingertips to rub fast circles where she needed it most. Alex made a strangled noise in the back of her throat and increased the speed of her thrusts. "That's so sexy, Claire-Claire. Show me how you play with your clit. Teach *me* what makes you feel best."

Claire rolled her hips against both their demanding hands. She bit her lip as her climax neared. "I want to come with you inside me."

"*Yes*, baby." Alex craned to suck on her breast, fucking harder. "Squeeze my fingers with that tight little pussy. Show me how you'll feel wrapped around my big, hard cock."

Claire jolted in surprise at this new element in Alex's verbal repertoire, particularly at how powerfully the image turned her on. None of her ex-lovers had been into sex toys, but she'd certainly imagined using them with Alex on numerous occasions. She wondered if Alex actually *had* a strap-on. The thought filled Claire with nervous anticipation, unleashing a hot flood that Alex used to thrust into her even deeper. Wiggling her hips to convey her eagerness, Claire whispered, "I've never had one inside me before. A toy."

"Seriously?" Alex pulled back to study her face. "Like, *never* never?"

Claire's cheeks heated under Alex's intense scrutiny. She shook her head and reluctantly paused her self-pleasuring. "Only fingers. And tongues."

Inhaling shakily, Alex glanced across the room at a trunk that sat next to the closet door before hanging her head with a sigh of resignation. "I'm afraid I'm too drunk tonight for the gentle, painless introduction to strap-on sex that you deserve, but maybe another time…"

"I would love for you to be my first." Claire lifted her hand from her clit to Alex's chest, pressing firmly against the spot over her heart. "If we don't regret this in the morning." She cracked a sloppy grin, relieved when Alex matched it. *We won't, will we?*

"With *that* experience to look forward to?" Alex moved her thumb to rest against Claire's recently abandoned clit. "I'm not sure I'm capable of regret."

Claire hoped the same was true for her. "I'll never regret that I got to be with you like this, even if it's only for tonight."

"I don't want it to be." Alex traced light circles around the sensitive bundle of nerves, then stroked directly over the pulsing tip. "I want to fuck you in every room of this house. On every surface. In every one of your holes, in every single way you've imagined for the past fifteen years."

Claire contracted around the fingers inside her, inducing Alex to ratchet up the intensity of her fevered touch. Despite how precariously she teetered on the edge of oblivion, Claire hated to let herself surrender because it would mean the end of the most magical night of her life. No drunken reassurance in the world would guarantee that she'd ever find herself in this position again. Unfortunately, though she tried desperately to hold off, Alex's practiced skill easily destroyed Claire's attempts at resistance. Another few firm, focused caresses from the fingers buried inside her, combined with pass after pass of Alex's big thumb over her clit, brought on a noisy, earth-shaking climax that left

Claire clinging to Alex—first for support, and then in an unspoken plea not to leave.

Alex brought her down from the peak gently, fucking her with a softer and softer touch until finally she slipped out of her altogether and cradled Claire's vulva in the palm of her hand. Heart hammering, Claire rested her forehead on Alex's broad shoulder and pressed her lips against a thrumming artery she found in her neck. "I always knew you'd be really good at this."

Alex laughed and tightened the fingers curled around Claire's waist. Her other hand remained where it was, holding Claire's pussy in a loose grip. "You know I'm kicking myself for wasting all that time telling myself I was too old for you, and Sarah would kill me, and you probably weren't interested anyway, right?"

Claire smiled against the smooth skin at the juncture of Alex's neck and shoulder. "Silly boi."

"You're really good at this, too. By the way." Alex squeezed her pubic mound, setting off mini aftershocks that ricocheted through Claire's body like tiny little bolts of lightning. "That really *was* the best head I've ever gotten."

Claire shuddered at the memory. "I could do that again," she murmured, lowering her hand to toy with the short, curly hairs at the juncture of Alex's muscular thighs. "Or something else. Anything you want."

Alex let out a regretful whimper. "As much as I hate myself for saying this...I'm sorry, but after the flight, and the wine, and the first orgasm...I don't think I can. Even though I want to, more than anything."

Claire withdrew her hand from Alex's lap and threw her arms around her shoulders in an impassioned hug. "It's okay. I understand."

Alex rotated them forty-five degrees, then carefully placed Claire onto the mattress so that her head rested on one of the two pillows near the headboard. "Will you let me hold you for a while? And sleep with me?" Alex crawled into bed next to her, rolling onto her side to give Claire a mischievous grin. "Naked?"

"Sure." When Alex reached for her, Claire curled up against her solid body with a relaxed sigh. "Should we be drinking more water?"

"Probably." Alex kissed the crown of Claire's head as she cradled her in a loose embrace. "I'll refill us before we fall asleep. Promise."

Chuckling at the sudden heaviness of Alex's voice, Claire murmured, "Sure you will." Not keen for the inevitable hangover that would result from dehydration, she summoned all her willpower to extricate herself from Alex's strong arms. "I'll refill us."

"Don't go," Alex pleaded sleepily. Her fingers trailed along Claire's leg as she crawled toward the end of the bed. "Your body fits so perfectly against mine."

Claire felt exactly the same way. "I'll be right back. Promise."

Alex held her eyes open, though it clearly took effort, and blew Claire a kiss. "Hurry."

It took Claire a few minutes longer than anticipated to locate their empty glasses, then the filtered tap in the kitchen, and then to mop up the water she spilled while stumbling back into the front room. By the time she returned to the bedroom, she wasn't surprised to find Alex passed out, mouth ajar, snoring quietly. Heart leaping at the sight, Claire deposited a glass of water on the nightstand next to what she assumed was to be her side of the bed, then sank down onto the mattress next to Alex before giving her a careful nudge. "Wake up, sleepyhead."

Alex grumbled, then pried her eyes open to flash a goofy smile. "Claire-Claire."

"It's me." Claire offered her the glass. "Drink up."

For a moment Alex simply stared at the water in confusion. Then she sighed and dragged herself into a sitting position. She set the glass aside after a few hasty gulps. "Thank you, sweet girl."

"You're very welcome." Trembling, Claire picked up her own glass and drained half the liquid in one go. Surprised to find Alex still conscious, still watching her, Claire finished the rest and put the empty glass on her nightstand. "Hopefully we won't feel like shit tomorrow."

"Hopefully." Alex caught Claire by the shoulder and pulled her down to lie on her chest. Excited by the hard nipple that jutted into the air mere inches from her lips, Claire struggled to restrain herself from attempting to initiate an encounter Alex clearly didn't want. "It would be nice to do this some more. Sober."

It *would* be nice, Claire agreed silently, not entirely convinced whether Alex would feel the same way once they'd slept this off. Or even that she herself would. *Well,* Claire's eyes drifted stubbornly shut, *I guess there's only one way to find out.*

## CHAPTER EIGHT

Claire woke up groggy, confused, and—for at least ten solid seconds—completely lost in time and space. Uncertain about where she was or what she'd done the night before, it took her more than a couple of minutes to gather the presence of mind to sit up and look around. She was alone in an empty bed she only vaguely recognized, completely naked, thighs and pussy sticky with half-dried juices. Alarmed, Claire pushed aside the minor headache she had just begun to notice as she fought to remember the series of events that had led her to lose consciousness in this place. After a few moments, the memory of her drunken romp with Alex hit her full force, knocking Claire backward to lie on the pillow she'd drooled upon while asleep. Groaning, she tried to decide how she felt about what they'd done now that the alcohol was out of her system.

*How do I feel? Like I need to pee, that's how.* Scrambling out of bed, Claire grabbed her glasses and ran to the toilet. She was already seated before it occurred to her that Alex's absence in the bathroom meant that she hadn't left Claire alone in bed in order to relieve her own bladder. Anxious about what that might mean, Claire strained her ears to detect any signs of life elsewhere in the house. *Where is she? Off trying to figure out what the fuck to do now, just like me?*

After a wistful, longing glance at the shower, Claire washed and dried her hands before she left the bathroom on a mission to find her clothes. It felt beyond strange, wandering around naked in Alex's bedroom without the benefit of alcohol-induced euphoria of the sort that might convince a person that sleeping with her best friend's older sister was a good idea. *Oh, God.* After a frantic search, Claire located her T-shirt and bra and tugged them back on. Bare-assed, she turned in a circle in an attempt to pinpoint where her pants had ended up. Then a flash of memory rolled over her. *The couch. I took them off near the couch so Alex could take my picture—after she went down on me.* Claire completed another revolution in the spot where she'd become temporarily rooted in place, conducting a panicked scan for something, *anything,* she could use to cover her pussy before Alex came back to check on her. *If she hasn't fled the scene entirely.*

She spotted the boxer shorts Alex had offered to lend her the night before, crumpled on the floor after being shoved off the bed at some point during their encounter. Fighting to maintain her outward calm, she grabbed the shorts and pulled them on, trying not to stain the material when she inevitably flashed back to her time on Alex's lap after she'd chosen to forgo wearing these very same shorts not twelve hours earlier. Shivering, Claire folded her arms over her chest and hugged herself for comfort. *Will Sarah be pissed off at Alex about what happened? At both of us?* She gripped her biceps tightly. *How badly did I screw everything up last night?*

Claire rushed into the front room, steadfastly *not* looking at the fateful couch where she'd seduced Alex while she searched the floor for her panties and jeans. Once she'd found both articles, she looked around to confirm that she was still alone, then stripped off Alex's boxers and tugged on her panties, followed by the jeans. She zipped up her fly clumsily, noticing not only her worsening headache, but also the dryness of her throat. *My kingdom for a cold glass of water.* She glanced toward the kitchen, finally noticing the savory aroma of eggs and bacon in the air. The subtle clinking of dishes from the other room confirmed that Alex was, indeed, cooking breakfast—and *not* actively escaping the scene of their crime.

That meant the decision was Claire's. *Run away or deal with this mess like a grown-up?* Paralyzed, Claire glanced at the front door, then back toward the kitchen. As though summoned by her silently overflowing angst, Alex emerged from the open doorway wearing a green tank top that showed off her muscled arms and shoulders, paired with boxer shorts that did the same for her powerful thighs and calves. Struck dumb by the sight of so much bare skin—*though not as much as last night!*—Claire froze, unable to offer even the most rudimentary of traditional verbal greetings. Not even a grunt.

Alex stopped at the sight of Claire, obviously surprised to find her standing there, silent and motionless. "Claire. Good morning! I didn't hear you get up."

One of Alex's humorous lines from the previous night trickled into Claire's consciousness, and she answered, impulsively, "Ninja reflexes." Blood rushed to her cheeks at the realization that she'd purposefully referenced their illicit encounter, however tangentially. "I wasn't sure where you were. Sorry."

Alex shook her head. "No need to be." She ran her gaze down Claire's fully clothed body, frowning. "Are you leaving? I raided Sarah's fridge so I could make us breakfast. I was just debating whether to wake you up by bringing you a plate in bed."

*She's so sweet.* Claire practically swooned despite her lingering uncertainty about how to respond. *Was* she leaving? She probably should. But now that she knew Alex hadn't simply run off and left her—that, instead, Alex had actually decided to cook them *breakfast* after everything they'd done—Claire found it impossible to simply walk away. She didn't want to be the one who made this situation weird, or any weirder than it had to be. The truth spilled out before she could come up with a smoother answer. "I...hadn't decided yet. Whether to leave."

"You should stay." Alex gave her an uncharacteristically shy smile. "Food will help with your hangover."

Reminded of her headache—and at the same time alerted to a mild queasiness in her stomach—Claire accepted the invitation with a shy nod. "All right."

"Great." Alex jerked her thumb toward the kitchen. "Want to eat in there, or would you still be interested in doing the breakfast-in-bed thing?"

Claire wanted so badly to let Alex serve her in bed, but now that she was fully dressed and painfully sober, it hardly seemed appropriate. "We can sit at the table."

"Sure." Alex gestured for Claire to follow her. "Come on. I'll make you a plate."

Claire entered the small kitchen behind Alex, then kept walking to sit at the small café table in the sunny breakfast nook across the room while Alex made her way over to a collection of still-steaming skillets on the stove. Scooping a generous amount of eggs, potatoes, and bacon onto two separate plates, Alex occasionally lifted her gaze to meet Claire's, her smile growing more nervous each time. Claire filled the silence with the first question that came to mind, Desperate to lessen the awkwardness created by their indiscretion. "Did you sleep well?"

"Like a very drunk, very satisfied rock." Alex carried both plates to the table and set Claire's down in front of her with an affectionate wink. "How about you?"

"I slept so hard I basically had amnesia when I woke up. I had no idea where I was for at least a full minute."

Pausing with her hand on the refrigerator door, Alex studied Claire's face while she took a first, tentative bite of egg. Her expression was almost painfully concerned. "You...remember last night, though. Right?"

Cheeks aflame, Claire nodded before ducking her head. "I wasn't *that* drunk."

"Good." Alex let out a literal sigh of relief and opened the fridge. "Would you like orange juice, water, or both?"

"A lot of water, a little orange juice. And something for a headache, if you have it."

"Not a problem." Alex grabbed a carton of orange juice, a jug of cold water, a bottle of ibuprofen, and a handful of cups, then brought everything back to the table. She sat down to pour two small cups of juice, then two taller glasses of water. "Other than the headache, how are you feeling this morning?"

"Pretty good, considering." Claire took a big sip of water, then popped a few ibuprofen in her mouth and swallowed. "I haven't been that drunk in years."

"Me neither. Luckily, I've never been all that susceptible to hangovers." Alex took a bite of potatoes and chased them with a mouthful of eggs. When Claire still hadn't said anything by the time she swallowed, Alex sighed and put down her fork. "How are you doing otherwise? Like, emotionally?"

Claire cleared her throat, staring at her plate so she wouldn't have to make eye contact. "That's...a little more complicated, I guess."

"Complicated how?" Alex's voice sounded hushed. Almost like she was holding her breath.

Mortified that they were actually going to *talk* about this, Claire sighed. "I...feel the need to apologize for getting so drunk and so...

so *silly*...last night. I know I was incredibly forward with you, even when you told me you weren't sure it was a good idea. Even when you worried that we would regret it." She speared a chunk of potato with her fork, then set the utensil down on her mostly untouched plate after her stomach rolled uneasily. "I think...I enticed you into something you knew better than to do. I took advantage of your inebriation." She swallowed past the growing lump in her throat, suddenly worried she might get sick all over Alex's kitchen table. "Honestly, I'm ashamed of my behavior. Ashamed, and sorry."

"No, *I'm* sorry." Alex's entire tone had changed. Instead of the amiable congeniality with which she'd served their breakfast, now she sounded mired in despair. "I shouldn't have let things get so out of hand. I could have stopped what happened, believe me. I just...didn't want to."

The unbearable tension in the room became too overpowering for Claire to handle. She pushed back from the table and started to stand, finally ready to make her escape, but Alex caught her wrist in a firm but tender grip that kept Claire from leaving. Fearful of what she might see, Claire tentatively lifted her eyes to meet Alex's.

"Do you regret sleeping with me?" Alex asked, vulnerable in a way Claire had never once imagined in any of her myriad fantasies.

Claire's cheeks burned hotter. Yet again, she had no idea how to answer. "Yes and no?"

"Well, I don't regret it. I sure thought I might, and believe me, I wish it had happened in a different way—a more deliberate, carefully chosen way—but I really had been nursing a wicked crush on you for a while now." Alex's gaze never wavered. "You didn't talk me into anything I didn't already want. You simply gave me permission to live out my biggest fantasy. And Claire...I *loved* being with you like that. I enjoyed every last second of it. You were always one of my favorite people in the whole world, but after last night..." She exhaled, shook her head, and slid her hand up Claire's wrist to tangle their fingers together. "Just...know that I would be interested to see where this goes. If you were willing to take that chance with me, I mean."

Claire's eyes welled with tears, blurring Alex's handsome features and also making her feel more fragile than she'd ever let herself be with another human being. *Ever.* "What about Sarah?"

"Sarah's a big girl. She can handle us dating." Alex lifted Claire's hand to her lips and kissed each finger in turn. "Is she your only concern?"

Every brush of Alex's full lips against her skin sent an electric charge shooting through Claire's body. Each successive shock eroded a little more of her resistance to the idea that Alex could actually want *her. For more than one night, even.* Claire shook her head in disbelief. "The biggest one. I think."

"What's another?" Alex set Claire's hand on the table without letting go. The muscles in her jaw bunched slightly. "I don't want to feel like I'm talking *you* into something you don't want. If you would prefer that last night be a one-time thing, I'll respect that. I promise."

Kicking herself for signaling any type of uncertainty about her feelings, Claire shook her head. The truth was, she *wanted* to date Alex—if only she weren't so afraid it could never actually work out. "Alex, at this point I've wanted to be with you for more than half my life. Literally. You *were* my sexual awakening." Barely managing a bashful shrug, Claire noted how much more excruciating it felt to confess this sort of thing while sober. "It's not that all I ever dreamed of having with you was one night, but…that's probably the best you'll get out of me. Because as much as I'd love to see where this might lead…I'm not sure you and I are all that compatible. Unfortunately."

"Oh." Alex hesitated, then let go of Claire's hand so she could pick up her fork and take another bite of egg. After she swallowed quickly, she added, "All right. I understand."

Something about the timbre of Alex's voice told Claire that she really didn't. "Alex, you don't want to date *me.* I'm a total geek, an introvert who's painfully shy at parties whenever someone actually manages to drag me to them. My idea of a perfect Saturday night is video games and pizza. Sex for dessert. After the *actual* dessert, of course, which is probably something chocolate."

"Claire—"

On a roll, Claire steamrolled over Alex's attempt to interrupt. "You've traveled the world. You're always going to some party or special event, always surrounded by beautiful women, always so calm and confident and *sexy* and comfortable in your own skin. I would hold you back. I would *bore* you."

"You're not boring." Alex's hand crept under the table to rest on Claire's knee. "And I told you, I'm ready for a change. I'm tired of living life at a hundred miles per hour. I'm ready to slow down. Ready to *settle* down."

Claire shook her head, refusing to accept that she might really have a chance to get everything she'd always wanted. "What happens when you change your mind?"

Alex exhaled. "I've known you for fifteen years, Claire-Claire. I *know* you. More than that, I respect you. Please believe me when I tell you that I would *never* try to pursue a relationship with a friend who means this much to me if I didn't believe she was someone I might potentially be able to love and cherish for the rest of my life."

Claire quivered from head to toe, the shock of Alex's bold pronouncement rolling through her like a nuclear blast. "Why didn't you ever tell me you felt this way?"

"At first, because I had a girlfriend. After that, because I was intimidated."

Claire shook her head again, pretty sure that she'd lost her grasp on the English language. "*Intimidated?* By me?"

"I hate to break this to you, sweetheart, but you've got this big, amazing, world-changing brain, and I'm…" Alex lifted one shoulder in a playful cover for the genuine flash of worry that passed over her face. "Well, I'm…an artist."

"You're brilliant! In your art and in life." Claire frowned at the nonsense Alex had allowed herself to internalize. "Honestly, *that's* the least intelligent thing I've ever heard you say. Intimidated by *me*." She scoffed. "Don't be stupid."

Luckily, Alex reacted to her diatribe with an amused chuckle. "I suppose we all have our insecurities. No matter how silly they may seem to others."

Claire nodded to indicate her understanding of the point Alex had so deftly made. She hesitated, then covered the hand that still rested on her knee, entangled with her own. "Sarah is my best friend in the entire world. She's my family. *You* are my family. I'm terrified to disrupt that…*any* of that…"

"It's your decision," Alex said patiently. "I think Sarah will be okay. I think—I *hope*—that you and I could be even better together than we are apart." She waited a beat, then said, "I'm not going to beg. I'll just say…I want you again, Claire. Sober. I want you *again* and again. As soon as possible, for as long as you'll have me."

Floored by Alex's unmistakable sincerity, Claire went boneless as she surrendered to her greatest desire. "Okay."

Alex cocked her head, leaning closer to search Claire's eyes. "*Okay*, okay? Or was that more of a 'you talked me into it, so okay'?"

Claire pushed her chair away from the table and stood. "May I sit on your lap again?"

"I'd like that." Alex scooted back to make room before reaching for Claire with outstretched arms. "Come here, baby."

Settling gingerly onto her firm upper thighs, Claire looped her arms around Alex's shoulders and clung tightly to their solid bulk. Glad not to have to worry about holding eye contact any longer, she put her mouth next to Alex's ear and whispered, "I want you again and again, too."

The powerful body beneath hers shuddered in reaction to the shy confession. Threading her fingers through Claire's hair, Alex tugged to gently encourage her into a position that brought their lips mere inches apart. Close but not touching, Alex murmured, "May I kiss you?"

Ever pragmatic, Claire wrinkled her nose. "I haven't brushed my teeth."

"I couldn't possibly give less of a fuck." Alex edged even closer. "Please? May I?"

Claire nodded and closed the distance between them to give Alex a timid little peck. Lacking the assertiveness to set their pace, she breathed, "Yes."

Alex brought their mouths together in a tender kiss, moaning when Claire's hands tightened on her shoulders in response. She ran the tip of her tongue over Claire's bottom lip but made no other attempt to deepen the contact. Instead, she dropped kiss after kiss on Claire's mouth and cheeks and chin and neck, literally showering her with the most reverent, worshipful caresses she'd ever received. Claire reciprocated each and every touch, every press of those full lips, using her whole body to communicate her hunger for their newfound intimacy. Eventually Alex broke away, panting hard, and whispered, "How's your headache?"

"What headache?"

Chuckling, Alex gathered her closer. "Did I kiss it better?"

She really had. Not only had the pain in Claire's head receded, but her unsettled stomach was also a distant memory. "You're an artist *and* a healer."

Alex drew back to look into her eyes. "On that note, you should eat a couple more bites. At least."

"All right." Claire turned back to the table without leaving Alex's lap. She picked up Alex's fork and took a little egg from her plate, then followed up by feeding the next mouthful to Alex. After that, she did the same thing with the potatoes. One bite for her, one for Alex. When Alex finally refused her turn, Claire ate the last chunk of potato and set the fork onto the nearly empty plate. "There."

Alex trailed her fingers down the center of Claire's back, triggering a rush of arousal that made Claire grateful for the layers of cotton and denim that separated her suddenly wide-awake pussy from Alex's bare thighs. "Now that our bellies are full and you're feeling a bit more settled, would you be interested in joining me for a shower?" Alex nipped at her earlobe. "Then perhaps we could go back to bed?"

Everything about this felt so much more precarious—and therefore more thrilling—without alcohol to dull her senses. Claire's pulse raced at the thought of getting naked with Alex Williams while they were both of sound mind and body. "Sure."

Alex stared at her with so much compassion that Claire nearly blurted *I love you* right then and there. "Only if *you* want to, for real."

Flushing at the sound of the familiar words, ones she'd spoken right before their first kiss, Claire murmured, "I want to, Alex. For real."

# CHAPTER NINE

In a stunning display of strength, Alex somehow managed to rise to her feet while lifting Claire with one arm under her knees and the other wrapped around her slim shoulders. "Good, because I'm not ready for this to be over yet, either."

Claire buried her face in Alex's shoulder as she was carried back to the bedroom, then into the bathroom. Alex set Claire on her feet next to the tub, grabbed two towels from the built-in closet, and turned on the shower in a single, smoothly executed motion. Awed by her impressive physical presence, Claire watched in silence until Alex eventually came to stand in front of her with a teasing wink. "Don't worry, Claire-Claire," she said, giving a polite bow. "I'll take off my clothes first."

Claire couldn't help but return her smile. "Lucky me."

Beginning with a goofy, seductive wiggle, Alex proceeded to perform a mini striptease, at first tugging her tank top off over her head, then shimmying her boxers down her long legs before she kicked them away with a flourish. Claire dissolved into giggles when Alex carried on the dance a little longer, finally concluding by spinning in place to shake her tight little ass from side to side. Alex directed a dashing grin over her shoulder. "Thank you. I'll be here all week."

Disarmed by Alex's casual ease, Claire inhaled deeply before pulling off her own shirt. To her credit, Alex focused on checking the water temperature instead of Claire's tentative disrobing, and when the time came for Claire to remove her bra and panties, Alex retreated behind the shower curtain with a little wave. "Come on in once you've psyched yourself up. Oh, and there's an extra toothbrush for you on the sink, if you want to brush your teeth."

Claire grabbed the toothbrush, still in its retail packaging, and tore it open to perform the fastest cleaning of her life. She stared at the cup that held Alex's still-damp toothbrush as she worked, wondering whether she made it a habit to keep extras around for a regular stream of unexpected overnight guests. *Or maybe she simply borrowed the toothbrush from Sarah, too, like the groceries. Alex might have lived a bachelor's lifestyle, but that doesn't mean you're simply one of many.* Annoyed by her perpetually insecure train of thought, Claire rinsed her toothbrush, stuck it in the cup with Alex's, and removed her glasses to set them on the sink. After only a momentary hesitation, she stripped off her bra and panties, then went to stand outside the shower. She raised her voice to be heard over the water. "I suppose it's silly to feel shy after last night."

"Nah." She could hear Alex ducking her head beneath the spray. "Not silly at all. Alcohol makes it *way* easier to be naked with someone new. I get it."

Claire took another deep breath and drew back the shower curtain so she could step inside. She returned Alex's welcoming smile shyly, folding her arms over her bare breasts as she stood face-to-face with her longtime crush. "You don't seem to be having any trouble."

Alex flashed a toothy grin. "Maybe I'm just better at hiding my anxiety."

"Maybe." Claire bit her lip when Alex stepped closer to take her by the forearms and guide her hands down to her sides so she could no longer shield her breasts. She watched Alex drink in the sight of her nudity, thrilled by the unmistakable hunger that darkened her eyes.

"You're even more beautiful this morning," Alex murmured. She wrapped an arm around Claire's waist to pull their lower bodies together so their hips touched. Her free hand drifted to settle on Claire's right breast, which she caressed lightly with her palm. "Reverse beer goggles. Doesn't usually work out that way."

Claire snorted yet couldn't help but succumb to the immense pleasure elicited by the compliment. "I think I'm starting to see why you've never struggled to get all the gorgeous women you want. They really don't come much more charming than you, do they?"

Alex waggled her eyebrows. "They may try, but no. I don't think they do." She rubbed her thumb over Claire's pebbled nipple, then used her index finger to pinch and twist the sensitive nub until a needy whimper escaped from Claire's throat. "I hope you know these aren't just lines I'm feeding you. I really *do* think you're breathtaking, Claire. You're *exquisite*. Inside and out."

Having no experience fielding such heady praise, Claire could only manage a self-deprecating smile. "You're just saying that because I let you take pictures of my pussy." Heat flooded her face the second the p-word passed over her lips, only to intensify when Alex burst into loud laughter.

"Oh, baby...*lots* of women let me take pictures of their pussies. It requires much more than that to win me over." Alex paused before her expression brightened comically. "Also, I'd *totally* forgotten we did that! I can't wait to look at those shots later." She gave Claire's bottom a few firm pats. "Maybe together?"

"Maybe." Certain she had to be fire-engine red at this point, Claire buried her face in Alex's shoulder to bask in the strength and confidence her new lover so effortlessly exuded. "I still can't believe last night actually happened."

"Me neither." Alex wrapped Claire in a tight, full-body embrace. "But I'm so fucking happy it did."

Secure within the circle of Alex's powerful arms, Claire found it impossible to disagree. "Me, too."

"Then let's get that sexy little body of yours nice and clean, sweet girl." Alex nibbled on Claire's neck, then her ear. "So I can take you back to bed and make love to you the way you deserve."

Claire quivered in anticipation. "All right."

Alex released her waist and bent to squirt a dollop of gentle cleanser into her palm. Claire faced the opposite direction without being prompted, smiling at the wall when Alex's strong hands massaged the soap into her back before reaching around to do the same for her breasts. Pressing a warm kiss to Claire's shoulder, Alex murmured, "You tasted amazing last night. Better than the finest wine."

Claire battled the instinctive embarrassment that arose and leaned back against Alex's broad chest as the hands on her chest moved down to smooth over the tops of her bare thighs. "I loved how you tasted, too." She held her breath when Alex's fingertips brushed over her pubic mound, tilting her hips to encourage a firmer touch on the next pass of her roving hand. "And all that dirty talk...you have a real way with words."

Cradling Claire between the legs, Alex tightened her fingers to give her a firm squeeze while simultaneously thrusting against her ass. Claire could feel the rasp of Alex's kinky pubic hair scraping her buttocks and bent slightly at the waist so she could back up even more firmly into Alex's crotch. Alex groaned, using the hand not on Claire's pussy to grab onto her hip and hold her steady. "You enjoyed those nasty things I said to you?"

Claire used both hands to brace herself against the shower wall. "Very much."

"That was me without a filter." Alex continued to grind herself against Claire's butt, clearly enjoying both their position *and* Claire's willing submission. "To be honest, I was concerned I might've offended you. This morning, I mean. When I woke up and…remembered."

"*Definitely* not offended. You're about to discover that this shy exterior has been perfectly crafted to conceal a downright filthy sexual appetite."

"Excellent." Moving the hand that cradled Claire's pussy up to support her stomach, Alex helped her stand fully upright so she could squirt a bit of shampoo into her long hair. "In that case, there was something else we talked about last night. I'm not sure whether you'll remember, or even if you really meant it…"

Claire searched her memory of their drunken encounter, an enjoyable exercise that only made her hornier. Not entirely certain *which* conversation Alex was referring to, yet reasonably certain she wouldn't have agreed to anything she couldn't also enjoy while sober, she prompted Alex. "Refresh me."

Alex removed the showerhead from its holder to rinse Claire's hair clean. When she was done, she put her hands on Claire's hips and turned her around so they faced one another. Then, looping her arms around Claire's waist, she bent and captured her lips in a lingering kiss. They broke apart and Alex murmured, "I want to come while I'm buried inside you."

Claire's legs weakened at both the comment and the smoky voice that delivered it. In a flash, the previous evening's brief exchange about strap-on sex floated back to her in a stream of images and sound bites that left her clinging to Alex's shoulders for support. "You mean…with a dildo?"

"I love wearing a cock. Love the way it makes me feel." Alex used her fingers to nudge Claire's chin up, forcing their eyes to meet. "But let me be clear. This isn't something I *need* from you. No pressure—really. There are all kinds of fun ways to make each other come, so don't you *ever* worry if you're not into any particular one of them. That said, last night you told me you wanted to try. That you…you wanted me to be your first." Alex swallowed and ran her knuckles along Claire's jaw. "If that's still true, I'd love to do that with you this morning." She searched Claire's face, then wound her hand in her hair to tug lightly. "I could teach you how to take my cock like the good girl I know you are."

Claire jolted at the impact of Alex's lewd comment, which had been delivered so naturally and without even breaking eye contact. Swaying on feet she could barely feel, Claire held tighter to those broad shoulders, overwhelmed by Alex's uncanny knack for tapping into the tone and spirit of her most cherished, most secret fantasy scenarios. Far more intrigued than frightened—though she *was* a little frightened— Claire pushed her hips into Alex's with a small nod of acquiescence. "I think I'd like that."

"All right. But at the risk of sounding like a broken record, I need to make sure you understand that I only want this if you do, too. Like, *really* want it." Alex cupped her hand around the back of Claire's neck and tilted her face up for a tender kiss. "And not just because you want to make me happy."

"I *do* want to make you happy, but that's not why I'm still interested." Claire initiated another brief kiss. "Believe me when I tell you that the idea of being fucked with a strap-on worn by Alex Williams has formed the basis for more than a few of my masturbatory fantasies over the years. You're not asking for anything I haven't already imagined giving you hundreds of times."

Groaning, Alex said, "But we could always wait." She moved forward, forcing Claire to back up until her shoulders hit the shower wall. Alex exuded a vaguely predatory air as she placed her palms on either side of Claire's head to cage her between muscular arms. "Until you're more comfortable. With me, I mean."

Claire couldn't quite imagine ever feeling comfortable in Alex's presence. She supposed she would eventually, if they continued to sleep together. Regardless of her comfort level, now that the idea had been raised, she couldn't think of anything she wanted more than the type of skillful introduction to strap-on sex Alex would undoubtedly provide. Appreciative of the concern, but more than ready to make yet another of her longstanding desires come true, Claire rose to her tiptoes so she could plant an impish kiss square on Alex's mouth. She dragged her fingernails down Alex's flank as they broke apart, triggering a noticeable shiver that Claire echoed unconsciously. Exhilarated by Alex's powerful reaction to her touch, Claire murmured, "Would you be willing to go slow with me?"

Alex nodded soberly. "Of course, Claire-Claire."

"Then I want to try." She encircled Alex's waist in a loose embrace and rubbed their pelvises together. "Right now."

Alex caressed her cheek. "I promise to make sure you're very wet, and *very* ready, before I put it in." She chuckled when Claire moaned wantonly at her phrasing, then pulled her even closer. "Maybe you'd like to sit on my cock and ride me. That way you'll have total control."

Claire dipped to lick Alex's right nipple. "Yes," she whimpered. "To all of it."

With a shaky exhalation, Alex retreated to allow Claire to step away from the wall. She cut off the flow of water with a few turns of an ornate brass knob, then grabbed Claire's hand and helped her out of the shower. Claire took the towel Alex offered and rapidly rubbed her body dry—except her pussy, of course, which seemed to have entered a state of perpetual wetness. When Alex rehung the towel next to her own, Claire's entire body tingled with anticipation. Resisting the urge to cover her nudity, she took Alex's hand and led them back into the bedroom. *Time to prove that I really do want everything she's willing to give me.*

Before Claire could say a word, Alex scooped her up and carried her to the bed, then deposited her on the center of the mattress like the most precious, fragile artifact ever uncovered. Alex sank down beside her and trailed a reverent hand from the base of Claire's throat to the juncture of her slightly parted thighs. "Thank you for trusting me," she said, huskily. "I'll do everything I can to deserve this."

Claire half chuckled, half whimpered at the tickle of Alex's blunt fingernails combing through the trimmed thatch of hair so very near her throbbing clit. "Of course I trust you. You're Sarah's big sister." She fisted her hands in the comforter and let her legs fall open. "I know you would never hurt me. Not intentionally."

"Never," Alex repeated with an emphatic shake of her head. She rested her hand on Claire's inner thigh, making her jump. Once Claire's breathing evened out, Alex moved cautiously to caress her slippery labia with the tips of her fingers. "I only want you to feel good."

"I do." Nostrils flaring, Claire lifted her hips off the mattress to encourage a firmer touch. "Alex, that feels *so good*."

Alex bent to Claire's chest, taking a hard nipple between her lips for a languorous suck. Her fingers dipped lower, first to trace Claire's tight entrance, then to gather enough of the abundant juices that flowed from her opening to smear across the rest of her swollen folds. Claire felt yet more arousal trickle out immediately, a never-ending stream of desire she hoped would ease the dildo's passage into her needy cunt. Uncurling the fingers of one hand so she could cradle Alex's head with her palm, Claire arched her back to force even more of her breast into the hot mouth that feasted upon her. Alex's grateful moan vibrated through her chest, causing Claire's clit to jump beneath her fingers.

Alex raised her head and licked her lips. "The wetter your pussy is, baby, the easier my cock will slide in." She brought her index finger down to Claire's opening, resting the tip just barely inside. "You want me to put my cock in here, don't you?"

Claire nodded, then gasped when Alex guided a single digit into the slim channel of her vagina. "Yes," she whispered, spreading her legs even wider. Folding the pillow beneath her head so she could more easily see Alex's hand between her thighs, Claire watched, fascinated by the sight of the thick finger gliding in and out of her. "Go ahead and use two."

Alex chuckled and bent to kiss her cheek. "Good girl." She withdrew her index finger, added the middle one to join it, then carefully eased them both inside her body again.

Surprised by their thickness, by how *full* she felt already, Claire exhaled shakily. "How big *is* your cock?"

Alex flitted her gaze to the trunk at the far side of the room and tilted her head thoughtfully. "The one I keep here hasn't been used in a long time—or really much at all, for that matter. To be honest, I don't remember."

Needing to know—and already thoroughly enjoying the way her pussy had to stretch to accommodate Alex—Claire put her hand on the muscular arm that flexed in time with every cautious thrust. "May I see it?"

"Sure." Alex brushed her mouth over Claire's, teasing her upper lip with the tip of her tongue as she slipped her fingers out of their snug new home. Rather than leave the bed immediately, she reached for Claire's right hand, gently loosening the fist it had formed before placing the fingers over Claire's sensitive labia. "Will you touch yourself for me, Claire-Claire? Don't be shy."

Despite her fuzzy recollection of having already done this for Alex once before, Claire couldn't help but feel bashful about masturbating in front of the woman she'd spent over half her life loving from afar. Only Alex's kind, beseeching eyes gave her the courage to use the pads of two fingertips to rub small, tentative circles around her own clit. Alex watched attentively, pushing Claire's trembling thighs farther apart, then carefully holding open her labia to get a better look. Claire exhaled in a rush, floored by her own boldness, not to mention the surety with which Alex handled her body. *Alex may not leave me any choice* but *to get more comfortable.*

"Keep playing with your pussy for me," Alex rumbled, glancing up with a rakish leer. "I'll be right back."

# CHAPTER TEN

Claire let out a mournful sigh at the loss of that safe, solid presence beside her when Alex finally got off the bed and went to the trunk. She stroked herself with an even firmer touch, her horniness outweighing her shyness at this point, while studying Alex's every movement with watchful, impatient eyes. "Hurry," she begged.

Alex tossed a cocky smirk over her shoulder. "Stick one of your fingers inside that tight little hole for me, baby."

Claire moaned and circled her clit even faster. After a moment, she realized that Alex was still watching her with an expectant look on her boyishly handsome face. "Oh," Claire murmured, then tentatively worked her index finger into her very willing opening. "All right." Gasping at the foreign sensation of penetrating herself in this way, Claire caught her lower lip between her teeth and gingerly fingered her own pussy.

"That's perfect, sweetheart." Wholly focused on Claire's self-pleasuring, Alex opened the trunk and rummaged through its contents without looking. "Are you almost ready for my cock?"

Claire was positive she'd never been so ridiculously wet. She wasn't sure she'd even *known* this level of arousal existed. "*Yes.*" Noticing that Alex was holding an object in her hands—an object that decidedly *wasn't* a dildo—Claire strained for a better look. "What's that?"

"The harness." Alex held up what appeared to be a pair of black boxer briefs. She reached back into the trunk. "And this..." Alex's face lit up for only an instant before her shoulders dropped and her mouth twisted into a mild grimace. "Is a little bigger than I remembered."

"Bigger?" Claire came up on one elbow without ceasing the motion of her busy fingers. "Let me see."

Alex produced a tan-colored dildo from within the trunk and dutifully carried both objects back to the bed. "Claire, if this one is too much for you, we can try some other time. We'll go to the store together and pick out a toy that's a little…slimmer to start."

Fascinated by the realistic-looking phallus cradled within Alex's big hands, Claire slipped her finger out of her pussy and sat up. She extended her hand without speaking, then gasped, mouth dropping open, when Alex passed her the surprisingly heavy object to inspect. "That *is* big."

"About seven inches long, one and three-quarters in diameter," Alex said. "Certainly not the *biggest* around, by any measure, but not exactly an ideal beginner's model, either."

Claire turned the dildo over in her hands, stunned by the attention to detail paid to the bulbous head, the veiny shaft, and the slightly wrinkled testicles. "Do you like the fact that it looks so real?"

Alex surprised her by turning a deep, lovely shade of pink. "Yeah," she mumbled. "I do."

Claire handed it back. "Put it on."

"Claire…" Alex accepted the dildo but made no move to equip it. "If I'd realized which cock I had at this house…"

"I still want to try." Summoning her bravest grin, Claire moved to the edge of the mattress so she could kiss the patch of short hairs between Alex's powerful thighs. "After all, it's not like I've never gotten myself off with thoughts of Alex Williams and her slightly-too-big cock before."

Alex exhaled, then shook her head. "Fuck…you are *full* of surprises, girl."

"Pretty soon I hope to also be full of *you*." Returning to the center of the mattress, Claire lay down on her back and resumed stroking her clit, then nodded at Alex. "Put it on."

"Okay." Alex picked up the shorts and fit the wide tip of the phallus through the hole centered over the crotch. "But if you don't like it…if it *hurts* or something…promise you'll tell me so we can stop. This will only be good for me if it's also good for you. All right?"

Touched *and* reassured by Alex's insistent concern, Claire stared at her with every bit of the desire she'd carried inside for the past fifteen years. "I understand. Now *hurry.*"

Alex opened the drawer of the nightstand and pulled out yet another object. This one was a silver, bullet-shaped vibrator, attached by a long, thin wire to a battery pack with controls. She grabbed a pair of fresh batteries from the same drawer, replacing the ones in the control pack before tucking the bullet into a pocket sewn into the interior of the shorts, over the crotch. Catching Claire's interested look, Alex winked. "That's mostly for my benefit."

Claire groaned at the implication of the set-up. Alex really *would* be able to come while inside her. Dipping into her own pussy to check her arousal, Claire hummed happily when her fingers came away coated in thick fluid. "I'm *so* wet for you, Alex." She watched Alex sit on the edge of the mattress and slip her feet through the leg holes of the assembled apparatus before she stood up to pull it on with one skillful motion. "I can't wait for you to come inside my pussy."

Alex turned to face her with the thick, rigid cock jutting proudly from between her legs. "You'd *better* be wet for this, sweetheart." She fisted her hand around the dildo and stroked up, then down its length. "I can already tell you'll be a tight fit."

Claire's clit pulsed beneath her fingers, causing her inner muscles to contract a handful of times before she was able to forcibly suppress her impending climax. "I'm sorry," she whispered, about both her relative inexperience and her current hair trigger.

Alex lowered herself onto the mattress and stretched out alongside Claire's writhing body. "No, baby. I *love* a tight fit." She reached between Claire's thighs, knocking her hand away so she could once again position her index and middle fingers against Claire's opening. "I just hope you do, too."

Claire threw her head back, moaning when Alex slowly drove both thick digits all the way inside her vagina, then crying out in surprise when the fingers spread slightly apart. It didn't *hurt*, not at all, but for a moment the pleasurable effect approached mild discomfort, before Alex's hand relaxed and Claire released a sigh that was part relief, part disappointment.

"Are you okay?" Alex murmured. She shifted farther down the bed until she could lick Claire's engorged clit. After at least twenty seconds of the most intimate kissing imaginable, Alex lifted her head and searched Claire's face. "I didn't hurt you, did I?"

"No!" Claire's hands flew up to cup her own breasts, where she pinched her nipples sharply to distract herself when Alex stretched her open again. "I like it."

"Should we try three fingers now?"

Already they were breaking new ground. The most Claire had ever taken from an ex-lover was two. Excited to give Alex the gift of her relative innocence, she nodded enthusiastically. "Please."

Alex withdrew her fingers, added a third, and carefully worked them back into Claire's slender opening. Once the initial sting of being stretched beyond her previous limit had receded, the feeling became pure pleasure, a fullness that hit all the right spots inside. Alex stopped moving once she'd buried her fingers as deeply as they could go, allowing Claire time to adjust. "How's that?"

Claire tightened her fingers on her own breasts and squirmed around on Alex's hand. "*Wonderful.*"

"Yeah?" Alex pulled out of her almost all the way, then pushed back inside with an excruciating lack of urgency. "Rub your clit again, sweetie. It'll help you relax."

Claire lowered her hand and stroked herself unselfconsciously, greedy for the pleasure of her own touch even if she didn't agree with Alex about the need to further relax. "I told you, it feels good."

Alex scooted farther up the bed, using the hand that wasn't buried inside her pussy to curl Claire's unoccupied fingers around the thick shaft of the dildo. "I know, baby, but you've never taken anything as big as me before. I won't lie. It may be a little uncomfortable in the beginning. The more relaxed you are, the better it will feel."

This was like a real, live version of her many "Alex Williams, the gentle, big-dicked teacher" masturbatory larks, right down to the patient, considerate dialogue that still somehow managed to sound vaguely lewd enough to make Claire soak the sheets. Pressing down on her clit, Claire gasped when her internal muscles responded by clamping harder onto Alex's big fingers. Nervous about the potential reaction to the reversal of all their hard work, Claire's muscles gradually unknotted once Alex bent to capture her lips in a lingering kiss while continuing to thrust her fingers within the gradually widening passage. Claire let her fingers rest lightly over her clit without stroking it, afraid to come before Alex managed to fit that impressive girth inside her body.

Breaking away from their kisses some time later, Alex whispered, "I'm going to let you be the one to put my cock inside. I'll lie on my back so you can straddle my hips. That way you decide how much to take— and how fast." She stared at Claire with an expression of unambiguous devotion, then smoothed a stray lock of hair off her forehead. "Best of all, it'll give me the opportunity to watch the brilliant Claire Barker ride my big, fat dick."

Claire lowered her hand to cup the bulge created by the fake testicles concealed within Alex's shorts. "Sounds like a win-win to me."

"Indeed." When Claire rose onto her knees, ready to make an attempt, Alex stopped her with a hand on her hip. "Hold that thought." She rolled toward the nightstand and pulled yet one more item out of the open drawer. Returning with a foil-wrapped square that Claire instantly recognized despite never having used one herself, Alex passed over the condom with a shy grin. "Put this on me first."

Claire raised an eyebrow as she tore open the condom. "Okay." She examined the circle of latex for a moment, trying to decide which end was up, then waited for Alex to settle fully onto her back in the center of the mattress before she fit the rolled ring over the wide head of the dildo. "Will it ruin the mood if I ask why?"

Alex folded one arm behind her head and lifted her other shoulder in a half shrug. "Good hygiene? Role-play?"

Sensing that Alex truly regarded her cock as an extension of her body in the bedroom, Claire rolled the condom down the ridged shaft, using both hands to stroke its length as though Alex possessed the necessary nerve endings to feel the seductive caress. Her impromptu hand job created a tantalizing visual, at the very least, as confirmed by the way Alex tipped her head back with a strangled groan. Taking a cue from the many fantasies she'd created to fill a lifetime of lonely nights, Claire settled into the role-playing she suspected Alex most desired with surprising ease. "Do you like it when I jerk you off like this?"

Alex used her free hand to click on the vibrator's controls, jerking a little when a quiet buzz filled the air. Teeth gritted in response to the sudden stimulation on her clit, she lifted her hips to push the cock through the small circle of Claire's hands. "I love it, baby. You're so good at this." She cupped Claire's breast in her hand, massaging the supple flesh with a possessive touch. "You know, if you can't accommodate me with your pussy, you could always use your pretty little hands to get me off." Grinning, she rubbed her thumb over Claire's bottom lip. "Or your mouth."

Inspired, Claire bent to place a tentative kiss on the tip of Alex's condom-sheathed cock. "Like this?"

"*Fuck*," Alex breathed. She used her hands to gather Claire's hair away from her face. "Lick the tip this time. Pretend it's a clit."

Claire grabbed the base of the dildo in her hand, then traced her tongue around the mushroom-shaped top. She raised her eyes to meet Alex's as she fluttered the sinuous muscle down the rippled shaft, teasing thoroughly before she finally popped the first couple inches of the toy all the way into her mouth. Only slightly unsettled by how much she had to strain her jaw to fit around its girth, Claire gazed up at Alex with all the adoration she felt inside.

"Oh, *fuck*." Alex locked her hand on Claire's head, uttering a helpless laugh. "I'm about to come already."

Claire took that as her cue to sit up and allow the cock to slip out of her mouth. "Oops."

"*No*." Cursing under her breath, Alex whined, "I didn't mean *stop*."

"I want you to come inside my *pussy*." Claire winked. "Not my mouth."

Alex growled and reached for her hip. "Sit on my face."

"As lovely as that sounds…"

"Just for a minute." Alex's fingers dug into her side, gently, as she attempted to urge Claire upward. "*Please.*"

She grew even wetter at the sound of Alex's urgent plea. "Well, if you insist." Claire crawled up to kneel over Alex's face, tickled that she was being begged for something she'd yearned so long to receive. She lowered herself onto Alex's waiting tongue, already anticipating the blissful pleasure of being consumed by her ravenous mouth. Humming when Alex's tongue slid into her, then squirming, Claire murmured, "*Oh*, I love that."

Alex's large hands curled around her thighs, then shifted to squeeze her buttocks when Claire began to rock back and forth on her busy tongue. Excited by Alex's enthusiasm, Claire ground down against her face, painting her forehead, nose, cheeks, and chin with the slick product of their shared efforts. Half giggling, half moaning, she teased, "See? I'm ready." Claire planted her hands on the headboard and dragged her slick folds up the center of Alex's face, then back down, marking Alex with her scent. "Are *you* ready?"

Aware that Alex couldn't speak with a mouth full of pussy, Claire lifted herself off her face to let her answer. After gulping in a few deep breaths, Alex rasped, "Beyond ready."

"Great." Claire clambered off Alex's face and moved down to straddle her hips.

"But first—" Alex lunged for the nightstand, retrieved a bottle of lube, and squirted a thick line down the length of the shaft. "There's no such thing as too much lube."

With a grateful smile, Claire balanced herself on her knees and reached between their bodies to grasp the slippery dildo in her hand so she could position it at her entrance. Inhaling steadily as the heavy pressure pushed against her slick opening, she bent to lie chest-to-chest with Alex, then rested her forehead on Alex's shoulder when she realized how big the toy was actually going to feel. "This might take me a minute."

Alex's hands came up to stroke her back. "There's no rush," she whispered. She trailed her fingers down to squeeze Claire's ass, encouraging her to rock against the rounded head of the cock. "I love how your body feels on mine. So warm, so soft." Her touch drifted to Claire's waist, then her upper back. "So *strong*."

Claire rolled her hips, using the hand that held the toy to guide its head just inside her opening. "And you're so *big*."

Alex dragged her blunt nails down the length of Claire's back before grabbing her hips. "Do you still want this?"

"More than anything."

## CHAPTER ELEVEN

Bracing herself, Claire sank slightly lower onto the wide tip of the dildo. She gasped when her body strained to accept its girth. "*Oh, God.*"

"Can you feel me sliding into your pussy, Claire-Claire?" Alex laid an affectionate kiss upon her hair. "Am I stretching you open?"

Claire moved the hand not holding Alex's cock to clutch her solid bicep, holding on tight as she took in still more of the unbelievable length. "*Yes.*"

"Do you like how it feels?"

"Yes." Claire cried out as the widest part of the mushroom-shaped head breached her opening. She forced herself to keep sinking down onto the dildo, suspecting that once she'd gotten this part inside, the rest would follow relatively easily. "Almost there."

Alex's hands landed on her back, one at the base of her spine, the other between her shoulders, holding her tenderly. "You're doing so well, sweetheart."

The praise helped to mitigate the mild discomfort that rolled through her lower body as the tip sank fully inside. "*Oh.*" Claire gasped, nearly incredulous when the rest of the cock slid right in. "*Oh!*"

Alex let out a strangled noise and raked her blunt fingernails down to Claire's ass. "*Very* good girl."

Pushing against Alex's shoulders, Claire raised her upper body so she could stare down into desire-filled blue eyes. "I almost can't believe you fit."

Eyes sparkling, Alex positioned her hands on Claire's hips. "It doesn't hurt?"

"Not anymore." Claire lifted herself up a few inches before slowly impaling herself a second time. "Actually…" She undulated her hips, attempting to ride Alex the way she'd seen women do in movies. "It feels *really* fucking incredible."

Alex groaned. "I'll say."

Relocating her hands to the mattress on either side of Alex's head, Claire leaned forward so her breasts hovered directly over Alex's gorgeous face. "Suck on them," Claire commanded, moving faster. "Play with my tits."

Alex beamed up at her. "My, my. Someone's not nearly as shy as she seems."

"Shut up." Claire bounced a little on the cock, then grabbed Alex's head so she could feed her breast to the hot, willing mouth waiting below. Taking the chance that Alex would allow her to turn the tables, however mildly, she said, "Be a good boi and do as you're told."

Alex drew Claire's nipple between her lips and gave it a firm suck, shuddering beneath her still-moving body. Claire echoed Alex's loud moans, unable to remember feeling so connected to anyone, ever. She angled her hips so her clit pressed more firmly against Alex's crotch, the vibration from the bullet within the harness arcing through her lower body like the most magnificent electric charge. Then she straightened, removing her breast from Alex's mouth so she could sit upright and fuck herself on the cock buried so impossibly deep within her pussy. She grinned shyly at the sight of Alex's awestruck expression, a mixture of potent desire and pure adulation.

"I don't know how I got so lucky." Eyes shining, Alex ran her hands over Claire's entire body, everywhere she could reach. "You're so fucking hot, Claire. In every way."

Unused to compliments of that nature, Claire nonetheless took Alex's words in stride. It was obvious they were truly heartfelt. "So are you."

One of Alex's hands snuck around to palm Claire's ass, then moved down to tease the sensitive skin stretched so tightly around her cock. "I had no idea you were such a cock-hungry little slut." She winked, as though to take any possible sting out of the naughty, clearly playful remark. "But you're going to drain me dry, aren't you?"

"That's my goal." Claire pouted, biting her lower lip as she rode Alex harder. "Am I doing this right?"

"Yes, baby." Having gathered wetness on her fingertips, Alex reached between Claire's thighs to find, then fondle, her erect clit. "I'm getting close."

Alex's fingers worked her clit like they already knew Claire's body by heart, triggering her inner muscles to once again clamp down, this time on the firm yet somehow yielding thickness of the dildo lodged inside her. The sensation was nothing short of incredible. "Me, too."

"That's right, baby." Alex rubbed faster. "I want you to get me off by coming all over my cock. Can you do that for me, baby?"

Already on the edge, Claire could no longer remain upright and fell forward onto her hands, pressing hard against the mattress on either side of Alex's head. "Yes, Alex."

"That's my girl." Alex's lower body surged, seemingly involuntarily, to thrust the cock up into Claire. With her hand trapped between their abdomens, Alex continued to stroke Claire's clit with vigor. "Milk my dick with that sweet, tight pussy."

The spark of Claire's climax ignited deep within her, rapidly spreading outward as her thighs began to quiver around Alex's hips. "I'm gonna come."

Alex's free hand came down sharply on Claire's butt to deliver a slap that startled her at first, before rapidly inducing the most tremendous orgasm of her life. Claire threw her head back and shouted—*loudly*—as she clenched around Alex's cock and unprecedented ecstasy scorched through her veins. Alex smacked her ass again, setting off another round of furious contractions that eventually left Claire breathless, yet also more determined than ever to make Alex come. Summoning all her remaining energy, she dragged Alex's hand out from between her thighs, grabbed her other wrist, and pinned both on the pillow next to Alex's head. She held Alex down with all her strength, savoring the concept of immobilizing her powerful new lover even if she knew that, in reality, Alex could escape the forceful hold without breaking a sweat. It seemed that Alex enjoyed her play-acting, too, judging by the wide flare of her nostrils and the tension in her trembling thighs.

"Now *you* come for *me*." Claire drove her hips forward, again and again, fucking Alex so demandingly she knew she'd pay for it later.

*Worth it, though.*

"Holy…" Alex tipped back her head and lightly tested Claire's grip on her wrists. "*Fuck me*, Claire-Claire."

"Don't worry, stud. I'm going to jerk your cock off with my pussy until you squirt—"

Alex's roar cut off her foray into truly gender-bending dirty talk, proof positive that her instincts were on target. Claire smiled big while she continued to jerk her hips into Alex energetically, rutting as though she were the one inside Alex instead of the other way around. The muscular body beneath hers stiffened, and quaked, until finally Alex escaped Claire's grip so she could cut off the vibrator's power before promptly melting into a human puddle. With obvious effort, she lifted both arms to drag Claire down against her chest, hugging her so tight she had no problem detecting the thudding of Alex's racing heart synchronized with her own. For at least a minute, neither of them spoke. Both tried to catch their breath.

Eventually, Alex said, "Please don't take this the wrong way—"

"Just what I love to hear after I make a woman come." Claire picked up her head, trying to cover her very real glimmer of anxiety with a lighthearted wink.

"But I never, *ever* envisioned how good sex with you would actually be." Alex shrugged and stroked Claire's back with an apologetic smile. "That's all. I clearly underestimated your abilities as a lover, and for that, I'm truly sorry."

Even as relief swept through Claire, she still had to ask, "So it was good for you, too?"

Alex rewarded her with a hearty laugh. "Let's just say it ranks right up there with the very best I've ever had. Considering who I'm with, probably *the* best."

Shaking, Claire cradled Alex's strong jaw in her hand. "Are you going to freak out if I end up falling in love with you?"

"Yes." Alex grinned. "In the very best way."

Despite her newbie status and the morning's mild hangover, Claire shocked herself by grinding her lower body into Alex's, so that the dildo shifted within her slick vagina to brush against a thrillingly sensitive spot deep inside. "Can you go again?"

Alex groaned, placing her hands back on Claire's hips. "I hope I'm fit enough for the challenge of dating a younger woman. As far as keeping up sexually, I mean."

Claire curled her fingers around the base of Alex's neck, gingerly. "I have faith in you."

"You're biased." Alex tickled her sides, forcing Claire to squirm off the dildo to get away. "On that note, I sure hope I live up to all these fantasies you keep talking about."

"Are you kidding? You already have." Getting onto her hands and knees, Claire took advantage of her growing comfort—and unrelenting sexual appetite—by flipping around to face the foot of the bed. Excruciatingly aware of the view she was offering to Alex, Claire supported her upper body with her forearms and thrust her butt up into the air. "Can we try doggy-style next? I've always wanted to do that."

"My goodness, Claire." Alex rose up onto her knees behind her, grabbing Claire's ass and carefully pulling the cheeks apart. "I really *have* underestimated you."

"I guess so." Claire wiggled her bottom enticingly. "Want to spend the day figuring out in how many ways?"

"Sold." Nudging the head of her cock against Claire's sodden pussy, Alex paused before pushing herself inside. "Let me take you out to dinner tonight? Somewhere fancy and delicious?" She edged forward, delivering the subtle threat of penetration. "On a real date."

"Sold." Claire dropped her head, exhaling under her breath as Alex slowly but forcefully eased the head, then the shaft, back inside her still-tight opening. She pushed herself up onto splayed hands, helping Alex by backing up the rest of the way, until her bare ass pressed against Alex's pelvis. Claire opened her mouth and released a soundless cry, overwhelmed not only by the eroticism of their position, but also by Alex's passionate touch when she reached beneath Claire's chest to cradle her breasts. Alex withdrew from her vagina almost languidly, then drove forward, using the hands on Claire's tits to tug her backward to deliver a more powerful thrust. Claire's mouth dropped open—

And at the same time, Alex's bedroom door flew open. "Hey, sis. Have you seen Claire today, because her car is—"

Horrified, Claire raised her eyes to where Sarah stood frozen with her mouth agape and her hand splayed over her heart. She couldn't help but wince at Alex's sudden retreat from her pussy, though the hasty extraction was performed with admirable care considering the shocking awkwardness of the interruption. Demonstrating remarkable poise under duress, Alex covered Claire's naked body with the comforter and quipped, "She's right here."

"*Holy. Shit.*" Sarah lurched as though the discovery had literally slapped her across the face. "What the fuck—how did…" She retreated a step, then turned and left the room while closing the door behind her. "Sorry," she called out, voice slightly muffled behind the wooden barrier. "I was *not* expecting that!"

"Neither were we!" Claire shouted back. Heart hammering, she leapt off the bed to once again search the room for her discarded clothing. "It started last night with a bottle of wine and—"

"Do we really need to gossip about this right now?" Alex asked. "Or should we wait until we're all dressed?"

Claire frowned at Alex, afraid of Sarah's reaction after such a major bombshell. She turned to the door, holding her breath while she awaited some indication of how Sarah felt about the seismic change in her relationship with Alex. "I hope you're not upset," Claire said in a more subdued tone. "This *just* happened. I would've told you about it as soon as I saw you again."

"I'm not upset, you dork." Indeed, she heard a genuine smile in Sarah's voice. "As long as neither of you breaks the other's heart, or mistreats someone I love, then I'm willing to adjust to this paradigm shift if there's any chance it'll make you two happy."

"I have absolutely no plans to break Claire's heart," Alex assured her, catching Claire's gaze. "I'm crazy about her."

"And I'll never intentionally hurt your sister," Claire added. She smiled at Alex. "Pinky swear."

"I believe you." Sarah adopted a teasing tone. "After all, you *have* loved her forever."

Claire blanched at Sarah's use of the L-word, as well as her revelation that Claire's desperate pining hadn't been as subtle as she'd hoped. "Crushed on her, yes," she protested weakly. "I wouldn't say *loved.*"

Alex shot Claire a look of mock sadness, lower lip thrust out and everything, then called to Sarah, "You *knew?*"

"You didn't?" Sarah snorted. "Anyway…I think it's kinda…cute. You two together." She waited a beat. "Not the part I just saw, mind you. *That* image will scar my retinas forever."

Alex whispered into Claire's ear. "If not, we have photographs for re-imprinting purposes."

Claire giggled, then bumped Alex with her shoulder. Still

concerned about her best friend, she put her hand on Alex's and said, "Should we all have lunch? We can get dressed—"

"Oh no, not on my account." Sarah snorted. "Honestly, Marcus and I were planning to lie down for a nap anyway. That fourteen-hour flight wiped us out."

"I'm taking Claire to dinner tonight," Alex said. "Maybe we could have a drink afterward? Or better yet, dessert?"

"Perfect." Sarah tapped the door, her amusement ringing through the layer of wood that separated them. "I hope you know I'm going straight home to tell Marcus every detail of what I just saw."

Claire blushed, but Alex simply chuckled. "Fair enough."

"I had no *idea*, Claire." Sarah's voice faded as she retreated. "Brava!"

Shaking with laughter, Alex wrapped a strong arm around Claire's shoulders and pulled her in for a warm hug. "Brava, indeed."

"She seemed okay." Claire chewed her lip and glanced into Alex's eyes for confirmation. "Right?"

"Yes, Claire-Claire. Everything is okay." Alex ran her lustful gaze down the length of Claire's still-naked body. "Everything will *be* okay. Except our sex, of course, which is downright *superb.*"

Won over by Alex's desire-filled eyes, Claire got back on the bed and resumed her former position on her hands and knees—this time facing the headboard. She glanced over her shoulder at Alex and raised an eyebrow like a dare. "We should still practice, though. Practice makes perfect."

Alex got onto her knees behind Claire, hands locking onto her ass and hip. "Told you. Nothing but a cock-hungry *slut.*" Without hesitation, she pushed her way inside Claire, who rocked forward with a rapturous moan. "Also, the girl of my fucking dreams."

Claire grinned into the pillow her forehead rested on, thrilled by the way reality continued to somehow, improbably, exceed even her wildest fantasies. No longer afraid of anything, at least for the moment, Claire spoke the truth she was relieved to no longer have to hide. "You're mine, too, Alex." She closed her eyes, euphoric when Alex plunged into her again. *You always have been.*

## CHAPTER TWELVE

Much later that night, Alex took Claire back to her place after a lengthy, expensive meal that Alex had insisted on paying for, at a restaurant Claire had been stunned they'd been able to get into on such short notice. It was a testament to Alex's success that they'd been greeted like VIPs, then treated to a tasting menu that consisted of delicacy after mouth-watering delicacy, before finally being presented with the finest dessert on offer, a chocolate concoction that quickly had Claire moaning and Alex signaling for the check. By the time they pulled into Sarah's driveway, the hand that had started the drive home on Claire's knee had traveled nearly to the juncture of her thighs, and it took all of Claire's willpower not to beg Alex to carry her off to bed and ravish her again.

"We should check in with Sarah," Claire murmured when Alex leaned over the center console to kiss her. "Before…anything else."

Alex groaned but then nodded. "You're right. We should."

"We said we would."

"You're right. We did." Alex released another low groan. "I underestimated how badly I'd want to be back inside you once I watched you eat that dessert."

Claire echoed her noise of disappointment. "Stop saying things like that or we'll never make it to Sarah's door."

"We *could* just meet her for breakfast tomorrow."

Tempting…but Claire shook her head. "No. I don't want Sarah to feel like us sleeping together is going to negatively impact our friendship—*or* the relationship she has with you. Blowing her off tonight would be a really shitty way to start things out."

"You're right." Alex played with the fine hairs at the nape of Claire's neck, making her shiver. "But is that all we're doing, Claire-Claire? Sleeping together?"

Claire shivered. "No."

"Good." Alex reached across Claire's lap and unbuckled her seat belt. "Come on. The sooner we fulfill our social obligations, the better. I'm dying to taste your sweet little pussy again."

Claire's face grew hot, and she just knew Sarah was going to tease her about her red cheeks when she answered the door. "Stop that."

"I thought you enjoyed the dirty things I say to you." Alex's soft lips brushed against Claire's ear as she retreated. "Do you really want me to stop?"

"Since we're about to see Sarah, yes." Claire blushed harder while imagining her best friend finding out how much she really did *love* Alex's filthy mouth. "Your sister is *merciless* whenever she discovers something new to give me a hard time about. The last thing I want to do is provide any additional ammo."

Alex snorted and climbed out of the convertible. "I hope you at least give as good as you get."

Eyes sparkling, Claire met Alex's gaze over the top of the car. "Well, I don't know. Do I?"

With a semi-tortured chuckle, Alex walked around the hood and gathered Claire into a heated embrace. "And then some."

The security lights around the house began to blink on and off, and seconds later, Sarah's sharp voice called out to them from the rear of the house. "Hey! Knock it off out there. I don't want anyone getting pregnant in my driveway. You hear me?"

Alex snickered, whispering to Claire, "Someone *really* needs to talk to her about the birds and other birds."

Claire giggled at the playful jibe, then stepped out of Alex's arms. "We were on our way to find you. I swear."

"I'm not sure I want any part of what you two have on your agenda tonight." Sarah stepped out from behind the corner of the house, smiling as they approached. "I get it, by the way. You're only at the twenty-four-hour mark at this point. I'm sure it's all you can think about."

"Pretty much," Alex answered. She snorted when Claire elbowed her gently.

"Actually, I'm thinking about you, too." Claire moved away from Alex and stood close enough to look Sarah directly in the eyes. "My best friend...who I hope really *is* okay with all this. I know it's incredibly sudden."

Sarah took her hands, squeezing briefly before letting go. "I'm okay, Claire. It's a little weird, yes, but I'll adjust." Her attention shifted to Alex and her smile widened. "The best part is that my sister's back home...I hope for good?"

Claire hoped so, too.

"That's the plan." Alex caught Claire's hand and interlaced their fingers. "Especially now."

Claire tried not to melt into a puddle of goo in front of both of them, but it proved to be a real challenge. She stared down at her feet, too overwhelmed to look at Alex, too nervous to meet Sarah's piercing gaze. Sarah grabbed Claire's free hand and pressed their palms together firmly.

"You know how badly I've always wanted you to find someone who deserves you, Claire." Sarah paused. "You too, Alex. Maybe this makes sense. Who better for my two favorite people to love than each other?"

As it had earlier, the appearance of the L-word made Claire antsy. Alex had such a long, varied sexual history—surely the last thing she wanted to contemplate one day into a brand-new relationship was the idea of *love*. Feeling the need to demur in case Alex had been spooked, Claire murmured, "Don't get ahead of yourself, Sarah. Like you said, it's only been twenty-four hours."

"Yeah, but I've known you for the better part of fifteen years." Alex wrapped her arm around Claire's waist. "I don't want to make you nervous or anything, but I pretty much already love you. *In* love... well, let's just say that's not too far behind."

For some reason, the idea that Alex would be so open with her feelings—in front of a third party, no less—simply didn't gel with the image she'd long held of her first crush as a globe-trotting, heart-breaking playboi. The consummate bachelor. No revelation should have been too difficult to believe by that point, not after last night, but Alex's enthusiasm for a shared future continued to mystify Claire.

Sarah let out a low whistle. "Well, I'd say you've got her hooked, Claire. Alert the presses. Yet another notorious bachelor *tamed*."

"Do me a favor, sis?"

Sarah gave Alex a shit-eating grin. "Yeah?"

"Shut up." Alex winked at Sarah and rubbed reassuring circles on Claire's back. "You okay, baby?"

Claire watched Sarah flinch subtly at the pet name, cringing a little on the inside. "Yeah. Just tired, I think."

Sarah chuckled lightly. "I'll bet."

"Do you need to head home?" For the first time that day, Alex appeared to feel awkward around her. "I'll understand if you do, though I'd love for you to stay…"

Sarah glanced back and forth between them. "I was going to invite you two inside for a drink. I'd love to tell you about what we did in Europe, if you wouldn't mind indulging me for twenty minutes or so. I promise to show you only a *few* photos. Maybe a dozen, tops."

Both sisters' eyes were on Claire, so she said, "I'll stay."

"Great." Sarah ushered them to follow her into the main house, entering through the back porch to the demanding cries of Willow, the disapproving orange tabby cat.

As Sarah shooed Willow aside, Alex bent to whisper in Claire's ear. "All night?"

Claire tipped her head, then whispered, "Yes."

"Lucky me." Alex's hand found Claire's ass and massaged a cheek.

Claire shook her head in mild disapproval, then grinned too brightly when Sarah turned to shoot them a suspicious look. "Are you guys making out back there?"

"Not yet." Alex gripped Claire's butt gently, then let her hand fall away. "I'm trying to control myself."

"Like I said, twenty minutes. Think you two can hold out that long?" Sarah rolled her eyes and led them into the bright kitchen, where her husband Marcus stood in the middle removing the cork from a bottle of wine. As they streamed into the room, the epitome of tall, dark, and handsome flashed them a white-toothed grin that contrasted beautifully with his flawless skin.

"Hello, ladies! And gentleman, of course." Marcus winked at Alex, who returned the gesture with a fond nod.

"How's it going, Marcus?" Alex sidled up to the bar that separated the kitchen from the den, pulling out a stool for Claire, then herself. "Glad to be home?"

"Yes and no." A loud meow drew his attention to his ankles, and he laughed while bending to pat Willow affectionately. "Willow's thrilled, of course."

"Yeah. I'm a pretty poor substitute, as it turns out." Claire sat down next to Alex, glad to have her so close. She rested her hand on Alex's knee, on instinct, wanting to stay connected. "On that note, *I'm* glad you two are home. I've missed Sarah in particular, both personally *and* professionally." She shot Sarah a wry grin. "As it turns out, running our company is super hard without you, partner."

"I feel the same way. No wonder we make such a good team."

They did, it was true. Sarah possessed a keen business mind, whereas Claire supplied the technical and creative know-how. When it came to raising money, managing budgets, drawing up contracts, and navigating other legalese needed to turn an innovative concept into an actual corporation, Claire had always felt lost and overwhelmed. Her expertise lay in product development, software engineering, and the tailoring of an accessible curriculum specifically targeted at aspiring female computer scientists and engineers. Their skills complemented each other perfectly, a serendipitous fact that had helped propel them to quick success.

"So…" Marcus set the bottle of wine on the counter in front of him, turning Claire's stomach a little. "I hear you two decided to give my wife a minor heart attack this morning."

"Yup." Alex snickered. "That'll teach her not to knock."

Frowning, Marcus shrugged at Sarah. "She's right, you know. You really should've knocked."

"Hindsight." Apparently noticing that no one was reaching for the wine, Sarah said, "Last night put you off wine? Would you prefer tea instead?"

"Yes," Alex and Claire answered in unison. "Please," Claire added.

"Probably smart." Marcus folded his arms over his broad chest and gazed at them with obvious amusement. "Sounds like you two had a pretty wild evening together."

"You have no idea," Claire muttered, automatically thinking back to the photos of her naked body that were currently etched into the memory card of Alex's camera. "Alcohol is a great and terrible thing."

"I have no regrets," Alex announced. She flashed a beaming smile at Marcus, but Claire knew she was the intended target. "Lowering our inhibitions allowed us to admit what we've both felt for a while now."

"In Claire's case, since she was approximately twelve." Sarah smirked in profile as she brewed the tea. "Alex, I'm almost positive she wanted you even before she grew boobs."

"*Sarah!*" Mortified, Claire covered her face with her hands. "You can shut the fuck up *anytime.*"

"Awww." Marcus's large, warm hand landed on Claire's shoulder, while at the same time Alex wrapped her in a tight, one-armed hug. "Go easy on poor Claire, love. She's feeling vulnerable."

This was exactly why she loved sweet, sensitive Marcus. He was a civilizing influence on her sometimes sharp-tongued best friend. "*Thank you*, Marcus. Have I mentioned lately that marrying you was the smartest thing Sarah's ever done?"

"Oh, I know." Marcus's rich, deep laughter brought an unthinking smile to Claire's lips that only grew wider when she watched him dodge the hard swat Sarah aimed at his admittedly cute ass. "I tell her all the time."

"He does, too." Sarah rolled her eyes. "So don't encourage him."

"For the record, I didn't start to think about Claire romantically until long after she grew boobs." Alex kissed Claire's flushed cheek, whispering, "They're beautiful, by the way."

Claire exhaled in a rush, overwhelmed to be the center of attention even among friends. "So when do we get to see those vacation snapshots we were promised?"

Sarah chortled. "Well, someone clearly wants to change the subject." This time Marcus let her pat his butt. "Honey, will you get your tablet? I want to give them the highlights before they run off to bone."

Marcus left Sarah with a kiss, and when she went to busy herself pouring tea, Alex leaned in and whispered, "But later you and I will talk about your tits some more, right? After this?"

Claire breathed out, shivered, and nodded. Blushing when Sarah turned to smirk at them knowingly, she fidgeted for a moment before welcoming Marcus back into the room with a wide, overcompensating smile. "You're back!"

"I am." He set the tablet on the counter, and then, after Sarah placed a mug of tea in front of both Alex and Claire, pulled out a stool for his wife. "You two ready for some crazy slideshow action?"

Ready for a very different kind of action, actually, Claire nodded anyway. After all, friendship came first.

❖

"Is your pussy sore?"

Having spent the past four hours together fully clothed, Claire found herself wholly unprepared to handle the frankness with which Alex asked the blunt question after they walked into the guest house forty minutes later. Awkwardly, Claire shrugged, tempted to lie for the sake of her libido. Yet she *had* been carrying a pleasant but noticeable ache between her thighs all day, one which she suspected would become less pleasant if she pushed herself too hard without allowing her body to recover first. "A little, I guess."

"I'm sorry." Alex managed to look both truly chagrined and roguishly satisfied.

"Don't be. We've had more sex in twenty-four hours than I've managed to get over the previous three years. It was bound to hurt a little."

"And I *am* bigger than you're used to." Taking her by the hand, Alex led Claire through her bedroom, to the bathroom. "Aren't I?"

Claire bit her lip when her clit pulsed, relishing the pleasurable clench of her sensitive inner muscles in remembrance of Alex's thick cock and the way it had penetrated her so exquisitely. So *deeply*. "Yes."

"But you took it anyway. *All* of it." Alex positioned Claire directly in front of the sink, then bent to turn on the faucet, filling the large tub Claire had admired just that morning. Straightening, she reached around Claire's shoulders to unzip the dress she'd thrown on during the brief stopover they'd made at her place before dinner. With a light smile, Alex stared into her eyes and dragged the zipper down to the small of Claire's back. "I was so proud of you."

To be perfectly honest, Claire was also rather proud of herself. "Thank you. I enjoyed every second, believe me."

"I'm glad. You know, you did such a good job taking care of me earlier, now I want to take care of you."

Shivering in anticipation of the singular joy that came from being Alex's sole focus, Claire whispered, "I'd like that."

Alex raised her arms to indicate the action she wanted Claire to take. "Then let's get that dress off...and you into the tub."

"Yes, sir." Claire shot Alex a smart-aleck salute after she'd pulled the dress over her head. "If you insist."

"It's a real hardship, I know." Alex checked the water temperature with her hand before returning her attention to the task of undressing Claire, first unclasping her bra, then sinking to her knees so she could remove Claire's already-damp panties. "Maybe you'll let me kiss you better before we go to sleep tonight?" Still kneeling at Claire's feet, Alex carefully pressed her lips into the curly hairs that helped shelter her tender labia. "If I promise to be *very,* very gentle?"

Claire sucked in an excited breath and gripped Alex's shoulder for additional support. Her other hand found the back of Alex's head, pulling her deeper into the space between her thighs. "Maybe," Claire murmured, then immediately belied her ambivalence by preventing Alex from moving her face away. "I do like the way you kiss."

Alex snuck out her tongue, sliding between the slick folds to elicit a choked grunt from Claire's suddenly dry throat. Then she sat back on her heels and gazed up at Claire with a mischievous glint. "That's all you get for the moment. First I want to pamper you a little. *Then* I'll let you come in my mouth."

Claire reached behind her hip and grabbed the edge of the sink for balance. As epic as her private daydreams about Alex had always been, how was it possible for real life to keep exceeding them? Overwhelmed, she whispered, "I really am going to fall in love with you, Alex." She stared down into Alex's earnest blue eyes, unexpected tears blurring her vision. "So I sure hope all of this is for real, because I honestly don't know what I'll do if it's not."

"Hey." Alex's warm expression melted into one of concern. She rose to her feet and drew Claire against her chest for a fierce hug. "I don't feel like I've been ambiguous about my intentions—or the way I feel. But in case I have, let me say, unequivocally: I want you to be my girlfriend, Claire Barker. Exclusively, and for as long as we're able to make this work, which I personally—and prematurely, I admit—hope will be forever."

Claire's heart thundered against Alex's solid chest. Had she really just hinted at *forever?* If Claire hadn't spent the better part of her life yearning for this exact moment, then perhaps that sort of bold declaration would be easier to accept as reality. It wasn't only that she'd always pictured—and in some ways, hoped—that Alex would remain an eternal bachelor. After all, even the biggest players choose to settle down on occasion. But for *Claire?* That part was what made this fairytale romance seem so improbable.

"Talk to me," Alex murmured. Pulling back, she wiped a stray tear from Claire's cheek, then caressed the side of her face with a big, compassionate hand. "Why is it so difficult for you to believe that your feelings are returned?"

"Because for more than a decade, they weren't." Claire lifted a shoulder, embarrassed by her obvious lack of self-esteem. Logically, she knew how unattractive that quality was—and the awareness only made her feel worse. "All I know is that I'm far from the prettiest or most exciting woman you've ever dated, let alone slept with. You have to understand, from my perspective…the idea that you're legitimately attracted to me has come from out of nowhere. That you actually want to *date* me, long-term, runs contrary to everything I know about your romantic history."

"Which isn't a lot." Alex kept her voice gentle but made the point firmly. "I'm willing to bet."

"That's true," Claire acknowledged. "But what I *do* know makes it difficult for me to believe that a hopelessly geeky introvert like me will be able to keep you happy."

"I told you, Claire-Claire, that part of my life—and with it, the desire to play around—is over…and has been for a while. Remember, I was celibate for ten months before you and I slept together last night. That was my *choice.* The same way I'm choosing to be with *you.*" Alex moved her hand, tugging on a lock of Claire's hair with the air of a big kid teasing her younger peer. "Not because of sex, by the way. Well, not *only* sex." When she grinned, Claire couldn't help but grin back. "But seriously…I could get sex wherever, if that's all I was interested in. I hope you know that I'm not the type of person who would fuck my sister's best friend for the sole purpose of getting my rocks off. Even if you don't fully believe in your own appeal yet, please believe in *me?*"

Claire nodded, struck by Alex's sincere, pleading tone. "I do."

"I think you're sexy, and smart, and funny, and an all-around good person. That's more than enough to justify the way I feel." Alex brushed her lips over Claire's forehead, then cut off the flow of hot water into the bathtub. "Now get in, darling girl. I'll be right back."

Struck by the realization that she was completely naked—while Alex continued to look dapper in dress pants and a vest—Claire hurried to do as she was told. She sighed as soon as she sank into the steamy water, pleased to feel her muscles relax one by one. After Alex rushed out of the bathroom en route to parts unknown, Claire reached between her legs and carefully stroked the sore flesh. The tentative contact of her own fingertips felt good enough to negate any thoughts of discomfort, leading Claire to muse that she'd probably allow Alex to do whatever she wanted tonight, consequences be damned.

"Fuck, you make a pretty picture."

Claire startled, shifting her attention to the doorway without ceasing the lazy motion of her fingers around her swollen clit. "I missed you."

"I see that." Alex loped across the room without tearing her eyes away from Claire's casual self-pleasuring for even a second. "Is that how you make your pussy feel good when you're all alone?"

Claire almost pulled her hand away, the intense scrutiny embarrassing her every bit as much as it turned her on. Instead, she gave in to her desire to entice Alex, shifting position so she could use three fingertips to massage large circles over her clit. "Usually."

Still rapt, Alex sparked the lighter she carried in her hand—undoubtedly the object she'd left the room to find—and set fire to a half dozen candles already positioned in strategic spots near the tub. Then she went back to the door, pausing with her finger on the light switch. "I had hoped to create a romantic ambience, but now I kind of hate to lose the light—and that view."

Chuckling, Claire lifted her hands above the surface of the water. "I'll stop."

Alex frowned, but still flipped the switch to plunge the room into flickering candlelight. "Not what I was going for."

"You know, I've never done that in front of anyone before you." Claire folded her hands on her stomach, demurely. "I'm not sure I understand how you can make me feel so comfortable *and* so nervous all at the same time."

"I feel the same way about you." Alex approached the tub, hesitated, then tentatively sat on the edge. She bent to open the cabinet under the sink, withdrawing a clean washcloth that she soaked with hot, soapy water and then rubbed across Claire's back. "Believe it or not."

Claire released a contented groan at the satisfying friction of the wet terry cloth against her skin. "That feels nice."

"Good. I love making you feel nice." Alex paused to roll up her shirtsleeve, then plunged deeper into the water, dragging the washcloth down until she reached the top of Claire's ass. Then she switched tactics, moving around to massage Claire's left breast, followed by her right. Eventually Alex abandoned the washcloth altogether, choosing to smooth her bare hands over Claire's heated skin instead. "Also, *you* feel nice."

Soaking up both the compliment and Alex's ardent caress, Claire murmured, "You should take off your clothes and join me."

Alex didn't hesitate. Stripped naked within seconds, she climbed into the water behind Claire and tugged her backward to rest against her broad chest. "Good call," Alex said a moment later. "This is even nicer."

Safe within the circle of Alex's well-muscled arms, Claire closed her eyes, then turned her face to search for Alex's turgid nipple with her lips. Latching on, she gave the hard nub a brief suck and then bit down cautiously. She grinned at the sharp inhalation she heard from above, delighted by the way Alex's whole body went tense until Claire finally released the breast from between her sharp teeth.

"I could stay like this forever." Whispering, Claire spoke from the heart.

"Me, too." Alex gave her an affectionate hug, then let her hands roam lightly over Claire's hips and stomach. "You looked so beautiful tonight at dinner. In Sarah's kitchen, too, for that matter." She trailed her fingers down Claire's belly to play with the short, kinky hairs at the juncture of her thighs. "But honestly? I'm thrilled to have finally gotten you out of that dress."

Claire managed a weak chuckle as Alex's deft fingers parted her labia and the tip of her index finger glided over the perpetually swollen clit hidden within. "Four hours of non-naked time too much for you?"

"For the moment, yes." Alex tickled her clit teasingly, then withdrew.

"But it's not *only* about sex," Claire reminded her.

"Hey. It's not called the honeymoon stage for nothing." Her large hands slid up to cup Claire's breasts and pluck the nipples. "Anyway, it's your fault for being so damn hot."

Claire stared down at Alex's thick fingers pinching the hard tips of her breasts and shuddered at the eroticism of the sight. Under Alex's expert touch, she did indeed feel hotter than hell. "You're the hot one. So fucking handsome wearing that vest and tie."

"You know, I seriously never realized you were so into butch women." Alex kissed the side of Claire's neck, lowering her right hand back to its previous spot between her trembling thighs. "Lucky me."

Claire's breathing caught when Alex tickled her pubic mound. "Pretty sure luck has nothing to do with it. I suspect that your very presence in my young life did more to shape my sexuality than either of us could possibly imagine."

"Are you saying I turned you gay?" Seemingly delighted by the idea, Alex fondled her sensitized folds with care.

"Maybe." Claire inhaled sharply when the fingers again brushed over her clit, then turned to hide her face in Alex's neck. "You certainly helped establish a standard no other woman has been able to meet."

"To be perfectly honest, I hope *I* can live up to that standard." This time, Alex's laughter carried an undercurrent of real anxiety. "I worry you won't find me nearly as enchanting in real life as you do in your many fantasies."

Twisting around, Claire planted a soft kiss on Alex's full mouth. "You've already surpassed my fantasies."

Alex smiled and captured her lips a second time. After they broke apart, she whispered, "But you haven't even seen me at my worst yet."

Even at her worst, Claire guessed that Alex was still every bit as wonderful as she'd always known her to be. "Maybe not, but I look forward to it."

Alex snorted. "Boy, have I got you fooled."

"Nah," Claire murmured, nuzzling the base of Alex's throat. "I just can't imagine you could possibly do anything to change the way I feel. The way I've *always* felt."

"Sure I could," Alex said soberly. "But I won't. At least I'll try not to."

Sitting up, Claire placed her palm on Alex's warm cheek. "No one has ever made me feel as cared for, and as cherished, as you have already. I don't think you're perfect, Alex, nor do I expect you to be. Particularly because I'm not perfect, either. However, you *are* the best I've ever had, in more than one way."

Their next kiss was fiercely passionate, initiated by Alex with a low, needy moan. Claire somehow ended up on her lap again, cradled within a possessive embrace that rendered her boneless with desire. When they broke apart minutes later, they touched foreheads as they heaved for air together.

Alex was the first to recover her voice. "You ready to let me put my tongue all over that sweet, sore pussy of yours?"

Claire shivered. "Yes, please."

"Then sit on the edge of the tub." Alex nudged Claire's shoulders to encourage her to move backward, then patted the wide corner of the tub next to the wall. "Right here, sweet girl. Legs open."

Blushing, Claire followed the suggestion despite her mild embarrassment about having her body so thoroughly exposed to Alex's desirous gaze. Grateful for the low light provided by the nearby candles, she rested her back against the wall and spread her thighs so Alex could fit her shoulders in between. She gasped when Alex grabbed her ankle and lifted her foot out of the water before setting it on the rim of the bathtub, an action that exposed her even further. She clutched Alex's shoulder for balance as her other foot received the same treatment. The positioning left her splayed open, her wet pussy mere inches from Alex's searching eyes.

Nervously, Claire whispered, "Do I look all right?"

"You look *exactly* right, Claire-Claire." Alex bent to press her tongue against Claire's puffy labia. Twitching at the sensation, Claire whimpered sadly when Alex pulled away far too soon. "You also look like a woman who's been recently fucked...hard."

Settling into the corner, Claire lifted her hips in a subtle invitation for Alex to resume. "Yeah. *Ow.*"

"Poor baby." Alex stuck out her tongue, dragging the tip from just above Claire's opening to the rigid point of her clit. "Show me where it hurts."

Claire dropped her hand between her legs, dipping in to ghost a trail around her opening. "Right here," she breathed.

"Your tight little hole?" Using her thumbs to hold the labia open,

Alex deliberately touched the tip of her tongue to Claire's aching vagina. Claire gasped, then shuddered as Alex worked the sinuous muscle slightly inside. She lowered her eyes to meet Alex's sparkling gaze, and for endless seconds neither of them moved nor spoke. Finally Alex withdrew, causing Claire to release a breath she just realized she'd been holding. Framing Claire's vulva with her thumb and forefinger, Alex planted another kiss on her now-slick labia, then followed up with a playful lick. "I'm not surprised, sweetheart. I stretched you open pretty wide around my cock earlier."

Claire emitted an embarrassingly needy noise at the lewd comment, bumping her pussy against Alex's mouth before she'd even finished her sentence. "Please."

Alex placed her palms on Claire's inner thighs, somehow managing to push them even farther apart. "Please what, baby. Please kiss your pussy all better?"

Reaching for her head, Claire pulled Alex, grinning, down into the abundant wetness of her cunt. "*Please* make me come."

"I can do that." Alex dragged her tongue around the throbbing clit. "I love how you taste, Claire. So *innocent.*"

Claire felt anything *but* with Alex's face buried between her thighs. The pressure in her abdomen built rapidly, and before long, Claire spasmed loudly into Alex's skillful mouth, coating her lips and tongue with the sticky result of her orgasm. Alex hummed contentedly as she lapped up all of Claire's juices, going directly to the source before returning to again lave the tip of Claire's clit. Muscles jerking, Claire whimpered in distress when her desire to keep going conflicted with her physical limits. "Alex…"

"Is that really all you've got for me, baby?" Alex smoothed her hands along Claire's inner thighs before slipping them, palms up, underneath her butt. Raising Claire to her face, Alex inhaled deeply, then smirked. "What if I just licked your ass this time? We'll let your pussy have a little break."

Claire's breathing hitched at the impossible sexiness of Alex's proposition. Despite her vague memory of Alex momentarily flirting with that particular act when they were drunk, she wasn't sure she could summon the bravery to allow such an intimate exploration while sober—even though she wanted to, desperately. "I'm not sure I'll be able to come again."

Alex kissed the sensitive crease between her thigh and her pussy. "That's all right. I'm willing to bet you'll love how it feels, regardless."

Probably true. Shivering, Claire held her lower lip between her teeth and sank back into the water, allowing Alex to gather her close for a heartfelt embrace. Claire closed her eyes and tried to memorize the utter rightness of the moment—how Alex felt in her arms, but perhaps more importantly, how *she* felt in Alex's. Struck anew by the uncanny aura of trust and comfort Alex engendered through her warm, steady presence, Claire gathered the courage to accept the gift she so badly wanted to receive. "Could we...do it in bed? So I can lie down?"

Because there was no way she would be able to stay upright with Alex's tongue in her ass.

"I like the sound of that." Alex kissed the back of her neck, then scraped her teeth over the same spot. "Shall we go there now?"

"If I can stand."

As it turned out, she couldn't. Or rather, not without a serious wobble that Alex immediately used as an excuse to scoop Claire up like a bride to be carried over the threshold. She was placed back onto the floor only long enough for a quick toweling off, and then Alex demonstrated her impressive strength by transporting Claire to the bed in the same manner. At Alex's urging, she turned over so she rested flat on her belly in the center of the mattress, then used her fingers to part her buttocks and expose her anus to the cool air. Before she had an opportunity to feel cold or even self-conscious, Alex lowered herself onto her belly between Claire's open thighs and buried her handsome face between the widely spread cheeks. Forsaking every other erogenous zone within reach, Alex licked in and around her anus for breathtaking seconds that stretched into minutes that seemed to extend into hours. Alex performed the selfless service with unwavering diligence, as though there was nothing else in the world she'd rather be doing—not even getting herself off.

"*Oh,*" Claire finally groaned, turning her face to the side. Her anus contracted beneath Alex's searching tongue, and her pussy echoed the convulsion an instant later. "Maybe I *will* be able to."

She could feel Alex's smile against her butt cheeks. "Then try. For me."

Lifting her hips, Claire bumped into Alex's mouth in an unspoken request for more. Her miraculous tongue quickly found its way back inside. Claire pushed her hand between her hips and the mattress, using her fingers to seek out, then stroke, her overworked clit. She gasped when Alex eased the first inch or so of her tongue into the tight, puckered opening, overwhelmed by the intensity of the pleasure created by their mutual effort. Whatever embarrassment Claire might have once felt about masturbating in front of Alex vanished, cured by her fierce desire to come as a result of this heroic effort.

It took her some time, whole minutes, in fact, to coax her exhausted body back to the brink. Having spent the majority of her day being fucked raw, Claire's pussy screamed for rest despite her mind's insatiable appetite for more. But eventually, Claire hastened her fingers, reached back with her free hand to yank on Alex's hair, and orgasmed with a loud shout that she feared would be heard up at the main house. Alex hugged Claire's thighs tight as she came, diving in deep for the full duration of her explosive climax, only breaking off the intimate kiss when Claire reluctantly begged her to stop. As Alex climbed up to collapse at her side, Claire rolled to face her, falling into her arms for a full-body embrace.

"I love you," Claire blurted. Then, despite all their heart-to-heart chats about why that was probably no big deal to say, she corrected herself. "Love *that*, I mean. You were right. I loved *that*."

Eyes glittering, Alex pressed her lips to the center of Claire's forehead and whispered, "I love you, too."

## CHAPTER THIRTEEN

Two weeks later, Claire was still resolutely in love. *Stupidly* in love. Which explained why she couldn't seem to keep her mind on work these days—to the point that her projects were beginning to suffer.

The gorgeous bouquet of flowers that her assistant had delivered to her desk moments ago didn't help. An explosion of bright-yellow and pure-white blooms, the arrangement came with the sweetest love note Claire had ever received.

> *Claire—This is how my heart feels when we're together. Thank you for the best two weeks of my life. Here's to many more.*
> *I love you, Alex.*

Claire reread the card three times, then forced herself to put it down so she would stop grinning like a lunatic in case anyone walked by her door.

Alex was like no one she'd ever dated. The sex was not only plentiful, but transcendent—always—and the time they spent out of bed was just as satisfying. They never seemed to run out of things to talk about. Alex made her laugh hard and often, and claimed to adore the fact that Claire made her think about the world in new and different ways. They liked the same types of restaurants, and foods, and television and movies (for the most part), and their musical tastes aligned well enough to make the prospect of future road trips not only bearable, but downright fun. Neither of them was sure yet whether she ever wanted children, nor were they anywhere close to seriously considering such a life-changing decision, but they both agreed that they should revisit the question a few years down the line, if they were still together.

Alex made Claire feel not only smart, which wasn't all that unusual, but also utterly beautiful and desirable, which most certainly was. Their bodies fit together perfectly when they cuddled, they both liked dogs a little better than cats, and after only fourteen days as a couple, Claire felt like she could tell Alex almost anything. She trusted Alex *that* much. On paper, at least, everything seemed perfect.

So why couldn't she get rid of this knot in her stomach? The one that urged her to wonder when this improbable relationship would inevitably fall apart? Things had seemed pretty great with Jane, too, at first—until the so-called "baby butch" decided that Claire wasn't exciting enough to keep in her life. Despite Alex's reassurances that she didn't feel—and wouldn't do—the same, Claire couldn't help but worry about what would happen once they faced their first real test as a couple.

Unfortunately, she had a feeling she was about to find out. Alex's gallery exhibition opened next week, and Claire had agreed to be her date even though the idea of rubbing elbows with glamorous art-world people made her want to vomit. She picked up the note Alex had written again, exhaling slowly as she read it for the fifth time.

*This is how my heart feels when we're together.*

Swallowing, Claire closed her eyes. If it meant keeping Alex, she would gladly brave an uncomfortable situation for a few hours. She just prayed she wouldn't embarrass Alex or do anything to cause her to realize that Jane had been right about how boring she was after all.

"Knock, knock." Sarah stood just outside her door.

Claire jerked to attention, then quickly tucked the card under a folder in the center of her desk while shooting Sarah a guilty look. "I wasn't asleep. Really."

Sarah snorted and, apparently deciding to take that as an invitation, strolled into Claire's office. She closed the door behind her. "You sure? I get the impression you've had a late night or twelve over the past couple weeks."

It was true. Quoting Alex, Claire said, "It's not called the honeymoon stage for nothing."

"I hope you don't mind me saying so, but…" Sarah dropped into the chair across the desk from Claire with an exaggerated shudder. "It's still pretty weird to think about you and my sister…like that."

"I don't mind." Claire moved the vase to the corner of the desk so the flowers wouldn't obstruct her view of Sarah's face. "It's still pretty weird for me, too, to be honest."

Sarah tilted her head. "Weird, how?"

"Weird in that I'm still not sure why Alex would want anything to do with someone like me."

Rolling her eyes, Sarah leaned forward to smack Claire's hand where it rested atop the surface of the desk. "Stop it. You're attractive, funny, *brilliant*, financially solvent, and have your shit remarkably together for a young lady of your tender age. Why *wouldn't* Alex want to date you?"

"Um, *you're* the one who showed me all those selfies she took with the flawless models she banged over the years. Can you blame me for feeling a little inadequate?"

"Claire, I showed you maybe *two* photos, possibly three, over the course of, like, eight or nine years. That said, yes, my sister *has* bedded some gorgeous women. But I've never seen her look happier *or* heard her gush about anyone the way she does when she talks about you." Sarah shook her head, then folded her arms over her chest while studying the bouquet Claire had moved off to the side. "Looks like she's doing all she can to make you believe that, too."

Claire nodded. "She's incredible."

"Well, I'm happy for both of you. Really." Sarah lifted one side of her mouth in a half-smile that conveyed a complex array of emotions. "Even if it *is* weird to know that my big sister is fucking the girl I used to practice kissing with when we were both thirteen."

Claire laughed at the sweetly awkward memory. Sarah had not only been her first kiss but also served as definitive confirmation that Claire really did like girls better than boys. Fortunately for their friendship, that brief foray into sexual experimentation hadn't extended past a handful of clumsy make-out sessions. Eventually Claire admitted that their rehearsals were causing her more confusion than she could easily handle. Sarah had reacted with grace and true friendship by accepting Claire's tearful coming out with a tight hug and the reassurance that her disclosure changed nothing about the bond they'd built over the previous year. And it hadn't. If anything, the fact that their close relationship not only survived, but *thrived*, in the aftermath of that adolescent indiscretion had long ago convinced Claire that even if everyone else in her life abandoned her, Sarah would always be there.

Sarah was her constant.

Smirking, Claire said, "If it makes you feel any better, you're *both* really great kissers. Maybe it runs in the family."

Sarah groaned. "Stop. *Please.*" Her laughter faded after a moment, and she took on a serious expression that signaled a change in topic. "Before I forget…and this is work-related, sorry…but did you get the email I sent yesterday afternoon?"

Claire tried to recall which messages had come into her inbox over the past twenty-four hours but drew a blank. A *complete* blank. As far as her distracted brain was concerned, she hadn't received an email for at least two weeks. Turning to her monitor, she opened her email client and scanned the first dozen subject lines. "I'm so sorry. When did you send it?"

"Probably around two o'clock?"

Claire located the message, which had been marked read despite not looking at all familiar. "Here it is." Skimming the text, she realized that she'd ignored an urgently worded request for an update on the requirements document she needed to deliver before they could start development work on the new module for their current smartphone app. At a loss, she tried to recall how close she was to actually completing the complex assessment and write-up. Finally, she met Sarah's gaze with an apologetic shrug. "I'm so sorry. I'll get the full requirements to you by lunchtime tomorrow. Will that work?"

Sarah gave her a relaxed smile. "Sure. I know you're aware, like me, of how time-sensitive this development effort is, given that we want to do a simultaneous launch with the updated website."

"I know. You're right." Claire sighed in exasperation at her own level of distractedness. "Sorry. I promise I won't always be like this."

"I get it. New love is all-consuming. It's overwhelming."

"And nerve-wracking." Claire dropped her head into her hands.

"And *wonderful.*"

"That, too." Looking up, Claire met Sarah's gaze with a warm smile. "I've missed you, by the way."

"I miss you, too." Sarah's smile stretched into an excited grin. "Hey, so Alex's new exhibition opens next week."

Claire's outward cheer melted away. "Yeah. It does."

"Do you know what you're going to wear?"

A lump rose in Claire's throat as she mentally reviewed her woefully inadequate closetful of choices. "Not really."

Sarah frowned and again leaned forward to touch Claire's hand. "You look nervous. Are you?"

"I'm not sure that's a strong enough word for how I'm feeling."

"Why?" Sarah squeezed her clammy digits, offering a small measure of comfort. "Because it's a social event, or because you're going as Alex's date?"

Rather than answer directly, Claire said, "What if I embarrass her? I mean, I don't know how to do stuff like this."

"Stuff like what?"

"Like be the girlfriend of someone who thrives on being the center of attention. Or talk about art. Or, let's be honest, make casual conversation with anyone, really, about *anything.*"

Sarah scoffed. "You and I have both spoken to roomfuls of investors asking tough questions, not to mention presented in front of crowds of kids and parents both large and small, and you've always held your own. Back in college, when I'd drag you to the bar against your will, you always looked and sounded totally relaxed and articulate even though I knew you were dying inside. Really, Claire, you're not nearly as bad as you think—not at all."

"Maybe, but Alex deserves more than 'not bad.'" Eager for Sarah's counsel, Claire fully unburdened herself. "Not knowing what to wear definitely freaks me out. But not nearly as much as the fact that I don't want to go at all. Don't get me wrong…there's nothing I want more than to be there to support Alex. But I worry she'll see how out of place I feel, and I don't want to ruin her night."

"I'll be there, too, you know. What if I promise to stick with you the entire time? That way when Alex gets pulled into random small talk with strangers, we can chat with each other." Sarah studied her with eyes full of infinite kindness, displaying a rare softer side that few people other than Claire ever got to see. "Also, I'll take you dress shopping this weekend. We won't rest until we find the perfect outfit for your first big event as the artist's girlfriend."

Somehow, Claire already felt a little better. "Yeah?"

"Absolutely." Sarah gave her a look she could only describe as bittersweet. "It'll be nice to spend time with you again."

Guilt flowed over Claire, making her cringe. "I'm so sorry. I know I've been pretty unresponsive lately…"

"Like I said, I get it." Sarah rose from her chair, leaning across the desk to tug on a lock of Claire's hair. "I'll cut you some slack for the first few weeks, but then I expect my best friend to once again be available for both business and pleasure. Deal?"

Claire also stood, sticking her hand over the desk for a brisk shake. "Deal."

"Good. But work on those requirements *now*, all right? I'd like to get them to the team tomorrow, or else I'm afraid we'll have no shot at meeting the deadline. It's tight enough as it is."

Bowing her head, Claire said, "Understood."

"As far as our shopping trip…Saturday? Lunch first?"

Claire battled a twinge of disappointment at the thought of not spending Saturday afternoon with the woman who currently consumed her every thought. *But remember, friendship comes first.* She smiled and nodded. "It's a date."

"Well, all right. Make sure you tell my sister that I've got dibs on you that day."

"Yes, ma'am."

Sarah walked to the door, opened it, and paused with her hand on the knob. "Relax, Claire, and try to *enjoy* all of this. After all, it's what you've wanted for pretty much forever."

Claire stuck out her tongue. "I *am* enjoying it. Anxiety, insecurity, and lack of a suitable wardrobe aside." It was uncanny, really. As long as she and Alex were together in the same room, her mind and body had no trouble believing that their shared future was bright. But whenever they were apart, doubt crept in. "I love her so much, Sarah. I just don't want to lose her. That's all."

"As long as you relax, sweetie, I don't see why you would. Besides, you know I'd kick her ass if she ever hurt you, right? Blood or not, you're my best friend." Sarah winked. "Now get to work. The sooner you write that document for me, the faster you can jump back in bed with your *lov-ah*."

Claire pulled a face at the teasing jibe. "Go away. You're distracting, and I've got *work* to do."

Sarah chuckled, then slipped backward out of her office. "Good girl."

Fighting a blush as similar praise from Alex—delivered under *very* different circumstances—rang in her memory, Claire turned to her computer and tried to remember where she'd saved the document she'd started drafting weeks ago. Drawing a blank, she glanced over at the door, relieved to see that Sarah had disappeared from view. After only a brief hesitation, she lifted the folder on the desk in front of her and retrieved Alex's card from underneath.

Then she read it again.

## CHAPTER FOURTEEN

Claire reached up to hold on to the headboard with one hand, then down to touch Alex's flexing stomach with the other, while she received the most vigorous pounding of her life. The pleasure was indescribable, building with every smooth thrust until she was sure—over and over again—that her body had finally reached its limit. But it never did, and Alex seemed determined to keep pushing until she either succumbed to her third orgasm of the night or else begged to stop. For now her impending climax remained frustratingly out of reach, but that didn't mean she was anywhere near ready to beg.

Alex slowed her pace momentarily, leaning back so Claire could easily see the thick length of the dildo sliding in and out of her slick pussy. When Claire lifted her gaze from their point of connection to stare at the striking face above her, Alex caressed the base of her throat and murmured, "I know you can do this for me, baby, and I need you to. I need you to come around my cock." Alex's free hand found her hip, gripping possessively as she plundered Claire's depths with increased urgency. "I'm not sure I'll be able to stop fucking you until you milk me dry."

Alex could stop—and *would* if asked, Claire knew—but knowing that only made the threat more tantalizing.

"I'm trying." Claire let go of the headboard and reached for her own clit. The distended nub was sensitive to the light touch, delivering equal parts joy and pain. Rubbing tiny circles, she moaned when the good feelings almost immediately overwhelmed the bad. Alex slowly withdrew from her body, pulling all the way out to rub the smooth, round head of the cock over her pulsing clit, further wetting the area for her fingers. Suddenly on the edge, Claire gasped, "I'm close!"

*Beep-beep.*

Claire frowned at the familiar-yet-foreign noise from across the room, then threw back her head with a groan as Alex forced the full length of the rippled shaft back into her vagina. "*Yes!*"

*Beep-beep. Buzzzz.*

Claire turned her head in the general direction of the infernal racket, growling as she felt her orgasm slipping away. "What the *fuck* is that?"

"Your phone." Alex tightened her fingers on Claire's hips and pulled out, then pushed all the way back in without missing a beat. "I think maybe you missed a call? Or a text?"

"I don't *care*," Claire wailed, frustrated by the delay of her long-awaited release. "Not about anything right now, except this."

*Buzzzz. Buzzzz. Buzzzz.*

With a muttered curse, Claire hooked her legs around Alex's narrow waist, crossing her ankles at the small of her back. "Fuck me, Alex. *Fuck me.*" She blocked out another beep from the phone while mentally plotting the murder of whoever felt entitled to her immediate attention at ten o'clock on a Sunday night. Her fingers flew over her clit while Alex obeyed her directive, delivering stroke after ecstatic stroke to hit *just* the right spot.

*Beep-beep.*

"*Fuck!*" Claire roared, pissed off as her orgasm retreated yet again. "What the *fuck?* Give me two more minutes, *please!*"

Alex's steady rhythm faltered. "Maybe you should—"

"No!" Claire drew Alex deeper inside with her legs, then used the hand not rubbing her clit to twist her own nipple demandingly. "Whoever it is can wait. I'm almost there."

*Beep-beep.*

Alex relocated Claire's hand from her breast to the mattress and pressed down on the wrist. She shifted to lie more fully atop Claire, so their chests touched, and breathed into her neck. Her hips rapidly established a new rhythm, hard and fast like before, and then she started to whisper hot, dirty words into Claire's ear. "Think I can force your slutty little cunt to come all over this fat fucking cock, Claire-Claire? 'Cause I do."

Claire moaned in delight, then groaned wretchedly at yet another alert from her phone. "Alex…"

Curling her hand around Claire's neck, Alex rubbed her thumb along the slender column of her throat in a subtly threatening manner that hinted at dominance without actually constricting the airway. "You wanted me to teach you how to get my dick off, didn't you? Well, this is how you get me off. Now *take it.* Work that cock with your tight little hole."

*Beep-beep.*

Claire closed her eyes and struggled to rub her clit faster, knuckles bumping into Alex's pelvis in the scant space between their bodies. Alex moaned, first pinning Claire's captured wrist down with even more force, then applying controlled pressure around the base of her throat. "That's right, baby, I love that. Squirm around on my cock. But only with your hips." She tightened her hold on Claire's upper body. "The rest of you stays right here, with me."

*Buzzz. Buzzz.*

Tears of frustration blurred Claire's vision at the same time Alex lifted her head to stare down into her eyes. Alex let go of her throat to collect Claire's tears on her thumb, then deepened her thrusts, moving impossibly faster. Sweat rolled down Alex's corded neck, evidence of her valiant exertion. "Rub your clit for me, sweetheart. One orgasm and I can stop. That's all I need. One wet, messy orgasm from your beautiful body and then I'll kiss away all your tears."

*Beep-beep.*

Claire's angry internal musings about repetitive smartphone-alerting tactics were abruptly silenced by the sudden beckoning of her release, now only seconds away. She hastened the fingers on her clit and cried out, "Yes! Yes!"

"Yes!" Alex echoed, lifting herself up slightly to allow Claire's hand more room to work. "That's it, Claire-Claire. Jerk your clit, just like I showed you. Remember that lesson? You did so well." She reared back without releasing her hold on Claire's neck and wrist, but altered her pace to deliver shallow, rapid thrusts. "You always make me so happy, baby. Always."

Claire quaked with the force of her massive climax, a tsunami of ecstasy that thundered through her body and left her boneless in its wake. She kept stroking her clit long after she felt like she couldn't take any more, never wanting the moment to end—stupid, persistent interruptions aside. But finally, as she drifted back to earth and reality settled in, Claire decided that she couldn't take the distraction anymore. Sighing in disgust, she withdrew her hand from between her thighs and raised her head to capture the full lips that hovered inches from her own in a brief kiss.

"Maybe I *should* check on that." Claire dropped her head back onto the pillow. "But let me tell you, it had better be important. Like, *really* important."

*Beep-beep. Beep-beep.*

Alex released Claire from her possessive hold, then braced her weight on her knees, reached between their lower bodies, and carefully withdrew the dildo from Claire's sodden vagina. "Personally, I'm of a different mind on that one. I hope it's *not* important, so that whoever's calling is in the wrong, instead of us for wanting to finish."

Claire exhaled when Alex rolled off to the side, then gathered her strength to sit up on the edge of the bed. Actually getting to her feet was going to take another minute or more of mental preparation. "Trust me. Nobody wants to deal with me when I've been left hanging. It's not pretty."

Alex grunted as she climbed off the bed. "Oh, yeah? So no orgasm-denial play in our future?"

"I mean, if that's something you wanted to do…" Claire frowned at another noise from her phone, then watched Alex cross the room to retrieve it. "There are probably only a few things I'd *never* try. I can't promise I'd enjoy being denied, though."

"Forced orgasms, then." Alex tossed a wink over her shoulder as she scooped up Claire's phone. "Feast, instead of famine. You down for that?"

Claire shivered at the thought of Alex giving her no choice but to come repeatedly, as many times as her body would allow. *Sort of like what we just did, but* more. Another shiver ran through her, raising goose bumps on her upper arms and chest. "Yes, please." Her heart leapt into her throat at the alarmed expression on Alex's face once she finally glanced down at Claire's buzzing phone. "What is it?"

"Sarah's calling—and it looks like she also sent a shitload of texts." Alex hurried to the bed and handed over the phone. "You'd better answer."

Claire fumbled with the large green icon on-screen, missing the call before it was sent to voice mail. "Damn it." She navigated into the missed-calls list, fuzzy-brained from the endorphins still flooding her system. Unable to focus, she caught a glimpse of Alex tugging off her harness and the attached cock next to the bed and hesitated with her finger over the call button. After taking a moment to appreciate Alex's nudity, she said, "You're so sexy."

Alex snorted and shot her an admonishing look. "Call her back, Claire-Claire. Before she gets any angrier."

Reminded of her best friend's infamous temper, Claire initiated the call. She brought the phone to her ear, staring at Alex's small, firm butt as she disappeared into the bathroom. "You should run a bath for us," she called out after her. "I can already tell that my thighs will be aching tomorrow."

"Tell me about it." The tub's faucet came on, and the resultant rush of water almost drowned out Alex's next comment. "You're going to keep me young, Ms. Barker. Either that or kill me."

Claire laughed, then realized belatedly that her phone was blaring a busy signal into her ear. Sarah had probably tried to dial her back at the same time, and their calls were conflicting. "Damn it," she muttered, then disconnected. "I'm having trouble with this phone," she shouted, lightheartedly. Rather than make another attempt and risk blocking Sarah's inevitable incoming call, she decided to check her collection of unread text messages instead. "I'm pretty sure you fucked my brains out."

"Well, that should level our intellectual playing field, at the very least."

Rolling her eyes, Claire opened her mouth to answer, then snapped it shut when her first missed text message from Sarah finally registered.

*911! Catastrophic failure of the main server. Ramona out of town & cell range, so she can't fix. We have that big demo for LA public schools tomorrow @ 7:30. Call me!!*

She didn't bother looking at the next message—one of about fifteen she'd received since Sarah had apparently started trying to contact her almost twenty minutes ago—and instead went into her contacts list to try calling again.

*Beep-beep.* An incoming message flashed across the top of the screen.

*Are you with Alex? She's not answering her phone, either. If you're ignoring me to fuck her, I'm going to be PISSED.*

Swallowing her fear, Claire started to push the green call button but stopped when an incoming call from Sarah popped up on the display. "Shit," Claire whispered, then answered with a rushed, "I'm so sorry. I tried to call back a few minutes ago, but I think we ran into each other. What happened with the server?"

"A few minutes ago?" Sarah's sharp tone made her cringe. "I've been trying to get ahold of you for nearly half an hour!"

"It looked more like twenty minutes to me," Claire said weakly. "I'm sorry. I was in the shower."

Fittingly, Alex chose that moment to poke her head back into the bedroom. "Water's ready when you are."

"That's Alex, isn't it? Did *neither* of you hear the phone?" Sarah's voice rose in frustration. "You know, it's great that you're finally getting laid on a regular basis, but we *still have a company to run!*"

Claire winced, realizing too late the mistake in allowing Sarah so much time to ruminate in her panic and resentment. Waving Alex away, she said, "*Sarah,* I'm sorry! I wasn't thinking about the fact that the calls might be related to that demo." In truth, Claire hadn't remembered the upcoming demonstration for their potentially huge new client at all, since she wasn't the one who had to give it. "Just tell me—"

"Wait, what do you mean, you weren't thinking my calls might be related to the demo? Were you *ignoring* me?"

Claire gritted her teeth at her own stupidity. "To be fair, I didn't know it was you."

"Nice." Claire could practically feel the steam coming out of Sarah's ears. "Let me guess…you guys were busy *fucking*, right? Like *always?*"

Claire bristled. Since they'd come of age, Sarah had almost always maintained an active sex life while Claire would sometimes go years without getting naked with another person. Company to run or not, she resented *Sarah's* obvious resentment about the way she'd been spending her time lately, especially after they'd spent the previous afternoon together conducting what turned into an hours-long quest to find the perfect outfit for Alex's exhibition. "*Always?* I'm pretty sure I spent most of yesterday with *you,* actually. *Shopping,* by the way, which you know I pretty much hate."

"Oh, okay. Well, I'm sorry I made you *waste* your Saturday doing something you hate. A real friend would have just left you alone. My bad, I guess, for wanting to help you find something to wear for Alex's show."

Sighing, Claire surrendered, uninterested in trying to further defend herself when the company was in crisis mode, and she knew she wasn't entirely in the right, anyway. "I really am sorry, Sarah, for not answering sooner and for what I just said about shopping. You know I love hanging out with you. And I had fun yesterday, really." She paused, then added, "I *love* that dress you picked out for me."

Sarah was silent for a beat. "And the shoes?"

Claire relaxed slightly at the audible thawing of Sarah's formerly icy tone. "The shoes are adorable." If not uncomfortable, she didn't add. "I love you, Sarah. I'm sorry it took me so long to pick up. I promise it won't happen again."

"It better not."

Claire sagged with relief upon being forgiven. She got off the bed and hurried to find the laptop she hadn't removed from its case all weekend. "Now, please tell me what's going on with the server."

## CHAPTER FIFTEEN

Five days later, Claire stood next to Sarah in front of a six-foot-tall likeness of her own vagina—postcoital and shiny with both her juices and Alex's saliva—and tried not to give away that she was the current subject of the lighthearted running commentary Sarah had been engaged in since they'd walked through the door. Casually, she replied to Sarah's lascivious appraisal of her aroused genitalia with a simple, "Yeah, she's okay."

Sarah snickered as they turned to face the small crowd of people clustered around Alex a few feet away. Both the women and men pressed into her space eagerly, ready to receive their moment of personal attention and—usually—a breathtaking grin before Alex moved on to the next fan. "Look at her work that crowd," Sarah murmured, shaking her head. "What I'd give to have half that charm…"

"Tell me about it." Even though Claire hated to abandon Alex among her admirers, especially with so many beautiful women clamoring for her girlfriend's undivided attention, she'd barely made it through ten minutes of small talk before gratefully accepting Alex's kind offer to stay on the sidelines with Sarah.

"How many of the women hanging on these walls do you think my sister slept with?" Sarah clapped her hand over her mouth immediately after she blurted the question. "Oh my God, Claire. I'm sorry." Indeed, she looked mortified about what would have been, admittedly, a very typical thing for her to wonder aloud about Alex's past life as a bachelor. "I shouldn't have said that. Especially not right now. I'm sorry."

Still feeling guilty over her professional inattention at the beginning of the week—even after having worked tirelessly to finally bring their main server back online, with all the lost data restored, a whole two hours ahead of the Monday-morning demo—Claire waved off the apology. "It's all right. I asked her the same thing before we slept together. The answer was one."

"*Really?*" Sarah didn't try to hide her disbelief at first. Then, apparently realizing how she sounded, she repeated, "Really," in a milder tone. "Well, she's clearly got impressive willpower." She shot Claire a reassuring smile, then gestured behind her at the most embarrassing image the gallery had on display—her own. "I mean, I'm almost ready to go down on this one, and I've never really even felt that particular urge before."

Claire couldn't prevent fierce heat from crawling up her face. "The last woman she dated—" She turned and pointed at one of the images of the narcissistic ex. "*Her*...I get the impression she hurt Alex badly—and it changed her."

"Her loss, your gain." Sarah gave her a kind smile. They both looked over at Alex again, who laughed politely at something a gorgeous young blonde with a plunging neckline had just whispered into her ear. With a gentle but firm shake of her head, she pointed over at Claire, then waved until Claire hesitantly returned the gesture. The blonde returned the greeting before shifting her attention back to Alex with a simpering pout. "Still beating them off with a stick," Sarah remarked mildly.

"Some things never change." Claire's stomach rolled as she again wondered how she would ever be enough for someone like Alex. With an entire world of willing lovers regularly throwing themselves at her, why would Alex ever be satisfied in a monogamous partnership with a hopeless introvert like her?

As though privy to her growing anxiety, Alex turned to look at Claire with her brow furrowed in obvious concern. *You okay?* Alex mouthed silently, across the crowd.

Claire nodded, wearing as big a smile as she could muster. The smile faded when Alex's expression suddenly tightened, first in surprise, then muted fear, then, finally, with markedly less-muted anger. Confused, Claire scanned the room for the source of Alex's distress and immediately zeroed in on a tall, statuesque brunette striding across the gallery floor like it was a runway in Milan. Almost afraid to receive visual confirmation that the stunning woman currently tracking her girlfriend like a heat-seeking missile was also the reason for her change in mood, Claire flicked her gaze back to Alex right in time to meet her stricken gaze. Nausea crawled up Claire's throat as a subtly deepening look of horror spread across Alex's handsome face as her eyes shifted from Claire to the newcomer, then back to Claire.

"Oh my God," Sarah whispered. "Do you think that's *her?*"

Claire opened her mouth, but her throat had gone too dry to produce words. She watched the woman approach Alex with a predatory smile, then pull Alex's stiff, unyielding body into a far-too-intimate embrace. Rooted to the spot, Claire only vaguely felt Sarah's hand settle on her back as the terrible scene unfolded in front of them. Alex drew back sharply at the unexpected contact, escaping the hug with an audibly harsh reprimand. "No, Vanessa. *No.*"

"That's her," Claire breathed. Her heart kicked into overdrive, thumping violently against her chest as she regarded the magnificent specimen who'd preceded her tenure as Alex's one and only.

"What are you *doing* here?" Alex seethed, eyes darting again to where Claire and Sarah stood staring at the nightmarish reunion. "You're supposed to be in Paris."

Vanessa followed Alex's gaze, briefly studying Claire's face before she scoffed and turned to say something Claire couldn't make out. By this point, Claire's face was so hot she could actually feel droplets of sweat rolling from her hairline down the side of her neck. Silently, she watched Vanessa take Alex by the arm and guide her away from the crowd, to a secluded spot over in the corner of the room. Shooting a backward glance at Claire, full of obvious trepidation, Alex tugged her arm out of Vanessa's grasp. Yet she continued to move toward the more-private location, even while resisting Vanessa's repeated efforts to reestablish physical contact.

*Probably to avoid making a scene.* Claire wished she could hear what was happening or even see Alex's face, but Vanessa's partially exposed back blocked her view as she and Alex occupied their new spot on the other side of the room.

"I don't like her," Sarah stated flatly.

"Me neither." Claire put a hand on her aching stomach, turning away from the heated conversation now playing out in front of a giant photograph of Alex's finger embedded within Vanessa's disgustingly flawless snatch. "I hate her, actually."

"Me, too." Sarah pulled Claire closer to her side for a firm squeeze. "Don't worry. You know Alex is blowing her off as we speak."

Alex tried to walk away from Vanessa, nearly proving Sarah's point, but Vanessa yanked her back with a vicious tug on her arm. Claire took a step forward at the sight, furious that anyone would treat a person they claimed to care about with so much disrespect. Especially at Alex's own exhibition. "That *bitch.*"

Sarah moved with her. "What do you want to do? I've got your back."

No matter how angry she was about seeing Alex be humiliated by a bitter ex-girlfriend, Claire wasn't sure she was up for whatever Sarah might be thinking. "I don't know. Maybe we should go rescue her? We could tell Vanessa that we need to talk to Alex about something important."

"Or we could tell her to fuck off, because Alex has a kickass girlfriend now...who just so happens to be you."

Claire froze. "Yeah. I'm not sure I can say *that.*"

When Alex tried to move away from Vanessa again, only to have her path blocked bodily, Sarah grabbed Claire's hand and dragged her toward Alex and her ex. "I can. Come on."

Alex greeted their arrival with a warm smile. "Hey, sis. Claire, baby, I was just about to come find you."

Vanessa simply glared, first at Sarah, then more venomously at Claire. "Do you mind? This is a private conversation."

Taking advantage of her distraction, Alex slipped past Vanessa and wound her arm around Claire's waist. "Actually, this conversation is *over.*" She kissed the top of Claire's head, holding her close. "Go ahead and enjoy the exhibition, Vanessa, if being here really *is* important to you for some reason. I'm not sure *why* it would be, given the way you left, but whatever. When it comes to you and me, though...we're done. *Completely.* Understand? I have nothing left to say to you."

Vanessa directed an angry scowl at Claire, who tried not to shrink under the venomous look of disapproval. "Because you're sleeping with *this* now?"

"Hey!" Sarah stepped forward aggressively. "Claire's twice the woman you'll ever be."

"Well, I wouldn't go *that* far, but now that you mention it, Claire *does* appear to enjoy her desserts a little too much." Vanessa delivered the withering put-down with a sickly sweet smile plastered across her perfectly symmetrical, breathtakingly angular face. She dragged her gaze down the length of Claire's body, making her feel downright hideous in the brand-new, form-fitting little black dress Sarah had picked out. "Not the type Alex usually goes for, but hey, when you're desperate for a slump buster—"

"Bitch—" Sarah snarled.

Alex cut off her sister's attack by launching a vehement defense of her own. "Vanessa, not only is Claire more beautiful than you, inside *and* out, she's just plain better in every way imaginable. Smarter, funnier, sexier, more ambitious, even *wealthier*—not that it matters. Quite frankly, I *never* felt for you what I feel for her. Not even close, actually. So do us a favor and *fuck off* before I ask security to escort you off the premises for stalking and harassment."

Vanessa turned up her nose, haughtily, while feigning an air of bored disinterest. "Fine, Alex. If you're not ready to talk things over like two reasonable adults, I certainly can't force you." She shot Claire a look of naked disdain. "Little girl, you feel special right now, but she'll use you up soon enough. Believe me."

"*Go,*" Alex roared, finally drawing the attention of the small crowd of people nearest to them. "*Now.*"

"Call me when you get bored with Velma." Vanessa winked and sauntered away. "I'll be in town for a couple weeks, at least. I have a suite at the Omni."

"Good for you," Alex said dismissively. She hurried to shepherd Claire into the next room, where they were greeted by yet another portrait of Vanessa's pussy. Wincing, Alex bent to stare into Claire's eyes, clearly searching for an honest reaction to the shitshow that had just unfolded. "Baby, I'm *so, so* sorry." She lifted Claire's fingers to her lips, kissing the knuckles urgently. "I had no idea she was coming tonight. *None.*"

"What a monster," Sarah piped up, still standing next to Claire. "I'm sorry, sis, but you've got *terrible* taste in women." She offered Claire a conciliatory nod. "Present company excluded."

"Yeah. I agree." Claire tried not to meet Alex's eyes, afraid to reveal just how shaken she was. "She was totally awful."

"You'll have to take my word for it, but she really was a lot nicer in the beginning."

"She must have been." Sarah raised her eyebrow at Alex. "Either that or you let the sex completely mangle your judgment."

Alex shook her head, cheeks turning pink as she first glanced at Claire, then stared down at the floor. "Whatever the reason, getting involved with someone like Vanessa was clearly a mistake. But it's *my* mistake, so the fact that my choices have come back to hurt you, Claire..." She raised her face, painfully hesitant to make eye contact. "I can't apologize enough. I know it wasn't easy for you to come here tonight, and I realize that Vanessa's attitude pretty much caused all your fears to be realized in the worst possible way. She had absolutely no right to speak to you like that, and frankly, if it wouldn't have caused too big a scene—or possibly led to my arrest—I would've happily smacked that stupid smile off her face." Alex captured Claire's hand and brought it to her lips. "I love you, Claire-Claire. You are *everything* Vanessa wasn't. Actually, forget Vanessa. You're just *everything*."

"Aww," Sarah cooed, only half teasingly. "You two are so *nauseating*."

Claire stuck out her tongue. "Shut up."

"You two are so *cute*." Alex smirked and put her other arm around Sarah. "My two favorite girls."

Sarah slipped from her grasp. "Don't drag *me* into this lovefest." Chuckling, she surveyed the room. "Does anyone else find it weird that the three of us are standing in a room full of vagina together?"

"Yes." Alex shifted her weight uncomfortably. "Now that you mention it."

Claire suppressed her laughter as Alex's eyes darted over to the photo of her finger-fucking Vanessa. "Same."

Hugging her, Alex said, "You know, you two can leave if you want. I could take a cab home."

Claire cringed at the thought of how expensive *that* ride would be. "That's not necessary. We'll stay."

"This is scheduled to go on another two hours." Alex glanced around at the crowd, which hadn't yet begun to thin. A couple of people on the periphery brightened when Alex's gaze passed over them, openly eager to catch her attention. "I really should keep working this room." She returned her attention to Claire. "But I hate to leave you alone again."

"I've got her." Sarah looped her arm through Claire's, easing her out of Alex's embrace. "I see that bitch again, she won't even have the chance to barf out a shitty put-down before I've dismantled her piece by piece."

Claire lifted an eyebrow, both impressed and slightly taken aback by Sarah's colorful threat. "Wow."

"Wow is right." Alex clapped her younger sister on the back. "Good on ya, sis. But don't do anything that'll get the cops called, all right?"

Sarah feigned exasperation, but with an amused snort. "Yeah, yeah."

Alex bent to give Claire a lingering kiss. "I love you, baby, and I promise we'll get out of here as soon as humanly possible."

Claire shook her head. "No. Enjoy your evening." She caressed Alex's cheek, then rose on her toes to kiss her lips one more time. "You've earned it. I love you, too."

Sarah stood quietly by her side as they watched Alex walk to a pair of nearby art lovers, who greeted her with enthusiastic hellos. Low enough that only Claire could hear, she said, "You know you've got a slammin' body, right? And you're *way* prettier than her. That bitch is just jealous that Alex is in love with you now." She tightened her arm around Claire amiably. "You're the cream of the crop when it comes to Alex's lifetime dating pool, and *Vanessa* knows it." She sneered Alex's ex-girlfriend's name.

As much as she appreciated the vote of confidence, Sarah *was* her best friend and thus not exactly able to judge with any objectivity. Claire returned her one-armed hug anyway. "I love you, too, Sarah."

"You'd better." Sarah released her with a kiss on her hair. "Shall we keep circling the room? Take in the feminine landscape, as it were?"

Claire chuckled, then looked around the gallery for a restroom. "Actually, I *really* need to pee. You?"

Sarah shook her head. "But I'll walk with you."

"Great." Claire kept scanning the room. "Do you have any idea where we're going?"

Sarah laughed. "Time to case the joint."

They found what they were looking for a couple minutes later, after they'd walked clear to the other end of the large building. A somewhat long line of women snaked from the restroom in the rear corner of the space, all waiting for what Claire guessed was only a handful of toilets.

Sighing, she stepped into the queue and waved Sarah toward a row of photos they hadn't yet seen. "Go ahead. Entertain yourself while I wait."

"You sure?" Sarah moved forward with her as the line grew slightly shorter. "I can stay with you."

"Sarah, I'm an introvert...not a child." She smiled to further soften the placid admonishment. "I'll be fine."

"All right, then." Sarah gave her arm a playful squeeze. "I'm off to see some pussy."

*The wonderful pussy of Oz!* Claire concluded silently, in song. She folded her arms in front of her chest and waited with her eyes slightly downcast, so as not to make eye contact and be dragged into conversation with anyone she didn't know.

Once it was finally her turn to step inside the restroom—which hosted two booths with floor-to-ceiling doors, both currently occupied—Claire reared back in surprise when she came face-to-face with Vanessa, who'd just finished washing her hands at the sink. Vanessa glanced up, rolled her eyes, then lunged forward to grab Claire's arm and pull her into the corner of the enclosed space. Shocked that she was being manhandled in the same way as Alex, Claire simply went along, until suddenly Vanessa backed her up against the counter and got right in her face.

"Look," Vanessa said, dripping with faux sweetness. "I'm sorry about before. The truth is, you seem like a sweet girl. Pretty enough, even, in your own way."

Claire swallowed a sharp retort she knew Sarah would've actually had the balls to utter. "Thanks?"

"In all seriousness, though, you're crazy if you think there's any chance you'll be able to keep Alex satisfied for more than a month or two. *Tops.* After that, your new-car smell will disappear. It always does." Vanessa tried to caress her cheek, but Claire jerked away. Chuckling, she said, "Let me guess: Alex gets off on your inexperience, right? I mean, it's pretty obvious you haven't been fucked a whole lot. Probably not until college, I'm guessing. And not all that much since then?"

Claire wrinkled her nose, then tried to sidestep the interrogation and flee the bathroom, bladder be damned. Vanessa caged her against the counter within surprisingly well-muscled arms, keeping Claire at her mercy. Whole body trembling, Claire stared hard into Vanessa's eyes and summoned up enough bravery to speak with slightly more volume. "*Stop.* Let me leave." She glanced around the bathroom, which had inexplicably emptied over the course of their confrontation. She wasn't sure whether anyone currently occupied the stalls. "Seriously, Vanessa. I don't want to do this with you."

Giggling, Vanessa mimicked her in the high-pitched voice of a little girl. "*Stop.* I don't want to *do this.*" She bit her lip, dropping her gaze down the front of Claire's cleavage-baring dress. "Is that how you get Alex off? By playing the innocent, unwilling virgin?"

Claire flushed as the jibe hit a little too close to reality. "That's none of your business."

"Oh, I bet Alex *loves* that game." Vanessa's smug grin faded. "For now, at least. I mean, innocence only lasts so long. At some point she'll have stuck her dick in you so many times it won't even be possible to pretend you're anything but her nasty little cock-slut. Once that happens, I'm not sure you'll have what it takes to keep her interested."

"You don't know anything about me *or* my relationship with Alex. Like the fact that I've known her *way* longer than you have. I mean, *years* longer. So don't talk to me about my girlfriend, because—believe me—I know her better than you do." Claire had no idea if that was really true, but she sure hoped so.

Vanessa chuckled. "Has she tried to fuck you in the ass?"

Claire tried again to escape from the prison of Vanessa's arms, but Alex's ex had no problem using her superior physical strength to block her. Heart thudding, Claire spoke without meeting Vanessa's eyes. "Do you want me to scream? I will."

"Ooh, do *that.* Have you figured out yet how much Alex appreciates a good, full-throated scream? And tears. She *loves* tears." Vanessa lifted her hand to trace a mocking finger over Claire's jaw. "I have to admit, when she told me she enjoyed rough anal sex, I was skeptical. But what can I say? I must be a masochist. I'm not sure I've ever cried harder or experienced so much pain inflicted by another person, but I loved every second of her cock in my ass if only because it got her off like you wouldn't *believe.* After, Alex told me it was the best sex of her life."

Caught between punching Vanessa in the face or bursting into tears, Claire simply stood there and stared. Her instincts urged her to disregard every word that came out of this woman's mouth, but for some reason, doing so wasn't exactly easy. Thus far, her sexual appetite had perfectly aligned with Alex's. But what if Vanessa was telling the truth? What if Alex wanted something Claire wasn't willing to give? *Even if Alex does get off on inflicting serious pain, that doesn't mean she'll require that from me.* The thought didn't reassure her as much as she wanted it to. *But if she doesn't get it from me, will she seek fulfillment somewhere else?* With *someone else?*

Vanessa wore a smirk of deep satisfaction. "Like I said, I'm pretty sure you don't have what it takes."

Angrily, Claire planted her hands on Vanessa's chest and shoved her backward just as two women entered the restroom. They hastily averted their eyes at the sight of their physical confrontation, rushing into the now-empty stalls. Giggling when she stumbled before regaining her balance, Vanessa stepped aside and let Claire go.

"Later, *Claire.*"

Claire hurried out of the restroom, dodging a handful of bodies that lingered outside the door before she plunged into the crowd in a desperate search for a friendly face. She scanned the room she was in, then moved on to the next one, where she immediately encountered an intensely concerned Alex. After excusing herself from a conversation with a balding man and a wealthy-looking woman, Alex rushed to Claire without hesitation. "Where's Sarah? What happened?"

"Sarah..." Claire glanced backward, trying to decide *where* her chaperone had gone. "Probably off looking at a vagina somewhere."

Alex's strong hand captured Claire's chin and forced her to make eye contact. "What *happened?*"

Claire realized that she didn't know how to have this conversation. Or maybe she simply didn't want to. Unfortunately, either way, she probably had to. If Vanessa ended up telling Alex that they'd spoken, Claire didn't want it to seem as though she'd tried to hide something. "I went to the restroom. There was a line and Sarah didn't have to go, so I told her I'd find her once I was done."

"And?"

"And I ran into Vanessa washing her hands." Claire shrugged, feigning nonchalance that was surely as unconvincing to Alex as it felt to her. "She was a bitch. But I already knew that, right?"

"What did she say to you?"

Claire noticed an attractive, middle-aged woman standing nearby, eyeing Alex in a way that made it clear she was smitten. Uncomfortable with the subject matter even *without* an audience, Claire shook her head. "It doesn't matter."

"Yes, it does." Alex swallowed and brought Claire's hand to her mouth for a tremulous kiss. "It matters a lot, actually."

Claire's attention drifted to their onlooker, who seemed a bit crushed about Alex's display of affection. "Alex, why don't we talk about this later? At home?"

Alex's jaw tensed. "Fair enough, but we *will* talk about this. Okay?"

"If you insist."

"Thank you." Alex laced their fingers together. "You sure you don't want to leave now?"

*And abandon you here with Vanessa? No, thanks.* Not wanting Alex to think she didn't trust her, Claire shook her head, smiling as best she could after the night she'd had. "No, I want to be with you." At the sight of a now-familiar flash of arousal in Alex's eyes, Claire stepped closer and traced a blunt fingernail over her arm. "I *miss* you."

Alex's breathing hitched. "I miss you, too, baby. A lot."

Greedy for proof that Alex really *did* desire her—*at least for now*—Claire got up onto her toes and whispered into Alex's ear. "Do you think you could take a super quick break? With me?"

Alex nodded, then turned to address the woman awaiting her attention. "I'm so sorry. I promise to come back and chat with you, but I need five or ten minutes with my girlfriend here."

The woman's delighted expression faded only slightly at the news of Claire's title. "No problem, Alex. I love your work!"

"Thanks. I really appreciate that." Alex's grin was radiant enough to power an entire city block. "Excuse us." She took Claire by the hand and led her away. "What kind of break? You want to grab some fresh air? We could find Sarah and take her with us, if you'd like."

As they neared the restroom, Claire had a better idea. *Vanessa must be out of there by this point, right?* Tugging Alex's hand hard enough to alter their trajectory, she led them into the bathroom, then into the stall that had its door ajar. Claire engaged the lock behind her before shuffling their bodies around so she could lower the toilet seat cover and sit down. Alex looked downright shocked when Claire reached to unbutton her pants.

"What are you doing?"

Claire smiled at Alex's hushed whisper. "You know what I'm doing."

"Baby." Alex's hands covered hers, preventing Claire from tugging the pants any lower. "Is this because of something Vanessa said to you?"

Hearing feminine voices gathered at the sink, Claire gestured for Alex to lean closer. In a whisper, she stated, "This is because I'm proud to be with you, I'm hot for you, and you deserve it." She licked her lips and stared into Alex's eyes as her girlfriend rose to her full height. "Do you not want this?"

Alex sighed and released Claire's hands. "Of course I do. I just don't want *you* to do anything you don't truly want to do."

*Like have my ass pounded?* Even as the thought flitted through her mind, Claire admonished herself for letting Vanessa get into her head. She pushed their disturbing conversation from her mind, yanking Alex's pants around her knees, followed by her boxer briefs. Then she moved forward, mouth open, to lave Alex's slick pussy with her tongue.

"Claire?" Sarah's voice echoed through the bathroom, causing Claire to straighten in surprise. "You in here? Alex?"

Alex opened her mouth to answer, but Claire pinched her thigh with a shake of her head. It was one thing to go down on her girlfriend in a semi-public restroom, but quite another for anyone to *know*. Hating herself for suggesting they ignore Sarah, particularly after the crashed-server fiasco, she decided that the only solution was to get Alex off as efficiently as possible. If she was quick about this, she could probably intercept Sarah at the other end of the gallery and convince her that they'd been walking circles around each other in the crowded space for a ridiculous fifteen minutes.

Focused on her goal, Claire opened her mouth again, desperate to prove to both herself *and* Alex that whatever shortcomings Claire Barker might possess, when it came to pleasing Alex she could be *more* than enough.

❖

When Claire and Alex emerged from the bathroom a few minutes later, it was at the very same moment Sarah happened to be walking past the door with a noticeable scowl etched across her face. Glaring in their direction—harder still when Claire nervously wiped her mouth with the back of her hand—Sarah stalked over to greet them. "*Really?*"

Claire put her hand on Alex's back and gestured toward the area of the gallery where she'd held court before their oral interlude. "Go ahead and find that woman who's waiting to talk to you. We'll see you in a bit."

Alex glanced at Sarah, then at Claire. "You sure?"

"What, you need to protect her from *me* now?" Sarah folded her arms over her chest. "Go on. We'll be fine."

Once Alex walked away, Claire turned to Sarah. "Sorry. I went looking for you after a particularly nasty run-in with Vanessa in the bathroom but found Alex first. We decided to find some privacy so Alex could help me calm down."

Sarah's expression softened, but only slightly. "I was getting worried. I couldn't find either of you anywhere inside—*including* the bathroom—or even outside, and then you weren't answering any of my texts. I started to think that maybe you two had ditched me here."

Guiltily, Claire remembered the phone tucked into her purse, which she'd muted. "I'm really sorry. We didn't mean to take so long. But you know we would *never* ditch you. *Ever.*"

Sarah shrugged. "It's easy to feel like an afterthought these days." She looped their arms together again, then snagged a glass of red wine from a tray one of the catering staff carried past and gave it to Claire. "What happened with Vanessa?"

Claire took a sip of the alcohol before answering. "She was primping at the mirror when I walked in. She grabbed my arm and pushed me against the counter and basically tried to intimidate me away from Alex."

"*Seriously?* What a tremendous cunt."

Claire nodded, ignoring her distaste for that particular insult. "She's not a nice woman."

"What did she say, exactly? To intimidate you?"

Claire blushed and shook her head. "Nothing I care to repeat."

"Did she threaten you?" Sarah scanned the room as though hoping to find and confront the target of her anger. "If she thinks that's how to win Alex back, she obviously doesn't know my sister very well."

"She didn't threaten me. Not really." Claire took another long drink. "Let's just say, she tried to convince me I won't be able to keep Alex satisfied…in the most graphic terms possible."

"Well, she's full of shit." Sarah patted Claire's arm. "Don't worry about what she thinks. And promise me you'll disregard every word out of her hateful mouth. She has her own motivation, which means that everything she says is suspect."

Claire nodded. "I know."

"But you're letting it get to you, anyway."

Busted, Claire reflected on the beauty and the frustration of having a best friend who knew her so well. "I'm trying not to."

"Just remember what I said earlier. Alex is *way* into you, Clarabelle. It's obvious—I'm sure to Vanessa as well, hence her aggression."

Claire stopped walking—right in front of her own self-portrait, she noticed too late—and pulled Sarah into a clumsy hug. "I love you. Thank you for being here tonight…and sorry again for making you worry."

Sarah returned her hug with a resigned sigh. "I love you, too. Sorry that dating Alex is more complicated than either of us realized it would be."

There were so many ways to parse that statement, Claire hardly knew where to start. Without asking, she knew that Sarah was referring not only to Claire's inexperience and insecurities running up against Alex's worldly, apparently vindictive past, but also the impact this new relationship seemed to be having on their friendship. Clinging more tightly to Sarah, she vowed, "It'll get better."

Hopefully in every way.

## CHAPTER SIXTEEN

Claire lay entwined with Alex on the couch where they'd had their first time, listening to one of the many albums it turned out they both loved while trading gentle kisses and murmured endearments during the brief lulls between tracks. In the two days since Alex's show opened, they'd spent every waking hour together. Though neither of them explicitly said so, it was obvious they both felt the need to reaffirm that the foundation they had to build upon was stronger than a bitter ex-girlfriend or even Claire's antisocial tendencies.

*Or perhaps I'm just projecting.* Claire raised her head to stare up into Alex's eyes, wishing she could peek inside her mind and know what she was really thinking. After they'd finally left the gallery on Friday night, Alex had answered all of her questions about Vanessa—at least those she'd been brave enough to ask—but Claire still hadn't summoned the nerve to reveal the ugliest details of her confrontation in the restroom with Alex's ex. She'd recited to Alex, verbatim, Vanessa's subtle put-downs about her appearance, the faux concern about her suitability for Alex, and her incisive remarks regarding Claire's relative inexperience and how what might appeal to Alex in the short term would fail to sustain her interest longer than a few weeks. Alex had assuaged Claire's fears first with all the right words to counter Vanessa's insinuations, then with a deft hand that reached between Claire's legs to induce a shattering orgasm after less than three minutes.

*I love you,* Alex had whispered afterward. *You're the smartest person I've ever known. You turn me on. You make me laugh. Your body fits perfectly against mine. I believe with all my heart that you truly love me and would never intentionally hurt me. So I honestly don't care that you'd rather stay home and binge-watch sci-fi reruns or play video games than go out dancing at the club or attend some pretentious art show. You* are *who I want, Claire-Claire. Only you.*

Even after all the heartfelt declarations—or perhaps *because* of them—Claire hadn't been able to stop thinking about what she *hadn't* yet shared about that night at the gallery. Specifically, the repulsive lie Vanessa told her about Alex's violent tendencies. The entire story had obviously been an attempt to frighten the competition away from the object of Vanessa's twisted desire, which meant it almost certainly wasn't true. At least not entirely true.

*But what if it is? What if it's at least* partially *true?*

For the sake of her future with Alex, she needed to come clean about Vanessa's accusation. That way she would be able to hear firsthand what Alex had to say about the matter, which would hopefully help her determine whether her ex-girlfriend's warning was a load of horseshit or a potential incompatibility to seriously consider.

Wanting to tread lightly, Claire closed the distance between their mouths to give Alex a deep, slightly wet kiss. Alex groaned at the contact, pulling Claire to rest fully atop her body. Pushing her hips into Alex's, Claire waited until they both sang the iconic closing refrain of the song currently playing through the speakers before initiating the conversation she'd been dreading all weekend. "Alex, could I talk to you about something Vanessa said Friday night? When she confronted me in the bathroom?"

Alex stiffened, instantly at full attention. "Please. Is this the part you didn't want to tell me before?"

"Yes." Face heating, Claire fought to maintain eye contact. *So Alex knew I was holding back.* "I'm sorry. I was too..." She searched for the right word but settled on "embarrassed."

Alex laid her cool palm on Claire's hot cheek. "Don't be. You can tell me anything." She swallowed, worry dancing in her eyes. "I just hope Vanessa didn't make you too uncomfortable or cause you to question how I feel or what I want."

Claire also swallowed. Now that the moment was here, she wasn't positive she could actually repeat Vanessa's vulgar claim. But she had to try. Without honesty, she and Alex were as good as done. "She wanted me to know that I wasn't enough to satisfy you or keep your interest. She said that once you'd put your dick in me enough times, the thought of my relative innocence would no longer get you off. And that's when you would ask me for…other things. Things I might not want to do but that you'd previously enjoyed with her."

Alex's throat tensed, and the blood appeared to drain from her face. She coughed, then whispered, "Like what?" Based on the fearful anticipation in her eyes, it appeared she might already know.

Placing her hand on Alex's shoulder, Claire answered, as calmly as she could, "Anal sex. But not just…she said you liked it rough. That you made her scream and cry, that it hurt…and that you loved every second of it." When Alex didn't respond but instead looked away, wincing, as though trying to decide what to say, Claire added, in a weak voice, "But I keep telling myself she's full of shit. She wants to scare me away from you."

"She *is* full of shit." Alex reestablished eye contact while subtly moving her hand from Claire's flannel-covered bottom to the middle of her back. "And yeah, she's *definitely* trying to scare you."

"But?"

"But I can't honestly tell you that was a *complete* lie. I mean, the part about me loving every second is absolutely *one hundred percent* false. Please know that. But did I fuck Vanessa in the ass with a strap-on? Yeah, I did." Alex paused to wet her lips. Then she cleared her throat. "The last thing I wanted was to cause her any pain. The entire thing was *her* idea, although I'd done it before with a past lover. Who *also* asked for it, by the way, and liked it, and didn't shed a single tear of discomfort throughout. I spent probably a full hour preparing her with my fingers and tongue, used a small cock and tons of lube, and barely moved once I was inside her. The first woman, I mean."

Though she attempted to remain open-minded to Alex's explanation, Claire's pulse raced at the news that even part of Vanessa's story was true. "But with Vanessa?"

"I tried to do it the same as the first time, since it was such a good experience for my ex-lover, but Vanessa was impatient. She wanted me to just shove it in after only a few minutes of preparation. She'd chosen a bigger cock for me than I'd worn the first time, which worried me a little, but she told me it was what she wanted. Vanessa had a lot of…dark fantasies. She begged me to take her hard and fast, to be merciless and verbally degrading and…*mean.*" Shuddering, Alex let her hands fall away from Claire altogether. "She pretty much backed into me as soon as I got into position. And yes, she screamed. She cried. But every time I tried to stop, or slow down, or pull out, she'd goad me into continuing by telling me what a worthless lay I was, how her ex was *so* much better than me, how I was selfish not to give her what she wanted. She asked for it—and I wanted to satisfy her—so I did what she told me to do."

"She's sick," Claire whispered.

Alex had gone pale. "You have no idea." She shivered, averting her eyes from Claire's once more. "When it was over, she made me hold her while she sobbed about how much it had hurt, how brutal I'd been. She reframed the entire encounter as soon as she orgasmed, casting me in the role of the overly aggressive butch and herself as the abused partner. It was absolutely insane, a total mind-fuck. I knew the sex hadn't been my idea, of course, but I still felt terrible. I even swore that I would do everything I could to make it up to her."

"Lying, manipulative, narcissistic…" Claire recited Alex's initial description of her ex-girlfriend. "I see that now. I'm so sorry she put you through that. The entire ordeal sounds awful."

"It really was. She made me feel like an evil person, at the time. Now, with the benefit of hindsight, I'm able to recognize that she was simply escalating an existing pattern I really should've noticed long before that night. Vanessa thrives on drama. She loves to play the victim. When she left me a month later, she claimed it was because she didn't know how to trust me anymore. Of course, she moved in with her new lover that very same day. Months later, a mutual acquaintance told me that Vanessa had confided in her that she'd concocted the whole scenario to cast me as the guilty party in our breakup." Alex's nostrils flared and her lower lip trembled. "It's hard to explain after all this time, but I had real feelings for her then. Not nearly as strong as what I feel for you, but still…I thought Vanessa and I were close. I thought we were *friends*. Being accused of betraying her trust in that way hurt me, badly."

"Well, if it helps alleviate any lingering guilt, Vanessa told *me* that she must be a masochist because of how much she totally *loved* giving you everything she claims I won't be able to."

Alex sat up slightly and they locked eyes. "Claire, I would *never*—"

A loud, clearly annoyed knock on the front door interrupted the mellow vibe of the music and broke the tension between them. They both turned to glance at the source of the noise. "It's Sarah," Claire decided, based on sound alone. "We have to answer it."

Bad timing or not, she wasn't about to ignore her best friend even one more time.

Alex grabbed Claire's hand after she disentangled their bodies and stood, before Claire could walk away. "Wait. Let's finish this conversation first."

Sarah knocked again, louder and angrier than before. Claire shook her head, frowning as she withdrew her hand. "I'm sorry. I can't blow her off this time. She's likely to kill me if I do."

Alex sat up, lips twisted into an irritated scowl. "No problem. I mean, it's not like we were talking about anything *important*."

Claire shot Alex an admonishing look. "Stop that. I just don't want to disappoint my best friend again. Her approval of our relationship is no less critical to its future than our ability to talk openly about your psycho ex-girlfriend."

Alex's scowl deepened as Claire went to open the door. When Sarah greeted them both with a facetious, "Oh, look! I actually exist," Alex immediately shot back a searing retort.

"We really ought to think about hanging out at your place more, Claire." Alex pinned Sarah with the kind of death glare only possible between siblings. "Fewer annoying interruptions."

"Oh, am *I* taking up too much of your time?" Sarah's answering glare slid from Alex to Claire, as though the two of them had spoken in concert. "I'm awfully sorry, I didn't realize. I mean, why *would* I, given that I barely see either one of you anymore? Except, of course, when you need me to run interference at a social event or, you know...*run our company while you fuck.*"

Claire flinched at the fire in Sarah's eyes. "Whoa. *Hey.* Alex said it. *I* didn't." Noticing Sarah's agitated state, Claire's stomach twisted when she realized that she knew exactly why Sarah was here—and so very pissed off. "Oh my God. We were supposed to meet today, weren't we? To go over the..." Though her memory faltered, she was suddenly, sickeningly certain that she'd neglected yet another important deadline. "The, um..."

"To finalize the TED talk we're supposed to give next month in

Austin?" Sarah threw her hands up in exasperation. "Claire, I put this meeting on your calendar *weeks* ago. You told me you needed time to gather data and generate statistics, so I gave it to you. I didn't harass you with constant reminders because I figured, you know, you're a *responsible adult.* Or at least you used to be. I wanted to give you the benefit of the doubt, but clearly you don't deserve it."

"*Hey.*" Alex's sharp tone pulled both their gazes to the couch, where she rose to assume a genuinely intimidating pose. "Back off, Sarah. Seriously."

Sarah swung her furious gaze to Alex. "*Back off? Seriously?*" She checked Claire's face briefly for a reaction, then advanced on Alex in a burst of unchecked rage. "Claire is my *business partner!* Not to mention my *best friend since sixth grade!* And until you decided you just *had* to sleep with her, she was also the most *reliable* person I've ever known. I'm sorry, Alex, but frankly, you're the worst thing to ever happen to her productivity. Not as though you give a flying fuck, but this TED talk is important to us. Not only could nailing it open new doors for our company, but the exposure alone will be absolutely *integral* to achieving our marketing goals this year."

"Fine, so it's important. But Claire's only human, you know? She's had a rough weekend, and after all the drama at the exhibition Friday night, well, it's understandable how this slipped her mind. Why don't you cut her a little slack?"

Sarah puffed up. "I *have* been. All kinds of slack."

While she appreciated Alex's staunch defense, Claire had to interject on her business partner's behalf. "Alex, Sarah isn't wrong. This TED talk—"

"*Sarah* is being a real *bitch.*" Alex's vicious comeback made it clear that she wasn't about to forgive her sister's need to interrupt their serious chat in order to loudly express her disapproval of Claire's work ethic. "I'm sorry the meeting slipped Claire's mind, but if it matters to you at all, we were right in the middle of a pretty important conversation of our own. One I'd like to finish, if you wouldn't mind getting the *fuck* out of my house."

Sarah pinned Alex with a withering look. "I *own* this house."

"Yeah, and that's starting to become a real problem for me."

Startled by how quickly sibling bickering had turned into

contentious, potentially life-altering anger and resentment, Claire stepped between Sarah and Alex with her hands in the air. "Time out. My turn to speak."

Two pairs of eyes turned toward her expectantly. Sarah muttered, "Finally, considering that this has *nothing* to do with Alex anyway."

Claire shushed Sarah, then turned to address Alex with her hand still raised. "Alex, I'm truly sorry that I didn't remember the meeting with Sarah before I decided to bring up what I did. You absolutely deserve a resolution to the talk we were having, but unfortunately," she shifted her attention to her business partner, "Sarah's right. Delivering a brilliant TED presentation will be critical for our company. I've known about this deadline for months and really have no excuse for letting today's meeting slip my mind." She took a cautious step closer to Sarah, trying to gauge exactly how much trouble she was in. "I hate to even ask, but would you mind giving me an hour or two to pull the rest of the data together? I'll meet you at the main house as soon as I'm ready. I'm sure we'll be able to whip this out in no time."

Sarah heaved a sigh. "Sure. I'll just tell Marcus that dinner isn't going to happen tonight because *you* were too busy living it up to take care of the *only* responsibility you had in this thing."

"Fuck off, Sarah," Alex muttered, collapsing back onto the couch. "*Please.*"

Once again holding up her hand to silence Alex, Claire said, "One hour, tops. There's no need to cancel your plans with Marcus."

"I guess we'll see. It depends on how long it takes us to get our shit together. At the moment, I don't have very high hopes. So just... hurry up."

"I will." Claire suppressed the urge to touch Sarah's arm for reassurance that she hadn't completely fucked up their friendship. "Sarah, I'm sorry. This will *never* happen again."

Sarah scoffed. "You're saying that a lot these days." Turning, she extended her middle finger at her grumbling sister. "Oh, and Alex? Go fuck yourself."

"Sarah, go *get* fucked. Use the next hour to do us all a favor and chill the hell out."

"*Alex,*" Claire said sharply. "That's *enough.*"

Alex glowered at Sarah until she stormed out the front door, slamming it behind her. Then she shifted her focus to Claire. "Come on. You know she was acting way shittier than the situation called for. So you're an hour late for a meeting. It's not the end of the world…or a good enough excuse to barge in here and yell at you."

Claire made eye contact with Alex, stepping closer so there would be no mistaking her sincerity. "Alex, I love you, but Sarah had a point. I'm your girlfriend, yes, but not first and foremost. I'm also Sarah's business partner—*and* her best friend. I've been those things for *years* longer than I've had the pleasure of calling you mine."

Though Alex bristled at her gentle correction, she also softened slightly. "Of course. I know that."

"The truth is, I've pretty much sucked at being Sarah's friend *and* her partner since you and I first hooked up." That in mind, Claire walked across the room to grab her laptop so she could boot it up. "That's on me, of course, but the point is, Sarah wasn't *wrong* to call me out."

"What are you doing?"

Claire set her laptop on the coffee table, then walked behind the couch to plug in its charger. "Getting that data ready for Sarah. I've already done some of what we need, but between you and me, finalizing the rest in only an hour will be a challenge." She sank down onto the couch, shooting Alex a wry smile. "One I have no choice but to overcome."

Alex snapped her mouth shut and glanced at the laptop's screen. Right as the operating system loaded, she said, "What I wanted to say before Sarah interrupted us was that I would *never* ask you to do anything you didn't want, sexually or otherwise. And although I would do almost *anything* you asked me to do, honestly, I could never cause you real pain. Even if you asked for it. I never want to hear you scream like that."

Claire dragged her eyes away from her computer with effort, paused mid-click over the icon of the database management tool she needed to launch. "Alex, I believe you. But do you think we could talk about it later? Like after the meeting?" She gestured at her laptop. "I kind of need to focus on this."

Alex exhaled through her nose, then planted her hands on the couch cushions to push herself standing. "Fine. I'll be in the bedroom doing some photo editing, if you need me."

"Okay." Claire nodded, barely listening as she started tapping out a query to retrieve a complex set of data. "Love you."

"I love you, too, Claire-Claire." Alex lingered in the doorway, obviously forlorn. "Are we okay?"

Unable to focus on two things at once, Claire answered Alex with a simple "Uh-huh."

The next time she looked up from her screen, Alex was gone.

## CHAPTER SEVENTEEN

The following week was a stressful one, largely because Claire barely spent any time with Alex. Or, at least, very few of her waking hours. Eager to prove to Sarah that Alex wasn't the worst thing to ever happen to her in *any* way, Claire threw herself into her work, even putting in over a dozen of the extra hours she'd long gifted to the company in lieu of having a personal life. She still slept at Alex's place, and they'd even managed to have sex once, late Tuesday night, but after Claire realized how tired she was the next morning at the office, she declared a moratorium on intimate encounters until the weekend to give herself a chance to catch up on her many lapsed responsibilities.

By the time Saturday rolled around, Claire was both ready and eager for a long, uninterrupted day with the woman she loved. Sarah and Marcus were visiting the redwoods with out-of-town friends, so spending time together was a blissfully guilt-free decision, making it far easier for Claire to relax and enjoy a much-needed reunion with Alex. Though they'd been able to finish their conversation about Vanessa—concluding that she was an unambiguously awful human being that neither one of them ever wanted to see again—they still hadn't had a real opportunity to reestablish the easy intimacy they'd settled into before Vanessa's reappearance and Claire's forgotten meeting had disrupted the sanctity of the perfect little bubble they'd retreated inside while falling in love.

When Claire awoke on Saturday morning, she craned to look out the curtained window of her apartment to discover an already vibrant blue sky. Rolling to face her still-slumbering big spoon, Claire grinned at the sight of her lover wrapped in the quilt her parents had given her as a high school graduation gift, to keep her warm at college. When Alex had insisted they spend Friday night at Claire's place so Sarah would be less likely to interrupt any drowsy lovemaking they might be able to achieve, Claire had initially balked at the slightly longer commute, but now she had to admit that it was *nice* to wake up and see naked Alex Williams in her bed.

Like she belonged there.

Alex opened her eyes and returned Claire's grin. In a scratchy voice, she rasped, "Hey. Good morning."

"Good morning." Claire lifted the comforter so she could slide her naked body against Alex's. Their limbs entwined naturally as they settled into the most comfortable cuddling position Claire had ever achieved. "Oh, that feels *good.*"

Alex tightened her arms, kissing Claire's hair. "It really, *really* does."

Neither of them rushed to initiate anything more intense than the tender embrace. For a few minutes, they simply lay chest-to-chest, Claire focusing on Alex's heartbeat while wondering whether Alex was similarly fascinated by the rhythm of hers. Then Alex's hands found her shoulders and stroked gently down her back, landing on her ass with a flirtatious caress. Claire drew back to meet Alex's eyes. Without speaking, she snaked her hand between their bodies and cupped Alex's vulva provocatively. "So...what do *you* want to do today?"

Alex swallowed noticeably, nostrils flaring as Claire brushed her fingertip across her prominent clit. "Um...I was actually going to suggest, *ah*—" Her fingers tightened on Claire's ass. "A picnic. At the coast."

Surprised to have received such a nonsexual answer to her blatantly suggestive question, Claire frowned and stopped teasing Alex's clit. "That sounds fun, but..." Claire removed her hand from between Alex's thighs and backed off slightly so she could watch her face. "You don't want to have sex?"

"Oh, I *definitely* want to have sex with you today. More than once, if I'm lucky." Alex moved closer to stroke Claire's cheek with the backs of her fingers. "But I also want to prove to you what Vanessa obviously doesn't understand: my interest in you goes a *lot* deeper than sex. You're not only my lover. You're my *friend.* So, as your friend, I want to take you out for a private, fairly secluded day away from our bedrooms, where we can work on our friendship—and not just our sexual skills."

Genuinely touched, Claire still felt her lip poke out in a mildly frustrated pout. "That sounds wonderful, Alex, really, and the sentiment is so sweet, but..." When Alex didn't complete Claire's thought, as she'd sort of hoped would happen, Claire endured a rush of embarrassment. "Do you think we could have at least *one* orgasm before we leave our bedrooms behind? It's been such a long week, and I'm *so* horny—"

"Say no more." Alex let her go, then drew back the comforter and crawled down the length of Claire's body. She nudged Claire's legs apart and rested on her stomach between them, making brief eye contact before dipping down to drag her tongue along Claire's inner thigh. "I don't intend to deprive you, baby. Only to spend today cherishing *every* part of who you are." She paused to lick another wet trail that stopped as soon as she reached Claire's labia. Pulling back, Alex murmured, "Not just *this* part."

Kicking the comforter farther down the bed so she could see everything Alex was about to do, Claire propped herself up on the pillows and spread her legs wider. "Fair enough." She grabbed the back of Alex's head, guiding her down to encourage another pass of her warm tongue. "As long as *this* part doesn't get neglected in the rush to demonstrate how you're not using me for sex."

Alex smiled against her wetness. "Oh, sweetheart, rest assured, I *am* using you for sex. But not *only* sex, see? There's also your brain, your personality, your sense of humor, your compassion—"

"Yeah, yeah." More interested in pleasure than compliments, Claire pushed Alex's face deeper into her pussy. "Let's talk about it later, in the car. We've got a long, sexless drive to the coast ahead of us, after all."

Alex nodded, then took Claire into her mouth without another word.

❖

"This was a fun day, right?"

Only fifteen minutes before sunset, Claire sat between Alex's spread legs on a blanket they'd laid out on the secluded beach where they'd chosen to conclude their evening on the coast. Safe and warm within Alex's strong arms, which were wrapped around her like a protective blanket, she answered without even thinking. "It was an *amazing* day."

They'd spent the drive singing along to a playlist Alex had made of all their favorite songs, but also chatting about anything and everything that came to mind. Over the course of the car ride, grabbing a picnic lunch from Alex's favorite seafood restaurant, then a tour of the small seaside town's cutesy shops, Claire had learned more about who Alex was as a person than she'd ever previously known. Alex shared childhood memories, anecdotes about how she'd built her career, her hopes and fears for the future, her general life philosophies, and even new details about her relationship with Sarah—which they'd blessedly patched up after last weekend's argument, though according to Alex, things still seemed a bit strained. By the time they ended up camped out on the beach waiting for the sun to go down, Claire was at least twice as in love with Alex as she'd been upon waking up that morning and, as Alex had so obviously intended, even more confident that the feeling was mutual.

"So you're not disappointed we didn't spend the day in bed?" Alex's body tensed subtly around Claire, as though bracing for her response.

Turning slightly, Claire glanced up at Alex with a playful smirk. "I probably wouldn't have lasted more than a few hours, anyway. After the crazy week I had." She stretched to peck Alex on the lips. "Besides, our Saturday isn't over yet."

"Good point."

Belying her light tone, Alex's answering smile was tinged with an emotion Claire couldn't identify, but which unsettled her nonetheless. She frowned and eased back to study Alex's face. "What's wrong? Did I say something to upset you?"

Alex shook her head unconvincingly. "Not at all."

"I did." Claire touched Alex's cheek, stroking the soft skin with her thumb. "Tell me."

Alex shrugged. Her gaze flitted away and she took a deep breath. "You…want me for more than just sex, too, right?" Her eyes shimmered as they reflected the orange light from the sinking sun. "I know it's stupid to need to hear that, but…" She swallowed, letting go of Claire with one arm so she could dab at the moisture on her face. "I guess I do." Sniffing, she looked directly into Claire's eyes. "Need to hear that."

"Alex, of *course*." Claire shifted farther to the side, facing Alex so she could loop her arms around her shoulders. "I love having sex with you, yes, but I never would've agreed to be your girlfriend, or told you I *loved* you, for goodness' sake, if this was only about getting laid."

Alex pressed her lips to Claire's forehead. "I knew that," she mumbled, almost to herself. "I'm sorry, I did."

"Don't apologize." Claire cradled Alex's face in both hands, drawing back so she could hold her gaze. "I'm the one who should be sorry for ever giving you any reason to doubt my intentions."

Alex shook her head, guiltily. "It's not your fault. This is all me… and my stupid insecurities."

"You have *nothing* to feel insecure about." Getting up onto her knees, Claire loomed over Alex before bending for a languorous kiss. When they broke apart, Claire whispered, "You're the *whole* package, Williams. Every last bit of what I need to be happy."

"Even though I have no clue what the fuck you're even *doing* every time I look at your laptop screen?"

Alex had made enough comments since they'd started dating to make it obvious that she suffered from a real lack of self-confidence about her intellectual abilities, but Claire hadn't understood how deep the anxiety actually ran until that exact second. "Alex," she said softly, "no one I've ever dated has known how to code. Believe it or not, not only is that *not* one of my prerequisites, but I honestly prefer being with a woman who will complement my personality, rather than emulate it."

Visibly regaining some of her swagger, Alex put her hands on Claire's hips to urge her to sit down straddling her lap. "There was this girl in high school, she graduated valedictorian our senior year. Lynn. She was *so* pretty. I had the biggest crush…but she made me feel like a fuckin' idiot once I actually worked up the courage to try to strike up a friendship. Thinking I needed an excuse for us to hang out after school,

I asked if she could help me with my physics homework, which was by far my worst subject. She ended up laughing her ass off at my various attempts to find solutions for the problems, telling me she couldn't *believe* I wasn't able to figure them out. Later it got back to me that she told all her friends what an absolute moron I was and that she couldn't even imagine actually being *friends* with someone as dumb as me."

Once again taking Alex's face between her hands, Claire pinned her with a serious expression. "Baby, I hate to say it, but you *really* did have terrible taste in women."

"Until you broke me of that bad habit, Claire-Claire, with your drunken seduction."

Claire giggled, then moved in for a slow kiss. "Alex, you're *not* dumb. So you're not much for physics—well, to be fair, most people aren't. Same thing when it comes to programming, or engineering, or any of the other things I have some expertise in that you find impressive. Not knowing that stuff doesn't make you a moron. It makes you a different person, with different interests, knowledge, and skills. Like the ability to mingle in a crowd of strangers in a way that causes absolutely everyone to fall in love with you."

Scoffing, Alex gestured at the sky behind Claire's head, then maneuvered her so their bodies faced the same direction. "Sunset is starting. I don't want you to miss it."

Claire shivered as the cooling sea breeze whipped against the front of her body, pressing her back tighter against Alex's chest. "It's getting chilly."

On cue, Alex produced the second blanket she'd brought along for the occasion. Shaking it open, she cloaked both of them in the warm material, then held the front closed over Claire's chest so she was encased from her knees to her neck. "Better?"

"The *best*." Claire released a satisfied sigh and relaxed into Alex's warmth as she studied the pink and purple clouds that framed the sun's dramatic descent. Without thinking, she murmured, "I'm really happy."

Alex enfolded her in an even more heartfelt hug. "Yeah?"

Inspired by a sky that grew more impossibly gorgeous by the second, Claire pushed aside her natural reticence about sounding overeager. "To be perfectly honest, Alex, this has got to be one of the happiest moments of my life."

"Mine, too." Alex kissed Claire's cheek, then rocked their bodies slightly in a way that helped to ward off the growing chill. "Let's make a deal. Every time life gets a little crazy, we'll remember this sunset. We'll remember how perfect everything can feel when we're together."

Claire rested her head on Alex's broad shoulder, agape at the natural beauty unfolding in front of them. "Deal."

"Excellent." Alex pressed a more deliberate kiss against Claire's cheek, then transferred both ends of the blanket into her left hand, dropping the right to rest between Claire's slightly parted thighs. "May I touch you?"

"Yes." Claire swept her gaze along the beach to confirm that they were still alone. Satisfied that no one was watching, she opened her legs, holding her breath as Alex popped open the button on her jeans. In deference to the anxiety Alex had *just* confessed, she added, "But only if you want to. I'm perfectly content with what we're already doing."

"Oh, I want to." Alex slipped her hand down the front of Claire's jeans, into her panties. She rubbed Claire's mound sensuously, teasing out her slick arousal. "Don't ever think I don't want to be inside you, because I do...pretty much all the time." Adjusting the angle of her wrist, Alex pressed the first inch of one of her long fingers into Claire's already slippery vagina. "You're so sexy, sweetheart. The way your hips move when I finger you, the sweet little noises you make."

Claire bucked against her hand with a muted whimper, unconsciously doing everything Alex had suggested. Chuckling at how easily Alex was able to exert her will, Claire struggled to keep her eyes open, loath to miss even a single second of the glorious explosion of color over the flat, blue horizon. "That feels so *good*, Alex. Please don't stop."

Humming with satisfaction, Alex whispered into her ear. "Not until you come all over my hand."

Claire bit back a loud moan and grabbed Alex's strong thighs for support as her internal muscles fluttered around the roving digit. "That may not take very long."

"Can't say I'm sorry to hear that." Seconds later, Alex removed the finger from her vagina, then withdrew from her panties altogether. Before Claire could voice her objection, Alex lifted her hand to her mouth and sucked on the wet digit with a lewd slurp. Then, waiting until Claire turned to watch, she used her tongue to very deliberately wet the finger next to it as well. "Lower your jeans to your knees. Unless it'll make you feel too exposed."

As they were still the only ones on the beach, not to mention hidden by the huge blanket, all Claire felt was grateful to have an opportunity to grant Alex easier access. "No. I can do that." Shimmying her waistband down until it bunched around her knees, Claire spread her thighs as wide as she could and waited for the return of Alex's fingers.

Alex didn't disappoint, running her saliva-coated digits across Claire's clit, then down to her opening, where she inserted just one until it was buried to the second knuckle. Searing pleasure rippled through Claire's belly, but soon Alex pulled out of her again. Placing her hand in front of Claire's face, Alex commanded, "Open your mouth."

Claire did.

Alex pushed both fingers across her tongue, forcing her to taste the somewhat pleasant flavor of her own juices. "Suck on my fingers, Claire-Claire. Get them nice and wet so they'll slide into your cunt more easily."

Moaning, Claire laved Alex with her obedient tongue. *How does she always manage to make everything we do feel so damn* sexy?

"That's right, baby. Ready for me to check if they'll fit inside you now?"

Claire quivered at the effortlessly provocative dialogue. The instant she nodded her consent, the digits slipped out of her mouth. She gasped when Alex touched her again, gently at first, before she worked both fingers into Claire's snug opening until they rested all the way inside.

Alex groaned, her fiery breath washing over Claire's skin. She pulled her fingers out nearly all the way before driving back in. "Well, look at that. Like a hot, tight glove."

Breathing harder on every stroke, Claire tried to move her right hand from Alex's thigh to rub her own clit, but Alex stopped fucking her so she could bat away the attempt at self-pleasure. "Please, Alex," Claire begged quietly. "I want to come for you."

"All right, but let me try first." Alex gestured to where she held the blanket closed around them with her left hand. "Will you make sure we stay covered?"

Claire grabbed the blanket from Alex, rearranging the thick fabric to better shield their lower bodies. "No problem."

"I owe you one." Alex scraped her teeth over the side of Claire's neck before lowering her left hand to stroke her labia. "Repayment incoming."

Claire's amused chuckle died in her throat when Alex's left index finger swiftly but carefully penetrated her vagina, followed by a second digit that stretched her open even wider. Alex moved her right hand to cradle Claire's pubic mound, curling her fingertips inward to circle the swollen clit. "*Yes*," Claire said in a bare whisper, afraid to let the sound of her gratification carry on the wind. "Just like that."

Alex's talented hands worked in tandem to bring Claire to the edge of release right as the dying sun disappeared below the horizon. Dragging her teeth across Claire's neck, Alex murmured, "Give it to me, Claire-Claire. Give me that sweet, yummy cum all over my fingers." She hastened the speed and depth of her thrusts, then pressed more firmly on Claire's throbbing clit. "Let me *feel* how much you love having me touch your pussy like this." Accurately gauging their arrival at the finish line, Alex nipped Claire's earlobe sharply, then, mere seconds after achieving penultimate synchrony with her hands, growled, "Just like I taught you, remember?"

Thighs quaking, Claire finally closed her eyes and let go with a silent, open-mouthed roar. She shook under Alex's caresses for what felt like forever, until the sky had grown dark and her muscles ached from the effort. Once she was certain she couldn't possibly withstand any more, Claire pushed Alex's hands away with a regretful moan. "Any more and I'll pass out."

Alex laughed, taking the ends of the blanket so Claire could pull up her jeans. "No, thanks. I have zero desire to get caught carrying an unconscious woman away from the beach, in the dark, with my hands smelling of her pussy."

Claire buttoned her pants before resuming her reclined position against Alex's chest. "Yeah. That's reasonable." She put her hand on Alex's thigh, high enough to cause a hitch in the rise and fall of the breasts pressed against her back. "On a similar note, would you mind if we went back to the car—if not one of our bedrooms—before I return the favor? It'll be much easier to suck you off without a blanket over my head and the fear of being caught to distract me."

"Sold." Alex stood up, pulling Claire along with her. "I'm willing to wait for a real bed—and privacy. I want to keep the lights on so I can *thoroughly* enjoy the show."

Claire flushed with anticipation. "How fast can you drive... *safely?*"

Alex answered with a grin that lit up the dark.

## CHAPTER EIGHTEEN

From the very first moment Sarah walked into their favorite restaurant and spotted her already seated at a table in the corner, Claire knew that lunch together would be rougher than she'd anticipated. Despite having had a truly heartfelt conversation after they'd finalized their TED talk, one that Claire had honestly expected to patch things up, mostly, Sarah wore a grim mask of wariness, distance, and sorrow that both tore at Claire's heart and raised her defensive hackles. Sure, she'd fucked up with Sarah more than once. Yet for the past week and a half, she'd not only shown up in her professional life every bit as much as she always had before Alex, but she'd also attempted to extend multiple olive branches to her best friend, every one of which had been rebuffed with vague excuses. Until, of course, Sarah had finally accepted this invitation to lunch.

Clearing her throat nervously, Claire stood when Sarah reached the table. "Hey, stranger."

"Hey." Sarah pulled out her chair and dropped into it with a weary sigh. "I can't stay very long. Meryl Weaver scheduled a last-minute meeting to review her designs for the new logo and branding. She insisted on two o'clock, because she has to pick up her kid from school by three fifteen." Sarah glanced over the menu they'd both memorized years ago, then dropped it to scan the room for their waitress. "Has anyone been over to take a drink order yet?"

"I got you water with lemon." Not wanting to start out contentiously, Claire nonetheless couldn't suppress her concern about Sarah's casual bombshell. "Also, what do you mean you're meeting with Meryl about the branding? Did you send me an invite I missed somehow?"

Lighting up at the sight of their waiter, Sarah gestured the attractive young man over to their table. "Hi! We're ready to order, I think." She spared Claire a momentary glance to confirm. "Yes. We're ready."

Once they'd ordered and the waiter walked away, Claire repeated her question.

"Well, no. I figured you were too busy." Sarah stared across the table at her blankly, as though excluding her from a *branding* meeting was a perfectly reasonable decision when it was *Claire's* sketchbook that had yielded their original corporate logo. After they'd mutually agreed on the need for a new one, Claire had simply assumed they would make the decision about an updated design together.

With a careless shrug, Sarah picked up the glass of water as soon as their returning waiter set it down, then took a long sip before placing it on the table in front of her. "I didn't want to give you something else to forget."

"That's not fair." Claire's throat burned at the injustice of the statement after she'd been trying so hard to change her ways. "I told you it wouldn't happen again—and it hasn't."

"So far." Sarah sat back and folded her arms over her chest. "Look, you can come to the meeting if you want to. It's not like I was planning to pick a final design without your input, anyway."

Biting back a sharp retort, Claire reined in her hurt feelings to protect their apparently vulnerable bond. "My calendar is clear this afternoon, so I'd love to join you."

"Great." Sarah shot her a tight smile. "I appreciate the support." Her tone made it clear that she intended the comment as a subtle jab.

Claire took a sip of water and counted to five. *I suppose I deserve this, right? Still?* She set down her glass a little too hard. "I really have been trying, Sarah. You see that, right?"

Sarah chuffed under her breath before granting her a begrudging nod. "*Trying* to give a shit about me and the company. Yeah. How's that working out for you?"

"Hey," Claire shot back. "Lay off. I've already apologized about being so distracted lately, more than once. It's not like you didn't pretty much disappear from my life for at least a month when you and Marcus first got together. Don't be a hypocrite by implying that being a little overly consumed by a new relationship makes me a shitty person or something. It doesn't. It makes me *human*."

"Yeah, well, when I met Marcus we'd just graduated from college. You were working long, terrible hours at that stupid start-up. I was doing social media for the club, part-time, and working at the freakin' public library. Things were a little different then. We had fewer responsibilities, to say the least."

"Look, despite a couple close calls, I've been *meeting* my responsibilities. I had that crashed server back up with time to spare before the big demo. I delivered the data for the TED talk to you only one hour after our meeting was scheduled—on a *Sunday*, don't forget, and after everything that happened Friday at Alex's exhibition. It slipped my mind, yes, but ultimately, my distraction cost us an hour. Tops." Claire sat up straighter, tired of being punished for mistakes for which she'd already atoned. "For the past week, I've been on top of everything that's been thrown at me. I've worked overtime. Alex and I barely saw each other. I tried to invite you to lunch three times, and each time you turned me down. I asked you to go for a drink after work. You had an appointment. I invited you to my place to watch one of our favorite movies. You didn't have time."

"Oh, so when *you* call I'm supposed to come running?" Sarah chortled without humor. "I get it."

Claire took a deep breath and tried to calm down. "What's *wrong* with you? Why are you acting like this? I thought after we talked last week..." She wished she understood what was behind Sarah's fresh anger. "I thought you were ready to forgive me."

Sarah exhaled harshly. "Look, Claire...I want to be cool about your relationship with Alex. I really do. But so far, honestly, it's been a real bummer. It feels like you've...abandoned me. Not just me, but the company. Like you've lost the passion we both shared for everything we were building together." She shook her head and scanned the room again, ostensibly for their waiter. "It just bums me out, that's all. All of it."

"For fuck's sake. I've been seeing Alex for a little over a *month*. You've barely given me any time to emerge from the haze before deciding to label me apathetic about my life's work!" Claire realized she'd raised her voice when the people at the table next to them glanced over before swiftly pretending not to be watching. Lowering her volume, she said, "I'm *really* sorry you've had to shoulder a *tiny* bit more of the burden for the past four weeks, but let me remind you, Alex and I hooked up the night before *you* returned from a two-week vacation in Europe with Marcus. Who do you think did absolutely *everything* at work while you were gone? Happily, I might add, so that you would have an opportunity to enjoy your time away from the daily grind with someone you love. Someone who makes you feel *good*."

Sarah rolled her eyes so hard that Claire half expected them to fall out of her head onto the table. "Give me a fuckin' break. That's not the same thing, and you know it."

"Yeah, because I've actually *been* at work for the past month."

"Physically, maybe."

Claire took a breath to respond but swallowed her comeback when their waiter approached the table with their food. She waited until he'd left before whispering, in a harsh tone, "You're being *so unfair.*"

Snorting, Sarah took a defiant bite of her sandwich. "Whatever."

"Sarah, since the moment we started the company, I've put *everything* into our business. You have no idea how many all-nighters I pulled writing the first version of the app. How many hours I logged setting up and maintaining the network during the constant upgrades and expansions we experienced during the first two years. How many times I slept in my office because there was no point going home when I'd just have to turn around and go back a few hours later." Claire pushed her plate aside as her growing resentment burned away her appetite. "I *guarantee* I've contributed more to our company than you have, and I'm not just talking about time. Also, I've never taken a two-week vacation. *Ever.* But now that I actually *have* someone in my life, you've had to pick up a little slack, and you can't handle it." Heart hammering, Claire's entire being shook at the fury in her best friend's expression—the same fury that coursed through her own veins. "I get it. I see how it is."

"Fuck you, *Claire-Claire.*" Sarah shoved back her chair and stood up. Fumbling for money from her purse, she tossed a few bills onto the table, then one last insult. "Seriously, go fuck yourself. Or my sister, since she's all you give two shits about anymore."

"Maybe I *will.*" Claire glowered at Sarah's retreating form, wishing she'd managed a better parting shot. Noticing the attention from every one of the tables surrounding them, she dug through her own purse for enough cash to cover the cost of her uneaten meal and dropped it on top of Sarah's contribution. Then she left, regretting that she'd invited Sarah to lunch.

## CHAPTER NINETEEN

Once she left the restaurant, Claire wasn't certain where to go next. Not to the meeting with Meryl Weaver, certainly. Though she hated to miss such an important discussion, she didn't think it was a good idea for her and Sarah to be in the same room together until they cooled down, especially with a third party present. Besides, Sarah had never actually told her where the meeting was. She could simply return to her office, of course, but that wasn't what she *wanted* to do. Devastated by her failed attempt to repair their friendship, Claire wanted someone to tell her that everything would be all right. She wanted comfort.

She wanted *Alex.*

Yet she hesitated. Sarah surely wouldn't be home for at least another couple hours, but Claire was afraid she'd somehow find out that her first instinct had been to run to Alex after their fight. Would doing so prove Sarah's point? Did she even care anymore?

Eyes burning with unshed tears, Claire got into her car and started to drive. When she realized what direction she was heading, she initiated a call to Alex with a voice command to her mounted cell phone. She would ask Alex to come to her apartment to reduce the risk of running into Sarah later, because no way could she handle another ugly confrontation today. Unfortunately, Alex's phone went straight to voice mail, indicating that it was either dead or powered off. Cursing, Claire debated turning around and going back to work for about a mile, before she decided, *Fuck Sarah. I'm going to Alex's.* She wouldn't need this dose of compassion so badly if not for her so-called "best friend," anyway.

Claire tried and failed to call Alex two more times before giving up and finishing the drive to Sarah's house. She rolled down the long driveway slowly, on alert for any sign of either Sarah's or Marcus's vehicle, but neither one of them appeared to be there. There was, however, a strange car parked next to Alex's that instantly set Claire on edge. As far as she knew, Alex hadn't planned to host anyone today. In fact, she'd announced just that morning that she hoped to spend the entire afternoon brainstorming ideas for her next independent project.

Claire frowned as she pulled into the empty spot on the other side of Alex's car. *Shit...does this mean I'm interrupting her?* She glanced over at the unfamiliar vehicle, trying to ignore the unease that stirred her gut. *And what, exactly, will I be interrupting?*

Alex would never cheat on her. She *knew* that. Whoever was here, Alex would almost certainly tell her about later. Chances were an old acquaintance had heard she was back in town and decided to drop by unexpectedly. No doubt in a completely platonic fashion. Claire nearly backed out of the driveway to test that theory, when suddenly the door of the guest house burst open and Vanessa emerged, donning a light coat that flapped open in the breeze to reveal the lacy black bustier she wore beneath. Claire's gut lurched at the triumphant smirk Vanessa directed her way when she spotted her sitting in the parked car.

Vanessa turned and said something Claire couldn't discern, prompting Alex to spill out the front door with a stricken, wide-eyed expression. "Claire!" she yelled loudly enough to be heard through the windshield. "This isn't what..." She shook her head, then vaulted over the porch railing to sprint toward Claire's car.

Laughing, Vanessa sauntered down the porch stairs with a sultry little swagger. *Oops,* she mouthed to Claire, right before Alex knocked on the passenger side window of her car to break her visual hold.

"Claire." Alex tried to open the car door, then bent to meet Claire's eyes through the glass when she found it locked. "Baby, she got here five minutes ago. I didn't invite her. She just showed up, hoping to..." Her gaze slid over Claire's shoulder, and her jaw tightened. "Well, you know what she was hoping to do. What you just saw was me kicking her out."

A knock on the driver's side window pulled Claire's attention to Vanessa's exposed cleavage, then her smug grin. "Thanks for letting me borrow your lover for a few. Such an efficient pussy-licker."

"*Goddamn it,* Vanessa!" Alex lunged around the front of the car, causing Vanessa to dance away from the vehicle with a startled giggle. "Stop fucking *lying!*"

Afraid to see Alex so livid, Claire opened the driver's side door and got out of the car to intercept Alex before she could pursue Vanessa any farther. "Alex, let's go inside."

Alex's powerful body trembled under her hands. "Just leave me alone," she shouted at her ex. "You're the one who dumped me!"

The humor disappeared from Vanessa's face. In an instant, she became a doe-eyed, vulnerable creature who very nearly evoked a measure of sympathy from Claire—and would've, if Claire didn't hate her so much. "You're right, Al, and it was the biggest mistake I ever made. You were the best thing to ever happen to me. I know there was a time when you felt the same."

Claire glanced up to see Alex's reaction, an ambiguous mixture of emotion that Claire felt too nervous to parse. Stiffening, Alex met Claire's eyes, then turned them both to walk back to the house. "Before you showed me who you really were, maybe. But not anymore. You made your choice, Vanessa. Live with it."

As they climbed the porch steps, Vanessa called out, "Don't forget to brush your teeth before you kiss the new slut hello."

Claire grabbed Alex's hand, dragging her into the guesthouse before slamming the door. Once they were inside, Alex let out an exasperated growl, then dropped Claire's hand and stomped across the room where she collapsed onto the couch. "I swear I had no idea Vanessa even knew where I lived, let alone that she'd actually have the balls to ambush me like this."

"I don't understand." Claire's voice sounded timid to her own ears as she crossed the room to sit on the arm of the sofa, slightly out of reach. "From what you told me, she pretty much accused you of domestic violence, if not outright sexual assault. So why does she want you back?"

"Honestly, Claire, I can't begin to explain the way she thinks. Like I said, we really did have a good thing going in the beginning. Before she shoved me away so hard it nearly broke me." Alex shrugged, staring up at Claire with troubled eyes. "Why does she want me back? I have no idea. The challenge involved? Because another woman has me? Because she's bored? Just because?"

Drained from her fight with Sarah and beyond disappointed

that Alex had only supplied more drama instead of the refuge she'd sought, Claire fought to keep her voice steady as she asked the obvious question. "Okay, but why does she think she even has a shot?"

Alex frowned, then reached out to touch Claire's thigh, gesturing for her to sit on the cushion beside her. "Because she lacks empathy and therefore the capacity to understand that what she did to me was beyond forgiveness. She also lacks the maturity to accept the fact that I'm in love with someone else." Drawing Claire tentatively closer with an arm around her back, Alex added, "*And* because she's used to getting exactly what she wants."

Claire snorted in derision. "I suppose when you look like that, the world *does* tend to fall at your feet."

"More often than not, yes, but I promise you, she won't get *me*." Alex pressed a kiss into Claire's hair before moving to brush their mouths together. Succumbing to her shameful fear that she might catch the scent of betrayal on Alex's breath, Claire instinctively flinched away. Alex stared at her with a crestfallen expression. "Claire, I didn't go down on her. You *know* I didn't." Her jaw tensed, hurt flashing in her eyes. "*Please* tell me you know that."

Claire nodded slowly, trying not to think about how very flawless Vanessa's face and body were, but rather about how beautiful Alex always made *her* feel, how desired, how needed. How *loved.* "I do, I'm sorry, it's just…" Overwhelmed by her shitty day, Claire buried her face in her hands with a muffled sob. "This has been the worst afternoon."

Alex's arm wound around her back again, holding on tight. "Did something else happen?"

"Sarah." Sniffling, Claire dropped her hands and turned to press her face into Alex's shoulder. "That's why I came to see you. I tried to call and warn you I was on my way—"

"But my phone died this morning, and I forgot to turn it back on after I plugged it in." Alex cursed under her breath. "If I'd known you were coming, I never would've even let Vanessa inside."

"Why did you?" Claire asked in a tentative whisper. That part she honestly didn't understand.

"I shouldn't have." Alex pressed her cheek against Claire's and rocked them gently. Back and forth. Back and forth. "It was a mistake. She said she wanted to apologize, which is *not* something she's really ever been known to do. I'm not sure whether I actually believed her, but…I was curious." She sighed, going rigid without releasing Claire from her embrace. "I don't know what I hoped to hear. That she knew what happened that night—with the rough sex—wasn't my fault, I guess. I wanted…"

"Absolution." Claire's body relaxed slightly within Alex's arms. She understood that. Honestly, nothing about Alex's explanation rang false. She brought her hands up to rest on Alex's shoulders, melting into the embrace. "I get it. Did she give you that, at least?"

"Actually, yeah. She did. She acknowledged that she consented to everything we did that night, that it was *her* idea, *her* plan, and her decision to ignore my repeated expressions of concern for her well-being because she was too full of pride to admit that she couldn't handle what she'd asked for." Alex's muscles gradually loosened beneath Claire's tender caresses. "She told me she was sorry she lashed out afterward. She was embarrassed, and in pain, and just…reacted. Apparently she was *so* embarrassed that she felt she had no choice but to break up with me a month later." She shook her head. "I know it sounds crazy, Claire, but it was like a *real*, sincere apology. It actually made me feel a lot better. She must have realized that, too, because the next thing I know, she lets her coat fall to the floor and tries to pin me against the wall wearing only…well, I'm sure you saw."

Claire wrinkled her nose. "She's bold. I'll give her that."

"That's a much kinder adjective than I would've chosen. She destroyed almost any goodwill she created with the apology." Sighing, Alex drew away until she could see Claire's face. "Now tell me what happened with Sarah. Did you two argue at lunch?"

"Yes. *Bad*." Claire's chin wobbled at the memory of the cold disassociation in Sarah's expression as she'd stared at her across the table. "Apparently she scheduled a meeting with the graphic designer for this afternoon to review the choices for our new logo and branding without inviting me. When I asked why, she said she assumed I was too busy and used the fact that I'd forgotten our TED talk meeting to justify excluding me from a critical discussion. I pointed out that I'd been working my ass off for the past week trying to catch up, then said it was unfair for her to keep punishing me for falling in love and getting distracted when she did the same damn thing with Marcus."

"She didn't agree?"

"Apparently things were different then. Now that we run a company together, work takes precedence over everything else, especially my romantic life, but not her two-week European vacations, obviously." Pulse racing, Claire inhaled evenly to try to calm down. "Alex, you have *no idea* how hard I've worked to make us successful. To be accused of 'not giving a shit' because I got sidetracked for a few weeks by the very normal, very *human* experience of falling in love… well, *it pisses me off.*"

"I'm sorry, baby. I'm sure she just misses you."

"But I'm right *here!*" Claire threw her hands up into the air, causing Alex's arms to fall down around her hips. "Do you know how many times I've tried to get together with Sarah this week? She's pissed at me for being absent so she decides to disappear on me to get me back. *Real* mature, right?"

Alex blinked sadly. "I'm sorry for picking that fight with her last weekend. I know that didn't help your cause."

"Well, she *was* being a jerk. Even if her frustration was justified."

"I haven't seen her much this week. I thought we'd patched things up a few days ago, but who knows?" Alex blew out an exhausted breath, then released Claire so she could slump over and rest her head against the couch. "Why do other people insist on making something that's so damn good feel so freakin' complicated?"

"Because they suck," Claire concluded, mirroring Alex's pose. They sat that way in silence for a minute, until Claire lost her battle with insecurity and asked a question she wasn't positive she wanted answered. "If we weren't together and Vanessa had come here with that same apology, and even the same attempt at seduction…would you have taken her back?"

Alex hesitated a moment too long before answering. "No." She paused, searching Claire's face, then amended her statement. "I really hope not."

Though she told herself she shouldn't, Claire felt unsettled by Alex's apparent admission that Vanessa still held some measure of power over her. If any part of Alex wanted Vanessa back, Claire couldn't help but feel outmatched. If Vanessa persisted, if she said all the right things and maybe even refrained from insulting Claire whenever she saw her, would Alex really hold out forever? Life with

Vanessa was quite obviously more glamorous than life with Claire, and more exciting, not to mention less complicated when it came to the health of Alex's sisterly bond and Claire's most cherished friendship.

Reading her mind, Alex clarified her stance. "I don't want to be with Vanessa, baby. *Ever* again. I want you. *Only* you."

"Even though our being together makes Sarah miserable?"

"She'll get over it." Alex took Claire's hand, squeezing gently. "We'll help her get over it."

"I sure hope so." Claire closed her eyes and exhaled at length in an attempt to release the stress of the day. "I hate fighting with her. I *love* her." She blinked, then stared into Alex's shining eyes. "I don't want to lose my best friend."

"You're not going to lose her, Claire. I promise." She lifted Claire's hand, pressing the knuckles against her face. "She loves you, too. So do I."

"I know." Claire's voice broke, betraying her uncertainty. "And I also knew this wouldn't be easy, necessarily, but I don't think I realized it would be so hard, either."

"You mean dating me?"

"I mean being in love with my best friend's sister." Wincing at the pleasure tinged with pain that passed across Alex's face at her words, Claire moved closer so she could touch her forehead to Alex's. "You have to admit that we're dealing with a lot of drama for a brand-new couple."

"But none of our own making. Or not much, at least."

Claire savored the warmth of Alex's skin against hers, leaning in harder to maximize the contact. "This is one of those moments when we're supposed to remember that sunset, isn't it?"

Alex chuckled softly and gathered her into a fierce, full-body embrace. "That's exactly right, baby. Hang onto that sunset with me."

"When everything was perfect," Claire said. *And easy.* After today, it felt like nothing about their relationship would ever feel easy again. "I wish we were on that beach right now."

"Me, too." Alex kissed her earlobe. "You know, we *could* go get in the car. We have enough time to drive there before the sun sets."

Claire considered the offer only briefly before shaking her head. "As much as I'd love to, I can't. I need to make sure I'm near a computer in case anything comes up at work. I probably shouldn't have even left the office at all, but I had to get away."

"I'm glad you did." Alex cringed. "Well, it would have been better to tell you about Vanessa's visit rather than have you witness it firsthand. But other than that…I'm *really* glad you did."

"On that note, I should leave soon. The last thing I want is to run into Sarah again today. Especially here."

Alex's face fell. "Oh…yeah. I get that."

"So…do you want to go to my place? We could sit next to each other in bed while we work on our laptops." Claire drew back to pin Alex with a preemptively admonishing smirk. "And I mean *actually* work, until at least five o'clock?" Taking Alex home to her bed wasn't likely to fix all her problems, but at least it would make her feel better in the short term.

Alex replied with a sober nod. "I'd like that more than anything, Ms. Barker."

"Then come on, Williams." Claire hooked her index finger in Alex's shirt collar before she stood, bringing her along. "We'll let the rest of the world fuck off for the day."

"Yes, *ma'am*."

## CHAPTER TWENTY

The temperature remained chilly between Claire and Sarah in the week leading up to the TED conference. They spoke to each other civilly at the office, but hardly at all outside of work. Despite her history of being absolutely miserable on the rare occasions she fought with her best friend, Claire held fast to her decision not to reach out and apologize first. As far as she was concerned, she'd said sorry too many times already—especially when she hadn't dropped even a single ball since the forgotten meeting that started this whole mess. No, Sarah owed *her* an apology this time, for ignoring Claire's sincere efforts to make things right *and* for being a big, fat hypocrite when it came to their romantic lives.

Unfortunately, Sarah had yet to offer even the slightest indication that she was ready to repair their friendship anytime soon. Although Claire knew that Sarah had to feel equally as distraught about the schism between them as she did, it appeared that she wasn't upset enough to ask for forgiveness. Still, when Claire's phone chirped its distinctive alert to signal an incoming text from Sarah the evening before their shared flight to Austin, she experienced a brief flash of hope that the ice had started to thaw. Then she read the message to discover it fully intact.

> *By the way, I called the hotel to try to change our reservation to two rooms. Unfortunately, they said no. Too many conferences and special events that weekend to accommodate us. I called around to a couple other hotels...same thing. Sorry. I'm not thrilled, either.*

Claire frowned so hard that Alex apparently noticed despite the laser focus she'd maintained for hours while editing a new series of candid photographs she'd started taking to document life on the streets of Oakland. Seated next to her on what had become her side of Claire's bed, Alex set aside her laptop and touched Claire's wrist. "What's wrong, baby? Bad news?"

Claire shook her head, then tilted the phone's display toward Alex so she could read Sarah's passive-aggressive missive. "She's acting like such a child. What, I'm so horrible she can't even share a hotel room with me?" She lowered the phone when Alex's concerned gaze returned to her face. "*She's* the one who picked that fight at lunch. Not me!"

"Oh, Claire. I'm so sorry." Alex's blue eyes welled with tears, the deep show of emotion catching Claire completely by surprise. "This is all my fault. That you two are fighting at all, I mean. It's not like I didn't know how Sarah would react to suddenly having to share her best friend with me. Even before the night you and I first hooked up, honestly, I'd thought about how messy it would be to actually try to date you. But my inhibitions were lowered, and now it *is* messy, and I'm sorry."

Nothing about Alex's speech made Claire feel any better. "So you're saying we're only together because you got drunk and fucked me? And, what, now you feel obligated to be in a relationship with me despite your many reservations?"

Alex blinked rapidly, like she was trying desperately to catch up. "What? No. Wait...*no,* Claire-Claire. I'm just saying...I'm sorry that my being in love with you has caused so many problems with Sarah. I never wanted that to happen because I know she's pretty much the most important person in your life. The thought that I've come between the wonder twins breaks my heart—that's all. Not enough to break yours, mind you, or my own, by bowing out of your life gracefully. If that's where you thought this was going."

Claire exhaled, forcing her shoulders to relax. "I'm sorry. I'm on edge."

"I know, sweetheart. It's all right."

"Not really." Smiling weakly, Claire picked up the phone and stared at Sarah's message while she tried to decide how to reply. "I love you, Alex. I'm just so *angry* at Sarah right now. And...sad."

"I'm sure she's sad, too." Alex rested her hand on Claire's thigh. "Not that she's been confiding in me lately, or really talking to me at all, but I know her. I know how much you mean to her. If she didn't love you so much, she wouldn't be nearly this pissed off, right?"

"True." Claire snorted. "Not sure how much better that actually makes me feel." She brought her thumb up to the phone's keyboard, then paused. "I just...want you both. I want everyone to be happy. Is that really too much to ask?"

"Not at all." Alex gave her thigh a light squeeze. "At least it shouldn't be."

"I know I fucked up. I know I hurt her feelings...but I can't fix anything if she refuses to give me a second chance."

"You're right."

Claire sighed deeply. "I hate this." Then she started to type.

*Sarah, I have no problem sharing a room. We are still friends, after all. Even if you didn't make me feel that way last week at lunch.*

Claire stared at the phone after she sent the message, waiting for the apology she'd all but rolled the proverbial red carpet out to accept. An ellipsis at the bottom of the thread signaled that Sarah was composing her reply. Nervously, Claire let her gaze dart over to Alex's laptop right in time to see her click on a private message on her social-media feed, filling the screen with the image of a young, nude blonde with a lithesome body and a come-hither smile. She held a handwritten sign that said, "Shoot me, Alex! (Or maybe just fuck me?)"

"*Hello,*" Alex remarked with a surprised chuckle. She glanced over at Claire and, finding her already looking, turned the screen to face her more directly. "I get unsolicited nudes on occasion from fans and aspiring models. Sometimes they're looking for a way into the industry, sometimes just sex. I never reply to them."

Claire couldn't help but stare at the sweet young thing who'd offered her body up to Alex's work and pleasure. The girl was flawless, perky, without a stretch mark, mole, or blemish visible anywhere on her magnificently proportioned body. *This* was what Alex got offered on the regular? Not for the first time since they'd started dating, Claire couldn't help but feel almost pathetically plain, and imperfect, and downright baffled about why Alex would ever choose her as a partner in monogamy. All she could say was, "Wow."

Alex deleted the picture, along with the message, as Claire watched. "If she's hoping to become a model, she needs to learn how to approach potential photographers in a more professional way."

"I guess so." Unsettled by the newfound knowledge that Alex received a steady stream of sexual offers from hot, naked women direct to her inbox, Claire turned her eyes back to her phone, where she found Sarah's reply waiting.

*Funny, I thought you were the one who stopped treating me like your friend first. We may have to share a room this weekend, but I won't pretend to like it.*

Fury reignited, Claire angrily typed out her last word on the matter.

*Let me know when you're ready to grow up and accept my repeated apologies. The only one fucking up our friendship right now is you.*

She put down her phone, determined not to look again even if Sarah replied. This was her last full night with Alex before she'd be gone for almost three days—longer than they'd ever spent apart since beginning their relationship—and her mood had almost completely tanked. Between Sarah's stubborn anger, Alex's regret about the role she'd played in the disruption of her sister's best friendship, and the recent reminders of Alex's easy access to arguably better options, Claire found it difficult to summon up the seductive mood she'd hoped to achieve at the end of the workday.

Alex closed her laptop and put it on the nightstand next to her side of the bed. Then she wrapped her arm around Claire and pulled her into the shelter of her strong embrace. "You know I'm immune to the sight of random, naked women, right? I've seen so many unclothed bodies. Hundreds. All shapes, sizes, colors. Nearly all of them absolutely gorgeous, I'll admit, but…" She pressed her nose into Claire's hair, kissing the top of her head. "Yours is the only one I love."

Grouchy about her impending departure at a time when Sarah hated her guts and model-beautiful threats to her status as Alex's one and only seemed to lurk around every corner, Claire accepted the reassurance with a halfhearted shrug. Then she sighed, contritely. "You're sweet. However, it's fairly obvious that I'm damn lucky you decided that what *really* gets your juices flowing is a big, sexy brain."

"While I can't deny that your big, sexy brain makes me hard, so does your body." Alex plucked the eyeglasses from Claire's face and deposited them on the nightstand with her laptop. With the technological barriers to intimacy cast aside, she dragged Claire into her lap and allowed her hands to roam over pajama-clad curves. "But I think you know that, Claire-Claire. I think I've made that *very* clear."

She certainly had. Reminding herself how unattractive a quality like insecurity *actually* was, Claire managed a genuine smile. "True. No one has ever made me feel as desirable as you do."

"That's because I *do* desire you. Always. Every minute of every day, whether we're together or apart." Alex kissed Claire's lips, then licked the upper one with the tip of her tongue. "I'm going to miss you while you're gone, baby. Like, *really* miss you."

Claire felt Alex's breathing deepen, felt the rising need emanate from her trembling body, and so forced away her malaise in order to give Alex what so many others clearly yearned to provide. "I'll miss you, too, sweetheart."

Alex kissed her way down Claire's throat, to her shoulder, then waited until Claire tugged down the top of her camisole to let one breast spill over before wrapping her lips around the hard tip. She traced circles around the pebbled flesh with her tongue, moaning happily as she tightened her arms around Claire's waist. "I love your nipples," she mumbled against the turgid skin. "You should let me photograph them sometime. Your breasts are so delicious. I could stare at them for hours."

Reading between the lines she was almost certain Alex hadn't intended to draw, Claire decided to offer a going-away present that would not only prove to Alex that she had as much to offer as any Internet bimbo, but also provide her a much-needed reminder of their connection in her absence. "Get your camera."

Alex lifted her head, excitement flashing in her eyes. "Yeah?"

"Yeah." Claire eased off Alex's lap, then tugged down her pajama bottoms and kicked them across the floor. "And mine."

Alex froze at the foot of the bed, glancing over her shoulder for confirmation. "You mean your camcorder?"

Claire nodded and began to slowly unbutton her top. "If that's something you'd be interested in."

"Are you kidding?" Alex scrambled off the bed and out of the room. "Be right back!"

Claire took a moment to school her breathing after Alex left, then finished unbuttoning her pajama shirt and dropped it onto the floor with the bottoms. Just as she reached to unhook the back clasp of her bra, Alex swept into the room with an urgent, "*No.* Leave it on."

Swallowing at the sureness of the command, Claire lowered her hands and watched Alex set up the tripod at the foot of the bed. "No faces, all right?"

"Of course." Alex pointed the video camera's lens slightly downward and looked through the eyepiece to gauge the shot. "Come sit at the end of the bed for me. So I can position this correctly."

Claire crawled down to perch on the edge of the mattress, facing the camcorder. "Like this?"

Alex checked the viewfinder, then made one last adjustment before rising to her full height. "Perfect. But first…" She bent to retrieve her DLSR camera, the same one she'd used to photograph Claire's post-cunnilingual pussy the night they'd first kissed. Lifting it playfully, Alex smirked. "I'd like to work in my preferred medium."

"You're the *artiste.*" Claire allowed Alex to pose her leaning back on her elbows, casually sexy, and blushed when Alex snapped a quick shot of her torso.

"And you, my love, are most definitely the art." Alex laid her down, placing one of Claire's hands over her abdomen, the other across her breast. She took another couple of photos, then peered over the camera. "Pinch your nipple. Get it nice and hard for me."

Claire seized her nipple through the padding of her bra, surrendering to Alex's will with a grateful shudder. Anything to forget the world outside this bedroom. "It feels nice."

"I'll bet it does." *Click.* Alex lowered the camera briefly. "Now sit up, on your knees."

Claire did as she was told, keeping her eyes downcast as Alex snapped away. "Is this good?"

"You're so beautiful, baby. Do you have any idea how badly I want to make you come right now?" Alex kept the camera pointed at her as she issued her next command. "Reach behind your back and unclasp your bra. Don't take it off until I tell you."

Flushing while she acted out the striptease her girlfriend desired, Claire tried not to dwell on why Alex seemed so at ease in this role. Every nerve ending in her body was so highly sensitized that even the brush of her own fingers against her heated skin drew a quiet moan from her lips, an exaltation that Alex captured in a series of shutter clicks.

"Now lower your bra, slowly. Tease me about revealing those soft, gorgeous tits." Alex licked her lips at Claire's best attempts to entice, taking a new photo every few seconds while she peeled away her bra. "God, Claire, you're breathtaking."

Cheeks hot, Claire tried not to compare herself to the photo she'd just seen on Alex's laptop screen, but it was difficult. Unable to accept the compliment when it felt so contrived, she silently dropped her hands to the waistband of her panties. After a beat, she conjured what she hoped was an alluring smile. "Do you want me to take these off next?"

Alex moved the viewfinder away from her face, then turned the camera off and put it back in its padded bag. "Nope."

Claire sat straighter, concerned that she'd ruined the experience with her flagging confidence. "I'm sorry. We can keep going."

Alex walked to the camcorder and flipped it on so a red light appeared above the lens. "Unfortunately, the time has come to teach you a lesson."

Claire swallowed, then scrambled into position, sitting at the edge of the bed where she knew the camera wouldn't see her face. "What lesson?" she murmured, also a little afraid to have her voice on film.

"The one about believing me when I tell you how pretty you are, or how much I love you, or how badly I want to fuck you—and *only* you."

Claire stared up at Alex as she came to loom over her. "I do believe you."

"No, you don't." Alex sat down beside her, then quickly grabbed Claire around the waist and wrestled her onto her stomach until she lay facedown across Alex's thighs. "But you will. Someday."

Claire's breath came out in hot, sharp pants, further warming her cheek where it was pressed against the mattress. She wriggled in Alex's grasp, painfully turned on by the knowledge that this masterful handling was being preserved on film for future viewings. Whimpering when Alex shifted their bodies so that Claire's bottom was in full view of the camera lens, Claire hid her face in the comforter and waited for whatever would come next.

Alex's hand came down on her bottom gently, in a feather-soft caress, but Claire flinched anyway. Alex chuckled. "Personally, I think you would benefit from some firm discipline. What do you think?"

Claire bit her lip as the strong hand stroked her buttocks with the utmost tenderness. She was confident that Alex would never do anything without her explicit consent, so despite the overt dominance being put on display, Claire knew who really held all the power in this scenario. *How many spanking fantasies have I had? Fifty? A hundred?* Plucking up her courage, Claire said, "I think you might be right."

"Might be?" Alex patted her left buttock, followed by the right. "Let's try this again. Shall I give you something to remember me by when you're gone? Each and every time you sit down?"

Claire's pussy clenched, sending a trickle of hot liquid flowing out to wet her panties. "Yes."

Alex repeated the teasing pattern, slapping Claire's left cheek, then the right, with slightly more force. "You're such a *bad girl*, letting yourself believe that any other woman would possibly catch my eye. How could they, when I have all *this?*" She moved her hand back and forth, harder still, landing two blows on each side. "That's why I'm going to fuck you in front of the camera tonight. I want to *show* you how hot you are. I want you to *see*." *Smack. Smack.* Alex paused. "After I finish spanking your cute little butt, of course."

Claire moaned at the next slap, a harder blow that left her skin tingling with heat. She squirmed away instinctively, gasping with conflicted delight when Alex easily wrested her back under control. Heaving, she went still and awaited the next semi-painful stroke.

"Baby." Alex ran her hand down the center of Claire's back and came to rest atop the swell of her buttocks. "Say 'bananas' if you want me to stop. All right?"

Claire nodded without lifting her face from the shelter of her hands. "Understood."

Alex's fingertips curled beneath the waistband of her panties. "I'm going to pull your panties down for the rest. So the next bit may sting a little."

Claire wondered whether the camera would be able to detect how ludicrously wet she suddenly felt. She nodded without speaking, tense with anticipation as Alex slid the panties down around her knees before yanking them off altogether. Jumping when Alex brought her palm down to rest on her naked bottom—barely making contact—Claire trembled nervously as she wondered when the discipline would resume.

*Smack.* Another slap that immediately followed the first cut off Claire's yelp of surprise. Neither one inflicted any real pain. On the contrary, her entire lower body sang with pleasure, heavy and swollen and ready for the thunderous climax she had faith that Alex would eventually deliver. Wantonly, Claire opened her legs in a not-so-subtle invitation, a move that caused Alex's fingers to inadvertently brush across her sodden labia on the next blow.

"Oh, my." Alex's throaty murmur raised goose bumps all over Claire's body. "What's *this?*" Her fingers glided over Claire's wet folds on their way to fondle her slick opening. "Is it really discipline if it makes your pussy gush like this?"

Without showing her face, Claire shook her head as she limply submitted to the thorough examination. She said nothing, unsure whether Alex actually expected an answer. The keen awareness that Alex's confident actions were unfolding under the camera's watchful eye stoked Claire's arousal to indescribable heights, causing her to groan more loudly than normal when Alex worked a single, possessive finger inside her body. She spread her thighs wider, eager for more.

"Oh, so *that's* what you want." Alex pulled her finger almost all the way out before pushing it back in—over and over. "You want me to finger your greedy little hole, don't you?"

Glad the camera couldn't see her bright-red face, Claire nodded without speaking. Alex withdrew from her entirely, grabbing her up like she weighed nothing at all, then repositioning their bodies so Claire faced away from the camera with her bare pussy on full display. Alex re-entered her with two fingers, and Claire lifted her head with a moan, no longer worried that the camera might record her face. She knew that her ass, Alex's flexing arm, and her finger-filled cunt now dominated the lens's field of view, a thought that made her spasm around the plundering digits in a precursor to climax.

Alex stopped suddenly, pulling out of her pussy before carefully easing her legs from beneath Claire's hips. Left alone on her belly in the center of the mattress, Claire nearly turned to see where Alex was going before she remembered that she didn't want the camera to capture her face. Before she could ask what was happening, Alex knelt beside her, stroking Claire's back and ass with quiet reverence before helping to position her with her butt stuck up into the air. "Good." Alex penetrated her with two fingers, slowly, while using her other hand to spread Claire's buttocks apart for the camera's benefit. "Rub your clit for me. Set your knees as far apart as you can so we'll be able to see what you're doing when we watch this together later."

Claire shivered and did exactly as Alex instructed. Her fingers were like magic on her clit, falling into her favorite, familiar rhythm while Alex filled her again and again with confident, masterful thrusts that swiftly drove her to a loud, messy conclusion. Fingertips dancing over her pulsing clit, Claire arched her back and came with a yell, contracting around the digits inside her just as Alex's free hand came down sharply against her bottom one last time. Quaking, Claire rode out her orgasm until she couldn't hold herself up anymore, then collapsed, bonelessly, onto her stomach in the center of the bed.

Alex chuckled and trailed her sure touch down Claire's spine, to the small of her back. "Did you like that?"

"Yes," Claire murmured. She pushed herself up onto her hands. "Do you want—"

Alex planted her palm between Claire's shoulders and forced her back down. "I want you to stay right there. The camera is still on. I'll be right back."

Claire released a shaky breath, then buried her face in her arms. Based on the sound of Alex rustling around on the other side of the room, she had a good guess what was coming next. Would Alex really pass up the opportunity to strap on her cock for their home movie?

Claire didn't dare look and show her face to the camera, so all she could do was wait and see.

When the mattress finally sank under Alex's weight, signaling her return, Claire tensed in preparation for whatever she had planned. Strong hands gripped her hips, dragging her backward until her feet dangled off the edge of the bed. Then Alex climbed on top of her from behind, the rounded head of her beloved cock pressing insistently against Claire's vagina.

"Do you want this?" Alex leaned over her, moving her hand between Claire's legs to rub her slippery folds. "You have to say yes before I'll put it inside." She used her wet fingers to slick the length of the dildo, preparing them both for what was about to happen. "Tell me to fuck you, baby, and I'll make sure you never forget who loves you."

Overwhelmed by a complex mixture of desire and emotion, Claire simply nodded. Then, when Alex didn't react, she said, "Yes. Fuck me."

Alex rose off her body and reached down to guide the tip of the cock into Claire's waiting pussy. "Spread your legs, sweetheart, as wide as you can. Let me watch that big dick slide inside your tight hole."

Claire pressed her face deeper into her arms, so fucking turned on and embarrassed and excited that she didn't know what to do with herself. "Yes," she repeated, wanting there to be no mistake about her desire. "*Fuck* me."

Alex drove the dildo into her, inch by torturous inch, while the camera recorded every second of the deliberate invasion. Claire pictured Alex watching this part later without her, no doubt with one hand shoved down the front of her boxer briefs, and nearly came from the image conjured by her fevered mind. The thought that Alex's deep, forceful thrusts were being captured forever on a sex tape that could very well come back to haunt her in the future only made the sex feel more dangerous—and therefore exciting. Allowing Alex to record this was an extension of trust that could truly bite her in the ass someday, no matter how their relationship played out, but it was also another of Claire's most taboo fantasies, realized at last.

Alex paused to readjust the angle of their bodies, positioning Claire so the camera captured the optimal view of the dildo moving in and out. "That's right, sweetie. Does it feel good?"

Claire nodded vigorously as she rocked back to meet Alex's next thrust. "*Yes.*"

A buzzing sound filled the air, and seconds later, Claire felt the residual vibration against her ass cheeks, and then, to a lesser extent, inside her pussy. More than the increase in stimulation, Claire loved having confirmation that Alex was building toward her own peak. Alex withdrew the cock from her pussy, then stuck it back in, then pulled it all the way out again. When Claire moaned piteously, Alex drove its entire length home at once, letting go of the base to grab Claire's hips and ride her forcefully from behind.

"I'm gonna come inside you." Alex grunted as she rutted against Claire's ass in an increasingly jerky rhythm. She moved one of her hands between Claire's thighs to brush her sensitive clit with the rough pads of her fingertips. "Are you ready for this, baby? Will you come with me?"

Claire wouldn't have guessed she was capable of another orgasm already, but Alex's deft touch quickly proved her wrong. Less than a minute later, her thighs shook so wildly she had to strain to support her weight as Alex slapped against her. She felt Alex go tense behind her seconds before her own climax hit, and they cried out in unison, Alex moving within her until Claire finally collapsed onto the mattress, bringing them both down in a sweaty heap. Alex pressed her lips to the back of Claire's neck, then her shoulders, covering the damp skin in worshipful kisses as her hips continued to cant softly against Claire's trembling bottom.

"I love you," Alex breathed into her ear, too quiet for the camera's microphone to pick up. "No one has ever made me come like you do. No one has ever felt so good beneath me, wrapped around me." Her hands smoothed up Claire's sides before sneaking under her chest to cradle her breasts. "No one ever *will.*"

Claire's breath caught. She turned her face to the side. "Shut off the camera."

"Yes, ma'am." Alex withdrew from her cautiously, then climbed off the bed to fiddle with the equipment Claire still refused to face head-on. "All right, it's off."

Claire turned to check that the red light had gone dark, sighing in relief when she discovered that their privacy had been restored. Alex wore a wolfish grin as she detached the camcorder from the tripod and flipped open the built-in screen. Studying the glow reflected by Alex's face and eyes as she rolled back the video, Claire cringed as the sound of their breathless moans and the slap-slap-slap of Alex's lower body against hers suddenly filled the air.

"Too soon!" Claire cried.

Almost simultaneously, Alex drawled, "Oh, that's fucking *hot.*" Turning the camera around, she showed Claire a shockingly pornographic image of one attractive woman being pounded by another. For a split second, Claire failed to realize that she was, in fact, one of those women. "Tell me you're not sexy, Claire-Claire. Tell me why it's crazy that I'd choose you." Alex turned the camera around again to watch a while longer. "I'll erase this video right now if that's what makes you comfortable, my love, but if you let me keep it, I guarantee I'll be jerking off to this the entire time you're gone."

"Nobody will ever see it but us, right?"

Alex looked up from the screen to cross her heart. "Scout's honor. I know how to encrypt files, believe it or not. I've had to do it for clients in the past. I'll protect this video with my *life.* I swear." Her eyes drifted back to their home movie. "It means everything that you trust me enough to have done this at all."

"I love you," Claire said softly. "I want to make you happy."

Appearing mildly stricken, Alex established immediate eye contact. "I love you, too. You didn't do this *just* to make me happy, right? I mean you wanted to do it, too…right?"

"Yes, absolutely." Claire gestured for Alex to get back in bed. "I didn't mean to suggest otherwise."

"Because we've talked about that before." Alex set the camcorder on her nightstand before climbing onto the mattress to gather Claire into a bear hug. "Remember? About how I only want what you're eager to give—and the rest isn't important."

"I remember." Applying pressure to Alex's chest, Claire urged her to lie flat on her back so she could rest her head on her broad shoulder. "But believe me, that wasn't anything I haven't thought about doing before. More than once, in fact."

Snorting, Alex kissed the top of her head and tightened the arm she'd wrapped around Claire's waist. "You never fail to delight, sweetheart. Of course, I have a feeling our amateur film will only make me miss you more." She sighed heavily, holding Claire closer. "*Three whole days?* I swear this is gonna be *torture.* No doubt I'll be spending pretty much the entire time dreaming of creative ways to welcome you home."

That remark elicited a big, genuine smile from Claire for the first time that night. *Mission accomplished.*

## CHAPTER TWENTY-ONE

For the first time in their professional lives, Claire and Sarah didn't share a ride to the airport before a joint flight, which only added to Claire's stress. While she appreciated the extra time with Alex during the drive to Oakland, she was preoccupied by her anxiety ahead of her performance at the TED conference, by far the biggest presentation she'd ever had to make. Normally she would lean on Sarah to get her through any pre-public-speaking jitters, in part by honing their delivery through repeated rehearsals, but this time she was on her own. She hoped they would run through their speech at least once or twice tonight at the hotel, but truthfully, she had no idea how this weekend would go, or even whether Sarah planned to talk to her at all.

After Alex left her at the airport with a long, passionate kiss, Claire checked in for her flight and walked to the assigned gate. She studied the other passengers already seated and waiting, unsure whether she hoped to find Sarah among them or not. Sarah could have changed her flight, given that she'd also attempted to alter their hotel reservation. With a tired sigh, Claire dropped into an empty chair at the end of a long row of chairs, resting her head on the wall behind her as she awaited the boarding call at least twenty minutes away.

Sarah arrived at the gate almost exactly twenty-two minutes later, immediately after the flight attendant called for their section to board. Claire stood and grabbed her bag, joining the line to show her boarding pass right behind Sarah. Hurt not to get even a simple greeting, Claire asked, "Couldn't change your flight?"

"Nope." Sarah didn't even look at her as she stepped forward with the queue. "Let's not make this into a huge deal, all right? We're both grown-ups. We can sit near each other for three and a half hours without incident, I should hope."

"*I* can." Despite the assertion, Claire wanted nothing more than to take Sarah by the shoulders and give her a vigorous shake. *Why is she being so unreasonable? What's* wrong *with her?* "I'm not the one who's so over-the-top pissed off."

Sarah turned and met her eyes as they neared the gate agent. "Claire, I don't want to do this with you right now. *Please.*"

Her voice hinted at some fundamental shift in attitude and conveyed a deep exhaustion that startled Claire silent. She remained quiet as Sarah handed over her boarding pass and entered the gangway to get on the plane. Once Claire entered the cabin, she checked her seat number and walked down the aisle until she found her spot, two rows behind Sarah, on the opposite side of the plane. *Apparently she was able to get at least one thing changed.* Claire sat down near the window, staring out at the tarmac while she waited for the rest of the passengers to board.

"Excuse me, miss?"

Claire glanced up at a young couple who stood in the aisle next to her row. "Yes?"

The taller man put on a sparkling smile before making his pitch. "Is there any way you'd be willing to trade seats with my husband here? We just got married last night and would *really* like to sit together."

Grinning at the palpable love in the newlywed's voice, Claire retrieved her backpack from under the seat in front of her and scooted toward the aisle. "No problem. And congratulations."

"Thanks," the other man said, flashing a brilliant grin. "You're the best!" He glanced at his boarding pass, then pointed at the empty seat next to Sarah's. "I'm in 10B. Right there."

Sarah's eyes widened when Claire went to claim her new seat. "Seriously?"

"Blame the newlyweds," Claire said, pointing behind her at the lovebirds settling into their upgraded accommodations. "I couldn't deny the request of such an adorable couple."

Sarah's frown gradually disappeared as she watched the new husbands bring their airport-sanctioned bottles of water together in a toast, no doubt to new beginnings. "They *are* pretty adorable."

Encouraged by the crack in Sarah's icy facade, Claire tucked her backpack under the seat ahead of her, then sat back with a weary exhalation. "So are you nervous about tomorrow? Because I am."

"A little, yes." Sarah went quiet for almost a minute, then sighed. "The presentation is solid. I have my part down cold. As long as you've been practicing your section…"

"I have." Claire tried to keep her instinctive defensiveness from entering her tone. "It would help if we could rehearse together, though. Maybe tonight, at the hotel."

"Sure." Sarah reached into the pocket on the back of the seat in front of her and retrieved the in-flight magazine, flipping it open to scan a random page with unconvincing interest. "That's probably a good idea, anyway."

"Great." Claire stared over at Sarah's downcast eyes, saddened anew by the apparent dissolution of their longtime friendship. Over a *girl*. Blinking away tears, Claire whispered, "I *really* miss you, Sarah."

Sarah sniffed, then set the magazine down to stare out the window instead. Claire knew her well enough to realize that Sarah was trying to hide her rising emotion. "Even though I'm just a lazy hanger-on to our company's success?"

For a moment, Claire had absolutely no idea what she was alluding to. Then she remembered their disastrous lunch date and the vicious turn their argument had taken. "I wasn't trying to imply that you haven't done your fair share for the company. Just that I've put in more than enough effort to be given the benefit of the doubt even after a month of being overly distracted by Alex."

Sarah cringed at the mention of her sister's name. "Let's not get into this here. All right? We're about to spend the next few hours trapped inside this steel tube, so how about we *don't* talk about my sister right now?"

Scoffing, Claire faced forward so she could rest her head against the seat. "Fine. Is this the part where you act like a grown-up? Because I'm a little confused."

"You're not the only one."

Claire stewed in silence for a few minutes, unable to stop thinking about what Sarah had just said. *A lazy hanger-on? I never called her that.* She chanced a sidelong glance at Sarah, who now stared out the window like she wished she were anywhere except seat 10A. *She knows I don't actually think that about her, right?* Praying she wouldn't be rebuffed, Claire took a deep breath and touched Sarah's shoulder. "Hey. May I say one more thing?"

"If you insist." Sarah kept her eyes fixed stubbornly out the window for a few seconds more, then turned to Claire with a defeated sigh. "What?"

"I really, truly apologize if I ever made it sound like your contribution to our company was in any way less than mine. I may have put in a lot of hours coding and dealing with all the technology, but let's be honest. I wouldn't even be *going* to this TED conference if it weren't for you. You've always been the one to push us forward into bigger and better things." Relieved to see Sarah's expression soften slightly, Claire continued. "You're the one who found our first big investors, the one who knows how to talk to the people with money, how to persuade them that they should care about our vision."

"*Your* vision," Sarah said. "You and I both know that you're the one who came up with the idea for the app in the first place. It was your passion about the need to help more girls embrace STEM careers that started everything. I'm just lucky you asked me to tag along."

Claire winced at the naked insecurity showing through Sarah's normally confident facade. Clearly her comments at lunch had tapped into a deep-seated vulnerability, an unfounded concern that Sarah had seemingly carried around for far too long. "Sarah, I obviously haven't done a very good job of letting you know how important you are— to me *and* to the company. Yes, I've poured my blood and sweat into our products and into defining the company's original direction, but you're the one who's propelled us to such incredible heights. We make a great team. Alone, I'm not sure I ever would've found a large enough audience for my work to have any of it make a real difference. But together, we're unstoppable. Truly. Regardless of my contributions, I'm one hundred percent confident that we wouldn't be where we are today without you. I know that, and I need *you* to know that I know that. Okay?"

Sarah actually dabbed at her eyes with the sleeve of her shirt. "Okay. I appreciate that."

"I said what I did at lunch the other day because I was angry about the implication that I simply didn't care anymore. I *do*. But I never meant to suggest that you weren't an equal partner in every way. You are." Claire said, weakly, "Look, I screwed up badly, more than once,

but my heart is every bit as into our company as it's ever been. And…"
She paused, taking a breath before opening herself up for yet another
painful rejection. "I love *you*. Even though I might still be kind of mad
at you."

The pilot's voice came on over the loudspeaker to announce that
they were in line for takeoff and would depart shortly. Claire exhaled
at the announcement, bracing herself for her least favorite part of air
travel. Beside her, Sarah tucked the in-flight magazine back into the
pocket of the seat in front of her. Then she reached over the armrest and
grabbed Claire's hand, lacing their fingers together in preparation for
takeoff—a routine they'd established years ago, as teenagers.

"I love you, too." Sarah gave her fingers a gentle squeeze. "Even
though."

Claire closed her eyes when the plane started to roll forward,
reassured by the familiar comfort of her best friend's hand in hers. Even
if all their problems weren't yet solved, she already felt a little better.

## CHAPTER TWENTY-TWO

Claire sat backstage at the convention center that was hosting the TED conference, fiddling with her phone to try to take her mind off the fact that she and Sarah were about to speak in front of hundreds of people who likely had no idea who they were and might or might not care what they were all about. They'd run through their presentation twice the night before and then again that morning, before spending the rest of the day attending other talks and networking with presenters in all sorts of different fields. Despite her usual introversion, Claire had enjoyed getting to know so many remarkable people, and the socialization had actually helped take her mind off her performance anxiety.

Alex had been texting good-luck wishes and romantic proclamations every hour or so, starting from the moment Claire landed in Austin up until a few hours before Claire and Sarah had been scheduled to speak. Claire wasn't surprised by the current radio silence, as one of the last incoming texts from Alex had informed her that she had to drive to San Francisco to meet with a potential buyer at the gallery. It sounded as though Alex might have a chance to sell the few remaining pieces from her *cunt* series, which would amount to a resounding affirmation of her decision to venture beyond the fashion shoots that had long paid her bills. Despite knowing that Alex was probably still busy, Claire glanced at her phone's screen every few moments while they waited to be called onstage, hopeful that she'd receive one last boost to her self-confidence from the person who made her feel like the most beautiful, brilliant woman on earth.

"You're like a teenager," Sarah teased her somewhat hypocritically, considering that she sat beside Claire perusing her own social-media timeline. "You two aren't *sexting*, are you?"

"*No.*" Claire turned the phone toward Sarah so she could see that she was telling the truth. "Just pep talks, pictures of cute puppies to help calm my nerves, that sort of thing. But nothing for almost three hours now."

Sarah snickered and turned her attention back to her own screen. "Here's a pep talk: We're going to kick this presentation's *ass*. Why? Because we're two badass bitches who know what the fuck we're talking about."

Giggling, Claire turned off her phone and focused on the always dependable source of comfort sitting in the chair next to her. "I suppose we are."

"You're damn right, we are! And we—" Sarah's panicked eyes darted up to Claire's face, then back down to the screen, before she hurriedly turned off the display and slipped her phone into her purse. "Okay. Why don't we rehearse your part one more time? Maybe that'll help."

Claire's stomach twisted with the sick certainty that something bad had just happened. "What's wrong?"

"Nothing." Sarah gave her a big, wide smile—bigger and wider than Claire had gotten from her in ages. "I just decided that a good friend would put down her phone and try to alleviate your anxiety."

Claire narrowed her eyes. "Bullshit. I saw the look on your face. What did you see?"

Cursing under her breath, Sarah blocked Claire from reaching into her purse to retrieve the phone. "It's not important. It'll keep until after our presentation…" Her frantic gaze darted to the clock on the wall. "Which is in *ten* minutes, Claire. All right?"

"Is it about Alex?" Claire couldn't imagine any other subject that would provoke such concern about her reaction. "She's not hurt, is she?"

"Of course not." Sarah shot her a scolding frown. "I wouldn't hide that from you."

"So you *are* hiding something from me?" Claire suddenly felt like she couldn't breathe. "Sarah, please, *tell* me. You can't *do* that and not tell me!"

"Goddamn it," Sarah muttered. She shifted to face Claire, grabbing both her hands and holding them tight. "Look, I'm one hundred percent positive that Vanessa is just trying to fuck with you. No way is this what she says it is."

Heart hammering, Claire tugged her hands from Sarah's and gestured wildly toward the purse. "Show it to me."

"*Fuck.*" Sarah reached for her phone, then stopped, turning back to Claire with a pleading expression. "Claire, listen to me. We're about to get on a stage in front of *hundreds* of people to try to sell the idea of our company and its vision to the world. I can't have you distracted right now. I can't let my stupid sister ruin everything we've worked for."

Claire closed her eyes, fighting not to lose her composure completely. Sarah was right, of course, but now that she knew there was *something* on social media for her to see, *something* Sarah seemed convinced Vanessa had posted specifically to devastate her, she wasn't certain she could get through their speech without knowing what that *something* was. As calmly as possible, she said, "I won't get distracted. I won't fuck up. Just please...don't keep this from me." Her hand tightened on her own phone, reminding her of its presence on her lap. "Or I'll go ahead and try to find it on my own."

Sighing, Sarah turned on her phone and flipped it around to show Claire two photographs of the same gorgeous couple, posted side-by-side. The first shot appeared to have been taken some time ago, when Alex's hair had been slightly longer and Vanessa's not as wavy. The women were transcendent as a couple, grinning at the camera like they both knew exactly how in love it was with their flawless visages. The other photo was more recent. *Much* more, based on the necklace Alex was wearing—a necklace Claire had given her only last week. The location tagged in the post was the art gallery where Alex had told Claire she was going before she'd gone silent over text.

Tonight's portrait was more candid than the first, taken selfie-style. Alex wore a vague smirk beside Vanessa's luminous smile, appearing to pose nearly cheek to cheek with her ex. The caption read, simply, Back together again. *#TheGeniusAndHerMuse*. According to the time stamp, the picture had been posted less than twenty minutes ago. Claire forced her throat closed against the bile that threatened to rise.

"You realize that Alex would never actually do this to you, right?" Sarah's voice barely penetrated the haze of her gut-wrenching pain.

Claire forced her eyes away from the phone, trying to convince herself it wasn't what it looked like—*again*—and that Vanessa was a twisted, manipulative asshole—without a doubt—but the truth was, whenever she looked at Vanessa's stupid face, it reminded her once again of everything she wasn't. Of everything Alex was giving up to be with her. What if Claire had been deceiving herself about this relationship's longevity? What if the damage she'd caused to her friendship with Sarah was in service of a relationship that could never really last, anyway? Even if Alex no longer wanted Vanessa specifically, an entire world of unbelievable, clearly attainable women was apparently always ready to fall at her feet. How long would Claire actually be able to keep up? Did she really believe that the occasional offer to make a sex tape would keep Alex interested indefinitely?

"*Claire,*" Sarah whispered urgently. "Are you okay?"

"Mrs. Weatherspoon? Ms. Barker? We're ready for you to line up backstage. You're on in two minutes."

Sarah grabbed Claire's hand, gripping hard. "Sweetie? Are you ready for this?"

Claire nodded and allowed Sarah to pull her standing. For a moment she swayed on her feet, mind racing as she tried to decide what the pictures meant—and whether what they meant even mattered with her oldest and closest friendship at risk. Presentation entirely forgotten, she struggled to comprehend that she was *literally* about to go out in front of a massive crowd to give a speech she and Sarah had been anticipating for months. But then she recalled her promise not to get distracted, not to fuck up. She thought back to the other times she'd let her feelings for Alex interfere with her responsibilities as Sarah's partner and best friend and, in doing so, how badly she'd let Sarah down. No matter how impossible it felt right then, she couldn't afford to let her romantic life interfere with their professional interests even one more time.

Exhaling in a rush, Claire powered off the phone and slipped it into her own purse. Then she shook her head from side to side, abruptly, before tightening her fingers on Sarah's. "I'm ready, yes. I'm also okay."

Sarah looked at her warily, the fear plain in her eyes. "You sure?"

Claire lifted Sarah's hand to her lips and kissed her fingers before conjuring up a smile full of bravado that was one percent sheer will and ninety nine percent bullshit. "I'm positive. Now come on, you badass bitch. Let's go prove to everyone that we know what the fuck we're talking about."

Sarah answered with a smile that spread slowly across her face and filled Claire's heart with unexpected joy. "*Fuck,* yes!" Sarah said enthusiastically. Then, lowering her volume as they entered the backstage area, she added in a whisper, "I love you, knucklehead."

"I love you, too." Claire gave Sarah's hand one last squeeze, then released her fingers so they could walk onstage to thunderous applause.

Together.

## CHAPTER TWENTY-THREE

Despite wavering once or twice, briefly, Claire managed to keep her phone off and out of sight for the entire rest of the evening. Sarah followed suit and did the same, undoubtedly aware that the only way Claire would get through the after-party attended by the other speakers was by ignoring the outside world completely. The opportunity to schmooze with fellow conference-goers had been one of Sarah's primary motivations for submitting their application to attend, so even though all Claire wanted to do was go back to the hotel, crack open a bottle of wine, and drink herself to sleep, she sucked it up and socialized for the sake of her best friend.

At around nine o'clock, shortly after Claire's thin hold on her emotions began to slip, Sarah took her by the arm and whispered into her ear, "We should get out of here. Go back to the hotel and celebrate in private."

Claire nodded without hesitation, but a fresh wave of grief and anxiety instantly tempered the surge of relief that Sarah's suggestion triggered. Unexpectedly on the verge of tears, she could only offer a clipped, "Yeah."

"Come on." Like the true friend she'd always been, Sarah looped their arms together and walked Claire out of the noisy club. She signaled to one of the cabs lingering outside, then put Claire into the backseat, giving the driver the address of their hotel while sliding in after her. Once they'd set off, Sarah leaned closer to Claire and murmured, "You know Vanessa's a lying bitch. Don't fall for her twisted bullshit by believing for even a second that Alex would go back to that asshole as soon as you left town. *Or* that she'd be okay with Vanessa posting a cute little reunion photo on social media even if she had." Sarah shook her head, disapprovingly. "Nuh-uh. My sister may be a lot of things, but never *cruel.*"

Claire dissolved into tears, despite conceding that Sarah had a point. "I know. You're right."

"Then don't cry, sweetheart." Sarah turned in her seat, cupping Claire's face in her hands to clear away her tears with her thumbs. "You'll call Alex once we get back to the room and straighten this whole mess out. Everything will be just fine."

Claire disagreed with a dejected shake of her head. "I'm not so sure anymore. My relationship with Alex…" Her chest heaved and she hitched a broken sob. Being with Alex had already cost her so much, yet despite everything she'd sacrificed thus far, her faith in Alex's repeated proclamations of fidelity and devotion still remained tenuous—at best. "Maybe it was all a really stupid idea."

Sarah's hand landed on her back and rubbed lightly. "Oh, Claire…" Before she could go on, their driver parked at the curb of their destination. Sarah handed him a small wad of cash from her purse, then grabbed Claire's wrist and helped her out of the car. "Let's talk about it upstairs."

Claire let Sarah lead her into the elevator and up to their room, too drained to do anything except comply. Now that the adrenaline surge from public speaking had passed and the crowds were gone, Claire had nothing left to distract her from the reality of a personal life that had somehow become too messy to handle. Once Sarah opened the door to let them inside their room, Claire marched straight to her bed and fell onto the mattress face-first. After a beat, she rolled onto her back with a heavy sigh.

Sarah locked the door behind them and went to the minibar to retrieve an undoubtedly overpriced bottle of wine. She popped the cork to pour a single glass, then sat on the edge of the other queen bed before offering the drink to Claire. "Here. Why don't you take the edge off?"

Claire sat up and tossed back a few sips of the passable merlot. Then she gestured at the bottle Sarah had left across the room, trying like hell to summon up a celebratory spirit. "Pour yourself a glass. Let's toast our perfectly executed presentation."

Smiling, Sarah stood, went back to the minibar, and returned with a bottle of water. After twisting off the cap, she held out the bottle so Claire could clink her wineglass against the plastic container. "It really *was* perfectly executed. I'm sorry I ever doubted you. You were phenomenal today." When Claire hesitated to toast, frowning at Sarah's uncharacteristic decision not to share the bottle of wine, Sarah simply tapped her water bottle on Claire's glass with a smile. "And to answer your unspoken question…as it turns out, I can only help drown your sorrows in spirit tonight because, well…I'm pregnant. Apparently." She shrugged, brightly, and took a long swig of water.

"*What?*" Sarah's casual bombshell snapped Claire out of her self-pitying fog. "You're…*what? For how long?*"

"Six or seven weeks. We found out only a few days ago."

Claire performed the mental math. "Marcus knocked you up in Europe. Romantic second honeymoon *indeed.*"

Sarah blushed, an unusual look for her always-confident friend. "That it was."

"Wow." Claire's already tumultuous emotions only intensified as she struggled to decipher her reaction to the news. She felt joy, naturally, and excitement—but also fear. Fear of change. Of the future. Of losing Sarah to someone else, even if that someone was a tiny, adorable reflection of Sarah herself. But mostly…*excitement.* "Guess this means I'll get my baby fix without actually having to reproduce." She leaned across the space between the beds to pat Sarah on the back. "Thanks for that. Seriously. You're a real pal."

Chuckling, Sarah deadpanned, "All for you, bestie."

"Wow," Claire repeated. She took another drink, then walked across the room with her nearly empty glass to grab the rest of the bottle. "Is Marcus excited?"

"Are you kidding me? He's pumped. The man has already picked out all the movies he wants to show his miniature geek-in-training, the books to read, the projects they'll build together—"

"Marcus *does* realize that he'll need to survive a few solid years of almost nothing but tears, diaper changes, and inexplicable bodily functions first, right?" With a grin, Claire sat back down on the bed and topped off her glass.

Sarah snorted. "I think he's hoping the kid will inherit his big brain. According to Marcus's mom, he was reading at eighteen months."

"Well, the baby's mom is no slouch, either." Claire sipped her wine slowly, not wanting to get too drunk, but eager to dull the edges of her lingering pain. "He or she will be absolutely perfect. And, if we're very, very lucky, a geek just like her daddy and favorite aunt."

Sarah's expression turned sad. "Claire, I need to apologize for getting so angry with you at lunch that day. Honestly, even if you *did* earn a little of my frustration, you certainly didn't deserve the full brunt of my hormonal craziness. Not that I'm making excuses for the way I treated you after all your apologies and attempts to reconcile, but I honestly feel like this pregnancy—"

"Apology accepted." Setting her empty glass on the nightstand, Claire shifted to sit on the other bed next to Sarah and wrapped an arm around her waist. "I'm sorry again for every time I ignored you or let you down when I was with Alex. It was wrong of me not to put you first, and stupid, and *so* not worth the distance it created between us."

"Hey." Sarah grabbed Claire's free hand and squeezed. "Yeah, it sucked, but you were right…it's not like I didn't get similarly swept up in Marcus, way back when. It's not *your* fault that I fell in love when I was young and irresponsible, but you had to wait until your personal life had long since taken a backseat to our mutual ambition." She stroked her thumb over Claire's, holding eye contact in a way that easily conveyed her utter sincerity. "And Claire, I don't expect you to always put me first. Honestly, you shouldn't. Not when you have someone you love as much as Alex—someone who loves *you.*"

"I appreciate your forgiveness." Claire let go of Sarah's hand to pour herself another half glass of wine. "I still screwed up. You *should* have come first. Always. Because, I mean, you *did* come first. Not to mention, you've always been there for me." She took a small sip of the potent liquid. "Even when I was this nerdy, socially awkward twelve-year-old who none of the other girls in our class wanted anything to do with. At least, not until you convinced them I was all right."

"Claire, I love you." Sarah's voice quavered with emotion, another unusual occurrence that Claire immediately attributed to surging hormones. "Always have, *definitely* always will. Now I'll admit… seeing you with Alex made me—*makes* me—kind of jealous. At times, *really* jealous. Not because she gets to sleep with you, obviously, but because she…gets to *have* you, I suppose." With a shrug, she admitted, "You've always belonged to me. *Only* me. And now you don't." She blew out a dejected breath. "Selfish, I know, but…what can I say?" Another shrug. "Sharing you sucks. Especially with my sister."

"Well, like I said, you may not need to worry about that much longer."

Sarah's expression tightened. "Why is that? I thought we agreed that Vanessa's full of shit."

"Maybe she is, but even so, that doesn't exactly make the idea of me and Alex any more realistic."

Sarah bumped into her shoulder with moderate force. "What's so unrealistic about you and Alex? It's obvious she's in love with you."

Claire deflected. "Why do you care if we break up? Don't you think it would make all our lives a whole lot simpler?"

"Mine, maybe. Not Alex's." Sarah screwed the cap onto her water bottle, tossing it onto the bed behind them so she could take Claire's hands in hers. "I'm going to go out on a limb and guess that you'd wind up pretty depressed as well—and probably even *more* distracted at the office."

She wasn't wrong. Claire lowered her face with a groan. "Yeah, well…I *do* love her. Even if I'm not terribly optimistic about how long I'll be able to keep her interest."

"Are you kidding me? I've never seen Alex happier." Sarah tightened her grip on Claire's hands until Claire reluctantly met her eyes. "Sweetie, why don't you turn on your phone? I'm willing to bet you'll find probably a hundred texts and missed calls from Alex offering a perfectly good explanation for what we saw."

Not yet ready to face Alex, even over the phone, Claire broached a new topic instead. "Did you know that Alex has prospective models sending naked pictures of themselves to her on a regular basis? Gorgeous young things desperate for the hotshot photographer to shoot them nude, or more." Claire knew she sounded a little silly, laying out all her insecurities like this for Sarah to summarily dismiss, but she so badly wanted to be convinced that her fears were unfounded. "The other night she showed me this photo one girl sent and it was like…" Her eyes watered despite the pleasantly detached buzz she'd managed to attain from the now half-empty bottle of wine. "How can I *compete* with obsessive ex-lovers and an entire Internet full of horny, goddess-like nymphs all desperate to get in my girlfriend's pants? I mean, I've never been with anyone for longer than a year. The last one dumped me because I bored her to death. Why would Alex stay when she could have literally *anyone* she wants?"

"Because she wants *you.*"

Claire tried to hold back her tears. "I wish I could believe that—or at least better understand *why* so I can accept it."

Sarah released a deep sigh. "Claire, honey, I know you're not exactly used to feeling hot or sexy or desirable, but believe me when I tell you that Alex absolutely sees you that way. I hadn't intended to ever speak of this aloud, but a couple weeks ago I suffered through a very…explicit…conversation with my sister that left me with *way* more information than I ever really needed about my best friend's proclivities. Suffice it to say, Alex thinks you two are wildly sexually compatible. She even told me you were 'the best she's ever had.' Frankly, I don't know why she'd lie about something like that. Especially to me." Sarah shuddered with residual revulsion. "No, she definitely wasn't lying. Trust me. I could tell."

Claire did trust Sarah, but trust alone couldn't undo the hurt and anxiety caused by Vanessa's post, nor dispel her concern that dating Alex would one day cause irreparable harm to her oldest and most important friendship. "At this point I guess it feels like…if I still don't feel genuinely secure in this relationship that I've repeatedly allowed to come between me and my best friend…" Claire lifted a shoulder. "Why am I even in it at all?"

Fat tears tracked down Sarah's cheeks, a development that clearly surprised them both. Not bothering to suppress the uncharacteristic show of emotion, Sarah pleaded, "Don't say that. Yeah, we've all experienced some growing pains while adjusting to the new dynamic among the three of us. But that doesn't mean I want you and Alex to split up. For one thing, I'm positive it would break Alex's heart. Like, destroy her completely. I get that Alex has slept around, kind of a lot actually, but the couple of times I've seen her commit to someone, she genuinely *committed.* And she's committed to you. Even if you aren't yet able to believe Alex, believe *me.* I will freely admit that there exists a dark, evil part of me that loves the idea of regaining exclusive access to your time and attention. That said, it would be unforgivably selfish not to convince you how *incredibly* stupid you're being about this."

Claire laughed without much humor. "Gee, thanks."

"I'm serious. Alex loves you, sweetie. She's *in* love with you. She says you're the smartest person she's ever met. She thinks you're beautiful, and funny, and great in bed, and fascinating to listen to regardless of what you're talking about, and you enjoy a lot of the same music, and movies, and you both love dogs…seriously, her list goes on and on. It's rather nauseating, to be honest."

Face hot, Claire struggled to keep looking into Sarah's shimmering eyes. "I love her, too."

Sarah sighed, a bit helplessly. "After that huge fight she and I got into when you forgot our meeting about TED, Alex was the first one to apologize, but she also warned me that she planned to stay with you as long as you'd have her and so I'd better get used to that idea and stop taking out my jealousy on her future wife. That was literally her response after I told her that unless she was a hundred percent, for *real* in love with you, I didn't think you two should date anymore. She called you her future *wife*."

Claire's heart stuttered. Alex had never mentioned marriage to her. *But she did to Sarah?* "Oh."

"She was serious, Claire. She wasn't trying to get a rise out of me or make me upset. She wanted me to know what her intentions were. That they were sincere—and wholly serious."

"Oh," Claire repeated in a whisper. "Is that why you still seemed so upset with me even though I'd felt certain we smoothed things over after the meeting I forgot? When I was trying so hard to make things right?"

Sarah looked at the floor. "I'm sorry. I was already missing you terribly, so when Alex essentially declared that her goal was to take you away from me forever, I sort of came unglued. Not out loud. I just…" She exhaled heavily. "I decided to prove to everyone that I didn't need you anymore, either. You know, exactly the way a mature adult *should* react."

Claire laughed and hugged Sarah around the waist. "I love you, and I don't blame you for getting freaked out. It's not like I've done a whole lot to inspire your confidence that our friendship can survive me falling in love with your sister."

"That's not entirely true. You *have* been trying. I just wasn't ready to forgive you *or* Alex yet."

"But you are now?" Claire's eyes welled over, her tears mirroring the ones rolling down Sarah's face.

"Yeah." Sarah wiped her cheek with her sleeve. "You two are

about to become my son or daughter's favorite aunts. And *my* life is about to get a whole lot busier. What kind of selfish asshole would begrudge her two favorite women their own happy endings...or her best friend a chance at a life of her own?"

Claire kissed Sarah's forehead, then her damp cheek. Sarah returned the kisses and drew her into a tight hug. Savoring their closeness after far too many days of unprecedented distance, Claire breathed out in relief. "I will be better, though. *We'll* be better."

Sarah released her with a final kiss on her cheek. "Damn right you will." Winking, she said, gently, "On that note, you should probably turn on your phone now."

Claire's eyes darted to her purse. "But...I'm scared. What if she *did* go back to Vanessa? What if something really *has* changed?"

"Then I promise you we'll kick my sister's sorry ass together."

Sniffling, Claire reached across the space between their beds and clumsily retrieved her phone from her purse. She powered it on, staring intently at the screen while it connected to the cellular network. After thirty seconds or so, dozens of new text messages began to pour in. Claire watched the notifications scroll one by one across the top of the screen, each containing a brief snippet of the missive it was alerting her to read.

*Claire, please call me! Don't believe anything you see until we talk. I love you. I'm sorry. Vanessa set up that meeting at the gallery. She ambushed me. You know she's full of shit, right? Call me, baby, as soon as you're able. I love you.*

She opened the conversation thread, confirming that the messages had begun to trickle in mere minutes after she'd turned off her phone to go onstage. This evidence of Alex's furious burst of visceral panic made Claire feel marginally better, even if she was still unsettled by the sight of what an aesthetically pleasing couple Alex and Vanessa made.

"Alex untagged herself in those photos," Sarah remarked, showing Claire the phone she'd also booted up. "They're not on her timeline anymore."

"Yeah. She texted me. A lot." Claire scrolled through the rest of the messages with a flick of her thumb.

*I really hope you left your phone backstage so I'm not interrupting your speech. But I can't risk letting you see something so hurtful without trying to warn you first!*

Clearing her throat, Claire summed up the content of Alex's frenzied explanation as given over the course of dozens of brief messages. "She says Vanessa contacted the gallery with a story about wanting to buy some of Alex's work but insisted on speaking to the artist in person before finalizing the sale. When Alex showed up for the meeting and started a conversation with the gallery owner, Vanessa suddenly swooped in to take a surprise selfie. They got into a big argument, Alex tried to take Vanessa's phone...anyway, she obviously freaked when she saw that Vanessa had posted the pictures online. She wants me to call her."

"You should." Sarah turned and pulled her hair aside to give Claire access to the back of her neck. "Unzip me?"

Claire tugged the tab of the zipper down to the small of Sarah's back. "You'll need a new wardrobe soon, huh?"

Sarah snorted. "Thanks for the reminder."

"Whatever, you know this'll be fun." Claire smiled up at Sarah as she stood to slip off her dress. "I'll even go shopping for maternity clothes with you. All day, if you want."

Raising an eyebrow, Sarah gave Claire's hair an affectionate tug. "You really *do* love me."

Claire grinned. "I really do, forever...partner."

"The feeling is mutual. And now that we're covered in all that sap, *partner*, I'm off to take my celebratory shower in preparation of a longer, even more celebratory slumber. Because as much as I'd love to party hard with you all night long, my pregnant ass is *beat*."

Claire slapped Sarah on her panties-clad butt as she walked away. "Go on. You've earned it."

"Now call my sister!" Sarah paused to admonish her when she reached the bathroom door. "And this time *believe* her when she tells you how much she adores your sexy ass, all right? Vanessa has nothing on you, believe me. Neither do all those other girls with the unsolicited naked selfies. It's long past time for you to let that fact sink into your thick, brilliant skull. The only thing that might eventually make Alex leave is your stubborn inability to believe how badly she wants to stay. Do you understand?"

Claire couldn't suppress a warm smile. No one could cheer her up better, or faster, than Sarah Weatherspoon nee Williams. "Aye-aye, ma'am."

"Remember, Alex is lucky to have you. You're a successful entrepreneur who recently gave an incredibly well-received TED talk. You're objectively attractive and are almost certainly more intelligent than anyone Alex has ever seen naked before. You're also my very best friend and the first girl I ever kissed." Sarah flashed her a lopsided grin. "And we both know how impeccable *my* taste is."

"That's true. Marcus *is* a certified hunk of man genius." Claire looked down when her phone buzzed in her hand, unsurprised to see Alex's number lighting up the display. "She's calling."

"Answer it." Sarah disappeared into the bathroom. "Keep an open mind, and give her a chance to explain. And if you need me for any ass-kicking duties—"

"I know where to find you."

## CHAPTER TWENTY-FOUR

Claire's smile faded as soon as Sarah closed the bathroom door. She swiped her thumb across the screen and brought the phone to her ear. "Hello?"

"*Claire!*" Alex let out what almost sounded like a sob. "Oh my God, Claire, I'm *so sorry* about today. About *everything* that happened today. Specifically, that selfie I'm not even sure you ever actually saw, Vanessa's vicious drama-making, and all those texts I vomited at you right around the time you were supposed to be giving your big speech. I just…panicked. Vanessa did what she did, and I absolutely melted down because I knew you were already nervous about us being apart, and about Vanessa, and about *me* in general—"

"I'm not nervous about you, Alex. I swear."

Alex choked out another sob. "Yes, you are, baby, and I get it. I really do. Between Vanessa and her *insane* head games, your recent discovery about the volume of naked come-ons I receive from fans, and my somewhat sordid romantic history, I understand why you would be wary. But I swear to you, Claire-Claire, I don't even want to *look* at Vanessa, let alone touch her."

"I know that." Claire didn't realize how much she honestly believed that until she said the words out loud. "Really, Alex, I'm not upset with you. It's not like I expect you to predict the diabolical actions of your ex-girlfriend or control what she posts online. That said, I'm *super* over that woman at this point. She really is the worst."

"The absolute worst." Alex breathed out slowly. "So…did you not see what Vanessa posted? I'm not sure how long it was up, but I untagged myself as soon as I realized what she'd done."

"No. I saw it. Sarah noticed the photos right before we went onstage. I forced her to show me what had caused her to react with such horror."

Alex hesitated a beat, then asked, cautiously, "And you really weren't upset?"

"Oh no, I *was* upset. Devastated, to be perfectly honest. Luckily, I was able to pull myself together for the sake of our TED talk—which went *great*, by the way. After that was over we had to spend a few hours at this party with the other attendees, so I didn't even have a chance to cry until we left the club. That was about thirty minutes ago."

"I'm sorry I made you cry," Alex whispered. "I *hate* that. I could strangle Vanessa for doing this to you."

"*You* didn't make me cry." Claire kicked off her shoes so she could lie down on the bed. "And yeah, I hate it, too. Any chance we could land Vanessa a new modeling job in scenic Antarctica, starting tomorrow?"

The sound of Alex's relieved laughter sent an intoxicating shot of pure happiness straight to Claire's heart. "I wish." After a moment of silence, Alex said, more seriously, "You know, now that you mention it…there are a few calls I could make. I must know *someone* masochistic enough to want to work with her, right?"

"We can only hope. I mean, she *is* pretty. At least on the outside." Claire put her hand on her stomach, which was finally beginning to settle thanks to the normalcy of their interaction. Gathering her courage, she decided to lay everything onto the table. "To tell you the truth, Alex, seeing those photos of you with Vanessa triggered a rather nasty case of self-doubt. Not that I necessarily believed you'd actually cheated on me…it was more that it's never been easy to believe that someone like you could truly feel passionate about someone like me, anyway. Long term, I mean."

"But baby, I've told you over and over—"

"I know you have, and I'm trying to tell you that I'm finally ready to believe you."

Alex hesitated before speaking. "Yeah? What's changed?"

"Nothing, really. Sarah did a rather effective job of talking me down tonight. Then she helped me remove my head from my ass." Claire smiled and closed her eyes, picturing Alex's handsome face close to her own. What she'd give to kiss those full lips tonight. "She reminded me of your character, assured me how much you loved me, said she didn't want us to break up because it would devastate both of us, but especially you—"

"You wanted to break up with me?" Alex sounded like she might be sick.

"No." Claire had never *wanted* to lose Alex. In the interest of transparency, she clarified her position. "But I did wonder out loud if maybe things wouldn't be better that way, for all of us. Especially for Sarah—and for my friendship with her."

"I'm surprised she didn't agree with you."

"Me, too. I think it helped that she and I had already smoothed things over by that point." Claire bit her tongue at the sudden realization that she was sitting on huge news that even Alex likely hadn't yet heard. Sharing the whole story of their reconciliation simply wasn't possible. She pivoted back to the subject of Sarah's intervention on her big sister's behalf. "Believe it or not, Sarah insisted that she's never seen you happier. She said you'd already made your intentions toward me pretty clear, and they were serious, and she couldn't imagine a scenario in which you'd leave me for Vanessa…or anyone else, really."

"She's right. About all of it." Alex swallowed audibly. "Vanessa was cruel, emotionally abusive, manipulative to an extreme…but you, Claire, you're precisely the opposite. You're everything I've ever wanted in a woman. *I love you.* Only you."

"I love you, too." Stretching her tense arms and legs with a satisfied whimper, Claire murmured, "I'm sorry you had to spend hours worrying about how I would react to Vanessa's stupid stunt. I can only imagine how difficult it must have been for you when you realized my phone was off."

Alex barked a harsh laugh. "I'm not sure difficult is a strong enough word. In related news, I might actually be in a cab on my way to the airport as we speak."

"What?" Claire opened her eyes and sat up on the bed. "Baby, no. That's not necessary, really."

"I made the decision before you turned your phone back on. I was afraid you weren't going to let me explain what happened, so…" She sounded a little embarrassed.

"So you decided to fly to Austin so you could do it in person, in front of Sarah?" Claire looked at the closed bathroom door, gratified to still hear the sound of running water. "She and I are sharing a room, remember? Everything else was booked up."

"I remember." Alex sounded relieved and disappointed at the same time. "Are you telling me I should ask the driver to turn around and take me home?"

"Even though I can't wait to feel your arms around me, that would probably be best." Claire sat back against the headboard with a tired sigh. "By the time you got here it'd be the middle of the night. We'd have to share a bed right next to Sarah's. It just…wouldn't be the reunion either of us wants. I'm flying home tomorrow night, anyway, which I agree sort of feels like forever, but it won't really be *that* bad. Especially since Sarah has us scheduled up until the minute we leave for the airport. We're supposed to have lunch with another pair of educators who did this amazing presentation about using virtual reality in a classroom setting. We chatted them up tonight at the party, super-sweet guys."

"Fair enough." Alex took her mouth away from the phone to say something in a muffled voice, then came back with a resigned sigh. "We're turning around."

"Sorry, baby." Claire couldn't fight the goofy smile that overtook her mouth when she realized that Alex had actually been ready to hop on a spontaneous red-eye flight to Texas for the sole purpose of ensuring that their relationship remained intact. "Believe me when I tell you that I want nothing more than to take off all my clothes, crawl into bed next to you, and just…wrap my body around yours for the rest of the night. Wouldn't that be *perfect?*"

Alex groaned softly. "I want that *so bad*, Claire-Claire." Her voice was like liquid smoke. "Where's Sarah?"

"Taking a shower." On cue, Claire heard the water turn off. "But she's nearly done."

"Of course." Chuckling, Alex murmured, "Not that I can exactly *resent* her for anything after learning that she helped save our relationship tonight."

"She really is a wonderful sister—and quite possibly an even better friend." Claire watched the bathroom door, waiting for Sarah to emerge. When it suddenly occurred to her that she hadn't noticed Sarah take a change of clothing inside with her, she went to Sarah's suitcase and dug around for a suitable pair of pajamas. "You and I have always been the most important women in Sarah's life. Now that we have each other, she feels left out and a little lonely. We're both to blame for that, to some extent. So let's do better, Alex. Let's *be* better. Sarah deserves that much from us, doesn't she?"

"I suppose she *did* have you first." Alex snorted in feigned, begrudging acceptance. "I'll work on my sharing skills, promise."

"We both need to make more time for her in the future. Separately *and* together. You down with that?"

"I'm down. Tell Sarah I'll plan a *Designing Women* marathon for sometime after you guys get home. Just the two of us sisters, like the good old days."

"Sounds like a rollicking good time." Claire walked to the bathroom carrying Sarah's flannel pajama bottoms and a thin camisole. The door opened as she approached, like they'd choreographed the exchange. Sarah poked her head out, eyes brightening when Claire offered her exactly what she was looking for. Winking at Sarah, Claire said, "Hang on a second, and I'll let you tell her yourself."

Eyebrow arched, Sarah leaned out of the doorway wrapped in a towel. "Tell me what?" she asked after Claire put her on speaker.

"That you and I have a date with Julia Sugarbaker once you get home." Alex spoke to her younger sister with palpable affection, clearly softened by the reports of Sarah's efforts on her behalf. "You, me…and a pan of brownies, perhaps?"

"Sold!" Sarah seemed to glow at the sound of Alex's good cheer. "I take it all is well with my two favorite lesbians?"

"Claire told me my situation was dicey earlier, for a minute, but that I have you to thank for talking her down. So thanks, little sis. I owe you one."

"Only one?" Sarah left the door cracked as she stepped back inside to drop her towel and slip into the clothing Claire had given her. "Pretty sure tonight was worth at *least* two."

"That bad, huh?" Alex sounded more amused than worried.

"It wasn't good." Sarah opened the bathroom door all the way, now dressed and ready for bed. "That ex-girlfriend of yours is a serious pain in the ass. I hope you figure out a way to get rid of her soon, because Claire deserves better than this high-school-level drama."

"You're absolutely right. She does." Alex released a heavy sigh. "I plan to spend the next twenty-four hours figuring out how to make this up to you, Claire-Claire. Getting rid of Vanessa will be my first priority."

"*Legally*," Claire clarified, perhaps unnecessarily. "Even if I *do* feel murder in my heart every time I look at her rotten face."

Alex laughed, uneasily. "I'll do my best to keep you away from her, then."

"Maybe you can file for a personal-protection order?" Sarah suggested.

"She may need to do something a little more extreme than be an insufferable bitch for a response like that." Claire hated to imagine how far someone like Vanessa might take her obsession with Alex, but remained hopeful that the situation wouldn't actually require legal intervention. "In the meantime, I'll keep my fingers crossed for that Antarctic fashion shoot."

"Good plan." Sarah stepped around Claire, squeezing her shoulder as she passed. "Now if you two will excuse me, I'm about to fall asleep standing up. All the stress and anxiety I've been carrying around for the past few weeks has suddenly vanished, so my body has apparently decided to plummet straight into recovery mode."

"Get some rest, Sare-Bear," Alex said tenderly. "Oh, and congratulations on the presentation. Claire said you guys killed it."

"We did." Sarah grinned sleepily, yet still held out her fist for Claire to pound. "Your future wife rocked that stage today. Like a fuckin' *pro!*"

"*Sarah,*" Alex hissed. "A little discretion, maybe?"

"Oh, please." Sarah gave Claire one last kiss on the cheek, then collapsed onto her bed with a noisy yawn. "Claire wasn't exactly freaked out the first time I said it, and right now she's smiling like a crazy person, so…" She made a lazy attempt to yank the comforter down far enough to allow her to crawl beneath before giving up with a tired grunt. "Why bother trying to play it so cool? If you want to marry my best friend, then marry my best friend already." Sarah's words slurred as she lost her battle with slumber.

Claire turned off the speaker right as Alex said, "For fuck's sake, Sarah! I may owe you one, or two, or whatever, but—"

"Alex." Voice low, Claire went into the bathroom and closed the door. "I'm pretty sure Sarah just passed out on top of her comforter. Literally. She was serious about being exhausted tonight."

"Based on her loose lips, I'm guessing she also had a little too much to drink at the after party?" Alex sounded vaguely annoyed, but mostly embarrassed. "I hope she didn't make you too uncomfortable with all that 'future wife' talk—"

"Not at all." Claire lowered the lid of the toilet and sat down. "Why would that make me uncomfortable?"

Alex stayed quiet for longer than Claire expected. "I mean…it shouldn't. At least, I hope it wouldn't."

"It doesn't. Honestly, uncomfortable is the last thing it makes me feel." Claire bit her lip and began to unbutton her shirt. "Optimistic. In love. Excited for the future. It makes me feel more like that."

"Oh, *really?*" Alex practically purred in response. "Well, in that case, here's a pre-proposal confession: I *definitely* consider you my future wife—and have for a while."

Claire juggled her phone from hand to hand so she could strip off her shirt. "I accept that."

"Good." Alex fell silent while Claire continued to undress. Finally, she murmured, "What're you doing?"

"Taking off my stupid dress clothes." Finally down to her bra and panties, Claire unsnapped the clasp behind her back and freed her breasts from their confinement with a contented moan. "Feels *so* good."

"Make another noise like that one and I may end up embarrassing myself in front of this nice cab driver," Alex rumbled under her breath. "I've been hard for you all day."

"I like the sound of that."

"Did I say all day? I meant since the second we said good-bye at the airport yesterday." Alex spoke in a bare whisper, no doubt so the cabbie wouldn't overhear. "I miss you like crazy. Like you wouldn't believe."

With a hum of pleasure, Claire said, "I can't believe how cold it is in this hotel bathroom. My nipples are puckered so tight they actually *hurt.*" She conjured up her most boldly flirtatious persona, heady with power over her ability to make Alex squirm. "I wish I could put them in your mouth. I'm sure you'd be able to make me feel all better with your hot…wet…tongue."

Alex swallowed loud enough to be heard. "You're killing me, Claire-Claire. *Dead.*"

Claire leaned against the back of the toilet, slipping her hand down the front of her panties to check her arousal. "I'm only a *little* wet at the moment, but I'm willing to bet your tongue could fix that, too."

"Damn it. I probably deserve this, right?" Despite her lamentation, Alex didn't exactly sound *unhappy* about Claire's special brand of torture. "But mark my words, woman, I *will* have my revenge one day. My sweet, sweet revenge."

Claire let out another moan, making herself sound as intentionally sexy as she could manage. "I have no doubt I'll thoroughly enjoy every second of whatever punishment you decide on."

"That's always the goal." Alex sounded wistful. "My bed felt awfully empty last night without you in it."

"As empty as my pussy feels right now?" Claire whispered quietly enough that Sarah couldn't possibly hear, even if she *did* wake up for some reason. "Without you inside me?"

"*Claire Barker,* unless you're ready for me to tell the driver he needs to turn back around so I can catch the next plane to Austin, you need to start behaving yourself." Alex scolded her sternly, yet the words carried an undercurrent of fondness that made Claire giggle with delight. "Have you put your hand in your panties?"

Flushed from both the wine and an unexpected surge of raw, cathartic *need*, Claire stroked her clit with a tremulous whimper. "Maybe."

"Bad girl." Alex didn't sound entirely disapproving. "You should be saving that for me."

Not exactly prepared to get herself off with Sarah in the next room, anyway, Claire stilled her fingers without removing her hand from her panties. "But I want to come *so badly.*"

"I know, baby." Alex's reassurance came out silky smooth. "Unfortunately, I'm not there to give that to you. Am I?"

With a groan of disappointment, Claire removed her hand from her underwear. "No…which is *lame.*"

"*Super* lame." Alex chuckled. "The good news is that I love you—and tomorrow night I'll be able to show you exactly how much."

"That *is* good news." Claire groaned, wishing she could skip tomorrow's festivities and fly straight home. "We should plan a weekend away together soon. No family, no ex-girlfriends, no obligations. Somewhere pretty, for when we take breaks between orgasms to look out the window."

"I like the way you think, Ms. Barker."

"Well, you *did* say you fell in love with my big brain." Claire's cheeks ached from happiness. Still tipsy from the wine, she tried to convince herself to do the smart thing and get some rest. "I should probably go to bed. There's this breakfast tomorrow, some networking thing…Sarah wants to drop in, of course. I just hope they have waffles."

Alex laughed. "Priorities."

"I wish we could stay on the phone all night." Claire closed her eyes, almost ready to succumb to the blissful pull of slumber. "I miss you so much."

"I miss you, too." Alex's voice wrapped around her like a cozy embrace. "But I'm glad you and Sarah get to spend this time together. Have fun tomorrow. Make sure she knows how much you love her."

"To soften the blow when you steal me for sex once we get home?"

"Exactly." Alex snickered. "I love you, Claire. Get some sleep."

"What are you going to do?"

"I'll be home in about a half hour. If Marcus is around, maybe I'll have a beer with him. Either way, I'll probably unwind by watching a home movie before I go to bed."

Alex's suggestive tone instantly clued Claire in to her meaning. "You mean *our* movie?"

"That's the one."

Claire licked her lips, tingling at the mere mention of Alex reliving their passionate encounter by herself. "Did you watch it last night as well?"

"Nope." Alex seemed particularly proud of that accomplishment. "I decided to save it. Figured night two would be the worst. Granted, I had no idea exactly *how* shitty being away from you would actually be today, or why."

"Well, I'm relieved you have access to that sort of audiovisual therapy when you need it most." Claire briefly considered asking Alex to wait until they were together again, as Alex had suggested to Claire, but honestly, she enjoyed the thought of Alex getting off to images of them fucking too much to pull rank on the issue. "I won't ask you to save it for me, but I do have one request."

"Anything." Alex said the word like she wholeheartedly meant it. "Name it."

"Set up the camera and record yourself while you watch. I want to see how you make yourself come when I'm not there to help." Claire spoke in a low rasp, voice roughened by the unprecedented amount of public speaking she'd done that day. "Will you do that for me?"

"With pleasure. I'll make it *so* good for you, too. I promise."

Claire whimpered in pure anticipation. "I can't wait to see that."

"I can't wait to show you." Alex chuckled when Claire failed to stave off a yawn. "You really should go to bed, sweet pea. I can hear how sleepy you are."

"Yeah." Claire grunted, disappointed by her lack of stamina. "Full disclosure: *I'm* the one who had a little too much wine tonight."

"What? *You?*" Alex snorted. "That doesn't sound like *my* Claire."

"Hey, now. Believe it or not, I've only gotten tipsy to drunk on *two* occasions over the past three years. You just happened to be around for both of them."

"Or, rather, I'm the *reason* for both of them." Alex was unmistakably dejected to have made that connection. "Maybe Sarah's right. Maybe I *am* the worst thing to ever happen to you."

"No. You're the *best*." Claire stood up, swaying unsteadily as the day caught up to her in a rush. "No more insecurities, remember? We're future wives. That means we can relax. We can just…be happy, together."

"*Are* you happy, Claire-Claire?"

Alex clearly needed to hear her say it, plainly and out loud. "*Ecstatic*, baby. Like I never thought possible."

"So am I." Not for the first time tonight, Alex sounded close to tears. "I love you. Thank you for trusting me today."

"You've never given me a reason *not* to." Claire gentled her tone, wishing she could reassure Alex with a long, heartfelt embrace. "I love you, too. Questionable taste in past lovers aside, the least you deserve is the benefit of the doubt."

Alex barked humorless laughter. "Questionable is a pretty charitable description, considering the monster Vanessa turned out to be."

"Don't be so hard on yourself. The worst monsters usually know how to disguise themselves until it's too late." Claire hesitated at the sink. "I can imagine myself falling for her act, too—along with that face and body—in a different life, where she might actually deign to hit on a geek like me."

"Yeah, well, you're *way* out of her league." Alex's disdain for Vanessa dripped from her every word. "Granted, you're also technically out of mine."

Claire snorted, but she knew Alex was trying to be sincere. "I'm almost certain your criteria for the perfect woman doesn't match hers."

"Thank God." Sounding resigned, Alex tried again to steer Claire in the responsible direction. "All right, baby…it's time to hang up. For real. You need to rest up for the late, *eventful* night I have planned for us tomorrow."

Claire wished she could leap forward in time twenty-two hours. "I can't wait."

"Me neither. Sweet dreams, my darling. I'll see you soon."

Beaming, Claire murmured, "Don't forget to record what you do when you get home."

"I won't."

When they finally hung up—at the count of three after a couple minutes of haggling over who should disconnect first—Claire felt a thousand times lighter than she had in days. Weeks, even. With her own body rapidly entering recovery mode, she washed up and used the toilet, tugged on a long T-shirt over her panties, then stumbled to the bed next to Sarah's for some blessedly unburdened sleep.

But not before covering Sarah with the spare blanket first.

## CHAPTER TWENTY-FIVE

Contrary to Claire's optimistic prediction, the following day *dragged*. Even though their breakfast options did include waffles, and lunch with the virtual-reality guys turned out to be genuinely fascinating, she found it nearly impossible to focus on much beyond her growing desire to go home. She'd never been the biggest fan of travel, anyway, preferring the comfort and security of her personal sanctuary to the novelty of faraway lands—like Texas—and this had been a particularly rough trip to withstand.

The sole bright spot of the entire weekend, beyond succeeding at their lofty goal of introducing the larger tech community to their company, was all the quality time she and Sarah had together. Even with as badly as she missed Alex, the weekend served as a valuable reminder that she missed hanging out with Sarah every bit as much. Being able to laugh with her best friend again, to gossip and consult and brainstorm and dream with the closest thing to a sister she'd ever had, made the temporary ache of separation from Alex far more bearable.

Still, once they'd arrived back in California at a little after seven thirty that evening, Claire was more than ready to part ways with Sarah for the rest of the night. When they finally pulled into Sarah's long driveway and saw Alex's car parked in front of the guesthouse, Claire opened her mouth to beg off in the most conciliatory way possible. But Sarah spoke first, frowning in disappointment as she scanned the property. "I wonder where Marcus is."

Claire barely had a chance to ponder that mystery before the sight of Alex bursting out of Sarah's house wearing an apron and waving a colorful potholder in an enthusiastic hello distracted her. Cheeks aching from the face-splitting grin elicited by the sight, Claire pointed out, "Alex probably knows."

"Alex is a *dork*." Sarah chortled as she unfastened her safety belt. "Look how *excited* she is." She guffawed harder. "Shit, look how excited *you* are."

"Shut up," Claire said, then added, "She *is* my future wife, you know."

"Yeah, yeah." Sarah gave her a playful, long-suffering sigh. "I know." She nudged Claire's shoulder, shoving her toward the passenger door. "Go on. I know you're *dying* to kiss her."

"I really am." Claire reached for the handle but then paused to glance back at Sarah. "Sorry."

"It's all right." A newfound peace shone in Sarah's eyes, helping to persuade Claire that she was sincere. "I get it. She's your second best option, given our tragically incompatible sexualities. And I mean, let's be honest, the second best Williams is *still* a Williams."

Claire rolled her eyes and gave Sarah a light punch in the bicep. "*So* nauseatingly modest, you are."

"Yup." Sarah pushed on her shoulder again. "Now go. Make out with my sister. I'm giving you a fifteen-second head start to spare myself the full show."

"Modest *and* generous." Claire wasted no more time, swinging open the car door as Alex rushed over with an eager grin stretched across her face. Swept up in strong arms that pulled her out of the vehicle and into a passionate embrace, Claire swiftly changed gears to properly greet the eldest Williams sister. "Hey there, stud." She struggled to catch her breath, overwhelmed by the ferocity of Alex's response to her arrival. "I missed you, too."

Alex eased back far enough to cup Claire's face in her big hands and pull her in for a deep, reverent kiss. When Alex finally broke away to draw a much-needed breath, her powerful body began to tremble against Claire's. "I love you," she breathed hotly into Claire's ear. "And I'm so, *so* glad you're home."

"Time's up." Sarah sounded far too delighted about shutting down their heartfelt reunion. "Unless you can direct me to my absent husband so I may also partake, any further kissy-face will need to wait until I'm safely indoors. At the very least."

Alex shot Sarah a sympathetic look. "Marcus got called in to the hospital a few hours ago. One of his long-term patients needed an unscheduled emergency surgery…he told me to tell you how sorry he is. He says he promises to be home before you go to bed, at the latest."

Sarah did a marvelous job of hiding her disappointment. If Claire didn't know her so well, she might not have recognized how badly the news crushed her. "Naturally. Timing is everything."

"I'm sorry, Sarah." Claire hesitated, unsure what to do next. Given that Sarah's emotions were already so close to the surface, Claire *really* didn't want to leave her alone to pine for the father of her unborn child. Not even to have hot reunion sex with Alex. With that in mind, she made the only decision possible. "Alex and I will hang out with you until he gets back."

Sarah waved away the offer with a lighthearted smile. "No worries. I'll be fine by myself."

"Nope." Alex plucked the apron she wore away from her chest, then let it fall back into place. "I've already made dinner for all of us. Vegetarian enchiladas, refried beans, and Spanish rice, so I hope you guys are hungry. The food will be ready in about ten minutes, if you want to get cleaned up first. Or change into something more comfortable." Wrapping Sarah in a bear hug, Alex rocked her back and forth with an affectionate growl. "Hope you don't mind that I borrowed your kitchen tonight. It was bigger than mine. With more stuff."

"I can't really complain if I'm getting food out of the deal, can I?" Sarah returned her sister's enthusiastic embrace, squeezing until Alex gasped for mercy. "Thanks for cooking, sis. I appreciate the gesture, especially when I'm aware that all you *really* want to do right now is Claire."

Alex released Sarah so she could lunge at Claire to capture her into a loose hug. "Crude, but mostly accurate. However, doing Claire *isn't* more important than making sure that both my favorite ladies get the homecoming they deserve." She steered Claire in the direction of Sarah's back porch, gesturing for her sister to follow. "Come on. I made you guys a banner and everything."

Sarah laughed when she stepped into the den and saw the sign Alex had hung over the door. "Congratulations, brainiacs!" Snorting, she cozied up to Claire in order to reward Alex with another hug. "Thanks for that, Princess Charming."

Alex wrinkled her nose in disgust at the nickname, then dissolved into a silly grin after Claire expressed her own gratitude with a brief, intensely sincere kiss. "You like it?" she asked, hugging Claire tighter.

Claire studied the handmade, colorfully lettered work of art. She suspected that Alex had spent the better part of her afternoon preparing this reception. The thought warmed Claire's heart to an extent she'd never dreamed possible. "It's perfect."

Alex initiated another kiss, which Sarah stubbornly ignored by walking toward the kitchen with her nose in the air. "Dinner smells *divine*." She disappeared into the next room. "Hope you guys don't mind if I eat in my pajamas tonight, because that's what I'm about to go put on."

"Have at it," Alex called after her, tightening her arms around Claire's waist. "This is *your* night, Sare-Bear! Be crazy, go wild!"

Claire snorted at Alex's over-the-top joviality. "*Someone's* in a good mood."

"Are you kidding me? You're home. All is right with the world." Alex dipped Claire backward over her arm and planted a tender kiss on her lips. "God, sweetheart, you look stunning. Somehow I'd forgotten how beautiful you actually are."

Shivering, Claire silently lamented the emergency that had taken Marcus away. "I want you, Alex. So badly it *hurts*." Arms looped around Alex's neck, she held on even tighter once she was back on her feet. "But even so, thank you for including Sarah in your dinner plans. I appreciate that so much. I'm sure she does, too."

"She'd better." Alex gave a joking wink and trailed her fingers down Claire's sides. "All I can say is that I hope you're ready for a late night, sweetheart, because I've got all *sorts* of plans for the rest of the evening. Most of which involve you and me and nobody else."

Claire backed away so she wouldn't succumb to the shameful urge to ditch Sarah and drag Alex back to the guesthouse for a long night of blissful fucking. "Hopefully Marcus will be home soon."

Alex advanced on Claire, reaching for her arm right as Sarah returned to the room wearing fluffy pink pajamas. Coming to a dead halt just inside the door, Sarah glanced back and forth between them with a suspicious lift of her eyebrow. "Bad time? Do you two need a rain check on the enchiladas? You're leaving the food behind, of course, if you abandon me to jump in bed together."

Alex and Claire walked toward Sarah as one, like they'd planned it, without touching or even looking at each other. "Don't be silly," Claire said, at the same time Alex reassured Sarah. "We're not about to let you enjoy those enchiladas without us."

Sarah grinned as they approached, then turned to lead the way into the kitchen. "Then let's go. The good news is, I can't *wait* to eat dinner while watching my sister and my best friend undress each other with their eyes."

Concerned that Sarah might actually be annoyed about their palpable desire to reconnect, Claire said, "I promise not to even look at Alex. No matter how adorable she may try to be."

"I don't really have to *try.*" Alex scoffed, then shot Claire a grin that went straight to her clit when she promptly forgot her promise and met her girlfriend's cocky stare. "Do I?"

"See?" Sarah smirked over her shoulder at Claire. "Modesty. It runs in the family."

"Lucky me, then, hooking up with the pair of you."

"No, lucky us," Alex said, drawing another pleased smile from Claire before she remembered she wasn't supposed to be looking. Eager for the distraction, Claire bent instead to greet Willow the cat when she entered the kitchen after them with a demanding chirp. "Why don't you two sit down and I'll serve you?" Alex said, stroking Claire's hair as she walked past on her way to the stove.

Claire tried not to let her imagination go wild with the intriguingly worded suggestion. She took a deep breath before rising to her feet, then walked on shaky legs to claim the nearest chair. "That sounds wonderful. I'm starving after that flight."

"*Serve* us?" Sarah pulled a face that hinted at how much fun she planned to have with any opportunity to give them shit. "There's no need to include me in your weird sexual innuendos, please and thank you very much."

"For God's sake, Sarah." Alex shook her head as she portioned out food onto the three plates she'd laid across the countertop. "Do you *have* to make this situation as awkward as possible?"

Sarah glanced at Claire's face, catching her bashful smile. "I think Claire kind of likes it. She thinks I'm funny."

"I think you're coping," Claire said truthfully. When Sarah sat down at the table with her, Claire reached across the surface to take her hand. "But you *are* kind of funny, if sometimes wildly inappropriate."

"*Kind of,* my ass." Sarah beamed at the plate of fragrant Mexican food Alex set in front of her. "Anyway, I should get some benefit out of this whole arrangement. If not ammunition, then what?"

"A sexually satisfied business partner?" Alex waggled her eyebrows at Sarah, apparently attempting to prove that she could give as good as she got. "An ecstatically happy, completely fulfilled older sibling?"

"I'll stick with the ammunition, thanks." Sarah took a bite of food, then threw her head back with an exaggerated groan. "All right, no more being mean to Alex tonight. That's *incredible*, sis. I had no idea you could cook like this."

Alex blushed and sat down to watch Claire take her first bite, immediately followed by a second. "I watched a video online to learn how. Like, ten times."

Everything on Claire's plate tasted absolutely divine. She managed to pause her chewing long enough to issue an honest, albeit succinct, review. "I'm a lucky girl."

Beaming, Alex picked up her fork and took a bite from her own plate. "Thanks. I'm glad you guys like it."

"I *love* it." Claire really did. With effort, she slowed down the speed of her bites, not wanting to make herself sick before she could enjoy the rest of what Alex had to offer. "This really is a wonderful way to come home."

Sarah nodded and continued to shovel food into her mouth. "The only thing that would make it better is Marcus."

As though summoned by the mere sound of his name, the door opened and in strolled the object of Sarah's desire. Grinning at the sight of his wife, he shrugged off his jacket and crossed the room to drop into the chair next to hers before she could even attempt to stand. "Sorry I'm late, baby," he rumbled hungrily. His lips brushed across Sarah's cheek, then her throat. He straightened to meet her eyes with an even brighter smile. "I missed you like crazy. How are you feeling?"

Sarah's gaze darted to Alex, which appeared to clue Marcus in to the fact that not everyone had been told the big news. He glanced at Claire with a cautious head tilt that she answered with a mouthed, *Congrats!* His radiant inner joy reminded her all over again why she loved that this man had found his way into Sarah's life.

"I feel great." Sarah gave Marcus one last kiss before she refocused on her plate of food. "Tired, of course. Relieved that the conference is over. Incredibly proud of my partner for a job well done."

Marcus leaned across the table to pat Claire's arm. "Sarah said you exceeded her wildest expectations yesterday. I've rarely heard her sound that proud of anyone, ever. Excellent job. I'm proud of you both."

Claire couldn't believe she'd managed the performance she had while her heart had been in such a fragile state. "I couldn't have done it without Sarah." She meant every word. "Your wife is a real superstar."

Sarah rolled her eyes, but Marcus wrapped her up in a loving hug, seemingly on the verge of shedding actual tears himself. "Don't I know it, Claire."

With a hushed sob, Sarah slapped Marcus's chest, then hid her face in his shoulder until she regained her composure. "Damn it, honey, you're going to make me cry."

Back from fixing Marcus a fresh plate of food, Alex sat next to Claire and watched the interaction with an odd expression on her handsome face. She popped an eyebrow at Claire, then cocked her head as though she'd detected that there was some piece of information she hadn't yet been made privy to. "I sense a disturbance in the Force."

Claire beamed at the geeky reference. "I really do love you, Alex."

"I know." Alex shot her a quick wink before returning her attention to her sister. "Is everything all right, Sarah?"

Sarah nodded rapidly, sitting up straighter to dry her eyes with her napkin. "Very all right. Yes. I'm sorry, I'm actually—"

"You're not sick, are you?" Looking concerned, Alex's eyes darted around as she studied Sarah's face, then Marcus's, then Claire's. "Or…" Her mouth dropped open. *"Pregnant?"*

Marcus whooped with laughter. "Thunder, stolen."

Sarah groaned, reaching across the table to slap Alex's arm. "You're the worst. Why do you always guess my big news before I can tell you myself? So anticlimactic."

"Sorry." Alex wore a shit-eating grin that didn't make her appear apologetic in the least. "But Sarah, that's *awesome*! I can't wait to hold your spawn. May I babysit? Can we name it Alex? That would work for a boy *or* a girl."

"Whoa, whoa." Sarah held up both hands, beaming. "One step at a time."

Alex caught Claire's gaze. "You already knew?"

"I found out yesterday, in Austin. After she refused to share a bottle of wine with me."

Alex took Claire's hand in both of hers, caressing her fingers lovingly. "I'll drink wine with you, Claire-Claire."

Claire chuckled, then fiddled with her fork to avoid looking across the table at Sarah and Marcus. "Considering what happened the last time we opened a bottle together, I'm not convinced that's an entirely selfless offer."

"I never claimed it was." Alex put her hand on Claire's thigh under the table. "But as you know, I'm never selfish when it comes to the things that *really* matter…"

Sarah raised an eyebrow at Marcus. "You see what I have to deal with?"

Marcus curled an arm around Sarah's waist while simultaneously attacking his own plate of enchiladas. "Don't be jealous, baby girl. You know I can be selfless, too." He swallowed one last mouthful of food and put down his fork, angling his head to nuzzle the back of Sarah's neck until she shivered and set aside her own utensils. "Yeah, you remember how it feels to be worshipped like the goddess you are. Don't you?"

"Check, please." Alex regarded the other couple with an expression of mildly horrified amusement. "Do you two need some time alone?"

Sarah and Marcus nodded as one. Then Sarah crinkled her nose, shooting Alex a pointed look. "Disturbing, isn't it?"

"A little, yeah," Alex conceded. "But I hope you have fun anyway." She grabbed Claire's hand and pulled her to her feet, causing her to drop her last forkful of food on the nearly empty plate. "We sure will."

Claire waved at Sarah and Marcus in a semi-daze, all too happy to follow Alex's lead if it led her closer to bed. "Love you, Sarah. Have a wonderful time tonight, both of you…and great job this weekend, again."

"You, too." Sarah leaned against Marcus to allow his roaming hands better access to her sides and back. "I'm proud of both of us."

Alex stopped at the refrigerator to withdraw one of four glass dishes containing what appeared to be heaven. "Chocolate mousse," Alex announced, nodding to Sarah. "I made enough for everyone. Enjoy."

"Oh, we will." Sarah practically purred when Marcus bent to nibble on her neck. "And then afterward, we'll have mousse."

"Congratulations again about Alex Junior!" Alex hastened Claire out of the kitchen at a speedy clip, murmuring, "Okay, yeah, that's *very* disturbing."

Claire giggled at Alex's very real discomfort. "At least you didn't have to share an apartment with her in college. Sarah didn't invite a *ton* of guys over, but when she did, my *God* were they ever loud—"

Alex handed the dish of chocolate mousse to Claire so she could plug one ear with her free hand, but declined to untangle her fingers from Claire's in order to block the other. "La la la."

"You're adorable." Emerging from the back door of the house into the crisp autumn air, Claire led Alex to the bottom of the porch steps before stopping to throw herself into strong arms that opened on instinct to catch her. Mousse held safely aloft, she whispered, "I love you."

"I love *you*." Alex held her tightly. Though she said nothing more, Claire sensed that this was a moment Alex had worried she'd never experience again—most likely during the five hours when Claire's phone had been turned off and Alex could do nothing but worry about how successful Vanessa's sabotage attempt might have been. Claire's heart had also been broken during that time, but at least she'd had plenty of real-life concerns to distract her from the pain of losing the most intimate connection she'd ever known. Alex hadn't.

Caressing Alex's lower back with the hand that wasn't holding their dessert, Claire stood on her tiptoes to whisper next to her ear. "Take me to bed, sweetheart. Show me how much you missed me."

Alex bent and slipped a muscular arm under Claire's knees to scoop her up into a protective embrace. "I'm going to do you one better than that, Claire-Claire. I'll show you how much I *need* you."

## CHAPTER TWENTY-SIX

They stopped in the kitchen long enough to put dessert in the refrigerator, and then Alex carried her to the front room—specifically, to the couch—where they'd first kissed. Claire was reluctant to let go of Alex's neck after being deposited onto the middle cushion, doing so only because she wanted to see what would happen next. Though she'd expected to be taken into the bedroom, it didn't escape her notice that her camcorder was sitting on the entertainment console, plugged into the television—an unusual arrangement that naturally piqued her interest. Content to let Alex explain, she placed her hands on her knees and smiled up at her girlfriend, body abuzz with anticipation.

Alex shoved the coffee table away from the couch, then sank to the floor at Claire's feet. "Mind if we hang out here for a while?"

Claire swallowed when Alex pushed her thighs apart and shuffled forward to kneel between them. "Hoping to recreate our first date?"

"Partially." Alex pushed a lock of hair off Claire's forehead, lovingly. "I thought I'd also premiere that charming indie film I promised to make for you. If you're interested."

Exactly what Claire had hoped to hear. "Yes. Very interested."

Appearing only mildly bashful, Alex stretched backward to grab the remote from the coffee table. "Now, I'm pretty sure I won't be able to actually stand *watching* myself get off, so I hope you don't mind me hiding my face while you do." She flipped on the television but left the video paused on the first frame before passing the remote to Claire. "Go ahead and press Play whenever you're ready."

Claire inhaled sharply when Alex's hands went to the button on her jeans. "Is it safe to assume that I'm to be your hiding place?"

"As long as you don't mind." Alex batted her eyelashes in a stunningly misleading show of innocence. She tugged down Claire's zipper, then grabbed the waistband of her jeans and panties, yanking both to her ankles, then off altogether. "*Do* you mind, Claire?"

She shook her head, hardly able to speak as she ascended once more into the heady, transcendent, altered state that always overtook her during sex with Alex. "No." Remembering the remote, Claire pointed it toward the screen and pushed Play as Alex dragged her forward by the hips to the edge of the couch, then bent to kiss her pubic mound with an appreciative murmur.

On-screen, Alex walked into the frame, and for the first time Claire realized that the camera was aimed at the very couch where she currently sat. In the video, Alex wore a tank top that showed off her arms and shoulders with a pair of blue jeans that accentuated her tight little ass. She sank down onto the sofa, smiled nervously at the camera, and rubbed her hands together for a few seconds before finally speaking. "So…we hung up about half an hour ago, Claire-Claire, and I'm sure you're probably asleep by this point." She cracked a tiny grin. "Or *trying* to sleep, at least."

Real-life Alex used her thumbs to spread open Claire's labia, touching her tongue to the hot, pink flesh concealed within. Claire moaned and set down the remote, running her fingernails over Alex's scalp before digging in slightly to keep her from retreating. She resisted the urge to close her eyes, too enraptured by the sight of lonely, yearning Alex on the television screen to surrender to that particular instinct. Alex's tongue played between her labia, then lower, circling her opening.

On film, Alex removed her tank top in what was clearly intended to be a striptease. "I'm about to watch our movie for the first time, baby, while I jerk myself off. But before I do…" She exhaled, taking on a sober countenance made even more striking by her partial nudity. "You know, I can't stop thinking about what you said on the phone earlier, about how you wondered today whether things would be easier for everyone if you and I broke up…" Claire stroked Alex's hair as she listened to the emotional monologue, heart breaking at the suffering in her voice. "It wouldn't be. Not for me, for damn sure, and not for you either. At least…I don't think it would be easier for you. I *hope* it wouldn't."

"It wouldn't," Claire affirmed in a soft voice. She whimpered when present-day Alex responded by licking up to her clit, then sucking languidly. "Baby, losing you would *kill* me."

One of Alex's hands moved to her inner thigh, holding on tight as she continued to lave Claire's pussy with her tongue. On-screen, Alex stared directly into the camera and, seemingly, Claire's soul. "You mean *everything* to me, Claire. Absolutely everything. I never imagined I would feel this way about the girl I used to chauffeur around in the backseat of that shitty car I owned during my senior year of high school, long before you and Sarah got your driver's licenses, but I *do*. The fact that I've known you so long only makes what I feel that much more intense. That much *better*." She took a deep breath, then said, boldly, "I want to marry you someday, Claire Barker. I want to be the person who loves you and takes care of you and makes you happy for the rest of your life." After a pause, video-Alex cleared her throat, a bit sheepishly. "So…I hope you want that, too."

"I do." Claire shivered, perfectly aware of the significance of her phrasing. She tugged on Alex's hair to force her gaze upward. Making eye contact, she pulled a self-deprecating smirk. "For the record, I *always* knew I could feel this way about you."

Real-life Alex gave her a silent wink, then got back to work as her two-dimensional counterpart stood to unbutton her jeans. Video-Alex addressed the camera with a mildly cocky grin. "In the meantime, I happen to have something you *definitely* want." She stripped off her jeans but left her black boxer briefs on. Sitting down on the couch, she opened the laptop on the coffee table in front of her and positioned it at an angle that allowed her to see the screen without obscuring the camera's view of her lower body. "I've gotta be honest, baby. I've been looking forward to watching this since we made it."

Claire blushed when the sound of their own amateur film came through the laptop, then moaned when the tongue inside her moved up to circle her throbbing clit. She was relieved not to have to look at Alex's face as the sounds of the spanking she'd received before leaving for Austin played for both of them to hear. Rather than focus on the movie-within-the-movie, Claire watched the way Alex watched the images of *them*, exhaling shakily at the sight of Alex's big hand creeping into the front of her boxers. Alex tore her gaze away from the laptop to look into the camera, breathing, "You're so sexy, Claire. I'm soaking wet already." To prove it, she withdrew her hand from her boxers and showed her shiny fingers to the camera. "See?"

Tilting her head back with a gasp, Claire reacted with a full-body shudder to the sensation of the real Alex sucking on her clit while using a single fingertip to toy with her sensitive entrance. "Yes." Claire answered the unspoken question. "Go inside me."

Alex slid into her at the same time movie-Alex pulled off her boxer briefs to reveal her naked body in all its muscular glory, saying, "I suppose I should give you the full show." She spoke to the camera— to Claire—in a low, sultry voice that caused Claire's pussy to contract around the finger lodged within and threatened to push her over the edge much too soon. Drawing one knee up far enough to plant her foot on the edge of the couch cushion, movie-Alex exposed her pussy in a shameless display that Claire could plainly see had been somewhat difficult for her to offer. But as Alex ran her hand between her legs, teasingly, her expression gradually became confident, likely because she knew the effect her actions would surely have on Claire later. "Do you like this, baby?"

"Yes," Claire whispered, to both the television and the woman between her legs. She moaned when Alex rewarded that answer by licking passionate circles around her swollen clit.

On film, Alex inserted a fingertip into her vagina, barely, while stroking her labia up and down with her other hand. She watched the laptop screen intently as she worked, biting her lip at the sound of their recorded lovemaking. "Damn, you've got a nice ass," movie-Alex groaned. "What I'd give to bury my face between those pretty cheeks right now."

With a wiggle of her hips, Claire squirmed farther onto Alex's finger and more firmly against her tongue. In a ragged voice, she murmured, "You're so hot, Alex. I *love* watching you beat off."

Alex responded by increasing the speed of both her finger and her tongue, smoothly matching Claire's intensity in a way that communicated so much more than words ever could. Her free hand came up to hold Claire's hip against the couch, preventing her from getting away when the sensation became overwhelming and her body attempted to escape. Transfixed by the recorded image of Alex's hands expertly working her own pussy, Claire tried to stave off her orgasm so she could come along with movie-Alex, but she finally had to surrender when her vaginal muscles contracted sharply—completely against her will—to soak Alex's face with a fresh flood of hot juices.

Alex hummed loudly around her clit, a wanton, animalistic sound that triggered wave after wave of ecstasy, curling Claire's toes and sending her hands flying to her own breasts. She pinched, twisted, and squeezed her nipples while riding out a series of shattering climaxes that eventually left her boneless beneath Alex's hands. Meanwhile the video played on, broadcasting the succulent vision of Alex following her into blissful release. For a full thirty seconds, movie-Alex's body quaked with pleasure, until finally she lapsed into a state of complete relaxation that made Claire sigh contentedly. The real Alex matched the mood on-screen by stilling her finger inside Claire, then slowing her dutiful tongue to deliver soft, undemanding licks along Claire's outer lips.

It took Claire some time to regain her composure, and longer still to summon the willpower to push Alex away. But she did, only to make a new request. "Let's go to bed." Claire waved for Alex to stand, then held out her hands so Alex could help her to her feet. "I want to make you come as hard as you did last night. I want to see your body get all tense like that again. I want to feel you *quiver*."

Alex drew Claire into a tight embrace as soon as she pulled her up, a move that clued Claire in to the fact that both their hearts were racing. "Anything, Claire-Claire. Anything you want, it's yours."

Claire wanted only what would make them both feel good. Nothing more. Lacing their fingers together, she walked Alex to the bedroom, delighted by the vocal admiration she received simply for taking the lead while bare-assed. She shot a smirk over her shoulder as they crossed the threshold, emboldened by Alex's reaction to her mere presence. "I want you." She stopped at the foot of the bed and released Alex's hand so she could undress. "Take off your clothes and lie on the bed."

A noticeable shiver ran through Alex as she hurried to obey. First she removed her shirt, then her socks, then her jeans and boxers, until she stood naked in front of Claire, whose modesty was still partially preserved by the long-sleeved T-shirt she'd put on in Austin that morning. Gratified by the sight of Alex's now-familiar yet consistently thrilling nudity, Claire trailed her fingertips down a muscled arm before gesturing at the bed with a jerk of her chin. Nodding, Alex crawled onto the comforter and settled down on her back in the center of the mattress, attention fixed on Claire's face.

Claire tugged her own shirt over her head, then cast it onto the floor before crawling to straddle Alex's narrow hips with her knees. Alex held her breath as Claire loomed over her without allowing their skin to touch. "I want us to make each other feel good," Claire said, balancing her weight on one hand so she could brush the backs of her fingers over Alex's cheek. "Do you want to do that with me?"

Alex nodded, lips parted as though she wanted to speak but simply couldn't. Her hands landed on Claire's hips, then slid around to squeeze her butt in a show of lusty enthusiasm.

Claire reached between their bodies to cover Alex's vulva with her palm. "May I touch you like this?"

"Touch me however you'd like," Alex whispered. "Just *touch* me." Her roaming hands cupped Claire's breasts and fondled them tenderly. "Or tell me how to touch you. Whatever you want."

"Whatever I want," Claire echoed. Given the frequency with which Alex took charge of their sexual encounters, she couldn't help but appreciate this attempt to demonstrate not only her boundless trust, but a genuine eagerness to please. Without any sort of road map in mind, Claire slid off Alex, lying beside her without removing the hand from between her legs. "I want to touch you." She rubbed Alex sensuously, then used her other hand to guide Alex's fingers to the juncture of her own thighs. "While you touch me."

Alex delved between her slippery labia with what felt like two fingers, so Claire did the same, tickled to discover that Alex was *beyond* soaking wet. Her rigid clit slipped this way and that beneath Claire's searching thumb, triggering Alex's whole body to jerk repeatedly in reaction. "Oh, fuck," Alex whimpered, hastening the speed of her own fingers on Claire. "Please, *please* don't make me come yet. Not so fast."

Taking pity, Claire lightened her touch and moved down over Alex's labia, until the tip of one finger toyed ever so carefully with her opening. Alex mirrored the de-escalation, gliding delicately across

Claire's folds before pushing deeper to penetrate her with just one digit. Not wanting to misread the situation, Claire asked, "Do you want me to put my finger in, too?"

Alex nodded again, licking her lips without speaking. She closed her eyes when Claire first breached her vagina with a fingertip, only to force them back open almost immediately thereafter. Staring at Claire's face as though genuinely enraptured by the very sight of her, Alex released a heavy exhalation as she accommodated the gentle invasion, then captured Claire's lips in a passionate kiss once she was fully inside.

Breaking away, Alex breathed, "I love you." The steamy, whispered words were filled with so much raw emotion they brought tears to Claire's eyes. "No one has ever made me feel this good before. No one ever will again."

"Me neither," Claire responded truthfully. "No one has ever made me feel like this." Relishing the snug fit, she withdrew her finger nearly all the way before pushing back inside. Alex worked her finger in and out of Claire with far less caution, clearly well aware by this point that Claire wasn't anywhere close to reaching her personal limit. "I love you, too, Alex. So much it hurts."

Alex made a soft, sad noise in the back of her throat and brought her thumb up to rub Claire's clit. "I don't want you to hurt, baby. I *never* want you to hurt."

"If the cost of feeling this way is an occasional bout with pain, I'll gladly take it." Again mimicking Alex, Claire stroked the pulsing knot of flesh under her thumb. "Anything to be yours."

"You *are* mine." Alex's hips canted into Claire's hand, signaling her impending loss of control. "To love, to protect, to care for…" Back arched, she used her free hand to tug on one of her pebbled nipples. "To have, to hold…" Laughing, she sped up her own increasingly clumsy thrusts. "Damn, sweetheart…I really blew my chance at pulling off a surprise proposal, didn't I?"

Claire bit her lip at the tantalizing rasp of Alex's callused thumb circling her clit. "S'okay. I like knowing that you want to marry me."

Alex kissed her, tenderly. "I want to make you my wife."

Claire's heart seemed to skip a beat, and at the same time, her pussy tightened around Alex's finger—which suddenly felt more like *two* fingers—foretelling her own imminent surrender. "Me, too." With every second that passed, it became increasingly challenging to articulate her thoughts, but she had to try. She needed Alex to understand how committed she was to the idea of their shared future, regardless of the act of cowardice she'd considered during yesterday's episode of extreme vulnerability. "We can make love like this…until we're old and gray."

"I can't wait." Alex kissed her shoulder, her neck, her lips. "Gray hair is sexy." She put her mouth next to Claire's ear, fingering her more urgently. "Your pussy's so ridiculously swollen. Your clit is rock hard." She wiggled her thumb from side to side. "Feel that? Bet I can make you come first."

"No," Claire wailed, disappointed to feel herself on the precipice as a result of Alex's graphic commentary. "*You* were supposed to go first."

"Well, I'm close." Alex nibbled on her earlobe, free hand closing over Claire's to guide her movements. "Stroke me like this and I'll come in your hand, baby. All over your beautiful fingers." Her hips rocked to counter every one of Claire's thrusts, chest heaving in time with the thumb dancing over her fat clit. "Talk to me, Claire-Claire. Say something dirty, and I promise I'll finish for you."

Claire kissed her way over to Alex's ear. "Later…after we eat that mousse…I'm going to ride your cock. I'm gonna—" She gasped, no longer able to hold back her own pleasure. "Put you inside me…and, *fuck me, Alex*…use your body to get my pussy off—"

Alex cried out before going almost eerily silent. Her whole body tensed, and then she erupted in a thunderous orgasm that made Claire laugh-sob in relief as she finally joined her. They each continued to work the other with their hands throughout their shared climax, free arms flung around each other's backs and mouths locked in an earthshaking kiss that intensified the tremendous, staggering joy that flowed around and between them. Claire pulled away only when she absolutely *had* to, to allow both her and Alex to gasp for much-needed air.

"Holy…" Alex trailed off, fingers still lodged deep inside Claire's sensitive pussy. "How are you so *gifted* at that?"

"I have an excellent teacher?" Grinning, Claire extracted her finger from inside Alex's still-fluttering vagina but left her hand resting atop her sticky labia. "You *do* have a real talent when it comes to telling—and *showing*—me exactly what you want."

"Thanks, but no, you were gifted even before I got to you."

Instead of removing her hand from between Claire's legs, Alex scooted impossibly closer. "That first night we were together...*damn*, sweetheart. I couldn't believe it. Sweet, innocent Claire, exposed for the sex kitten she actually is."

The best part about Alex's praise was that Claire actually believed it. "No one ever made me feel like a sex kitten before you."

"No offense, but I'm pretty sure that means they were doing it wrong."

Claire's giggle turned into a whimper when Alex finally began to withdraw her fingers. "Wait."

Overtly pleased, Alex popped an eyebrow. "Wait?" She slid back in, until her second knuckles pressed firmly against Claire's heated flesh. "Now what?" Before Claire could decide whether her body was capable of withstanding more, Alex repeated the action—pulling out, then pushing in. "Do you want *more?*"

The way Alex asked the question, Claire expected to feel some measure of unthinking shame. But all she felt was greedy. "I was gone a long time."

Alex shot her an exaggerated pout. "Almost three days."

"That means we have three days to make up for."

"I suppose you're right." Alex shifted to lie on top of Claire, staring down into her eyes while she continued to perform the skillful hand job. "You're a dirty, dirty girl, Claire-Claire. Asking for my fingers *again*."

Claire shuddered with wicked satisfaction. This wasn't going to take long, primed as she was by her two previous climaxes. "You said... anything I wanted." She wrapped her arms around Alex's shoulders and raked her fingernails down the length of her broad back. "I want *you*."

"You have me." Alex plunged into her even faster, sliding her free arm beneath Claire's shoulders so she could lift her up to press their chests together. "For as long as you desire."

Claire moaned between fevered kisses. "That...feels...*incredible*."

"So do you." Rubbing all her most sensitive places at once, Alex sank her teeth into the juncture of Claire's neck and shoulder. Then she ran her tongue over the spot she'd bitten, soothing the tingling skin. "Last year, after realizing I had this totally inappropriate crush on you, I finally started to let myself go there in my head. I imagined being with you in all *sorts* of different ways. Some of those fantasies have already come true." She twisted her fingers inside Claire, angling to hit a spot that caused both of Claire's thighs to shake uncontrollably. "Some remain to be explored." Claire grabbed Alex's wrist, overwhelmed by its relentlessly ecstasy-inducing movements. "However, not one of my fantasies was even half as satisfying as reality turned out to be."

Claire snaked her hand between their pelvises to fondle the thumb that still caressed her clit. "Agreed."

Alex kissed her cheek, then touched their foreheads together. "I want you to come for me, sweet girl. One more time. Just focus on how it feels to have your tight little pussy filled up by my big, thick fingers. I'm stretching you open, aren't I, baby? Maybe next time I'll have you take something bigger. Something *harder.*" She sank farther down Claire's body, trailing a string of kisses across her chest before laving a painfully erect nipple with her fiery tongue. "You'll take whatever I give you, won't you, baby?"

Predictably, Alex's suggestive speech helped trigger an explosive orgasm every bit as much as the precisely wielded fingers that massaged her throbbing cunt to completion. Claire moaned, then gasped sensually, undulating her body beneath Alex's in a way that swiftly reduced her big, strong lover to a trembling, panting sack of dead weight atop her. Clenching around Alex's invading fingers, Claire let out a gratified sigh and wrapped Alex in an exuberant embrace. "That was wonderful," she said, giving Alex a ferocious squeeze. "*You're* wonderful."

"You are." Alex pressed her lips against Claire's neck, then eased off her limp body to collapse at her side. "Phew. That seriously rocked my world. My heart is beating like crazy."

Claire held her hand above Alex's breast to check for herself. "It sure is."

Alex covered Claire's fingers with her palm. "This is what you do to me, sweet girl. All the damn time."

Beaming, Claire stared up at the ceiling instead of into Alex's eyes. It was easier that way. Unsurprised by how bashful Alex's unabashed praise made her feel, Claire changed the subject as subtly as possible. "We should eat that chocolate mousse now. Right?"

Alex snorted in amusement. "Worked up an appetite, did we?"

"I did." Claire rolled onto her side to meet Alex's gaze. "Plus, I need energy for the next round."

"There's going to be another round?" Alex's eyelids, which had started to droop, shot open. "Damn, girl. You really are *insatiable.*"

"Hey, you promised me a 'long night' of sexing." Claire sat up and patted the center of Alex's chest. "I figure you've got at least one more orgasm in you. I'm hoping to find it with my mouth."

Alex sat up beside her with a melodramatic sigh. "If you insist."

Glad to be home and again immersed in the natural, easy flow of their relationship, Claire gathered Alex in her arms and repeated her words from earlier—almost certainly not for the last time. "I do."

## CHAPTER TWENTY-SEVEN

Claire tested Alex's grip on her wrists, releasing a ragged gasp when she realized just how thoroughly she'd been pinned. Flat on her back next to a coffee table still cluttered with cards and small metal pieces from the tabletop game she'd spent the morning teaching Alex how to play, Claire struggled to recall how they'd wound up on the floor. After two hours of competitive taunting and lots of shared laughter over Alex's treacherous-but-ultimately-amateurish strategies and Claire's win-at-all-costs attitude, a single, stray comment had propelled them into a heated kiss, initiated by Claire and eagerly escalated by Alex. She couldn't remember *what* Alex had said to light her fire, only that she'd been too overcome by lust to focus on taking her next turn. She had no regrets about cutting short another winning round, either. As much fun as her first two victories had been, this new game they were playing felt far more exhilarating.

Kissing her way down Claire's collarbones, Alex tightened her grasp on the slim wrists she held against the rug. "The rule was loser takes all, right?"

Claire tried again to wriggle out of the firm hold, but Alex was far too strong. Not that Claire actually wanted to escape. "I'm not sure I remember that particular stipulation."

Having already stripped Claire of her pajama pants during their passionate make-out session, Alex yanked Claire's arms over her head so she could grab both wrists in one hand. She dropped the other hand to massage the sodden crotch of Claire's panties. "Maybe I invented it. That said, I like the idea. Loser fucks the winner."

Claire took advantage of Alex's decision to multitask by pulling her wrists apart as hard as she could while simultaneously bucking her hips in an attempt to throw off the heavy form on top of her. If anything, Alex's weight grew even more overbearing as she flattened herself over Claire, retaining total control with apparently effortless calm. Claire gasped, genuinely short of breath. Inexplicably, the rising panic of her body's instinctive struggle only made her pussy wetter.

Alex brought her mouth to Claire's ear. "Loser fucks the winner. Do you accept the terms?"

Licking Alex's temple, the first bit of skin she could reach, Claire murmured, "What does the winner get?"

"The winner gets to come for me." Alex curled her fingers around the strip of fabric covering Claire's pussy and moved it aside. The cool air hit her slick labia, making Claire whimper. When Alex shifted her hand to play in her wetness, teasingly, the whimper became a full-throated moan. "Do you accept the terms?"

"Yes." Claire tried to arch against the light touch, but Alex had her almost completely immobilized. This demonstration of Alex's superior strength caused her heart to thud so hard and fast it actually frightened her a little. With their chests pressed together as tight as they were, she knew Alex had to feel it, too. "What are you going to do to me?"

"*Everything*," Alex said, which told Claire nothing at all. "Will I have to restrain you, or do you promise to cooperate?"

Claire's cheeks burned as a fresh gush of wetness leaked out of her vagina, onto Alex's hand. "I'm…not sure yet."

Alex smeared the hot juices all around Claire's labia, then her vulva, then her inner thighs. "You're so *messy*, Claire-Claire. Please do as I say, sweetheart, and lie *very* still while I clean you with my tongue." She released Claire's wrists, backing away slowly as though waiting for a reason to change her mind. "Can you do that for me? Please?"

Leaving her hands clasped above her head, Claire laughed helplessly when another minor flood created even more work for Alex. "Yeah. You'd better hurry, though…the conditions down there are getting wetter by the minute."

Alex relaxed into a cocky grin. "Excellent. I welcome the challenge." She pushed the front of Claire's camisole up under her neck and licked her left nipple, then the right. After returning to give each one a brief suck, she moved lower, approaching her final destination with a wanton growl. "Open your—"

The doorbell rang, startling them both. Alex banged her hip on the nearby coffee table only an instant before Claire gave her shoulders a frantic shove, as though she expected someone's parents to barge in and bust them. *Well, technically...I guess she* is *someone's parent now.* Claire smiled in spite of her best friend's unfortunate timing. She whispered to Alex, "That's probably Sarah."

Alex dropped her face into her hands and shook her head. *"Damn* her." Then she sat back on her heels, tossing Claire the pajama pants that lay crumpled on the floor beside them. "I need to start putting a sock on the door."

"Or we could look for our own place," Claire suggested, articulating a steadily growing desire without allowing herself to second-guess how it would be received. "Maybe we could find something nearby, so we'll still be close when the baby comes, but far enough away to make frequent drop-ins less of an issue."

"I like the way you think." Alex planted a kiss on Claire's nose, then clambered to her feet wearing a good-natured scowl. "All I know is that this better be important. That was a *really* hot little game we were playing just now."

Claire stood up before Alex reached the door. Using her fingers to comb through her mussed hair, she attempted a hasty and most likely futile cover-up of what they'd been interrupted doing. "Agreed. We'll pick up right where we left as soon as she's gone. But be polite. Don't rush her out of here."

"Deal." When Alex threw open the door, the big grin that had been plastered across her face died a swift, terrible death. She moved to shut the door, but a toned arm immediately shot out to hold it open. Angrily, Alex snarled, "What are you doing here?"

Claire took a step forward, then froze in place when Vanessa ducked under Alex's arm and swept inside with a roll of her eyes. In a voice dripping with confidence and false affection, Vanessa said, "Alex, dear heart, please. There's no need to be so dramatic."

Alex's mouth hung open as Vanessa stepped into the front room and briefly locked eyes with Claire, then turned back to address the woman she'd come to see. Before Vanessa could say anything, Alex demanded, "Get out of my house. *Now.*"

Vanessa giggled as though Alex had delivered an exceptionally funny punch line. "Oh, sweetie. I'd hardly call this a 'house.' Not that it isn't a darling little cottage, I'll admit. But as a full-time living situation?" Clucking her tongue, Vanessa turned in a circle and scanned her surroundings with a dismissive frown—Claire included. "You can and *have* done so much better. I mean, obviously." Turning her back to Claire, Vanessa approached Alex like she actually expected a warm reception. "Remember how happy we were those two months we shared that hotel suite in Milan? You can't tell me that you'll ever find that again *here*. With *her.*"

Infuriated that Vanessa would be bold enough to attempt to win Alex back *right in front of her*, Claire cleared her throat to interrupt, but Alex beat her to it. "You know, I *thought* I was happy in Milan. But whether or not you believe it, what you and I had then doesn't even come *close* to what Claire and I share. I'm going to say this one time, Vanessa, and I'll use small words I'm certain you'll be able to understand." Alex threw back her shoulders, utilizing her extra couple inches of height over Vanessa to strike an intimidating pose. "I'm never coming back to you. I don't even want to speak with you. Consider this your final warning: you need to leave us alone. If I have to go to the police and report you for stalking, I will. But this little game of yours ends today. I'm not playing anymore."

Vanessa scoffed. "*So* dramatic," she said, folding her arms over her chest. "I give this two more months, tops, before you realize how bored you are of fucking the same pathetic nerd night after night."

"*Enough.*" Claire's anger erupted before she even had a chance to weigh what she wanted to say. "That's *enough.*"

Vanessa swiveled around slowly, an evil smile stretching across her face. "It speaks."

Alex protested. "Vanessa, don't."

"*Enough,*" Clare repeated in a snarl, silencing everyone. Never had she been so consumed with rage, not once in her entire life. The emotion scorched away her ever-present social anxiety, her introversion, the typically awkward struggle she always faced to find the right words during moments of conflict or humiliation, and left behind only fiery anger fueled by righteous indignation. The constant attempts to break them up were bad enough, but interrupting their mind-blowingly fantastic impromptu sex to insinuate that Claire was a bad lover... well, she couldn't let that stand. Crossing the room to stand toe-to-toe with Alex's ex-girlfriend, Claire channeled a bitchy self-assurance that seemed to catch everyone in the room off guard. "Hi. Vanessa, right?"

The facetious question elicited an unimpressed lift of one precisely manicured eyebrow. "You know who I am."

"Uh-huh. Look, Vanessa…" Proud of her ability to so far match Vanessa's bitchiness pound for pound, Claire hesitated only momentarily before going all in with her new persona. "I'm afraid you interrupted Alex at an extremely inopportune moment. She was right in the middle of giving me something I really, *really* need. Now, when I don't get what I need, I tend to get…grumpy." She twisted her lips into a cruel smirk, praying that Vanessa wouldn't see how full of shit she (mostly) was. "And nobody wants that."

Alex moved closer to Claire's side while nodding in enthusiastic agreement. "Trust me, she's right. *Nobody* wants that."

Almost unconsciously, Claire shot out her hand and smacked Alex on the toned backside of her upper thigh. "Quiet," she barked, and to Alex's credit, she didn't laugh or even crack a smile. She simply obeyed, falling silent and staring down at the floor.

Vanessa eyed Claire suspiciously, as though trying to decide whether she needed to reassess the competition. "I can't stay, anyway. My agent booked me a job in New Zealand that'll last at least a month. I have another job lined up in New York after that, so…" She attempted to catch Alex's gaze, but Alex's attention remained stubbornly fixed on her feet. "The plan was to ask you to come with me, but I'm getting the impression you're too whipped to make your own decisions. At least for the time being."

"Alex can make her own decisions." Claire flicked her sharp gaze over to Alex's downcast face. "Love, do you want to leave with your terrible ex-girlfriend, or would you rather stay and finish licking my pussy?"

Alex jolted visibly at her blunt language but didn't hesitate to lift her face and answer. "Finish."

"Good choice." Claire turned her steely gaze on Vanessa even as her heart threatened to beat out of her chest. Adrenaline surged through her veins, causing her to tremble from head to toe. *Did I really just say that?* Fighting to remain composed, she sniped, "You should leave. Have a safe flight."

Vanessa pulled a sour, unattractive face that made Claire feel, definitively, like the superior choice between the two of them—by any measure. Angling her body to block out the sight of Claire, Vanessa touched Alex's arm lightly, which triggered Alex to flinch away. With a sigh, Vanessa said, "Alex, I'll call you when I land. I really *would* like to talk. Maybe the distance will help you feel more comfortable with the conversation."

"There's nothing to talk about," Alex ground out, still avoiding eye contact. She took Vanessa by the arm and forcibly marched her toward the door. "Good-bye."

Vanessa jerked out of Alex's grasp, then placed both hands on Alex's chest and shoved. Hard. "*Fuck you,* asshole." Alex stumbled backward, inciting Claire to rush closer to the altercation. Before Claire could insinuate her body between theirs, Vanessa gave Alex another shove that sent her crashing into the wall. "Don't forget that *my* pussy is the goddamn foundation of your recent success. You'd better fucking appreciate all I've done for you, because believe me, anything I've given you, I can also take away. In fact, nothing would give me more satisfaction."

Claire wedged her body in front of Alex's, unconcerned for her own physical safety with Alex's on the line. "Step back, skank, or I'll knock you the fuck back." Driven by mindless fury unlike anything she'd ever endured, Claire thrust out her chest and lumbered forward to make good on the threat. "Understand this: having a passably attractive snatch doesn't entitle you to bully my fiancé back into your bed."

"*Fiancé?*" Vanessa covered her obvious shock with a derisive snort, walking backward as Claire steered her in the direction of the front door. "That's hilarious, sweetie. Really. I mean, you're cute and all, as far as geeky losers go—not that *I'd* touch your cunt with a ten-foot pole—but…come on. There's not a chance in hell that Alex will really settle down with someone like *you.* Not when she's had someone like me…or, for that matter, any of the other dozens of gorgeous models I happen to know she's banged. A couple of whom I *helped* her bang."

Reaching around Vanessa's hip to open the door, Claire mustered a smile full of pure, condescending pity. "I'm sorry, *sweetie.* You made a huge mistake when you dumped Alex. Like, a *colossal* one. I know it, and you clearly know it. Fortunately, your loss is my gain. So please, Vanessa…stop embarrassing yourself by chasing someone who obviously doesn't want you anymore. It's time to accept that now I'm the one on the receiving end of Alex's magnificent cock, and you… well, you'll have to go elsewhere in search of whatever pale substitute you can find. Because this, what you're doing? Is pathetic." She placed her hands on Vanessa's shoulders and attempted to force her backward through the open door.

"Let me help, Claire-Claire." Alex stepped in, leading Vanessa out onto the porch by the arm. "Have a nice life, Vanessa. Enjoy New Zealand."

Vanessa tore away from Alex. "Whatever. Have a nice life with… with…*Velma* there."

Claire snickered at Vanessa's sudden lack of teeth. "Right," she called after her. "Velma, like from Scooby Doo. I actually got the reference the first time you made the comparison. Don't worry, though. It's still every bit as hilarious the second time around. Well played."

"Drop dead, whore." Vanessa seethed, beyond artifice and therefore clearly uninterested in her usual, more subtly cutting brand of vitriol. "I hope Alex rapes your filthy asshole until you bleed…all over her *stupid, fake* dick."

Claire blinked, startled but ultimately unmoved by Vanessa's vicious parting shot. "Wow. You know, you really *are* the ugliest person I've ever met."

"Same here." Alex nudged Vanessa toward the porch steps before retreating inside the house to wrap her arm around Claire's waist. "I hope you can be happy someday. I'm sorry you're not already."

"Fuck you, Alex." Vanessa's face had turned a deep shade of red. "You're the *worst* at eating pussy, by the way, and—"

Alex slammed the door shut and engaged the deadbolt, then looped her arm through Claire's to walk them deeper into the house, until they could no longer make out the words of Vanessa's final, furiously delivered diatribe. By unspoken agreement, they continued walking until they reached the bedroom, where Claire sank onto the edge of the bed, and Alex blew out a heavy sigh before kneeling at her feet.

"You all right?" Alex brushed a lock of hair away from Claire's face, cautiously, as though she might shatter to pieces. "I mean…that was fucking *crazy.* Also, kind of amazing. But mostly *crazy.*" She gave an incredulous snort, then shook her head and wrapped her fingers around the back of Claire's neck to give her a light squeeze. "Seriously, *are* you all right? It's okay if you're not. Honest."

Claire shrugged and held up her hands so Alex could see how badly they were still shaking. "That really was…" Lacking a better description, she settled on Alex's. "Fucking *crazy.*"

"Yet, as I said, also kind of amazing." Alex grabbed Claire's hands and held tight to the trembling digits. "Holy shit, Claire. I had *no* idea you had a performance like that in you."

The mere mention of all she'd said and done in front of Vanessa caused Claire's cheeks to bloom with blistering heat. "Me, neither." She remembered Vanessa's cruel words and the way she'd physically assaulted Alex, and her momentary shame receded. "I can't imagine why you wouldn't want a nightmare like that in your life anymore. Seriously, honey, she makes me so *mad.*"

"I guess so!" Alex chuckled, not so subtly curling her fingers around the waistband of Claire's pajama pants to shimmy them down her legs. "For the record, what you just did was *incredibly* hot. You're damn sexy when you get all bossy and possessive like that. Not to mention the part where you leapt between us to protect me." She grabbed the hem of Claire's shirt like she was going to remove it, but paused instead to stare up into Claire's eyes with an expression of undying love and devotion. Chin wobbling, Alex broke eye contact when a tear spilled over to track down her cheek. "Truly, Claire, I don't think anyone has ever made me feel that loved before. That *safe.* So…thank you. I know that couldn't have been easy for you, to say the least."

Claire used her thumb to wipe away the lone tear. "Actually, it was. Frighteningly so. At least, easier than I ever would've expected it to be." When Alex looked at her in wonder, Claire lowered her hand from Alex's face with a bashful shrug. "But then, standing up for the woman I love *should* be easy. Don't you think?"

Alex rose to her full height, tugging Claire's shirt over her head as she went. "*I* think," she said, pressing on Claire's shoulder to urge her to lie flat on her back, "That even before that very rude interruption, I loved you so intensely it was sometimes hard to breathe."

Swallowing in anticipation, Claire searched Alex's eyes for the steadfast acceptance she knew she'd find. "And now?"

"Now, somehow, I love you at least twice as much." Alex crawled on top of her, the denim of her jeans brushing roughly against Claire's exposed labia. "My favorite part was probably when you spanked me for speaking out of turn. Who knew you had a saucy little dominatrix inside you this whole time? Who knew I'd actually *enjoy* it?"

Claire raised her eyebrows, intrigued by the casual confession. "Oh, *really?*"

Alex slid her thigh up and down, spreading around Claire's abundant wetness. "Really." Turning pink, she balanced on her hands to better control the rhythm of her lower body. "I'm not saying I'd definitely enjoy giving up control or that we even need to try that if it's not something you'd be into, just..." She gradually came to a stop between Claire's legs, gazing down at her with a heartbreakingly vulnerable smile. "What you did was surprisingly exciting. Seeing you put Vanessa in her place like that. Playing along with your badass-bitch act."

Smirking, Claire caressed Alex's flushed cheek. "Who says it's an act?"

Alex swallowed, jaw tense under Claire's fingers. "Does that mean you *do* want to take a turn on top?"

Still high from the exhilaration of her run-in with Vanessa, filled with brand-new confidence, Claire grinned at the unexpected realization that yeah, actually, she did. Even better, the idea didn't intimidate her at all. "Only if you *genuinely* think you might get off on that."

Alex rolled off Claire to lie at her side. "Based on how hard I am simply from wondering, it appears I genuinely do."

"I doubt I'll try anything you'll find *too* intense, but if you're uncomfortable, say 'red.'" Claire sat up to scan the room for inspiration as far as how to approach her new role. Struck by the inherent eroticism of emphasizing Alex's masculinity while at the same time asserting her own feminine dominance, Claire crawled across Alex's side of the bed to withdraw her cock, harness, and vibrating bullet from the drawer of the nightstand. "Now suit up like a good boi."

Alex accepted the objects with a shiver. "Yes, *ma'am.*"

"Okay. I really like that." Grinning, Claire reclined against the headboard to watch Alex strip off her clothing and put on the cock. "I could get *used* to that."

"We'll see." Despite the disclaimer, Alex didn't seem altogether unhappy about the idea. She slipped the bullet into its special pouch in her shorts and then, after a brief hesitation, handed the control pack to Claire. "Here. I suppose this belongs to you."

Claire accepted the gift with an approving nod. "Lie down on your back. In the center of the bed, please."

Licking her lips, Alex did as instructed. Tethered to Claire by the cord connecting the vibrator in her shorts to the battery pack in Claire's hand, she settled into position gingerly, as though anticipating that Claire might flip the switch at any moment. Claire waited until Alex was fully reclined, and then some, before ending her anticipation by turning the vibration onto the lightest setting. Only enough to tease. Alex jerked at the unexpected stimulation, her firm muscles tensing in a way that ignited Claire's pussy like liquid fire. She reached behind Alex's back to tuck the control pack into the waistband of the harness, then straightened to run her fingers over her own sensitive labia.

"I was told you've never done this before," Claire said, slipping into her novel new role with ease. "That you would need to be shown how."

Alex's hips surged, desperately seeking relief via the thick cock that jutted up from between her legs. She choked out a strangled groan, staring at Claire with wide-eyed surprise. "Yes." Her voice quavered on the word. "Yes, *ma'am*."

Moved by the raw vulnerability on display, Claire rested her palm atop Alex's trembling stomach and rubbed the soft skin tenderly. "Since you're new, we'll start by building up your stamina." She slid her hand down Alex's abdomen to take hold of the thick dildo. Applying downward pressure to the wide base, she ground the vibrating bullet deeper into Alex's pussy. Once she had Alex moaning, Claire slid her fist up and down the shaft, repeating the motion over and over in an expertly pantomimed hand job. "After all, I don't want you to come as soon as I put you inside me. I expect a nice, long ride. Do you understand?"

Mouth agape, Alex studied Claire as though truly seeing her for the first time. "Yeah."

Claire let go of the dildo, drew back her hand, and delivered a sharp slap to the heavy shaft. It wobbled from the impact, making Alex groan loudly. Embracing her no-nonsense alter ego, Claire raised an eyebrow and got up onto her knees to loom over Alex's supine body. "I said, *do you understand?*"

Alex answered with a rapid nod. "Yes, ma'am. I do, ma'am."

"Good." Claire reached between her own thighs and rubbed her fingers through the seemingly endless wetness she found there. Then she grabbed Alex's cock, twisting her grip as she worked the shaft vigorously. "Maybe I should put your dick in my mouth. To make sure you won't explode the second you feel something wet and warm wrapped around it."

Alex's chest heaved, each breath coming out harsher than the last. "Ma'am, I *might.*"

Claire privately celebrated the honest concern behind Alex's warning. "If you do, I suppose I'll have no choice but to sit on your face while I wait for you to recover. Once you do, we'll try again." That Alex would never actually *get* soft was hardly the point. The rosy hue of Alex's cheeks confirmed that Claire's threat had achieved its intended effect. Gratified by the sight of such a powerful woman under her complete control, Claire took a condom from the nightstand and unrolled the thin sheath over the impressive length of the dildo. Afterward, she bent to give the head a quick, flirtatious brush of her lips. "Do you like that?" Claire pressed her mouth to the same spot, then drew away with a sensual flick of her tongue. "When I give you sweet little kisses all over the tip?"

"Please." Alex's left hip rolled beneath Claire's hand. "I need to come."

"Not yet." Claire opened her mouth and bent to engulf the first few inches of the dildo between her straining lips. Her pussy tightened when Alex cried out above her, tangling her fingers in Claire's long hair tightly enough to pull. Claire lifted her head and allowed the dildo to slip out of her mouth so she could shoot a disapproving frown at the now-squirming Alex. Once she'd forcibly removed the hand from her hair, Claire slapped Alex's dildo again, harder than before. Shuddering at the punishment, Alex dug her heels into the comforter, then balled her hands into white-knuckled fists at her sides. Claire issued a deadly serious reprimand in her iciest tone. "Don't you *ever* put your hand in my hair." She gave Alex's cock a rough yank, then ground its base into the still-buzzing bullet. "*Ever.* Now, tell me you're sorry."

Alex's solid thighs quivered next to Claire's busy hand. "I'm sorry." Her back arched when Claire tugged on her again. "I apologize, *ma'am.*"

"Damn right you do." Too aroused to further prolong the anticipation for either of them, Claire let go of the dildo so she could straddle Alex's hips. Once in place, she stared into Alex's eyes and seized the base of the cock to reposition the bulbous head until it nudged against her vagina, heavy and insistent. "Remember what I told you, my *big*, strong boi." Hanging onto Alex's broad shoulder with her left hand, Claire sank onto the dildo with an unintentional whimper. Then she lowered her upper body to lie chest to chest with Alex while she waited for her pussy to adjust to its girth. Impressed by Alex's willingness to follow orders, Claire whispered, "You'd better make this last for me." Hips swaying, she straightened gradually, staring hard at Alex the entire time. Claire grabbed Alex's big hands and pinned them against the comforter, encouraged by the passionate movement of her hips, then bent to breathe into Alex's ear. "Because if you don't—"

Alex never got to hear the rest of Claire's threat, because—out of nowhere—she suddenly tensed, threw back her head, and climaxed with a hearty roar. Muscles convulsing, Alex tried at first to slip out of Claire's grip, then simply froze, still quaking, beneath her still-moving lower body. Secretly chuffed that her final command had proven too difficult to obey, Claire held Alex down with even greater strength, rocking her hips in an increasingly driving rhythm. She grinned at the distinct disappointment that colored Alex's cries of ecstasy, tickled by the possibility that she'd legitimately managed to force Alex into orgasming against her will. Going on pure instinct, she let go of Alex's left hand to slap the puckered tip of her breast, initiating a smooth transition from giddy to chilly.

"I *told* you not to come." Claire administered swift punishment in the sharp twist of Alex's turgid nipple. "*Bad boi.*" She slowed her hips to fuck herself more tenderly. "You know what happens next, don't you?"

After a visible fight to regain control of her breathing, Alex lifted shame-filled eyes to meet Claire's look of censure. "I'm so sorry. I really…" Jaw set, she lifted her free hand to touch Claire's forearm, seemingly caught between embarrassment and genuine awe at what had just transpired. "*Really* didn't mean to do that. Didn't *want* to do that. But you were so…" Alex released a shaky sigh, the soft buzzing in the air hinting at the source of her continued distress. "*Fuck*, Claire-Claire, you're so sexy."

"It's all right, love. I forgive you." Claire settled her weight atop Alex's narrow hips until the large cock was fully embedded within her fluttering pussy. "That said, I'm not even close to finished with you yet. Now answer the question—but this time with the appropriate level of respect."

Alex wetted her lips with her tongue. "I'm sorry, ma'am. I forgot..." Her body jolted as Claire ground her clit in circles against Alex's pelvis. "Forgot the question."

"I asked if you know what happens next? Because you chose to climax before me?"

Alex started nodding a full five seconds before she was apparently able to summon the presence of mind to form sentences. "I remember, ma'am. You said...you'd sit on my face, ma'am."

"That's right." Taking pity, Claire cut the power to the vibrator and eased off Alex's cock, offering a brief moment of respite before she repositioned her pussy over Alex's waiting mouth. "Give me *lots* of tongue. Start with some light licking and sucking, on my labia at first, then my clit, but only after I give you permission." She lowered herself onto Alex's searching tongue, groaning languidly at the eager heat that enveloped her slippery folds. "When I decide you're ready, I'll try riding your cock again. See if we can help you last longer next time."

Alex moaned into her center, nodding in agreement while simultaneously sliding her tongue along Claire's labia to her opening. The muffled noise she made sounded vaguely like an impassioned, "Yes, ma'am."

"That's exactly right, good boi." Claire took a few moments to enjoy the treatment she was receiving, then reached behind her hip to give Alex's nipple a firm tweak. "Suck on my clit. Not too hard..." She squirmed deliberately atop Alex's mouth, helping her find the perfect spot around which to wrap her lips. "Yes. Just like that."

One of Alex's hands drifted up to rest on Claire's hip and gave her a cautious squeeze. Instinctively, Claire rose onto her knees to allow Alex the opportunity to gulp a few lungfuls of fresh air. Taking advantage of the break to straddle Alex's face in the opposite direction, she first reintroduced the vibration inside Alex's shorts at medium strength, then captured her unflagging cock in both hands so she could fondle it suggestively. Jerking the dildo the same way she had earlier, Claire returned to her former position on Alex's face with a joyful sigh. "I can *definitely* keep this up all night. How about you, stud?"

Gentle fingers caressed her ass—both hands, on both cheeks— the thumbs deftly tracing the shape of her buttocks in a way that conveyed both love and desire. The reverence of Alex's touch made Claire's entire body erupt in goose bumps, which only pushed her closer to orgasm. Not yet willing to give in to her growing need, Claire bent to take the tip of the dildo into her mouth once more, bobbing up and down on the shaft in an effort to match Alex's oral intensity with reciprocal action. When Alex dug her nails into Claire's butt, communicating sudden panic, Claire straightened and then climbed off the bed completely.

Sweaty and sprawled across the mattress, Alex Williams was a magnificent sight. Her cheeks, chin, and nose glistened with Claire's juices, evidence of servitude that she made no move to wipe away. Hips dancing in response to the merciless vibration concealed within her shorts, she watched Claire with dark, glittering eyes. "I'm ready for you, ma'am."

"Ready for *what*, exactly?" Claire's fingers glided over her clit, nearly frictionless, aided by the ridiculous pool of wetness that coated her pussy and inner thighs. "To feel my snug little cunt wrapped around that monster you keep between your legs?"

"Oh my…" Alex bucked sharply, narrow hips canting into the air. "*Yes*, ma'am. Please, ma'am…fuck me. Put my cock inside your pussy and *fuck me*."

Claire touched Alex's chest first, easily detecting the accelerated heartbeat beneath her palm. She soothed Alex with a soft shushing noise, followed by a lingering kiss against her warm, sticky cheek. "It'll be all right, sweet boi. Take a deep breath. You don't want to blow your load all over my tummy, do you?"

Alex screwed her eyes shut like she was fighting not to lose consciousness. She whispered, "No, ma'am," then keened when Claire seized her cock again. "But Claire…*ma'am*…"

Indulging a purely evil desire, Claire slapped the head of the cock against her slippery labia, then wiggled it side to side, lewdly, in a showy performance for an audience of one—who still hadn't opened her eyes. Claire put her free hand inches away from Alex's cheek, hesitating only briefly before delivering a light tap that instantly captured Alex's wide-eyed attention. "Watch me."

Alex sank her teeth into her lower lip as Claire leaned back and to the side, using the extra space to deliver a punishing slap from the dildo against her pussy. She followed up with another, lighter smack, then rubbed the head over her sensitive, soaked folds. Alex's hands flew to her face, covering her eyes and mouth as she let loose an almost wholly soundless scream. Unable to wait any longer, Claire placed the dildo at the entrance of her vagina and carefully lowered herself onto the full length of the wide shaft. Once seated atop Alex's pelvis, she rocked against the muted vibration inside the harness with wanton abandon, reaching a hand back to pull one of her butt cheeks open in an effort to draw Alex's cock farther inside her body.

"I'm sorry, ma'am!" Alex yelped, clearly agitated. Her hands found Claire's hips, bringing her down forcefully onto the cock while simultaneously thrusting upward to impale Claire to the hilt. "I tried… I'm *trying!*"

Acutely aware of the heavy, slightly wrinkled faux testes Alex had brought flush with her ass, Claire ground down with her clit while at the same time giggling at the euphoric joy of forcing her girlfriend to spill into her prematurely for a second time. Eager to make Alex blow, she captured both of her nipples between her thumbs and forefingers, rolling and pinching the pebbled nubs into rock-hard peaks. "You see, I really don't care. *Trying* isn't anywhere close to good enough. But don't worry. I'll teach you to obey."

Teeth gritted, Alex rode out the rest of her orgasm in silence. A few droplets of sweat trickled from her hairline down to her neck, a sight that literally made Claire's mouth water. In love with the vision of Alex covered in a dewy sheen of perspiration, Claire picked up the vibrator's control pack and dialed the intensity to the highest level. With a strangled shriek, Alex launched into a brief struggle that made Claire feel as though Alex were a prize bull and she, her courageous rider. Fighting to regain control, Claire wrestled with Alex until she somehow managed to recapture her wrists and force them down onto the mattress next to her head.

Clair scolded her. "Stop *fighting* me. If you want to properly satisfy a woman, you'll have to learn how to push your desires aside for your partner's. I need you to do that for me *immediately.* Got it, *boi?*"

Alex opened her mouth, from which a broken, unintelligible moan emerged. Excited to have obliterated her experienced lover's self-control, Claire increased the urgency of her movements along the subtly vibrating dildo that stretched her open. Nearly finished off by the next few concentrated strokes, Claire battled her disappointment as she realized she also wouldn't be able to hold out much longer. She abandoned the improvised dialogue, then focused on lasting as long as possible—above all else.

Claire held back long enough to make Alex come again—and then *again*. After the third orgasm, tears were leaking steadily from Alex's gorgeous blue eyes. Soon it became impossible to determine where one orgasm ended and the next began. Alex's body never stopped twitching as exclamations of agony and ecstasy burst intermittently from her raw throat. Eventually, she gasped, "Please! Please! No more, ma'am, no more. I can't...*stop!*"

The anguished plea—from which their safe word had been conspicuously omitted—brought on a reality-shattering climax that instantly turned Claire's bones to jelly, leaving her draped helplessly across Alex's broad chest for the duration. She scrambled to turn off the vibrator while coming down, mildly concerned about Alex's prolonged exposure to too much unrelenting stimulation. Alex sagged in relief the second the bullet went still, sucking in mouthfuls of air to ease her heaving lungs. Still contracting around the dildo, Claire rocked against Alex with a sensuous roll of her hips, savoring the last of her orgasm before it finally receded.

Alex wrapped Claire in a desperate hug that kept her firmly in place. "*Claire,*" she murmured, pressing damp kisses across her cheek. "*Claire.*"

With a start, Claire realized that Alex was crying for real. She returned the tight embrace with passionate ferocity. "I love you, Alex. Are you all right? I didn't hurt you, did I?" She sat up slightly, awed by the palpable emotion with which Alex stared back at her. "Or go too far?"

Shaking her head, Alex sank her fingers into Claire's hair and pulled her down for a deep, emotion-filled kiss. Claire kissed back hungrily, surging against Alex with an unthinking thrust of her hips. Not wanting to get too carried away before checking in more closely, Claire broke their kiss and balanced her weight on hands planted next to Alex's head. "Talk to me, stud," Claire whispered, making deliberate eye contact. "Was that okay?"

Alex brayed helpless laughter. "Yeah, baby. *More* than okay." She sniffled, dabbing her shiny face with the corner of the comforter. "I've never done *anything* like that before. I mean…ever." She dropped the blanket and fingered a lock of Claire's hair, then repeated, in a tremulous murmur, "*Ever.*"

"But it felt good? These are tears of satisfaction?" She was pretty sure Alex had enjoyed it but still held her breath while awaiting the answer.

"It felt absolutely *amazing.*" Alex loosened her arms, sliding her hands down to give Claire's bottom a light squeeze. "You ready to disembark?"

"Not yet." Claire cried out when Alex reacted to that bashful confession by dragging her higher up the dildo by a couple of inches, then slamming her back down. After a brief fight to catch her breath, Claire dragged the blunt fingernails of her left hand down Alex's side. "I thought it was amazing, too."

Alex's left hand stayed on her ass while the right moved to intercept Claire's light caress. Lacing their fingers together, Alex kissed Claire's knuckles with a throaty chuckle. "Stop that."

Certain that she'd found a ticklish spot, Claire rested her upper body on Alex's so she could test her theory with her free hand. Alex chortled madly, then grabbed Claire's other wrist and held both hands behind her back so she was completely immobilized. Using the only weapon she had left, Claire jibed, "Sensitive, are we?"

"I'll show you sensitive…" Alex released Claire's right hand to attack the skin around her hip and ribs, only to give up with a muttered curse when Claire managed not to react. "Brat."

Yanking both wrists out of her slackening grip, Claire pinned Alex down by the shoulders and rolled her hips against her, eliciting a brief, strangled moan. "But I'm *your* brat."

"That you are." Alex reached for Claire's ass again, sighing in contentment when the possessive touch was allowed. She patted the left cheek, then the right, then tightened and relaxed her grip on each buttock in turn. Her expression turned thoughtful. "It felt so strange to be that out of control. Not *bad* strange, really. Just…different. To be honest, I was a tiny bit afraid, at first." Blowing out a long breath, Alex shook her head in a rapid back-and-forth motion in an apparent effort to restore her equilibrium. "But—and I mean this, Claire-Claire—I've never come that hard, let alone that *much*. You absolutely ravished me, baby…and I adored every single second of the experience."

Claire tried not to be too obvious about the fact that Alex's praise had puffed her up to the point of bursting. "I'm so glad. I mean, I've never done anything like that before, either. I sort of made it up as I went along."

"You sure?" Alex uttered a hoarse chuckle. "Because that's actually pretty hard to believe. Not that I'm seriously doubting you, but…" She exhaled again. "*Wow.* You were perfect. Like, so unbelievably sexy I still can't fully wrap my mind around any of what just happened." Snorting, she said, "Don't *ever* buy into the bullshit suggestion that I might get bored with you someday. How could I, when you're full of constant surprises? You're just…everything, sweetheart. Absolutely *everything.*"

In light of the multiple orgasms and uncontrollable tears, Claire no longer had any trouble believing every word that came out of Alex's mouth. Mildly embarrassed nonetheless, she directed a light slap to the center of Alex's chest. "All right, all right. Thank you, but that's enough for now."

"Really?" Alex broke into the toothiest grin ever. *So* many teeth. "Because I'm willing to try to go again. I mean, unless you're too tired."

"That sounds like a challenge." Claire's competitive spirit flared back to life, overriding the mild achiness of her muscles. "Are you challenging me?"

"I suppose I am." Alex smacked Claire on the ass, hard enough to make the skin tingle as the blood rushed to the surface. "Tell me how you want it, and I'll give it to you."

Claire began the painstaking process of extracting the dildo from her pussy, collapsing next to Alex as soon as she was free. After waiting a beat to recover, she nudged Alex aside so she could stretch out on her belly in the center of the bed. Folding her arms beneath her head, she made a bold request. "Get the lube. You're going to slide a finger into my ass—just one—while I rub my clit. Once I make myself come, you can fuck my pussy from behind." Shooting an impish wink over her shoulder, Claire added, "Feel free to talk dirty throughout."

Muted fear in her eyes, Alex cleared her throat but made no move to retrieve the bottle of lube. "Yeah? You're sure?"

Claire propped herself up on one elbow and ran her other hand over Alex's tense stomach. "It's always been a fantasy of mine."

Alex's gaze drifted to Claire's butt, then flitted back to her face. "I'll be *so* careful."

"I know." Claire laid her head down on her arms. "I trust you, Alex." Unable to suppress an anticipatory grin at the sound of Alex rummaging through the nightstand drawer, she snuck her right hand beneath her lower body and used three fingertips to find and circle her swollen clit. With her left hand, she parted her buttocks by moving one cheek aside. "Let me help you learn to trust yourself again."

A single, lube-covered finger brushed against Claire's exposed anus, causing her to shiver at the very same time that Alex bent to whisper hotly into her ear. "Yes, *ma'am.*"

## CHAPTER TWENTY-EIGHT

*Nine months later*

"We should have hired a puppy sitter."

Claire snickered at the woeful expression on Alex's face, which amused her only slightly more than it tugged at her heartstrings. "Riley will be fine, sweetheart. I promise. We left her with a peanut-butter-filled toy, her favorite pillow, a bowl of water, and a get-out-of-jail-free card if she happens to have an accident while we're gone. I'm sure we'll be at Sarah's for only a few hours."

Alex nodded without looking away from the road. They were less than a mile from Sarah's house—as well as Alex's former bachelor pad—and so she remained on high alert while scanning for the hard-to-see driveway. "I know." Alex let out a heavy sigh. "I just…miss her. A lot."

Claire tipped her head back and laughed. She felt the same way, of course, but Alex was just so…so *enamored* with their recently adopted puppy. Her devotion to the scruffy little cattle dog-poodle mix was not only positively adorable, but also *way* too much fun to tease her about. Lightly, Claire remarked, "I swear, I'm beginning to think that you love the dog more than you love me."

Alex put her hand on Claire's knee and gave her a brief squeeze before retaking the steering wheel so she could turn onto Sarah's long driveway. "Don't be silly, love. Riley isn't the one wearing my ring, is she?"

Claire glanced down at her left hand, where the wedding ring Alex had slipped onto her finger nearly three months ago glimmered in the golden evening light. Warmed by the sight—not to mention perpetually stunned by the reality—she still couldn't pass up this opportunity to give Alex some more shit. "No, but Riley *is* wearing a custom-made collar that you designed yourself. I'm thinking that's pretty much the same thing."

Alex parked at the end of the driveway, right in front of the guesthouse that had been vacant for the past eight months. Then she took the keys out of the ignition and reached over the center console to gather Claire into an affectionate embrace. "Aww. Well, *you're* the better conversationalist, if that helps. To be fair, though, she *is* the superior fetcher…"

Claire pushed against Alex's shoulders, turning her face away from her wife's playful attempt at a kiss. "Nope. Maybe you should go kiss *Riley* instead."

"But she always uses *way* too much tongue." Alex wrinkled her nose, then stole a brief peck when Claire momentarily lowered her guard to giggle. "Also, *gross*."

"So you need me around for political discussions and gross kissing stuff, but Riley is an otherwise perfectly adequate substitute? Got it."

"Hey, now." Alex pinched Claire's nipple through her shirt. "Don't I always make the 'gross kissing stuff' worth your while?"

"I suppose you do." Claire melted into Alex's touch, wishing that they'd found time for a quickie before leaving home. "How about we stop talking about the dog?"

"If you insist." Alex cradled Claire's breast in her hand and moved forward to successfully capture her lips in a heated kiss.

A sharp knock on the driver's side window broke them apart. Carrying her nearly two-month-old daughter in her arms—while clad in a flattering black cocktail dress—Sarah bent to shoot them both a disapproving frown. "Do you two need some time alone?"

"That's very thoughtful of you," Alex said as she rolled down her window. "If we could just use your guesthouse for maybe ten minutes… fifteen, tops—"

Claire leaned across Alex's chest to give Sarah a sunny smile. "Hey there, Mama. *No,* we don't need time alone. And *yes,* I do want to hold baby Gracie, thank you very much."

Sarah gestured them toward the house with her chin. "Then get out of the car, slut, and take her from me. Preferably before she leaks on my dress."

Leaving Alex with a hasty peck on the cheek, Claire scrambled out of the passenger-side door and rushed around the front end of the car with her arms held out in invitation. "Come here, little bug. Let Auntie Claire cover your adorable face with kisses."

Alex emerged from the driver's side as Sarah transferred the precious bundle into Claire's arms. "Don't worry, Gracie. Auntie Alex will protect you."

Sarah chuckled, shaking out her arms with a relieved sigh once Claire unburdened her. "Gracie says she's gotten more than her fair share of kisses from you too, Auntie Alex, so she's not sure she actually believes that."

"Clever girl." Throwing open her arms, Alex drew Sarah into an oppressive bear hug so she could plant noisy kisses all over *her* cheeks and forehead. Following a brief, weak struggle from Sarah, Alex released her from the embrace and jumped back to neatly dodge Sarah's incoming fist. "Unlike her mother, who never saw it coming."

"Jerk," Sarah replied, lovingly.

Alex shot her a sparkling grin. "You look beautiful tonight, sis."

"You really do." Claire rubbed her lips across the top of Gracie's downy head and breathed in deep. "How are you feeling? Manage to sleep for more than two consecutive hours yet?"

Answering by way of a tired groan, Sarah wrapped her arm around Claire's waist to give her a friendly squeeze. "Ugh, I wish. And thanks for the kind words, you two, but I've gotta tell you…beautiful is the last thing I feel these days."

Claire walked beside Sarah as they made their way to the house, with Alex lagging slightly behind. "I'm sure Marcus disagrees."

Marcus met them at the door wearing an impeccably tailored suit and a brilliant smile. "Disagrees with what?"

"The suggestion that your wife looks anything less than gorgeous tonight." Closing the door behind them, Alex greeted her brother-in-law with an exceedingly masculine handshake, followed by a bro-style hug. "You're looking pretty sharp yourself."

"Thanks." Marcus clapped Alex on the back. "And you're right, because my wife is *never* anything less than gorgeous."

Sarah snorted. "That's the sort of talk that got me pregnant in the first place."

Angling Gracie's tiny body so her father could kiss her soft head, Claire cooed, "Hey there, daddy. Ready for your first date night as new parents?"

"*Very* ready." Marcus kissed Claire's forehead after Gracie's. "Thank you both so much for volunteering to babysit. Believe me, we truly appreciate it."

The four of them migrated into the kitchen, which now overrun with baby-related supplies. Sarah grabbed her purse off the counter, along with a sheet of paper upon which she'd hand-printed a meticulous list of notes. Apologetically, Sarah handed the paper to Alex. "I'm pretty sure you both know what to do, but I wrote out a few instructions just in case."

Claire waited for Marcus to pull a chair away from the table so she could sit with Gracie in her arms. "We'll be fine, Mama. Don't worry."

"I'm not *worried,*" Sarah protested, making it clear that she was—at least a little.

Alex wrapped Sarah in a much gentler hug than she'd given her in the driveway. "It's your first time leaving her in someone else's care. I understand. It's *totally* normal to be anxious about this, but I promise that Gracie is in the very best hands."

Claire shot Marcus an amused smirk. "You see, Alex is able to empathize because she recently went through the same thing when I forced her to leave our new puppy home alone for the first time."

Sarah snorted in amusement but hugged Alex even more tightly. "I know she's in the best hands. There's no one in the world I trust more than you and Claire." She let out a weary sigh. "Just…text me a few photos of her while we're gone?"

"Count on it." Alex slipped out of Sarah's arms and went to sit at the table next to Claire. She held out her hands, raising an eyebrow hopefully. "Is it my turn yet?"

Claire carefully passed Gracie to Alex, heart overflowing at the sight of her big, strong, butch wife cradling the tiny infant girl. Standing, she crossed the room to give Sarah a proper hug. In a low voice, she murmured into Sarah's ear. "By the way, the VR guys sent a rudimentary sample build of the new project for us to review. So far…

well, it's really impressive. I'm confident we made the right decision to partner with them."

Sarah tightened her arms around Claire's waist, rocking her back and forth in excitement. "*Yes!* That's fantastic news. Thank you." She eased back to study Claire's face. "When do you think we'll be able to launch? Before third quarter?"

"Hopefully. I meet with them on Monday to go over change requests and finalize a couple of last-minute additions to the features list. I'll let you know more then."

Sarah's countenance sharpened as she slipped into strategic mode. "If we can come in ahead of—"

Marcus cleared his throat. "Honey, our reservation is in thirty minutes. As much as I'd love to let you spend the rest of our romantic evening talking shop with your business partner…"

"*Fine.*" Sarah blew him a flirtatious kiss. "Work can wait."

"Work can *definitely* wait. I've got things well under control at the office. I was simply offering you an update, not requesting your precious mental resources." Claire rubbed soothing circles on Sarah's lower back. "Don't worry about anything tonight except showing your husband a good time. Alex and I have been looking forward to this all week. We love hanging out with our little sweet bug." Her voice had devolved into pure, syrupy baby talk by the time she cooed the nickname near Gracie Weatherspoon's delicately sculpted ear. "Maybe Gracie and Auntie Claire will read a book together later."

"My camera's out in the car," Alex told Sarah. "I figured I'd bring it along so I could try to get some shots of Gracie smiling. Maybe also a few of Claire and Gracie being adorable together."

Sarah clapped her hands and broke into a genuine smile. "Oh, I'd *love* that."

"Cool. I'll walk you and Marcus out so I can grab my camera." Alex nodded to Claire, then carefully handed her the baby after Claire had sat back down.

Claire waited until Sarah came over to kiss Gracie again, then said, "When's her next feeding?"

"Soon. Like, probably in about twenty minutes." Sarah's forehead creased. "Sorry."

"Don't be silly. I *love* feeding my favorite baby in the world." Claire stroked Gracie's impossibly soft cheek with one fingertip, grinning when she elicited a smile that already reminded her of Sarah. "And now I don't have to wait."

"You'll want to try to put her down for the night in about two hours. We won't stay out too long. Maybe we'll even make it back before she falls asleep."

"Not if I can help it." Marcus snuck his arm around Sarah's waist, urging her toward the door. "You'll get to see her soon enough, for the first of her middle-of-the-freaking-night feedings. Until then, you're *mine*."

Snuggling into his side, Sarah teased him. "You know you're not getting lucky for at least a couple more weeks, right?"

"Baby, I *already* feel lucky." Marcus bent to kiss the top of Sarah's head. "I'm *always* lucky, with you by my side."

Sarah bumped him with her shoulder. "Even with happy valley off-limits?"

"Always," Marcus repeated, soberly. He paused ahead of the doorway to let Sarah step through. "However, I feel compelled to point out that there's more to sex than intercourse." He looked over at Alex with a devious, mildly sheepish grin. "Just ask your sister. I imagine she's well-acquainted with all sorts of creative possibilities."

Alex glanced backward at Claire with an expression of mock alarm before following Marcus out of the room. "Are you seriously asking me for advice on how to get off without penis-in-vagina sex? Because I will provide it, for Sarah's sake."

Claire bent to speak quietly to Gracie as their voices faded away. "Well, *that* was inappropriate subject matter for a little bug like you, now wasn't it?" Uproarious laughter from the other room brought a warm smile to Claire's face. "Then again, your mommy and daddy love each other *very* much. And when two grown-ups love each other..." She stared down into Gracie's dark, unfocused eyes. "You know what? That's a talk for another day. Like, in about ten years or so. Hopefully I won't be the one who has to have it with you."

She bobbled Gracie in her arms, grinning when the infant's eyelids drooped heavily. A quiet *click* from across the room alerted her to Alex's return, and she held her pose through another few clicks before she lifted her face to wink at her wife. "Get anything worthwhile?"

Alex turned the camera around so she could study the display as she crossed the room. "More than worthwhile." She dropped into the chair next to hers and held the camera so Claire could see. "You're never *not* breathtaking, but when you're holding Gracie?" She blew out a shaky breath, then put the camera down to give Claire a reverent kiss on the cheek. "My heart fills up with so much love I feel like I might literally explode."

Claire drew back to meet Alex's gaze. "Is this your way of telling me you want a baby, too?"

Alex chuckled but then sobered almost immediately. "If you want to have a baby together someday, I'm willing. If not, I'm content to live vicariously through my sister—and be the best aunt ever."

"*I'm* the best aunt ever." Claire scoffed, not entirely under her breath.

"Maybe we're tied," Alex suggested.

"Maybe." Claire rolled her eyes lightheartedly, then moved on. "Honestly, I'm not sure yet about a kid. Right now I'm enjoying our honeymoon phase too much to willingly give it up."

Alex released a low hum of pleasure as her hand found Claire's thigh beneath the table. "Believe me, love, you're not the only one who's enjoying that."

Claire bit her lower lip when Alex's fingers slid farther up her thigh in a blatantly suggestive caress. "Priorities," she murmured, bouncing Gracie again. "On that note, why don't I put the bug in her car seat so we can get her dinner going?"

Alex withdrew her hand, then smoothly took Gracie out of Claire's arms so she could transfer the precious cargo to her cushioned carrier. After securing the tiny, wiggling body inside, Alex planted a gentle kiss on Gracie's head before dropping back into the chair next to Claire's. "I'm just saying, if you ever decide you're game for parenting with me, I could be persuaded."

Grinning, Claire leaned in for a kiss. "Really, being the cool aunt is all I need at the moment. I'm able to get my baby fix without losing any sleep *or* our rockin' sex life."

"Our sex life *is* pretty rockin'," Alex said, returning her hand to its original position. "And yes, absolutely, priorities." She cleared her throat as her fingertips crept closer to the juncture of Claire's denim-clad thighs. "Unfortunately, my wife is *so* mind-blowingly hot—and *so* crazy talented in bed—that I worry our honeymoon phase may just last for the rest of our lives. I mean, we haven't slowed down yet, almost a year later, and the sex only gets better as we go."

Claire released a helpless whimper when Alex teased her with the barest hint of pressure along the seam of her jeans, over her pelvis. Then she wet her lips and played along. "Oh, dear. Yes, I see how that might complicate things."

Alex nuzzled Claire's neck. "Do you?"

Claire's breathing hitched. "Yes, but…" She inhaled sharply when Alex's free hand landed on her other thigh. "What a wonderful dilemma to have, really."

Alex tightened her grip on Claire's thighs and captured her lips in a passionate kiss. The kiss lasted for less than ten seconds before a shrill cry sent their rising passion crashing back to earth. Giggling after they broke apart, Claire gazed over at Gracie with a lighthearted scowl. "Yeah, I'm not ready for one of you yet. Not when it's so much fun to hang out with Auntie Alex whenever and however I want."

Alex pushed back her chair and stood. "I'll get the bottle ready."

"Thanks, Auntie Alex. You really *are* the best!" Claire chirped in the cartoonish voice she'd assigned to Gracie the day after she was born. She unbuckled the carrier's restraints, then scooped her niece into her arms. To her utter delight, Gracie's dramatic scowl instantly transformed into an open-mouthed smile. Still speaking for Gracie, Claire said, "Except for Auntie Claire, of course. *She* promised to show me all the *Star Wars* movies the very second I'm old enough to appreciate them."

Alex, who'd already taken a few steps toward the fridge, paused to double over with laughter. After taking a moment to gather herself, she returned to the table and wrapped her arms around Claire from behind. Bending, she put her lips to Claire's ear and whispered, "I love you more every day, Claire-Claire. That's why I'm keeping you forever."

"I love you, too." Catching a glimpse of her left ring finger as she soothed their niece, Claire leaned back to soak in the warmth of Alex's unambiguous devotion. "Forever," she echoed, long past any hint of doubt.

With her best friend's sister.

# About the Author

Meghan O'Brien is the author of multiple lesbian romance and erotic novels, including *Infinite Loop*, *The Three*, *Thirteen Hours*, *Battle Scars*, *Wild*, *The Night Off*, *The Muse*, *Camp Rewind*, and the novella *Delayed Gratification: The Honeymoon*, all from Bold Strokes Books. She is also the author of a veritable cornucopia of dirty stories, published both online and in various print anthologies. She lives in Northern California with her wife Angie, their son, and a house full of animal companions.

# Books Available From Bold Strokes Books

**Forsaken Trust** by Meredith Doench. When four women are murdered, Agent Luce Hansen must regain trust in her most valuable investigative tool—herself—to catch the killer. (978-1-62639-737-8)

**Letter of the Law** by Carsen Taite. Will federal prosecutor Bianca Cruz take a chance at love with horse breeder Jade Vargas, whose dark family ties threaten everything Bianca has worked to protect—including her child? (978-1-62639-750-7)

**New Life** by Jan Gayle. Trigena and Karrie are having a baby, but the stress of becoming a mother and the impact on their relationship might be too much for Trigena. (978-1-62639-878-8)

**Royal Rebel** by Jenny Frame. Charity director Lennox King sees through the party-girl image Princess Roza has cultivated, but will Lennox's past indiscretions and Roza's responsibilities make their love impossible? (978-1-62639-893-1)

**Unbroken** by Donna K. Ford. When Kayla and Jackie, two women with every reason to reject Happily Ever After, fall in love, will they have the courage to overcome their pasts and rewrite their stories? (978-1-62639-921-1)

**Where the Light Glows** by Dena Blake. Mel Thomas doesn't realize just how unhappy she is in her marriage until she meets Izzy Calabrese. Will she have the courage to overcome her insecurities and follow her heart? (978-1-62639-958-7)

**Her Best Friend's Sister** by Meghan O'Brien. For fifteen years, Claire Barker has nursed a massive crush on her best friend's older sister. What happens when all her wildest fantasies come true? (978-1-62639-861-0)

**Escape in Time** by Robyn Nyx. Working in the past is hell on your future. (978-1-62639-855-9)

**Forget-Me-Not** by Kris Bryant. Is love worth walking away from the only life you've ever dreamed of? (978-1-62639-865-8)

**Highland Fling** by Anna Larner. On vacation in the Scottish Highlands, Eve Eddison falls for the enigmatic forestry officer Moira Burns despite Eve's best friend's campaign to convince her that Moira will break her heart. (978-1-62639-853-5)

**Phoenix Rising** by Rebecca Harwell. As Storm's Quarry faces invasion from a powerful neighbor, a mysterious newcomer with powers equal to Nadya's challenges everything she believes about herself and her future. (978-1-62639-913-6)

**Soul Survivor** by I. Beacham. Sam and Joey have given up on hope, but when fate brings them together it gives them a chance to change each other's life and make dreams come true. (978-1-62639-882-5)

**Strawberry Summer** by Melissa Brayden. When Margaret Beringer's first love Courtney Carrington returns to their small town, she must grapple with their troubled past and fight the temptation for a very delicious future. (978-1-62639-867-2)

**The Girl on the Edge of Summer** by J.M. Redmann. Micky Knight accepts two cases, but neither is the easy investigation it appears. The past is never past—and young girls lead complicated, even dangerous lives. (978-1-62639-687-6)

**Unknown Horizons** by CJ Birch. The moment Lieutenant Alison Ash steps aboard the *Persephone*, she knows her life will never be the same. (978-1-62639-938-9)

**The Sniper's Kiss** by Justine Saracen. The power of a kiss: it can swell your heart with splendor, declare abject submission, and sometimes blow your brains out. (978-1-62639-839-9)

**Divided Nation, United Hearts** by Yolanda Wallace. In a nation torn in two by a most uncivil war, can love conquer the divide? (978-1-62639-847-4)

**Fury's Bridge** by Brey Willows. What if your life depended on someone who didn't believe in your existence? (978-1-62639-841-2)

**Lightning Strikes** by Cass Sellars. When Parker Duncan and Sydney Hyatt's one-night stand turns to more, both women must fight demons past and present to cling to the relationship neither of them thought she wanted. (978-1-62639-956-3)

**Love in Disaster** by Charlotte Greene. A professor and a celebrity chef are drawn together by chance, but can their attraction survive a natural disaster? (978-1-62639-885-6)

**Secret Hearts** by Radclyffe. Can two women from different worlds find common ground while fighting their secret desires? (978-1-62639-932-7)

**Sins of Our Fathers** by A. Rose Mathieu. Solving gruesome murder cases is only one of Elizabeth Campbell's challenges; another is her growing attraction to the female detective who is hell-bent on keeping her client in prison. (978-1-62639-873-3)

**Troop 18** by Jessica L. Webb. Charged with uncovering the destructive secret that a troop of RCMP cadets has been hiding, Andy must put aside her worries about Kate and uncover the conspiracy before it's too late. (978-1-62639-934-1)

**Worthy of Trust and Confidence** by Kara A. McLeod. Special Agent Ryan O'Connor is about to discover the hard way that when you can only handle one type of answer to a question, it really is better not to ask. (978-1-62639-889-4)

**Amounting to Nothing** by Karis Walsh. When mounted police officer Billie Mitchell steps in to save beautiful murder witness Merissa Karr, worlds collide on the rough city streets of Tacoma, Washington. (978-1-62639-728-6)

**Crescent City Confidential** by Aurora Rey. When romance and danger are in the air, writer Sam Torres learns the Big Easy is anything but. (978-1-62639-764-4)

**Becoming You** by Michelle Grubb. Airlie Porter has a secret. A deep, dark, destructive secret that threatens to engulf her if she can't find the courage to face who she really is and who she really wants to be with. (978-1-62639-811-5)

**Birthright** by Missouri Vaun. When spies bring news that a swordswoman imprisoned in a neighboring kingdom bears the Royal mark, Princess Kathryn sets out to rescue Aiden, true heir to the Belstaff throne. (978-1-62639-485-8)

**Love Down Under** by MJ Williamz. Wylie loves Amarina, but if Amarina isn't out, can their relationship last? (978-1-62639-726-2)

**Privacy Glass** by Missouri Vaun. Things heat up when Nash Wiley commandeers a limo and her best friend for a late drive out to the beach: Champagne on ice, seat belts optional, and privacy glass a must. (978-1-62639-705-7)

**The Impasse** by Franci McMahon. A horse-packing excursion into the Montana Wilderness becomes an adventure of terrifying proportions for Miles and ten women on an outfitter-led trip. (978-1-62639-781-1)

**The Right Kind of Wrong** by PJ Trebelhorn. Bartender Quinn Burke is happy with her life as a playgirl until she realizes she can't fight her feelings any longer for her best friend, bookstore owner Grace Everett. (978-1-62639-771-2)

**Wishing on a Dream** by Julie Cannon. Can two women change everything for the chance at love? (978-1-62639-762-0)

**A Quiet Death** by Cari Hunter. When the body of a young Pakistani girl is found out on the moors, the investigation leaves Detective Sanne Jensen facing an ordeal she may not survive. (978-1-62639-815-3)

**Buried Heart** by Laydin Michaels. When Drew Chambliss meets Cicely Jones, her buried past finds its way to the surface. Will they survive its discovery or will their chance at love turn to dust? (978-1-62639-801-6)

# boldstrokesbooks.com

# Bold Strokes Books

Quality and Diversity in LGBTQ Literature

victory
EDITIONS

*Drama*

MATINEE BOOKS

SCI-FI

E-BOOKS

MYSTERY

erotica

SOLILOQUY

EROTICA

YOUNG
ADULT

BOLD
STROKES
BOOKS

LIBERTY
EDITION

*Romance*

# W·E·B·S·T·O·R·E
## PRINT AND EBOOKS

www.ingramcontent.com/pod-product-compliance
Lightning Source LLC
Chambersburg PA
CBHW032210030726
47494CB00020B/939